He caught sight of Gerten, getting out of a taxi some distance down the street and walking towards the restaurant in his awkward but determined way, filled with good intentions. The Colonel caught sight of Laing ten yards before the door and smiled as he raised his hand to wave. Laing waved back.

At the same time, he noticed a Thai with a sunken face, dressed in dirty clothes, standing near Gerten. The man was fumbling with a bag. He pulled out of it a homemade-looking pistol and put it to Gerten's head. Laing tried to focus on what he saw happening and opened his mouth to shout a warning, but the sound was frozen by an explosion . . .

Also by John Ralston Saul:

THE BIRDS OF PREY*

THE PARADISE EATER*

THE NEXT BEST THING

**Published by Ballantine Books*

BARAKA

John Ralston Saul

BALLANTINE BOOKS • TORONTO

ISBN: 0-345-36400-7

This edition published by arrangement with The Dial Press/ Doubleday, Inc.

Printed in Canada

First Ballantine Books Edition: October 1989

For Adrienne

BARAKA: an Arabic word meaning divine luck; God's grace communicated; a form of causality and the means by which it can be appropriated for oneself; a state of blessedness.

. . . the question is not how to get cured, but how to live

Conrad

On a certain day He will call mankind to Him and say: "Where are those fellow-Gods of Mine?"

The Koran

PART 1

ONE

That night, Martin Laing dreamt of Cosima for the first time since leaving New York. In colder weather he dreamt often and vividly. This time, lying naked, uncovered, enclosed as much by the walls of his hotel as by the oppressive heat of Hanoi, the story was confused.

He was in the heart of the city, walking across the water of the Central Lake towards the pagoda on the island. The colonial buildings around the shore were dripping with green mould after twenty-five years of neglect. Mr. Ngo was at his side, shorter and slighter even than in real life, and he was saying something Laing could not hear, something whispered, when a war canoe pulled up between them and Cosima rose from among the young oarsmen. She was clad in water and as she rose the water slipped away from her.

For an endless moment he saw her wonderful neck revealed as he had seen it revealed when they first met, like a porcelain river tinted soft brown, with her tiny collar bone invisible. The water slipped farther from around her shoulders down towards her breasts. Her shoulders were the most beautiful things he had ever seen and he had fallen in love with them before he loved her. He remembered wondering, when he had seen her for the first time, whether the light olive colour could possibly continue without change over her body. That was eleven years ago, long before he knew that he might have her. As her breasts became clear, she leapt into the air, revealing the small waist and then her sex, scarcely covered by a few dark hairs. She landed between himself and Ngo. Laing reached out to stop her being touched by the Vietnamese, and found himself naked, on top of her, on the long wooden table in the meeting room, where the air was like a wet, tepid sponge. Down one side sat the seven Vietnamese. Down the other were the large, untidy forms of Morley and Smith—why Anthony Smith? even within his dream he wondered—all watching while she and he heaved about, groaning. She called out to him, her eyes, wide open, slowly turning into ceiling fans, which turned faster and wider until they swept the dream away.

Three days before, Laing and Morley had flown into Hanoi, the worn rock pinnacles that jutted out of the rice paddies disappearing behind. The earth rose up to meet them, a deep green fungus slit in half by the runway and infected on either side with black sores that materialized into bomb craters. They were a decoration left by the war, finished four years before.

Laing peered out of the window. His face seemed aggressive, an impression created by his state of mind. In truth, his fair skin, light brown hair and slight frame made him like a rare bird unsuited for the sun or any extreme conflict. And yet, at thirty-five, exposure to the world had left no visible scars. His nose was northern and strong enough to create a determined cast, as did the unquestioning way he carried his body when he walked. It was only in his eyes that a touching layer of vulnerability showed through, the expression of a man who sought the protection of friendship or love.

He could see no buildings, only charred walls where there had once been the control tower of the military airport and the hangars. A mass of vines had already risen out of the ground to swallow and digest these remains. In the mud at the edge of the runway, a small crowd of Vietnamese stood waiting beneath the sun.

It was 17 May 1980 and they were waiting for this plane, the weekly turn-around flight from Bangkok to Hanoi; indeed, the only commercial flight of the day. There were two ways into the country; the other via Moscow. As for landing at the military airport, there was no choice—the runway of the civil airport was still a maze of bomb craters.

Although it was not yet eight, the moment the door opened a sullen humidity weighed upon the passengers, a humidity that would build until released by the afternoon rain. Laing was followed down the ramp by his assistant, Morley; both of them in shapeless grey suits, blue cotton shirts and unremarkable ties—a Madison Avenue style designed to disguise the body and merge the individual into a type. In Morley's case, there was no disguise, because he was shapeless. In Laing's, the illusion was complete. Only naked could you see that he was a lean, good-looking man. He was willing to wear this disguise in order to belong; but having had to force his way into that world from the outside, he wore it as an unnatural disguise, uncomfortably.

At the bottom of the ramp they were welcomed in English by a minor official who was delighted to see them, delighted to use his vocabulary of fifty words, delighted in every way, but Laing saw that he was nothing more than a nursemaid. They made their way off the runway to a muddy path that led to a mud parking lot.

Without passing immigration or customs, they were driven, sweating, over fifty miles of narrow roads, skirting around Hanoi. A sea of paddy fields engulfed them, broken only by brown rivers and single-file military bridges, which still replaced those destroyed by the American bombing. Each bridge was backed up with a jam of trucks, carts, bicycles and a few thirty-year-old official cars like their own, with stained lace doilies on the seats and sunscorched curtains on the side and rear windows. They passed a work gang made up of elegant girls in pink blouses, repairing the crumbling road.

It took two hours to reach the civilian airport. Although its runway was still out of commission, a small colonial terminal was standing. The Americans were made to wait, then to fill in endless forms, then to answer questions and, when that was finished, they set off again across the rice paddies towards the outskirts of Hanoi. It was a depressing beginning.

After another two hours, they drew up in front of a rundown French villa rather than their hotel. Laing smiled to himself. He had insisted they arrive in Bangkok a few days early, to get over the thirteen hours' time change before going on to Hanoi. At least he felt in shape to work.

The villa was the headquarters of Vietnam's Oil and Gas Directorate. Paint was peeling off the façade and where there had once been a garden, there was scrub grass. They were met upstairs by the manager, Ngo Van Cu, with a cold formality which passed for civility. His height and slightness were that of a boy and his skin, like polished ivory, fixed this impression of frozen youth. He was probably fifty, but he looked younger than Laing's thirty-five. Ngo waved them into his office, which had once been a bedroom, and sat them in colonial armchairs. He had no idea who they were or why they were there; all he had was a message instructing him to see them. Again Laing smiled. Their way had been prepared more discreetly than he could have hoped. The problems at the airport had come from ignorance, not malevolence.

James Moffett, the man Laing worked for, had arranged everything through Eastern Europe. He had told his contacts there nothing, except that he needed a favour. He had credit stretching back over thirty years. Laing and Morley had picked up their visas in Warsaw, before flying back to Paris and on to Bangkok.

Laing began in French. He had decided in advance to do this, as a concession during the first conversation. "I am from the American company, Western-Oriental. We have oil and gas interests around the world. As you may know, we held two permits for offshore exploration from the Government of South Vietnam."

Mr. Ngo interrupted. He had indicated that they should drink the small glasses of coffee which had been placed before them. After that, he raised the tone of his voice. "Illegal permits! And the criminals have been swept aside." He said this in an elliptical way, floating over the language which a Frenchman would have used with hard precision. He spoke as though telling a joke.

"Exactly," Laing replied. "You may also know that we struck oil ten days before Saigon fell. From our own point of view, we stupidly announced as much."

Ngo laughed carefully. He liked brusque acceptance of facts. He also liked people who could talk about their own errors.

"The point is, Mr. Ngo, we want back in." Laing sat forward. Although he spoke evenly, his body communicated lithe intensity. His eyes did the same, fixed on Ngo like blue lights.

"The illegal contracts drawn up by the criminals are dead. We don't recognize any rights granted by them."

"Mr. Ngo, we discovered oil. We know where it is and probably a great deal more. We have all the maps which, making up for our earlier error, we did not leave behind. We want to come to an agreement with you on mutually beneficial terms." He sipped his coffee. It was triple strength and bitter, an exaggerated leftover from colonial days. He put it down. "The past is as dead as the past can be."

Ngo laughed again and, in a calm manner, delivered a tirade. "If the past died so easily, Mr. Laing, your company and other American companies would have been what you call 'back in' three years ago. Instead, your country vilifies us.

You try to exclude us from the World Bank. You turn the United Nations against us when we save the people of Kampuchea. You go to the criminally hypocritical extreme of backing the Khmer Rouge in order to annoy us. And, Mr. Laing," he pulled out their passports and papers, which had been kept by their guide at the airport, "you arrive scarcely announced, with visas mysteriously completed in Warsaw. Your intention is a secret, at least to me. And why? Because your government still persecutes us with the . . ." Ngo hesitated.

"Trading with the Enemy Act," Laing volunteered.

Ngo spread his arms in a disarming way, "I don't even know who you are."

Laing drew a letter from his inner breast pocket and passed it across his glass of coffee. "This is from someone in Hungary who is well known to your Party Leadership, including Mr. Pham Van Dong." He mentioned the Premier without emphasis. "Neither our names nor the company's are used. Unless you think I'm a pickpocket," Laing smiled, "you'll find it a satisfactory introduction." He sat back in his chair.

Ngo read the letter, folded it and put it in a file with their passports. "What can we do for you?" The letter had put him slightly off balance, so he maintained his coldness. "You want to explore. We would be delighted to have you here. Your government says no. That is full circle."

"Our company has many manifestations. With a little time, we might be able to create a situation that would allow you to get on with exploration."

"But we can get on with it, Mr. Laing. Every week the Japanese are here, the French, the Canadians, the Italians. We have already agreed with some of them on their old blocks."

Laing leaned forward again, with what he knew was the main point. "Western-Oriental's friendship is a different matter. We could affect your relations with the United States. And what we have, you know you won't get from the others. For a start, our financial strength. All you have to do is hold back our old blocks and those around them."

Ngo pulled himself to his feet and glided across the room towards the door. "I think you should go to your hotel. While you rest, we shall organize your visit."

He came down the staircase of the villa with the Americans. The wife of the French colonial official who had built it would have done the same with her female guests, after they had powdered their faces at the end of long evenings. Evenings spent talking about France—a France not seen for years. It was so hot—Laing had once been told by an old widow who had emigrated to the United States after Dien Bien Phu rather than face the reality of her childhood memory of France—it was so hot, that for months you could not think of making love. The most passionate of affairs became verbal or emotional. The physical was a practical impossibility.

TWO

Their hotel floated, like a dragonfly, over a lake on the edge of Hanoi. It was a present from the Cuban government and brought a strange, jarring, Caribbean note to the green water. Farther down the shore there were villages of stucco houses built out over the bank on stilts and aged green by the humidity. A Romanesque church blended into the scene of soft decay, as if it had been there for 800 years instead of fifty.

Laing stripped the bed to its bottom sheet, pulled off his clothes and stretched out. A damp film appeared on his pale skin, highlighting the lines of his ribs and the smooth curve down across his belly. He willed himself to think of nothing and waited immobile through the rest of the morning and the early part of the afternoon, trying to adjust his mind to the intricately spliced heat.

An envelope slipping under the door startled him from this reverie. He leapt to his feet, too quickly in the humidity, caught himself and continued slowly. It was an invitation to dinner typed with an old fashioned typewriter on thin waxy paper. A twinge of relief went through him as he reached for his files to review the case again.

This was the first time he'd been sent out on his own—not to carry on negotiations already well down the line, but to initiate them. Moffett hadn't told him why he was being given the opportunity. Laing had guessed. He was enough of an unknown to get there unnoticed, and if something went wrong, he was junior enough to be jettisoned. Whatever the reason, it was his case and Laing intended to do it his way.

Moffett would have played a combination of experience, favours owed and gambler's instinct. He didn't like business school methods and he didn't like business school boys, nor did he hire them. These likes and dislikes were so widely known that Laing had never been able to understand why Moffett had taken him on.

But the older man was more careful in his prejudices than he appeared. If he took a liking to a candidate, he put Personnel onto chasing up their backgrounds. In a country like America, there are few secrets, so Moffett knew that Laing came from a borderline white collar family in Chicago, that his mother had run the family, had made certain Laing went to good schools and had pushed him to go to McGill in Montreal.

What he didn't find out was that Laing's mother had long regretted her marriage to her ineffectual husband. Only the birth of a son had strapped her to it. Her husband's inability to rise out of a clerical position had made it impossible for them to escape their working-class neighbourhood. Laing's mother had neither let Martin forget that he didn't belong there nor allowed him to make friends among their neighbours. She had managed to get him enrolled at various good middle-class schools some distance from their house. Her life was devoted to getting her only child to and from these places every day, while looking for another one which might give him a better education. His first school experience was that of being picked on by a gang of boys because he didn't belong. This had led to a fight with their leader, a fight which, to his own surprise, he won. From then on, each time he changed schools, he expected a new fight and, providing it was one to one, he believed he could win. His childhood was spent as an outsider. Even after the fights, he was never part of the world within his schools, because he had not the money to do what the other students did nor could he be in their neighbourhoods after school when they developed their friendships. He grew up alone, determined not to be alone, determined to find the balms that would soothe his childhood wounds.

He came back from McGill to Harvard, where the Masters of Business Administration provided him with a class, even a world of his own. Moffett knew that syndrome well. There was no need to be from somewhere or be related to someone, because the MBA spoke for itself. Moffett wasn't against that kind of ambition. He was just against the kind of people who channelled their ambitions in that direction.

Laing, however, had something about him. His vulnerability was the first thing Moffett had noticed. It was human and intelligent. But there was also an intangible strength. Moffett sensed it—a fire burning inside that would drive him on when others stopped. He also had wonderful taste in women, but Moffett had discovered that later.

In the late afternoon, Laing took Morley out onto the terrace, out of hearing. Moffett had offered one piece of advice: as the only visitors to Hanoi were people negotiating with the government, everything that could be bugged would be bugged.

They walked past the swimming pool, planning as they might have planned a Case handed to them in the anonymous classrooms of Harvard. No one swam. There was no lifeguard, no deck chairs. Apart from the lime-green water in the pool, the site was abandoned. They sat in the shade on the ledge of the terrace hanging over the lake and laid everything out. The problems could be guessed at before the negotiations began and the possible solutions could already be weighed. In order to have the negotiation played by the rules, Laing had only to draw the Vietnamese into his definition of the Case.

That evening they were taken to another government villa and led straight to the dining room, where Ngo met them. He was a different man. Effusive. Concerned about their comfort in the hotel. He introduced six other Vietnamese, then made them sit down at the table, where plates of shrimp and vegetables had been laid, along with a very sweet soft drink.

Laing took the lead in the conversation. He talked about Western-Oriental's capabilities before turning to what he thought could be done in Vietnam. "Our first and only well here flowed 2,400 barrels a day. Respectable without being exciting. Other factors, including our seismic tests, show that you have reserves of at least six billion barrels. Malaysia and Indonesia have already found ten billion barrels in the neighbouring waters. With production of as little as a million barrels a day, you would cover your annual trade deficit and have a billion dollars over."

He might have added that they were sitting on potentially the largest untapped basin in the world. But that would have pushed their price up. Or he could have told them that doing the deal would be a giant step forward in his own career, carrying him well out of Moffett's shadow. He could not allow it to fail.

A steamed carp appeared, large enough for twice their number, its stomach stuffed with vegetables. Green onions poked out of its mouth, setting off the curled whiskers.

The only Vietnamese to interrupt was Ngo, and to Laing's surprise, he did it in English. The surprise showed, to Ngo's obvious pleasure. He liked little jokes. Before Laing could ask, he explained that he was a Southerner and had had dealings with Americans while working in the South Vietnamese Ministry of Trade.

Laing guessed that, apart from being the official spokesman, he was also the man to concentrate on. The Americans encouraged him to talk to find out more and Ngo obliged by entertaining them with the story of his years as an informer for the North. There was a touch of cynicism in his account, which the Northerners did not seem to notice, let alone share. Mr. Ngo was a man who knew how to make a deal. Perhaps his friends would make sure it was kept.

Early the next morning they were driven into the centre of Hanoi. There were few cars, but the streets were filled with people on bicycles. The buildings were a mixture of provincial architecture from every region of France, interspersed with pagodas. Everything was covered in stucco, once cream coloured, which had gone mouldy after twenty years without paint. This and the ornamental lakes produced an atmosphere so sleepy and charming that it was hard to accept Hanoi as the capital of a country that had defeated the United States. They passed a monumental colonial government building and beside it a Catholic church with cows tethered inside.

Farther down the street they stopped at a two-story building which had once belonged to a trading company. Ngo met them and led them to a narrow room without windows. It reminded both Laing and Morley of the neon-lit hall, on the first floor of the Aldrich building at Harvard, where they had argued out so many of their Cases.

The meeting began before the onslaught of the worst heat, but it was only an hour before this cool illusion was dispelled. Two ceiling fans, dating from the French occupation, turned slowly, offering the suggestion of slight relief from the ninety-eight percent humidity and the temperature rising well over

100°. The walls, painted a light blue gloss, had a spongy appearance that came from too many coats applied in the climate of the Far East. Laing had hung his jacket over the back of his wooden chair, but his tie stayed knotted and his blue shirt buttoned, constricting his skin. The freckles were lost in the red flush and the clean leanness of his face was somehow distorted.

Morley's jacket was also over the back of his chair, which didn't stop him sweating profusely. His handkerchief was already soaking. Morley was Laing's first recruit to Western-Oriental. Like Laing, he came out of the Harvard Business School—in fact, had just graduated. Laing had brought him to Hanoi because they approached problems in the same way, making him a perfect sounding board.

Across the long wooden table were the seven Vietnamese in open-necked white shirts. At one end of the room, on the wall, was a photograph of Ho Chi Minh; at the other, a large wall clock dating from the 'thirties. Ngo sat in the middle.

Laing wanted one of two things from the Vietnamese. Either time to set up an apparatus that could bypass the Trading with the Enemy Act. Or time to work on its being revoked—at which point, Western-Oriental's reward would be a favoured position in Vietnam.

The Vietnamese wanted something now and they made that clear. Ngo in particular was vociferous. "Why should we wait," he laughed, midway through the morning, "while you mess about? If you take as long to return as you did to leave, we shall have a very long wait. Why shouldn't we give your blocks to those who can come now?" Ngo punctuated his words with precisely used hands and consciously placed smiles. The effect was of great charm. He might have been an old friend.

Laing knew the Vietnamese didn't want to do that. Their policy was to get America back in—because of its economic riches and as a counterweight to Russia. Oil was a good place to start, but these men still wanted something now, something tangible.

Ngo continued to react to Laing's advances throughout the day. Laing was conscious of that, but he didn't notice how closely he was being watched. Ngo thought himself a good judge of Americans, after dealing with them for years in Saigon. He found in Laing none of the false optimism or big talk or idealism mixed with corruption that had been so common in those days. What Ngo didn't notice was the vulnerability—it was too foreign to him—but he saw the drive and ambition. It sparked an idea within him. As the idea grew, he concentrated on Laing, trying to judge whether he had correctly understood the man's character. The more he concentrated, the more he seemed to feel Laing's ambition was the driving force, drowning all other qualities; but, Ngo had not forgotten that Americans were so filled with contradictions they themselves didn't understand, that any approach would have to be made carefully.

At noon, Laing and Morley were driven back to the hotel to rest and eat. The restaurant was filled with crowds of Russian technicians, sweating their way through bowls of meat chunks in thick sauce served by Vietnamese girls, moving like flying fish among the whales. The Americans escaped onto the terrace to rehash the session.

Across the deserted cement deck and the empty green pool, they could see someone slouched in the shade in a chair which must have been carried out from inside. It was a large ill-disciplined body in crumpled clothes. The person's hands and face stood out—pale with pink blotches, perhaps from the heat. In one hand was a half empty glass, in the other a cigar. On the deck beside him were a bottle of soda and a bottle of brandy.

From the advantage of the shade he watched them move hesitantly forward before veering off to the side. Then he called out in an American accent, which had something dissected about it:

"Martin!"

Laing stopped and looked back. At first he said nothing, then walked quickly towards the shade. "Is that you, Anthony?"

Anthony Smith rolled to his feet with surprising agility. "Of course it is. What are you doing here?"

They embraced in a clumsy way that Anglo-Saxon men can sometimes manage and then realized that Morley had come up behind. Laing introduced them, but he could see the shine of contempt in Morley's eyes as he examined Smith's dissolute figure; so he added, "My greatest and oldest friend." As that made no impact, Laing told him to wait and drew Smith away.

"What are you doing here?"

Smith smiled with the conspiratorial warmth that Laing remembered and whispered, "Railways. They all need to be rebuilt. I have a client—well, you can imagine. And you? You I would not expect to find here."

"Oil. You keep your mouth shut, Anthony."

Smith shrugged. "Who you dealing with?"

"Ngo?" Laing said the name as if it were a question.

Smith put his arm around him, the odour of the cheap cigar enveloping them both. "Good. I hear he's looking for a pension."

"You know him?"

As Smith shrugged again someone called from across the deck. A group of Vietnamese were standing in dark suits. Behind them Laing could see two large new limousines.

"I'm off," Smith said affectionately. "This is the big farewell. Witness the black suits; I must have done the deal. Give my love to Cosima." He smiled the same smile and disappeared across the deck, where he was respectfully led to the first car.

Morley appeared out of the shadow, from where he had been watching. Laing said, "He and I went to university together." Then he saw that Morley's eyes were still filled with contempt, an automatic reaction when unsure of his ground, and Laing couldn't stop himself adding, "That man could do three deals in the time you draw up one of your plans." It wasn't what he'd meant to say, nor had it anything to do with his friendship for Smith. But he wanted to sting Morley in a way that the man could understand and therefore feel. Even so he felt embarrassed by his own words and didn't look to see Morley's reaction. Instead he led him to where Smith had been seated and they began to go through the morning's session.

This rehashing became a habit as the talks stretched on. Two and or three times a day they would go outside and sift through the session's words and gestures—looking for an opening, afraid of missing a conciliatory indication.

Curiously enough, Morley was consistently better at mapping out the case; perhaps because he was fresh from daily torture sessions doing just that beside the Charles River. Laing recognized in him one of those machines that respond automatically to the business school system. He himself had found it difficult because it meant constantly curbing his own instincts and limiting himself to their structure. He did it for one reason—their method ran most of the United States—but he resented the facility with which less intelligent machine-minds could master things. Laing had had to try harder, and had eventually mastered his own mind.

By noon on the 19th, the third day, he was sure the elements were in place. All he had to do was wait for the Vietnamese to provide the solution.

At the end of the last session of the day, Ngo invited him to stroll over to the Central Lake. They walked out of the building and along an avenue shaded by trees. The paving had broken up into gravel. Laing rose above the crowds of people who, despite their poverty, wore bright colours. Around him he heard the words "American" or "Yankee" and turned defensively. Their expressions were friendly.

Ngo rested his hand on Laing's arm. "The great American dream makes it difficult, even for us, to hate you long," he said in his halting English, and with surprising warmth. "Of course, we have less reason to hate you as we didn't lose."

Laing stopped and moved slightly away to look at him. Quietly, he replied, "I'm not a man of great emotion. I represent my company interests. We don't love or hate. We find oil on reasonable terms."

Ngo abruptly started walking again. Laing didn't enjoy the role he was playing. He made a point of remembering that it was just a role and hoped it was convincing. The lake was fifty yards ahead.

"What we need, Mr. Laing, is an investment." There was still warmth in Ngo's voice. "That is what you cannot give us, so perhaps we can give it to you."

Laing smiled to himself. They were right on schedule.

Ngo led him to the shore, where old men with wispy beards and bowler hats were seated on benches. Two painted war canoes filled with students raced from a pagoda on a small island to an ornamental bridge at the far end of the lake. Once there, they turned and raced back. Ngo drew him away, his hand now slipped through Laing's arm.

"You Americans already have a large investment in our country. However, it has not been available for you to develop, on your behalf and ours." Ngo laughed indulgently at Laing's perplexed expression. "Part is scrap metal. I could show you some of that at the War Museum. The rest is operational. Five billion dollars' worth, Mr. Laing. Would you like to see it? I know it will give us ideas."

THREE

Ngo and Laing left the city the next morning, 20 May, on what was described as a sight-seeing trip. The other Vietnamese had apparently agreed to a day off and Morley was told to stay at the hotel, in bed. The heat had got him down just enough for it to be easy to leave him behind.

They sat silent in the back of a pre-Second World War cannibalization as it weaved through the streams of carts and bicycles and peasants coming and going on foot, blocking the narrow road or resting in the ditch under French planted trees. Left to himself, Laing stared at them and was surprised to see no war wounds—no one-legged men, no scarred faces. He shifted to ask Ngo for an explanation, but found him turned away and unapproachable. For the first time, Laing found the Vietnamese nervous, unsure of himself.

It took three hours to drive another seventy miles along the straight French roads, through rice paddies interrupted only by occasional villages. Ngo said nothing throughout all of this. It was as if he were so anxious to please that he couldn't bring himself to talk until he had seen Laing's reaction to whatever he was being taken to see. From time to time they passed a Catholic roadside chapel, used as a shed or locked up. Before one of them was a twenty-foot statue of St. Michael killing the dragon; both of them struggling like monsters dropped from outer space into the Orient.

It was afternoon before the car turned off onto a newly paved road which led to a compound enclosed by a high wall, with barbed wire around that. The soldier on the gate knew Ngo and opened it without hesitation. Inside there was a large open space surrounded by five warehouses. Ngo leapt out of the car and almost trotted to the closest, where he threw his weight against the side of the door. As it slid open, he pushed the American forward.

Laing's eyes were blinded by the sudden shade. An odour of metal and grease mixed filled his nostrils until he felt it difficult to breathe. Then, as his eyes adjusted, he saw outlined in the ray of light from the open door massive, grotesque forms towering over him, like barbaric gods. Ngo pushed him forward again and Laing took a few steps that echoed through the sombre light. The forms gradually became cannons, swollen to what seemed a monstrous size.

At first he couldn't speak. He walked slowly forward and touched the side of one, tentatively, as if these dormant monsters had power over him. The metal was cool and clammy and he withdrew his hand in discomfort. He had never actually seen armaments except on parade or on the screen. "What is this?" he managed to say. Even touching didn't make them real.

From behind, Ngo shouted out, "An American supermarket!" He laughed and climbed up onto one of the cannon, like some Pan tickling the armpits of a greater god, and read out its identification mark. "More precisely, they are M107-175 mm self-propelled cannons." He jumped down. "Come on."

The next warehouse was divided into rows of shelves, six levels high, stacked with machine-guns. Ngo grabbed one of these and dropped into a firing crouch, swirling to point it at Laing. Like a child, he shouted, "Bam, bam, bam. You're dead." He laughed again and Laing couldn't stop himself laughing back. "These, Mr. Laing, are M60-E2s, fifteen thousand of them. But need I tell you? You must know your own country's products."

Behind were rows of mortars. They walked on to the next warehouse, where the shelves were loaded with boxes.

Laing looked around, increasingly intrigued and disturbed. "What's inside?"

"Let's see." Ngo found a crowbar and threw his weight into prying open a case. It was filled with rifle ammunition. "Any other requests?"

He wandered down an aisle, Laing behind, until the American stopped at a series of larger cases. "This one?" Ngo went to work with his crowbar and discovered anti-tank shells.

The Vietnamese had relaxed now that he'd seen Laing's reaction. "If my memory serves me right, we have 130,000 tons of your ammunition. This place is only one of the depots spread around the country. You were so generous in your going away presents."

The next warehouse was filled with grenade launchers, forty-five thousand of them according to Ngo, and the last with anti-tank weapons. Laing was silent as they walked back to the car, still caught in the trance of the zombie-like gods who had somehow spoken to him. He had expected to see something strange, but nothing so strange as this. In any case, it wasn't his move. Not yet.

Ngo broke the silence, "You see the size of your country's investment here, and yet there it is," he waved behind them, "sitting around not even earning interest! We must capitalize on this. Here." He pulled two sheets of paper out of his trouser pocket. "You can read these in the car and think about how we might structure our deal."

That night Laing dreamt the same dream. He walked again across the water on the Central Lake with a miniaturized Ngo. Again a war canoe pulled up between them, Cosima rising naked from among the oarsmen and finishing in Laing's arms as they writhed on the long wooden table in the meeting room, the seven Vietnamese watching on one side, Morley and Smith on the other. Abruptly Smith stood up and put out a hand. Was it a protest or an encouragement? The gesture woke Laing. In the darkness he could feel his body covered in cold sweat, isolating him from the turgid heat of his room. The air was filled with the sound of mosquitoes who had found their way through the screens and hovered, waiting to attack.

Slowly the humidity withdrew its cloud from his brain, leaving only the unease with which he had gone to sleep. Suddenly he understood. Anthony Smith was the man who could help him. This was Smith's kind of game, one which Laing knew would only be safe if played with a friend on his side.

FOUR

James Moffett, the senior-vice president, looked around the table at the seven other members of Western-Oriental's Executive Committee with an expression of benign elegance that disguised his anger. Beside him was the President, Robert Erlich, untidy and overweight. Behind them, on the walls, were paintings of oil rigs, which the company reproduced on their Christmas cards. They were Erlich's choice.

The President moved to end the weekly meeting, his face radiating a childlike determination to seduce those about him, that they might forget his ugliness. "No more business? No chicken shit?"

Moffett leaned forward, an arm on the table, a cuff of fine pink voile poking out of his sleeve. "What about the North Sea deal?"

"We'll have to postpone it to next week." Erlich sounded ready to overturn the earth to please a friend, if only that were possible. "I mean, Fell's obviously not going to make it."

Moffett could see that and suddenly he understood why. Fell couldn't control the meetings, so he was neutralizing them—forcing delays in the hope that he could control the decisions in private. It was the third time in two months.

"I need an answer now." Moffett still appeared benign, but he could feel the others getting nervous as they sensed a confrontation and that amused him.

Erlich pushed himself as far back into his chair as he could to escape the question, his chin falling like a broken-down waterfall into his buttoned-down collar. "Come on, James. We can't decide without Fell. We need a financial report."

The door opened and Fell's secretary slipped in to hand Erlich a note. The President read it and looked around the table, searching for support in their eyes, which he found averted. "He's still tied up."

As the girl headed for the door, Moffett stopped her. "Tell us, young lady, do you know the North Sea file?"

"Yes, sir." She answered without thinking.

"Good. You typed the report?"

Erlich broke in, "You can't do that, James."

"Watch me." Moffett was still smiling.

The girl understood her error and began moving towards the door and escape. Moffett repeated his question, forcing her to reluctantly admit she had.

"What was the recommendation?"

"I don't remember, sir." They could all see she was lying, so he let her go.

"Well," Moffett said, his charm miraculously developing a hard edge, "the girl would have remembered a no. And Fell knew the agenda. If he has not sent word, then he must not think it important. I need an answer. Is it approved?"

No one said anything, because no one wanted to be used as cannon fodder between Moffett and Fell.

Erlich laughed. There could have been a beer can in his hand. "Christ, James, for you it's approved."

Everyone relaxed.

The President shoved his chair back from the table and rolled to his feet, ready to entertain his flock so that the incident could be forgotten. "Now can we get the hell out of here?"

After a decent interval Moffett walked out of the room, the murmur of voices turning off as the door shut. He walked down the corridor alone. It was Tuesday, 20 May 1980 and—he did a rough calculation—he had just sat through his 740th Executive Committee meeting.

They would chat on for another ten minutes, then move down the carpeted hall the other way to the officers' dining room. There, surrounded by paintings—the choice of the wife of a past Chairman of the Board—they would lunch well. Moffett had chosen the cook some years before. He liked to tell himself that he had lost all pleasure in those lunches when the last president—the first to be a geologist—refurbished the room in Long Island traditional. That wasn't true.

Someone he scarcely knew passed him in the corridor and said hello, with warmth and deference. Moffett touched the elevator button. It didn't light. He noticed that his hands were cold. Air conditioning meant that his hands were always cold, of which elevators reminded him.

The cabin was panelled in dark oak, old English style. Rather than lower his eyes, he closed them, opening them again six floors below where the executive elevator stopped. He turned right, into the corridor of the forty-seventh floor, walked ten yards, touched another button and a few seconds later entered the general elevator. Some employees recognized him and consciously made more space. He reflected that in other countries, because he stood well and dressed well, they might have offered that space by instinct, without recognizing him.

Below, one of the security guards blocked his way. "I don't see your driver out there, Mr. Moffett."

"Thank you, Norman. I did not order my car."

He walked through the third bank of swinging doors—he chose a different set every day—passed the marble encased beds of miniature trees and stopped on Seventh Avenue.

Moffett looked up at the sky. It was a sharp blue, broken by meringue-like clouds blowing in from the sea. People who didn't look up forgot that New York was a seaside town.

He had not only lost all pleasure in the lunches, but also in the Executive Committee meetings. He had enjoyed them when they were still what they were meant to be: the closest thing an oil executive had to public acclaim. The officers had gathered to report their successes, to plan, to argue for new initiatives, to repair errors. There had been few secrets because too much was at stake. But he no longer enjoyed it. Not because he was no longer successful. He was. And the company grew bigger every year. It was clear that 1980 would be no exception; in fact, the word big no longer seemed to apply. Sometimes he thought that the size was putting him off, but that was just an excuse. He wasn't romantic about money.

Moffett walked down a few blocks, past a Puerto Rican squeezing thick, bright orange juice on a cart by the kerb in the sunlight. It looked delicious, but he never bought it. The petrol fumes and street odours began to fill his lungs, chasing out the pasteurized office air and bringing him to life. He walked east on Fifty-fifth, cool in the shadow of the buildings, with a May breeze at his back.

There were secrets at the meetings—hidden agendas moving like worms of self-interest through the corporate brain, distorting its aims and upsetting Moffett. The others thought he no longer cared, now that he was fifty-five, five years older than the new President, and would never be more than what he was—the second most powerful man in the company. They mistook for disinterest the ease with which he held onto the power that had been in his hands for so long. The first few years on top he had worked hard to stay in control; but now, so much was assumed. It was easier every day.

And in spite of all those things which bothered him, Moffett was remarkably at peace with himself. He was conscious of who he was and what he had accomplished. Let the others dress like serial numbers to avoid attracting attention, he would continue to dress well. Let them mask their power in the mysteries of corporate structure, he was happy to deal with his as the raw thing that it was. Let them eat tasteless, meaningless food, he would continue to please his stomach. Let them hire technocrats with computer minds, he would continue to hire generalists if his instincts told him they were right.

Moffett recognized that his vision of the world was being encroached upon, but it didn't greatly concern him. When he saw another corner of his bastion drop away into the chasm, he noted it but suffered little. Instead he reinforced the remaining defences. Even if his eye was increasingly and invariably drawn to new evidence of decay, he managed to enjoy his own life with self-conscious calm and disguised ambition.

A solid man, not tall but large in an American way, he strode along, looking around, slightly up into the air. He felt most people looked down or straight ahead, seeing only the ground floor. Streets were dressed for them, like women with their panties down around their shoes. He saw New York, above the ground-floor disguise, as a fantasy of Florentine palazzos and Victorian Christmas cakes, floating in a mist over the passer's eyes.

Most of his success was like that. He kept his eyes on the general picture and the main line. That meant he managed to get the company into countries before anyone else knew there was a reason to be there. He also got the company out, after the profits and before the nationalization or revolution. He did this by not becoming one of the boys, by keeping apart.

When he reached the corner of Madison, the vagaries of Western-Oriental had almost been forgotten. He passed the New York Animal Mortuary. In the window there was an offer left over from April: "50% off for Easter." On the far side of

Lexington, the company had ceased to exist and an image of Cosima Laing took its place.

It went through his mind that, like David, he had sent Martin Laing to Hanoi to leave his wife unprotected. He enjoyed the idea, but the truth was that he believed Laing could pull it off. Moffett was obsessed by the Vietnam deal. He suspected it might be his last spectacular coup, not because he was old, but the world was tightening up. Once he had played on the fringes every day; now he was hemmed in by paper politics. Of course, Vietnam involved turning the law, but he considered it a stupid law kept in place by stupid men. At a certain point the law would change, by which time Moffett would be way down the track ahead of his competitors. In his experience, a prophetical turning of the law usually produced income, especially if his intuition had led him to choose the right man to do the job. He was convinced that Laing would break free from his business school mentality and produce.

None of which meant he wasn't interested in the man's wife. At Forty-ninth and Third, hidden from the street, there was a courtyard called Amster Yard. It took another five minutes to walk there, passing an office tower under construction on the corner of Fiftieth. On the other side of an iron gate, a carriageway led into a long, narrow garden—a mass of green. He walked down to the end and sat on a bench.

The frame of the new office tower loomed above, destroying the nineteenth-century illusion of the garden. He sat still, a healthy, weathered figure. Martin Laing had a house that backed onto the Yard; too expensive a house for even his best manager; but it belonged to his wife, whom Moffett had met a few times, always with her husband.

The odds of a chance meeting were not too bad. Cosima was an architect and from their conversations he knew that in the morning she often worked on plans at home, before walking to her office, on Forty-seventh near Madison. He was too old to saunter up and down the street in the hope that she might come out. That would be silly. He corrected himself. That would be even sillier than what he was doing. Moffett knew himself to be awkward in approaching women, but once the approach had been made the awkwardness passed. He sat there, counting the windows of the houses around the garden, until the right moment seemed to have come.

Walking deliberately out of the courtyard, he turned left towards Second Avenue, past an apartment building, then four brownstones, one of which was hers. They were set back from the street. Then two more small buildings and the Avenue. She didn't appear. He crossed Second and kept walking until he hit the East River at Beekman Place, where the sight of the pretty little street gave him a moment of pleasure. On the river, a tug was pulling two barges piled with garbage, gulls circling over the floating hills and diving down to snatch refuse. He turned back the same way for one more pass.

As he approached the houses, a door opened. It was just as he remembered—for no explicable reason, she stood out from the objects around her as if she had an extra dimension. He didn't know whether that dimension was in his perception or truly hers, but he felt something turn over in his stomach, the way it had when he was a young man, though that was probably because he was approaching her the way a boy might. He saw that she wore a belt to accentuate her very small waist, which went so well with an enquiring mind. That was, he admitted, a personal idea which needed no explanation. Moffett walked quickly past the steps, just before she came down.

"Mr. Moffett. What are you doing prowling around here?"

He turned back and smiled.

"Simply prowling. And you, Cosima, what are you doing going out at midday?"

"I'm not a great lover of questions." She was almost his height and when she looked straight at him, the way he wished the members of the Executive Committee would, he realized that he had no idea how to handle her. She was walking in the same direction.

"Have you heard from Martin?"

"Nothing," Moffett replied. "He will be back this week. His visa runs out. I am sure Hanoi is not the best place for telephones or telegrams."

"So that's where he is." Her voice was filled with surprise.

Moffett turned to Cosima. "Well, if Martin did not tell you, I hope you will not tell him I did."

"Mr. Moffett, I have you in my power." She took his arm in a relaxed way—neither attaching herself nor taking a lead.

He looked at her again, but couldn't interpret her expression. "Then come and have lunch with me."

"You're in my power, remember? I'll do the inviting, but not today."

"Egotists live to be old men, but do not leave it too long."

They were at the corner of Third and Fiftieth. She pulled her arm free, waved goodbye and walked on down the Avenue. He noticed that her black hair flowed straight for a few inches before curling away from the even-coloured skin gliding over her high cheek bones. She was wearing a blouse and a skirt made of different fabrics embroidered together like a fractured painting. And her ankles, like her waist, were set off by long delicate curves.

He was sorry she'd said no, but at least there was the promise of something in the future and the morning's distaste was gone from his mouth. Besides, he actually liked eating alone.

Moffett walked across the few blocks to Grand Central Station. He bought a paper and went down the winding stairs—keeping his hand off the brass railing—through the crowds in the great hall and on down into the Oyster Bar.

When he ate alone, he ate there. His colleagues would have thought it unsuitable. He chose a seat in the noisiest part, under the echoing, white-tiled vaults, and ordered a dozen Cotuit oysters with a half bottle of Kenwood white. The perfect American meal. Beside him, two men were eating from deep soup bowls filled with oyster stew, butter swimming on top of the cream.

It struck him as curious that Laing hadn't told his wife. But then she might have been covering for him. She was smart enough, that he knew because he had gone to the trouble of finding out about her. The Amster Yard house had been a wedding present from her father in 1974. That was curious, because she and Laing had overlapped at McGill for two years in the late 'sixties, apparently without anything happening between them. Her father had made a fortune out of automobile parts and Cosima was the love of his life. His wife, Cosima's mother, was a social object, ensconced in a big house on Long Island, creating a past which involved forgetting her immigrant grandparents and discovering an obscure noble extraction in Italy.

When Cosima's father died in 1975, his wife was left in isolation on Long Island. Cosima was her father's daughter. Moffett had worked out another thing. Living in his wife's house was just one more needle to drive Laing on. That needle, among others, had convinced Moffett that Laing would succeed in Vietnam. As for Cosima, she appeared to be so devoted to him that she hardly concentrated on her own life. His ambition consumed hers.

Moffett opened the *Times* and chose a heading at random.

Gonorrhea Resistant to Penicillin
Shows Abrupt Rise in New York

His eye skipped through the article.

1,372 cases of this totally resistant strain which produces a penicillin-destroying enzyme . . .

He picked up a shell, smelled it, and slid the oyster onto his tongue, to be squeezed before slipping down his throat.

FIVE

The last romantics in the world were American men, the masters of eternal expectation. Cosima had always believed that, but meeting Moffett reminded her. She had a more cynical friend who called it the mad man syndrome—rational people could never be sure what they would do.

Her friend found it annoying, because she felt threatened. Cosima was amused. She dodged her way through the honking of a traffic jam on Park Avenue, past a Checker cab carrying an illegal election sticker—"Carter's I.Q. is lower than Inflation." She was late for a meeting with a music promoter, who was coming to see a fourth set of plans for his sound studios.

Moffett had made her think of the way she had first noticed Martin Laing, apparently by accident at a dinner in New York —that was long after they had actually first met at McGill. She had been delighted by how hard he tried and had quickly realized that Laing tried that hard at everything he did. It wasn't endearing, but it was a declaration of life. She saw him as someone who didn't live in expectation but gave of himself. She knew no other person of whom she could say that. At thirty-three, Cosima believed she was well acquainted with what used to be called love. Whatever it was, she and Laing missed each other when apart without being suffocated when together. They allowed habit to play no role. They spent a lot of time concentrating on themselves and each other and their lives. That was the point of doing well in America. The real prize was time, not money.

It wasn't that she expected never to love another man; in fact she wasn't very interested in calculated expectations or exclusive visions. What she felt for Laing was anchored as a physical presence somewhere deep inside; a love that she couldn't express except through emotion and through her body.

However great her intelligence, Cosima was neither an intellectual nor what was ordinarily called an ambitious woman. She was an associate in a large firm of architects, which on the surface wasn't much of an accomplishment. But the fact that most of her friends from architectural school were more successful didn't bother her and, curiously enough, they didn't see themselves as having done better. Cosima always appeared to be embraced by the arms of success. She had never bothered to compromise or to struggle to fit into the kind of mould that would have sped her along. Somehow that same physical sense which expressed her emotions for Laing made her believe her time would come. Even when her friends took her ideas and used them in buildings because they were in a position to do so, she didn't mind. In fact, she was delighted. Envy was something she didn't understand.

As the only woman associate in her firm, all the fringe projects seemed to come her way. They had been coming ever since she'd passed her Architectural Board Exams three years before. That had taken some time because she'd failed Design two years running through lack of interest in the architecture of pre-digested formulas. The architects on the examining board hadn't been looking for the answers that she gave. Not that her ideas were radically different. She found simply that they were eliminating the interesting questions by making them irrelevant.

She had passed the third time, thanks to Laing's pushing her off to a crammer who knew what the examiners wanted. He could describe exactly what fire station they were waiting to hear about; where the emergency exits should be; how many flower boxes on the upper floor; how many square inches of toilet per fireman.

Once she had leapt this last hurdle, the senior partners stopped asking her to do the potato peeling part of hospital projects. They could see the day coming when there would have to be a woman partner in the firm and they thought she was the right person to groom for the honour. Just to be sure, they had given her an office down at the end of a corridor and were waiting to see what business she could produce. When peculiar projects came to the firm they were sent along to her, as little presents.

Cosima had always told herself that she didn't mind. Her calm but insistent optimism made her act as if everything were all right, while everything that was wrong built up inside. Periodically she exploded without warning and everything changed.

For the moment, she accepted being treated as the partnership clown. The one problem she admitted to was being the only woman in the firm and that for a specific reason—loneliness. She had to find her friends elsewhere—old classmates from Brearley who were far from her everyday life or architects who had gone through city college with her. But her working day was one of isolation.

She arrived to find the music promoter waiting patiently beneath the electronic ticker tape which ran along one end of the reception area, carrying excerpts from great architectural writings. "It is desirable to introduce taste into an art which shows so much—Jefferson," was flashing across. The walls of the room were hung at varying angles, disorienting the eye and encouraging people to sit down or leave.

He smiled when she arrived and jumped to his feet. He had an inoffensive face, even pleasant. She suspected the reason he had rejected the first three plans but still came back was that it prolonged their conversations.

They talked inconclusively for most of the afternoon, at the end of which he asked if she were free for a drink. The invitation was expected. There was always an invitation. She refused effortlessly, without thinking and without wounding him, despite a distant politeness.

SIX

By the time Laing left Hanoi, he was overwhelmed with a sense of victory. From an impossible situation, he had pulled not only success but the springboard to his future. All the elements were in his hands and he was determined to keep them there when he arrived back in New York on Saturday, 24 May, so exhausted by the pressure-cooker humidity of Hanoi and the long flight that he collapsed into a sixteen hour sleep.

Late on Sunday morning, he awoke to find Cosima sitting up beside him, reading. The sun streamed into the bedroom, reflecting off her skin. He put his arm around her waist—with an instinctive relief he always felt, that she was still there—and slid closer until he smelt the faint rose scent of her perfume.

"Tell me!" she said. "If Moffett can tell me where you've been, you can tell me what you did there. Come on." She began tickling him.

He grabbed her hands and held them down as he kissed her. "No. I can't. At least not yet, even if Moffett has a loose tongue."

"All right, Martin, all right!" He let her go and she sat up again. "Anyway, it's your body I'm interested in, not your mind. I can always have lunch with interesting men." She took his head in her hands and kissed his eyes. "I missed you," she said. "I missed you more than I realized."

"What about pangs of jealousy?" He made it sound like a joke.

She looked at him, surprised. "Why should I be jealous? I love you."

He lay back and ran his right hand from her neck over her shoulders and breasts.

"*La poitrine pensante*," she said. The thinking breast.

Monday was 26 May, Memorial Day, so the office was closed, leaving Laing twenty-four hours to write his report. Cosima had asked him if he wanted to accept a dinner invitation for Tuesday evening. It was from a friend of his: a junior vice-president in a small bank. He said no. He could only concentrate on this one thing and told her to go alone; not only to that, but to the collection of cocktails and gallery openings and other tidbits that made up their normal life. On Tuesday he sent the report over to be typed and telephoned to say he wanted to see Moffett the next day, if the senior vice-president was available. Morley had been told to stay at home until after that meeting and to show no signs of life.

Moffett was eager to be available. He came in at nine and waited, slouched behind his desk, leafing through the report. His delicate mauve and blue striped shirt seemed out of place in Laing's idea of a corporation; but then, so did the ochre-coloured walls and the elegant eighteenth-century American furniture. He sat down and waited until Moffett looked up genially.

"This is wonderful, Martin. Eighteen months to get a substitute company together or the Act rescinded. A good, quick pay out. First call on the surplus oil. A few decorative niceties about training local personnel. Now tell me, why are they doing it?"

Laing described what he had seen. The economic crisis. Vietnamese hatred of the Chinese and distrust of the Russians. Their desire to see America back economically as a counterweight. "As for specifics," Laing passed him two typed pages. "Morley knows nothing about this."

Moffett placed the sheets side by side on the leather-framed desk blotter which covered most of his desk and was used as an over-sized doodling pad. He leaned forward and began to read, following the lines with a red felt pen, his editing trademark. He underlined words here and there:

100 A-1H/1E Skyraiders
51 F-5A/B Fighters

90 M-551 Sheridan Light Tanks
791,000 M-16 Rifles . . .

"What is this, Martin?"

"Five billion dollars' worth of armaments. We, that is America, left them behind."

Laing described Ngo and exactly what they had seen in the warehouses. With Moffett's questions, if took half an hour, at the end of which Laing said, "The heavy material I didn't see. They keep it separate. The 636 jets and transport planes, the 900 tanks, the 466 helicopters and, well, it's quite unbelievable."

Moffett sat forward over his desk, analysing Laing's words. "And what was this tour in aid of?" There was a quizzical expression on his face.

"They want us to sell some of it for them."

Moffett stared at him doubtfully. "They do or he does?"

"Is there any 'he' in a country like that?"

"You tell me, Martin. In my experience, there is anything anywhere."

Laing chose to ignore the question. He knew Moffett had a tendency to get at problems by going round them and attacking from the rear. He was determined to stick to the main line. "The point is, they want money up front before they'll do our oil deal. I told them the Act made that impossible; not to mention government and press scrutiny into what oil companies do with their funds. I told him we had escaped what for other companies had been a disaster and we had no desire to be plunged in now."

Thanks to Moffett, they had escaped unscathed. Companies who listened to their economists and money men had been crucified like innocent children. As Moffett put it, the technocrats had been victims of their own contempt for history and ideology. Their naïve politics had consisted of workable solutions, as if there could never be a day of reckoning.

"The trouble is," Laing said, "Ngo's centralized little world is so far removed from our subtleties that he doesn't understand the improper use of funds."

Moffett interrupted him, laughing. "You forget, we were impregnating half of Vietnam with American subtleties until five years ago. And the French were there until 1954. Ngo seems to have understood something. If not, why this ingenious proposition?"

Laing relaxed. Moffett had seen the opportunity. The young man played his trump card. "According to Ngo, if they provide us with a commodity to sell on their behalf, there's no reason for Western-Oriental or its money to be involved. Everything could be done anonymously."

"Then why not sell it themselves?"

"To whom? Their own army used a bit of the equipment against the Chinese and the Khmer Rouge. But they have the strongest force in South Asia without any U.S. equipment. So they've given some M-16s and mortars to guerillas in Thailand and other odd groups. All of which accounts for ten per cent of the stock. They can't sell to their neighbours because their neighbours are the enemy. The Communist countries in Europe don't want American weapons. And to top it off, they don't want to attract attention."

Moffett picked up the list again. He paced around the office reading it through.

196 VH-1B Armed transport helicopters
36 A1-1G Cobra attack helicopters
30 A1-1G Unassembled in crates
780 M-113 Armoured personnel carriers
940 Landing craft, patrol craft, other naval vessels . . .

"Unbelievable. Do you have prices on these things?"

Laing produced a book called *Arsenal of Democracy.* Moffett sat down behind his desk and began looking up items. The capacity of each weapon was described, along with recent prices on the official and the open market. Ten minutes later he looked up.

"How much do they want?"

"One hundred million net."

Moffett slapped his desk in surprise. "Peanuts." He made a few calculations, in red, on the blotter. "Some of this material is worth two or three million a piece. But why would they bother, Martin? They have a two-billion-dollar trade debt. One hundred million is nothing."

"I know. Perhaps they want proof that we're serious. Perhaps they think they'll have something over us; something they could threaten to leak if we didn't co-operate down the line."

"That might be, Martin, but it is peanuts to them and peanuts to us. We can cover our expenses with a small percentage of the sale. And we can fund the up-front costs through any number of offshore banks without any possible trace. The mechanics are easy. When the sale is made, the money flows through and we leave enough behind to cover the funding. The question is, do we want to do it? Have you checked up in Washington?"

"Yesterday. Foreign Weapon Supply at the Pentagon—I used total discretion."

"Martin. I assume as much." He sounded annoyed.

"The Pentagon believes most of the arms have fallen apart or at least been seriously neglected. They think everything is sitting out in the fields rusting."

Moffett was on his feet again. "Typical. They cannot understand how to fight without spending billions on frills. What else?"

"They're blacklisted. In '75, after Saigon fell, the State Department warned all allies and countries receiving U.S. aid that if they bought any of the weapons friendship would be damaged and aid cut off. Of course, that was five years ago and they haven't got a great reputation for follow through."

"There are only two cogent points," Moffett said smoothly. "One. The arms business is government business. It is tightly run. The private dealers are mere flies on the carcass. Do we want to get involved, even for a one-shot deal? Two. How do we do it? Or rather, who does it for us? I do not know the business and I do not want to know it. This is hardly the time for amateur night at the Bijou, nor can we hire just any professional. The last thing we would want is to have the word out on the street."

Laing ignored point one. "I'd like to organize it, if you'll give me the go ahead. You handed me the negotiation when there was nothing. Now all you have to do is let me complete it. You can always shed me if I make a mistake."

Moffett looked at him, surprised, almost wounded. Then his face froze. "I could and would. You have an annoying habit of saying the unnecessary."

Laing found that Moffett didn't always react logically to his ideas. He apologized before going on. "I have an old friend who could play the intermediary. He isn't an arms dealer, but he's in that sort of business and is perfectly trustworthy."

"What is his name?" Moffett was delighted that Laing had worked the whole thing through before coming in.

"Anthony Smith. We were at McGill together."

Moffett jotted down the name, with the intention of having him checked out, and mused, almost to himself, "I should really like to lock up those offshore blocks. They are worth this sort of risk. But your Mr. Ngo is on the make. You say he is a Southerner. A month in Saigon was enough to turn the straightest man into a crook. You forget, I put the deal together for the original drilling in '74. How do we know Mr. Ngo won't just take the money and run or simply not deliver?"

Laing had asked himself the same question and not found a convincing answer. He gave Moffett his arguments with all the assurance he could muster, "Ngo may well be on the make for all or part of the money. That doesn't mean he won't deliver the leases. The deal is too complicated for him to be doing it without other people being involved at all levels. What does it cost them to deliver the leases, if they get the money? It's almost easier than not delivering."

Moffett smiled. It was exactly the argument that had been going through his mind. "Perhaps. One thing about Communists; they are so naïve about capitalism that they never break a deal. For them, it is like playing Monopoly. As no one really owns anything, there is no need for betrayal. Let me think about it."

In the fading light at the end of that day, the walls of Moffett's office took on a warm glow. He paced the length of the windows, reading through his old Vietnam files with the energy that the scent of a new deal gave him.

The geologists' reports were as encouraging as he remembered. Underneath was the original press release announcing the discovery. The local manager had stupidly mentioned the strike to some hawk at the embassy in Saigon, who had pressured him to announce it, arguing that the discovery was vital news which might encourage the Vietnamese to fight harder and make Washington give greater support. If the war were lost, the discovery would be lost; so the manager went ahead before checking with New York. Moffett had been furious. Any fool could have seen the game was over. He fired the man within twenty-four hours and pulled the rig out a few days later.

At seven he went into his private bathroom and noticed, in the mirror, signs of unexpected fatigue. Mulling over what to do, he went downstairs where his driver was waiting. The traffic went smoothly until Madison near Fifty-sixth, when they hit a jam.

Moffett couldn't see what he had to lose. If Laing wanted to be a hero, all the better. The young man had guts and if he succeeded he'd be well on the road, to . . . well, Moffett knew that road. The exercise would be good for Laing—a dose of reality, something beyond textbooks.

The car drew up in front of his apartment building, on Park Avenue at Seventy-fifth. Moffett climbed out, but hesitated before going in. He finally decided to walk for a while and turned off the soulless avenue towards Lexington, up a few blocks and over to Third. On Eighty-seventh he dodged a neat pile of dog faeces, placed in the centre of the sidewalk. The campaign to make owners pick up after their dogs was already slipping from people's memories. For a fad, it had lasted quite a few months.

It was Laing and Laing's deal that kept him walking. Moffett knew it appeared strange, even to himself, that he should have chosen this particular young man to push ahead into the vacuum that would be created the day he retired. But he had been looking for someone who had that intangible kernel which could make him a man of real power—power that emanated from within, not the corporate structural creepy-crawly kind. He had sensed from the beginning that Laing might have it. There was his training against him, but training was something to be flung aside in the face of reality.

Moffett took himself as an example—he had studied literature. Now, when people discovered this, he said it was his interest in new plot lines that had drawn him to the oil business. If they had any intelligence, they laughed.

What bothered him about Laing was not his training, but that only a certain breed of men seemed to want that training. To his mind, these Masters of Business Administration, these technocrats, these computer print-out geniuses, were all men who would have been bookkeepers fifty years ago. Now, because society needed their talents, they were becoming men of power. What was the phrase? If Byron were alive today, he would be a rock star. Moffett chuckled almost out loud. If Uriah Heep were alive today, he would have a Harvard MBA and be running a corporation. Moffett looked up at some condemned buildings. Or he'd have been Secretary of State, like that fool Kissinger emulating Metternich, one of the greatest failures of all time. Both of them had rushed from country to country creating artificial arrangements and technical victories, as if restructuring the world to suit themselves would change anything. The flow of history had effortlessly washed away both their empires of cards. Moffett couldn't convince himself that Laing belonged to that section of humanity.

At Ninety-fourth, near Second, there was a vacant block.

He walked over to the fence surrounding it and stared in. Laing wasn't really one of them. He just wanted to be. He could therefore be rescued. The vacant lot was a vegetable garden filled with a hundred little plots of cucumbers, beans and carrots. Tiny stalks of corn had just come up. Moffett wondered whether Europe had been like this after the plague passed, the cities disintegrating into large villages. Of course, that was an unheralded blow of disease. But time was now like a disease, striking down civilizations in fractioned moments, where once it had taken centuries. He remembered the brownstones that had stood there five years before. He even remembered when they had not been slums, twenty years before.

Why not go ahead?

SEVEN

Moffett telephoned Laing the next morning. He wanted a full report within twenty-four hours and would take the project to the Executive Committee on 3 June, the following Tuesday.

Laing didn't trust the older man to make the hard sell. He might trade Vietnam off against something else, or get it through with strings attached, or agree that someone should oversee both the project and Laing. When the report was finished, he sent one copy to Moffett, then telephoned David Fell and asked to see him.

Fell was the sort of man who enjoyed setting up meetings then keeping people waiting outside his office, a minor destabilizing technique. Laing avoided that humiliation by suggesting seven-thirty on Friday morning.

David Fell's childish habit might have seemed out of place in a man who was considered by all to be much more than successful. At the age of forty-two, Fell loomed already as the successor to the President of Western-Oriental. As Vice-President, Finance and Corporate Planning, he stood third in the hierarchy. He was also a reasonably good-looking man—tall, with a slightly muscular build—although looking at him the idea of physical strength didn't come to mind. This was because he regarded exercise and sport as a competition between men rather than the pursuit of excellence.

He brushed his hair straight back, which left a curious impression. From the hairline to the crown of his head, the growth was remarkably thin and often betrayed a red rash and peeling skin; perhaps a case of delicate flesh, perhaps of stress breaking out through a surface not under intellectual control.

Like Laing, he was a graduate of the Harvard Business School. Laing had tried to get a job with him when he first went to Western-Oriental; not because he liked Fell or wanted to work for him. It was just that he knew the senior MBA in the company was the right star to be under. They would all rise together.

Laing knew all about Fell. He had left behind at Harvard a myth which was laid out before all the students as an example from the moment they began there. Fell had been one of the most brilliant products of the system. Stories abounded of how he had treated the school as if it were itself a Case to be solved. The odd professor even admitted that they had taught him nothing. They had merely refined his tendencies.

His fame had been made eternal by one incident in particular, which involved the method he chose to deal with the only student who rivalled him. Rather than compete, Fell set out to destroy his credibility. Each time the man presented a case, Fell jumped up to undermine his arguments. For months, he miraculously found weaknesses to exploit and magnify, until everything else was forgotten.

The man reacted like a rabbit running before a train. He worked harder and harder to eliminate his weak spots, without realizing that Fell's comments were malevolent. In the end, only the attacker's reputation as an outstanding student remained. The one winnable defence would have been to attack Fell's own work, which had fallen off while he concentrated on his enemy's. But at the time no one noticed that because their eyes were fixed on the sparks from the battle.

The rival became increasingly nervous over the months; he began to show his stress and then to break down. Eventually, he appeared to be begging for execution. One day, near the end of term, Fell rose and moved effortlessly from destroying the man's arguments to ridiculing him personally, in a way that could only be done when the victim was already on his knees. The other students saw what was happening and gave a subliminal cheer for this final blow.

That night, the man threw himself from a high enough window to lie in a coma for two days before dying. The less talented people in the class blamed it on Fell—that was what Fell's supporters said. The winner was in the front row at the funeral and privately blamed the pressure put on by the professors. He meant what he said.

The students of Laing's day argued that Fell was justified because he had proved the other man inferior, but the story of Fell's victory had always left Laing uncomfortable. He preferred not to think about it.

When he got to Western-Oriental, his choice was unavoidable. Two myths dominated the company and everyone who worked for it—Moffett and Fell. Their rivalry was freely talked about, as was their hatred for each other.

But Laing saw it as something far more important. Fell was gradually taking over the company for the new men with their new ways. He was a crusader on behalf of the MBAs, on behalf of their way of doing things.

For Laing, the myth of Moffett was the myth of an almost extinct beast who survived on judgement and willpower alone. He rejected everything Moffett stood for. Fell was reality. Fell's successes were Laing's successes. It was only a matter of time until a total victory was won—reorganizing, restructuring, eliminating the non-business school bodies one after the other until none were left. Laing wanted to be on the winning side, so he shrouded his doubts.

But when he had first gone to Western-Oriental, Fell had had no place for him. At their first meeting, the Vice-President had encouraged him to take what was offered, while promising to keep an eye on his career.

Fell was neither loved nor understood, which was as he wished. Always calm and understated, he conveyed a sense of profound aggression. To control a conversation, he would suddenly inject a few words or a question accompanied by a meaningless but acute stare, which was usually enough to put the target off balance. It was as if his eyes were bald. There wasn't the slightest hint of doubt within them. His tactic was to discredit the person's line of reasoning by any means before introducing his own.

He had incited a rationalization of the company, which meant diversification and minute restructuring into small operating units. The Board was delighted. The days of the high rollers, with their big risks, were in the past. Minimal risks and quarterly profits were the soul of the new system. Fell's secret was that the units were of his making and only he understood the relation between them.

Behind these tactics was an honest delight in pure destruction. At that moment, when others were disoriented, he could gather up the meaningless, shattered fragments and remould them into a new order—the order he had decided upon before the destruction. Pure reason was applied when men were being unreasonable.

The night before his meeting with Fell, Laing tried to decide what to say to him as he sat silently with Cosima, lost in his thoughts until midnight. Their drawing room was painted in shades of terracotta. Cosima said it was to remind her, during the New York winter, of Italy. There were a minimum of comfortable chairs with simples lines, silver blinds on the windows and lacquered tables, empty except for one or two objects on each. Cosima liked to be surrounded by clean space.

Laing hardly noticed when she asked his advice. She said she felt she was not really building anything. She had done what her partners wanted for three years and it consisted of rearranging bedrooms. She wondered whether changing firms might help. When he turned aside her question, to avoid thinking about it, she buried the idea and with it a touch of resentment.

Through the windows she could see the skeleton-like concrete pillars of the office block rising up on the far side of the yard. She had organized the residents to fight the promoters. Each time she focused on its outline, she felt, as if it were fresh, the sense of failure that had washed over her when it became clear that her neighbours were protesting only to get a higher price for the loss of their privacy.

In the clarity of solitude, she repeated to herself what had been going through her mind for weeks—everyone has to serve time, but she had become an architect because she believed in certain things. In the back of her mind there was some sort of vision, but they had tried to banish it even from there.

The refrain of a school song went through her mind.

"We're Brearley born and Brearley bred and when we die, we're Brearley dead."

Fell's office was at the opposite end of the floor from Moffett's. It was also very different—his standard desk was covered in files, as were two metal side tables and all but one of the wooden chairs. Fell worked hard and used a great deal of paper.

He listened to Laing's story in silence, offering no sign of interest beyond an innocuous stare and eventually a disinterested question. "Why tell me? Surely, it falls within Moffett's domain. He'll bring it to the Executive Committee."

Laing hadn't expected obtuseness. He wondered whether he'd gone too far and said, with a hint of nervousness. "Of course, but one wonders whether Mr. Moffett really appreciates the opportunity? I have the feeling he has moral compunctions about the arms trade."

"Moffett? Morals? Come on." Fell leaned forward and fixed his eyes on Laing as if he were in another world, auditioning for a part he had no reason to expect.

Laing fidgeted with a jacket button. "I wonder," he said, "whether he would prefer someone more his style to handle it?"

"Ah. He might take your chance away?" Fell suddenly looked understanding. "I'll see that he doesn't. Agreed? But you keep me informed. And do it your way, Martin. Don't let them interfere." He went back to reading a report, which meant the meeting was over.

Laing went away pleased. In his office, he made a detailed memorandum on the conversation, sealed the sheet in an envelope and asked his secretary to put it in his personal, not corporate, Vietnam file. He was very exact about his records.

Fell turned the conversation over and over in his mind as he tried to make something of it. He picked up his phone and dialled Morley. Five minutes later the young man was in his office, sitting in pudgy submission, allowing himself to be cross-examined about the Vietnam trip.

Morley had kept him fully informed on everything that went on in Moffett's department since shortly after he arrived in the company. Fell only wished he had arrived sooner, because he was the kind of person who could be perfectly controlled. Morley's ambitions were so straightforward that Fell knew exactly what each of the young man's words meant. One day he would make a reliable vice-president.

Laing was another matter. There was something there that Fell couldn't get a grip on. The man's emotions and drives were too complicated. He couldn't be relied upon to do what was expected.

To Fell's surprise, all Morley knew was that the official negotiations had finished abruptly with an agreement that came out of nowhere. When Morley questioned this, Laing had explained that he and Ngo had worked out their differences on the day off, away from the pressures of the negotiating table. But Morley had a feeling there was something else, a missing element that was being kept back. Fell impatiently filled him in on the arms deal and made him feel he had failed without actually saying so. He instructed Morley to keep his eyes open for any developments.

EIGHT

"What makes us powerful?" Moffett asked. "Our style not our money. We can do what we want because nobody understands what we are doing."

Moffett lay on a sofa in the President's office, late on the afternoon of 2 June, just as he did every Monday afternoon, running through the agenda for the Tuesday morning Committee meeting. The President, Robert Erlich, slouched in an armchair with his feet on a low reproduction "Georgian" table. Erlich wore a tweed coat and a blue button-down cotton shirt, which suited his paunchy body. He was drinking gin with a hint of vermouth.

Moffett was still talking, with a Scotch in his hand, "the mystery part I love. I do not mean this new religion of organization. Organizational mystery is the refuge of a fool. They create a structure capable of doing real things only if you accept their definition of their organization as reality."

Erlich laughed because he was used to this needling. "James Moffett, ageing adventurer and prick. What are you going on about? We still control the company. It's still going in our direction."

Moffett had a headache and was tired. He persisted in these meetings only because they left Fell hamstrung before the Executive Committee even met. He pointed his glass at Erlich. "Bob, you have the consistency of a fly after fresh droppings. Why else would you be President? When they finished restructuring this place, what direction will it be going in? I have no idea. And I am supposed to be your senior and respected counsellor, the man with whom all secrets are discussed. But do you know what the secrets are, any more than I do?"

Robert Erlich had been the most popular man in Western-Oriental for years. He was a brilliant geologist who could smell oil at a thousand miles, but he wasn't a man of direction or vision. Choosing him had been popular with everyone—an oil man's oil man, they said—but he knew what it meant. The Board didn't know what to do with the company, which was why they didn't choose Moffett, the logical candidate. They knew what he would do.

"Did you see this garbage?" Moffett pulled out of his pocket a page from the company magazine with a paragraph circled in red. "Listen to this:

> 'Corporate leaders are truly men without a country as they strive to overcome irrational nationalist constraints and integrate the world.'"

Erlich nodded awkwardly.

Moffett persisted, "Are you *trying* to bring people down on us?"

"Come on, James, it's not that bad. Besides, it's true, we're anational, not multinational." Before Moffett could say anything, he shifted the subject. "Hey, what do you think about Thomson? Fell wants to prosecute him for that information he gave. He says we got a good case, it being privileged stuff."

"Of course Thomson gave information." Moffett had never had headaches. For the last six months they had been coming at unexpected moments and he couldn't tell how bad they were because they were pounding on virgin territory. "I am a mere politico, Bob, a negotiator of deals. You are the messiah-cum-geologist. You know what happens when one of your type believes there is oil to be found where no one believes it exists. He becomes a prophet. If he has any guts, when his company shuns him the way Jerusalem shunned Christ, he picks up his bags and heads for Rome. You should know. That was how you came here twenty-two years ago. Why? Because you converted me and I converted them and the company made a lot of money."

"I thought about that last night." Erlich nodded, a boy pleased at having worked it out for himself, with an honesty he could allow himself in front of Moffett, not the others. "Your great Colombian coup. There I was, blowing my career, changing companies on a dumb belief, making my first important discovery, and then some flaky dictator wants to take it all away. I was trying to remember his name."

"General Ramos."

"Nuttiest dictator I've ever run across. But then they're not my line. You think this Vietnam deal could be as big?"

"Bigger." Moffett had already sold him on Vietnam; at least, he thought he had. He could never be sure until the Committee meeting was over. "You watch this boy Laing. He will do the deal the right way and I shall have him ready for your job in another year."

Erlich laughed, but his mind was still on Colombia. "Dictators are your line, James. But Ramos could have had his percentage and lived happily ever after. You never told us how you did it, except there were $200,000 miscellaneous expenses on the books at the end of the year. You did it for almost nothing."

"I did not tell because it was not quite as smooth as the old boys here thought." Moffett tried resting his head on the back of the sofa. He hated reminiscing, but at least it reminded Erlich that theirs was an old alliance. "It was easy enough to find the right colonel, with a bit of a chip and a few brains. The price was nothing. He could see the real profit would be in the royalties. I helped him get organized, since I knew Ramos's movements. I was seeing Ramos every day, in what he euphemistically called negotiations. He spent most of the time insulting me, usually across some foul lunch served on silver plates.

"Two days before the coup, he started asking me how well I knew the Colonel. I said he was a charming young officer who played cards well, which helped me pass the time and cost me a bit of money. He kept grunting and making clicking sounds with his tongue. A very annoying man. Anyway, I, shall we say, acted precipitously—otherwise known as panicked. Your first real discovery, my first real crisis.

"I sent a message to warn the Colonel. I told him I would wait at the airport in the company plane—a tacky old Dakota. The President, of course, had me watched. He heard I was racing for the airport—because I was stupid enough to tell the driver to step on the gas. Fortunately the messenger I sent to the Colonel went unnoticed. Ramos probably thought he could deal with us separately. First the foreigner, who was paying. That would demoralize the Colonel. Then a little internal spring-cleaning. The soldiers picked me up at the airport, a bunch of goons with their safety catches off.

"Half an hour later Ramos arrived, shouting as he came through the door, making his men aim their rifles at my head, in a circle, you know, so that if they fired, they would kill each other. I was so scared, I just stood there, speechless. Apart from an incapacity to talk, I am lucky enough not to show fear—it comes out as stubbornness. My Colonel had not wasted a second. He arrived with a regiment and surrounded the terminal. So there I was in this dirty shack with the President and twenty goons, while three hundred soldiers waited outside. All they had to do to take over the country was open fire, with me an unfortunate casualty. Luckily the Colonel was naïve enough to think W-O would not pay up if I were killed and Ramos knew I was his only card. So they arranged a truce, just the three of us in the air controllers' office, to see if a deal could be done—you know, Ramos on a plane, no mess, no fuss. After three minutes of rather strained conversation, the Colonel pulled out his pistol and shot Ramos in the head."

Erlich started. "With you there?"

"Blood and stuff over my face and ruined my jacket. Red on beige is most unattractive. I emptied the pockets and dropped it on the floor. With Ramos dead, his supporters did not argue, so we celebrated in the President's palace that night."

"You made both of us vice-presidents." Erlich's remark was forced. He hadn't expected the end of the story.

Moffett scarcely seemed to hear him. "Ramos was irrelevant. What was it Stalin said? In the end only death wins. As for our Mr. Thomson, if we had explored where he wanted last year, he would have stayed and the discovery would be ours. If we prosecute and win, no senior oil executive will be able to change companies. We shall have total control over our people, which is fine, if we want them. But supposing we want someone at Gulf or Occidental? He will be untouchable. What happens to building the best company with the best people? And eventually, someone will appeal against our control over his personal life as an infringement on their human rights. And we shall lose."

"That's right. That's right." Erlich let loose his confusion. "But why do you think Fell wants to push it? To scare people? Shit. It makes us look like fools." He pursed his lips.

"Why?" Moffett suddenly came alive. "Because he cannot believe that someone who does not get his way here can simply step outside and get what he wants elsewhere. Fell and his technocrats defined this system as if there were no reality beyond their illusionary balloon. They react like children before what we know are the hard breaks of making a mistake."

Erlich nodded without agreeing. Moffett saw this and persisted.

"You just cannot see it, can you? Look, Fell and his band of Harvard MBA cronies see themselves as the gunslingers of the modern world, but all they are is sophisticated grease jockeys. Highly paid mechanics. They tinker. They replace parts. They tune up. They invent more complicated circuits to do the same thing. But only they know that. They invent a vocabulary to dignify their work by making it incomprehensible to us. And all that has nothing to do with reality."

Erlich got up and walked around the white sofa and the Chinese rug lying on the brown carpet to pour himself another gin. He changed the subject. "I've been looking at the preliminary quarterly profits. We might want to get an ad campaign on the road before they come out. Fast."

"The embarrassment of success." Moffett raised his glass. "Something about, 'Trust us, we love you.' Or was that last year? Something about, 'Your energy future is in our hands. Profits are not a dirty word. They pay for our research into the future.' What I suggest is that we postpone the hotel deal. And that we go ahead with the foundation."

"For Christ sake, what's that got to do with it?"

"The sooner we throw a big chunk of money into our own non-profit organization, the sooner we shall be paying a lot of nice people to write and talk about the right things. We pull their teeth. We make friends. They become our fulltime PR campaign."

"We can't postpone the hotel deal or we'll lose it." Erlich looked uncomfortable.

"Who says?"

"Fell says."

"Of course he does." There was contempt in Moffett's voice. "Do you realize this will be our eighth investment outside the industry in seven years? Hotels, timber, life insurance, copper, pulp and paper, department stores, cinemas. The money men say diversify. We diversify."

Erlich laughed. "With any luck, we'll be out of the fucking oil business before the crackdown comes."

Moffett was on the edge of exploding so he said nothing. Neither of them knew how to go on. They didn't let their arguments get out of hand. Moffett drew back. "How is your wife? Any better?"

"She's fine. You know Liz. There's always something wrong. I guess digestion is easier to deal with than the back."

Moffett nodded. Erlich had a tired marriage, from which business helped him to escape. Or the other way round. He was long overdue for what Moffett called the Bendix Washer syndrome—trading in his wife for another model, the same make but new. All Moffett's business friends had divorced and married younger versions of their first wife. He couldn't work out why. Inability to learn from mistakes? A question of taste? Sentimentalism? A desire to relive their youth now that they had money?

Moffett half mumbled, "I was running through the industry figures last week. You may remember that OPEC revolution in '73." He saw Erlich smile. "Remarkable memory. The economy of every Western nation was destroyed while our profits went up seventy per cent. We and the other six majors had net profits of $7 billion. Taxes $.6 billion. By 1977 the net profits were up to $10 billion. Taxes, well . . ." He flicked a hand as if it were unnecessary to mention them. "Our profits continue to climb while our sales decline. And why does the government leave us so much profit? Because we are going to reinvest it in oil and find new reserves to free them from the shackles of OPEC and discover wonderful new forms of energy. What did industry spend on R and D last year? Eight per cent of profits, the lowest of any industrial sector. What are we doing with the profits? Buying department stores."

Erlich began to look impatient. "Come on, James. We put a fortune into coal."

Moffett cut him off. "Into coal reserves, Bob. We are tying up the reserves, just like Atlantic Richfield and the others. You know we are going to do damn little with them until the price goes up. Between us, we have fourteen of the twenty key reserves and we are going to sit on them until the government is hungry. Or should I say desperate."

"That's garbage. You seem to forget we have a coal producing company."

"Exactly. Two years ago we bought one of the biggest companies and what happened? Their production dropped twenty-five per cent while production in the independent part of the coal industry rose twenty-five per cent. I brought the matter up in the Executive Committee. Fell dodged and you mumbled."

"Come off it," Erlich pouted.

"God knows, Bob, I love to see us all blooming like a monstrous rose. But a smart man takes care. He does not raise too much hatred and envy in the hearts of others. He makes friends. He plays the larger game, not just his own, so that they believe he is a team player. Your systems men cannot see that. They have us on an infallible golden path, built out of their illusions."

"Shit, James! Bullshit! Who's going to crack down?" Erlich sat forward and waved his arms as he spoke. "This dumb government? Carter loves coal. Takes his advice from Atlantic Richfield. They have bigger reserves than we do. And if by some freak that ad-man Reagan should win, what's he going to do? He'd marry us if he could. We win both ways this fall. Even if you are right in theory, the reality says they'll leave us alone until you and I are long gone. What are you moralizing for? Look at that Colombian deal. Twenty years of production for $200,000. You call that a good deal for them, Mr. Moffett? And this Vietnam business? You call that honest? Your Laing, is he Jesus Christ reborn? Could have fooled me. How does that make you better than a number crunching technocrat?"

Moffett jumped to his feet, his head pounding. He walked to the bar and poured another Scotch. "Because, you old bastard, we took responsibility for what we did, even if it scared us. I vomited up my dinner that night after I left the Colonel-become-President. Your systems men have no idea what they are doing. They only know what the system does. And since machinery is immune from responsibility, nobody carries the can."

Erlich slouched back into his chair, suddenly morose. "You haven't lost your touch yet, James. Play the game a bit. Don't leave me here alone."

NINE

With disappointment, Moffett saw it was only six o'clock when he left Erlich. He took a pile of foreign newspapers from his office and locked it behind him. Downstairs, he told his driver to take him to the Century Association, where he climbed to the first floor and installed himself in a corner of the large drawing room. He avoided the reading room on the other side because he liked to read where other people talked. Maurice brought him a Scotch without being asked.

Moffett had joined the club years before, when old friends from Yale offered to put him up. Theoretically, it was a place for literary people and Moffett was one of the few members who neither wrote nor published; although from the oil industry's point of view he was too literary. He had wanted to join because none of the members knew him in business. He could sit in the drawing room for hours, the panoply of paintings staring down at him, and no one would walk up to exchange gossip.

He drank one Scotch slowly, followed by a second quite fast. His headache gradually disappeared. At seven-thirty he got up, went downstairs and his driver took him home.

James Moffett's wife, Isabelle, had smooth, well looked after skin and an embracing way of speech—like considered honey. She had never been able to understand why her husband would not let them move from their apartment. He had had it before they were married, thirty years before. Being five years younger than him, she had not felt it right to suggest anything too quickly. But as the years went by, when she did suggest it, he changed the subject or made a joke about her grandiose tastes.

Not that there was anything wrong with it—a large place in a good building. It was simply too much like the large Park Avenue apartments of too many other successful New York businessmen; the difference being that they were vice-presidents or presidents of smaller firms or successful lawyers. They were not senior vice-presidents of a major oil company.

The apartment had been redecorated with every ounce of her taste, until it was as carefully arranged as her hair or her make-up. She came from an old New England family. That meant she had no desire to see the eighteenth-century of France or England as testimony of her taste. Instead, much of the apartment was furnished with pieces of Federal furniture, which Moffett also liked. The first investment they had made together was a set of maplewood chairs from Philadelphia, with an intricate design of flowers painted on the oval backs, to be used around the dining room table. At first, she had hated the dining room because it had no windows; but in the end it was an advantage. Moffett had so many pictures to hang.

Isabelle Moffett was proud of her husband and he no longer loved her. They were a much admired couple totally loyal to each other. They were admired for the harmony with which they pursued such independent lives, an indisputable sign of great devotion.

He arrived a few minutes before eight, when they usually sat down to dinner. Although Isabelle did not really care about food, she knew he did, so a cook appeared each afternoon to ensure that he got what he wanted.

Their conversation was a litany of her day, leaving him to eat in silence. While his wife's syntax was simple, even direct, her thoughts were intricately interwoven. He found it impossible to interrupt as she laid out her minefield and leapt deftly, without warning, from one secret safe spot to another. There had been a time when he had been happy to listen to her—not for what she said, but simply because the sound of her brought out his feelings. Now he felt nothing. The sound fell to the floor and lay there. He noticed again how little he missed his two daughters, now that they had not only grown up but married and left the city, one to England and the other to Los Angeles. They were like carbon copies of his wife, but then he had left it to her to rear them. In those days he had travelled almost permanently. A remark of Isabelle's made him glance up. She had thick, fine hair and warm eyes, when she chose to look at someone. He could still see what had drawn him to her.

He looked about the windowless dining room at the walls covered in naïve paintings that he had bought over the years from American and Caribbean painters. Now he wondered why. They weighed on him, an indistinguishable mass of unformed talent. People had vented their spleen on the unsuspecting canvas with almost aimless energy.

"I think we should get rid of all these paintings," he said.

She looked at him, neither agreeing nor disagreeing. "I thought you loved them."

"Apparently I don't."

"Those two gilt oval mirrors, James, you know the ones, with the wheat sheaf crown, would look very nice in here. They must be about the same period as the chairs, I should say."

TEN

The Executive Committee met on Tuesday morning at ten. Moffett always made a point of arriving in Erlich's office thirty minutes early, in case he had weakened on some question overnight. They walked together down the hall to the conference room, Erlich rolling at a forward tilt on the balls of his feet, his arms bent at the elbows, his fists up, like an overweight boxer crossed with a guppy.

The other five members were waiting. Erlich gave a general greeting from the door and made his way around the room with a series of jokes, as if working a night club audience.

He ran an informal meeting, pushing people on through the long agenda. There was a final look at the hotel chain acquisition; a discussion on whether to buy a second network of cinemas; and a request from the Canadian subsidiary to move ahead on a heavy oil project. It was a request which Moffett simply relayed to them.

Erlich exploded at no one in particular. "Those dumb asses up there, we've told them to hold off. James, what's the Canadian government heavy oil subsidy?"

"They give us $16 a barrel on top of the normal price, plus depletion on development costs, plus they will help finance the upgrading plants."

"It may sound great, but we all know in another year or so it'll be greater. We already told them to sit on it. It's bad enough having to deal with Arab and Black nationalists. If even the Canadians start getting trouble . . . Christ, it's too close to home. Just tell him, James, what's his name . . . ?"

"Ferguson."

"Just tell him we don't give a fuck what his passport says. I mean, does he want the job or doesn't he?" Erlich liked to lose his temper once in each meeting. It was his clumsy way of showing power.

Moffett calmly deferred, "I think, Bob, that we can move on to the next item."

Vietnam was near the end of the agenda. Moffett presented the project with perfect equanimity, lest they realize how important it was to him and up the stakes. He gave out no paper. "Under the circumstances, I think things should remain oral." He didn't mention who had gone to Hanoi, simply what was offered. It was easier to sell the project on his own responsibility. He had asked Laing to come and wait outside once the meeting started, so that when everything was approved he could bring the young man in, introduce him and give him full credit.

The House Counsel, at the far end of the table, spoke up first with the unruffled air of someone who had never sought a brief. His job was to cover the angles. "It runs a little near the bone. I'm sure it's doable, James, but is it doable without ramifications?"

"We would only make the one sale," Moffett replied. We do it at arm's length. We tie up the best offshore blocks."

"How at arm's length?" he persisted.

"We put one man on it, informally, you understand. He receives nothing, signs nothing, touches nothing. Our man finds an individual to manage the company, someone who knows the business. That man buys an offshore shell company and gets working funds through local arm's length borrowing. He doesn't even know who we are. The bank does, but no document links us with the bank. He spends the money, receives the arms, sells them and banks the hundred odd million. He then transfers one hundred exactly into an unnamed account at the same bank, where the Vietnamese do with it what they will. He pays the company's debts with the balance, including his own fee. That empties the account. He folds the company. Story over."

Erlich began clapping. "Like a poem, James, Another Moffett miracle in the making. Go ahead. Just don't tell us anything about it till it's over."

Moffett was about to bring in Laing when Fell spoke from down the table. He had a way of moving so that everyone's attention was drawn. He paused, to make them uncomfortable, then spoke,

"Who negotiated this miracle?"

"I was coming to that. It was Martin Laing . . ."

Fell cut in, his face immobile, his lips moving in disbelief. "Sounds like he deserves some credit. Maybe he should finish the job."

An old poem went through Moffett's mind:

> I do not love thee, Doctor Fell,
> The reason why I cannot tell . . .

"That was my intention," he replied.

"Good, James." Fell could hardly be heard. "Good to hear about the rising young."

Moffett was about to lash out when he felt himself go cold, his anger turning inwards. He drew a red circle around the notes before him and closed his folder. The poem wouldn't go away:

But this one thing I know full well,
I do not love thee, Doctor Fell . . .

Moffett turned to Erlich, an ice-like shield across his face. "I shall have to skip the rest of the meeting. I have an appointment downtown."

Seeing that something had happened, Erlich vainly tried to soothe the air. "We can leave the rest until next week. Nothing but chicken shit."

Moffett stood up, fuming. Fell had made him look like an ageing virtuoso stealing a young man's credit. It must have been planned. Laing had probably gone to see him. They all thought alike. No—even in anger, he corrected himself—reacted alike.

He strode to the door, pulled it open and waved brusquely at Laing to come forward. The motion was so unfriendly that Laing thought all had been rejected, that somehow he was to be made a scapegoat. He came uncertainly into the room. The older men around the table stared up at him, most of them not knowing who he was. Moffett put a hand firmly around his arm and moved him towards Fell.

"Here is the man you are eager to congratulate." His voice was above its normal pitch, almost out of control. "I asked him to wait outside on the off-chance you might feel inclined. Mr. Fell, Mr. Laing. The Vice-President is an admirer of yours. I leave you in his care."

Moffett turned and walked out of the room leaving the door open. In the hall he moved blindly, ignoring a secretary who greeted him. Only in his office, behind his desk, did he try to calm himself. For the first time, he questioned whether Laing was the right man. Why risk so much on someone whose loyalties were confused. Moffett could feel ambition rising again within himself, like the desire of youth. This wasn't just another deal. He needed the success, not for them, but for himself. There was something else. He knew this kind of game was uncontrollable once the players were let loose. Everything lay in the first move.

He forced himself back through his own arguments and found that they still stood—Laing's confusion would be swept away by the demands of action and he was still the only man in sight who could do the job. Then the ache of regret crept through Moffett's body. Why had he acted so stupidly at the meeting? Why had he lost control? That was exactly what they wanted.

PART 2

ELEVEN

Anthony Smith lay on a series of raised cushions under a jacaranda tree in his friend Sayed Idrissi's garden. He was re-reading *Moby Dick*, a cigar in his mouth, waiting for notice of yet another final meeting. In a group, Smith would have passed unnoticed. Here, isolated, his dark hair set off the pasty quality of his skin. He was soft, almost pudgy, and sweated lightly in the morning heat of the Moroccan summer. It was Friday, 6 June, and a brandy and soda sat on a low table beside him.

Idrissi always insisted that Anthony should stay at his house, a sprawling maze of rooms, modern but finished with a Moorish touch. Smith didn't argue. Time was an invention of a different kind outside the West. In Rabat, time was properly passed in the company of friends.

He looked up to see the houseboy walking towards him beneath the trees, an envelope in his hand. Smith finished the page before closing the book. He was looking for a passage which, he remembered, began:

Oh, Time, Strength, Cash and Patience!

He took the envelope and ripped it open. There was a Telex inside from his one-woman office in London, relaying a phone call from Martin Laing. Would Smith contact him urgently.

They hadn't spoken since running into each other in Hanoi and the gap before that had been a year. Laing was one of the few New York friends he kept up with, although Smith's constant movement meant there had been periodic silences over the last sixteen years. Yet no matter how long these gaps, they had always been able to pick up where they had left off, which Smith believed was a sign of true friendship; and he was an expert on friendships. He devoted himself to two things in life—enjoying his friends and doing deals, in that order. It was a formula for survival he had come to by natural inclination.

The operator took thirty minutes to get the call through to New York. When both men were on the line, Laing wasted no time,

"Can you come to New York?"

"I can't, Martin. What's up?"

"We'll pay your way."

"Don't overdo it." Smith expected Laing to be eager; that was one of his charms. "I can't. Not for a couple of weeks. What are you up to, Martin?"

"It's too complicated for the telephone. Would you mind if I came to Rabat?"

"I'd love it. When will you come?"

"Saturday."

"Tomorrow?" Smith didn't disguise his surprise.

"I'll leave this afternoon."

TWELVE

"Rabat consists of two worlds," Karim Farid would say, "the twelfth century and the nineteenth. I am acquainted only with the former."

From the small gazebo in his garden, where he received friends—and he had reached an age where he received no one else—he could see down through his miniature terraces of orange trees, rose bushes, pomegranate and jacaranda trees with their weeping flowers, across the Oued Bou Regreg as it flowed into the Atlantic. On the other side of the river were the walls and roofs of the town of Salé, untouched by the modern world.

Protected inside the Casbah of the Oudias at the end of a series of narrow alleys, with high stone walls behind him and the cliff edge before, he maintained his illusion of timelessness. His house was cooled in June and through the summer by the Atlantic breeze, which carried the scent of his mimosa into every room. In the winter he went south, across the Atlas Mountains to Zagora, in the valley of the Dr'aa on the edge of the Sahara.

Karim Farid's life was not one of solitude. His friends came to see him, and below, on the banks of the Bou Regreg, thousands of people walked on the sand, while small boys swam just inside the breakwater.

His physical appearance had years before become one with his state of mind. At seventy-five, he was an ageless figure; tall, slightly stooped, with a cautious, solid walk. He was fleshless without appearing drawn—more preserved—with a closely clipped beard. Despite his reputation as a man of learning and religion, he had gone through three wives and was enjoying his fourth. He had also been a resistance leader in the struggle for independence.

Sidi Karim, as he was addressed out of respect, sat on a wicker chair. He faced inland that Friday afternoon, through one of the four open doors. He was protected from the wicker by two cushions—one beneath and one behind—and was drinking tea from a glass. His worn djellabah was of cream wool, so finely woven that you could see the long, frayed tunic beneath, and the knee-length white bloomers beneath that. His feet were kept warm by a pair of short, striped socks and slipped into babouche—yellow leather slippers.

"Stop talking, Moulay Sayed. Find us some figs." His English was rudimentary. He had learnt it in the 'forties, as a protest against the French colonialists.

Moulay Sayed Idrissi jumped out of his wicker chair and left the gazebo, which he had given to Karim Farid twenty years before—a present to a friend and a mentor. Around the inside, over the doors, words from the Koran were carved.

> For those that fear the majesty
> of their Lord there are two

gardens planted with shady trees.
Which of your Lord's blessings
would you deny?

A large, beefy man of forty-nine who enjoyed life by throwing himself into everything and laughing at whatever happened, Sayed Idrissi searched aggressively through the three fig trees for fruit which was split open with ripeness. He had flung a grey striped djellabah over his Italian shirt and trousers before coming to Karim Farid's house.

"Let Anthony find the fruit," he shouted over his shoulder. "What does the Book say? 'Take neither Jews nor Christians for your friends.' And he's the youngest."

Idrissi picked a handful of figs and tossed one towards the gazebo, giving Anthony Smith just enough time to lunge forward. The American ambled back to his place.

"Which proves unbelievers can catch," Karim Farid remarked. "Now tell us what happened."

"My view was coloured by ignorance." Smith spoke in French, which was easier for the other two to follow, with a slightly American accent, each word perfectly clear. He had developed the same hesitation in English. Although American, he had the disjointed cadence of someone who has not lived in his own country for years. "In 1971 I was twenty-six and in Morocco on business. I had an introduction to Moulay Sayed from a friend in Paris. Despite his great age—what, forty?—we got on. He thought I needed contacts. I knew I did. He got me invited to the King's birthday party. At the time it seemed to me a grandiose gesture. I hadn't yet realized what a tight little ship this country is. The doors open or the doors shut. That was long before he introduced me to you, Sidi Karim."

The old man was peeling the skin off a fig in long thin strips. He looked up politely, then broke the fig into four pieces and slipped them into his mouth, one by one.

"It was July. We drove off in his Mercedes in open shirts, thank God. Even on the coast, the heat was unbearable. With all those California bungalows, Skirat was not quite my idea of a summer palace, but the setting, in the gardens by the beach, made up for it. And the party was marvellous. Moulay Sayed introduced me to a collection of useful people, which turned out to be a waste. Half of them were dead by the time the party was over. The great General Oufkir was wandering about like a mythical figure—remember, the Ben Barka kidnapping was still fresh history. He was so ugly, he was perfectly handsome. He had the face of a ravenous hawk and yet his charm was overwhelming. You almost expected to be asked to dance. Blood on his hands and delightful manners."

Idrissi shouted, "Get on with it, Anthony." He poured three more glasses of tea.

"In the early afternoon, about this time of day, we were inside one of the bungalows with a dozen or so people. Out of the sun. I was talking to a friend of Moulay Sayed's who was getting married the next day. We heard shouts and what I thought were flags snapping in the wind. Three young soldiers ran into the room, firing at the ceiling. I dropped my plate and froze." Smith's voice had a calm that made him appear to be whispering.

"They ordered us outside into the courtyard around the swimming pool. Hundreds of other guests were already there, plus the bodies of guards strewn on the ground. Two officers, who seemed to be in command, told us to lie down. I caught sight of Oufkir melting to the stones with the rest of us. Moulay Sayed whispered to me, 'Can you see the King?' That was who they wanted, because they sent soldiers through the crowd, making us turn over on our backs to see our faces. When I was turned over, I looked straight up at a boy who couldn't have been more than eighteen. They were all officer cadets. He was sweating, petrified, although I was the one on the ground with a rifle pointed at me. Eventually the two colonels decided that the King had escaped and rushed away themselves to attack the key strongholds around the capital. They left the cadets in command. We were told to stay on the ground and anyone who moved would be shot.

"The lucky people had escaped right at the beginning by running down the beach. Frankly, I was so terrified I couldn't have moved. Moulay Sayed kept whispering to me that we should try to escape before the sun fused us to the stone. Without officers, the cadets were getting nervous, firing at the least excuse. Bullets kept whistling overhead, as people shifted and were promptly killed. Moulay Sayed's friend, who was getting married the next day, was lying next to us. He went funny in the sun—I suppose he had eaten and drunk quite a bit. Suddenly he clambered to his feet and announced, 'I've got to go now or I'll miss my wedding.' The impetus from the bullets threw him across me, blood pouring everywhere. His body lay there for the rest of the afternoon, which, apart from the blood, protected me from the sun and the stray shots. Moulay Sayed was going crazy. The fellow's face, mouth gaping open, had fallen inches from his own.

"What saved us was what we didn't see. A cadet who was checking in one of the bungalows opened the door of a toilet to find the King before him. Hassan stuck out his arm and said, 'I am the Commander of The Faithful. Why do you not kiss my hand?' The boy collapsed to his knees. Within fifteen minutes the King had rallied the cadets and taken over the palace. Ninety-three guests were dead. Hassan disappeared into the night, while Oufkir brushed himself off and set about putting down the revolt. Now that's *Baraka*. The King has always had more than his share of divine luck. *Baraka*. That should be his theme song."

"Who would sing it?" the old man asked, with a sudden smile. "What did you think about, all that time on the ground?"

"That I should be more careful about accepting Moulay Sayed's invitations." He bit a piece out of a fig. "And that the only reality is physical pain."

Sayed Idrissi breathed in an asthmatic way before breaking in sarcastically, "Christian pessimism. Think! They died, perhaps they will go to heaven. You lived. In fact, you joined a select group by being there and surviving. Did you do your deal?" His voice was rising.

Smith nodded. "I believe I did."

"And did I, your friend, live?"

"I believe you did."

"Well?" Idrissi demanded.

"Stop shouting," Sidi Karim interrupted. "It does not suit you to shout."

Idrissi fell into a chastized silence, while Smith said, "I've always had trouble with your fatalism."

The old man stopped him with a small sharp movement of his hand. "I am not a fatalist. Pessimism is a sin. I accept the past because it has happened—it is God's will. You Christians do not accept the past. You and the Jews are pessimists and grudge holders. We are the most optimistic race in the world. I do not understand your dark side."

"What?" Smith snapped.

"If you understood yourself better," the old man replied, "you might be able to understand us."

Smith blushed, ashamed of having risen so quickly. He

found himself thinking of his conversation that morning on the telephone with Martin Laing. There was an optimist. There was a man who understood himself. Smith looked up brightly. "Your figs, Sidi Karim, are wonderful. It must be the ocean air and your voice."

The old man insisted. "What I do not understand, Anthony, is why you spend your life selling other people's belongings in other people's countries. I am happy that you give us a month here, a week there. But you always have, Moulay Sayed explained it to me, a deal to do. You will become the man of other men and lose yourself. You should go home."

Smith hardly let him finish. "This isn't a time to go home. We Anglo-Saxons have a mythical hero, Beowulf, who spent his life fighting other people's battles. 'For him who trusts his own merit it is better to visit distant lands.' His words not mine."

"You trust your own merit?" the old man asked.

"I visit distant lands."

Karim Farid laughed, a small, dry laugh. "Moulay Sayed, pick some fruit to take home."

"But we have too many in our garden."

Karim Farid waved him out. "Yours have no sea air and they grow from new trees in newly tilled soil. I admit these are not so good as in my garden at Zagora, but there the desert air caresses them."

Idrissi went into the garden, where he found five large purple figs. "I shall eat them as if they were history and truth." He laughed.

Smith rose and kissed Karim Farid's hand as it was withdrawn with humility. Idrissi followed suit.

THIRTEEN

Idrissi's Mercedes was waiting at the monumental gateway of the Casbah. He got in beside the driver, a dried, stubborn looking little man, while Smith climbed in behind. As they started down the hill and around the walls of the old medina, a man who had followed them unnoticed out to the gateway made an entry in his notebook. Then he disappeared back inside the Casbah to a place from which he could watch who called on Karim Farid.

"How much longer do I wait?" Smith asked from the back seat, pleasant but insistent.

Idrissi twisted to face him and answered in a calming tone, "Not a great deal longer."

"Not much, Sayed?"

"Not much." Idrissi turned away to shout at his driver, although he himself didn't know how to drive, "Can't you pass those cars? Come on, let's not take all day!"

"For God's sake, Sayed, leave the man alone. We're in no rush. What about my bid?" Smith pulled out a short cigar. He lit it as he talked.

"It may surprise you," Idrissi said, slightly irritated, "that I have other things to do than shepherd your buses through the bureaucracy."

He looked at his watch and took a powerful transistor radio from the floor. Moments later he had tuned into the five o'clock news from Paris.

The driver took the high road, dominated by the mausoleum of King Hassan's father, who had led the country to independence in 1954. They passed the Fortress of the Chella on one side and the King's palace on the other. Beyond the prison-like silhouette of the Hilton, they came to Souissi, the new district.

Those who ran the country had built their villas there on large properties surrounded by high walls. They said they needed air and space. In fact, they wanted to show that they, the old ruling famlies, had won the great race for material prosperity. Fez, their old capital, with its villas and palaces, had been abandoned to great-aunts and country people. But the Fassi still ran Morocco, the way they had run it for a thousand years, with their own particular finesse.

Sayed Idrissi came from one of the great families of Fez. He was descended from the Prophet Mohammed and, because of that, people gave him the courtesy title of Moulay. There, he had gone to one of the country's two senior schools—two was all the French permitted. From those years, he knew half the people running Morocco.

The French had allowed no local university and had controlled which students went to which universities in France. Idrissi had applied for Paris and Politics. They said no. He had applied for Paris and Philosophy. They still said no—still too suggestive of subversion. He had applied for Paris and Medicine. They said no, unless he went to the provincial university in Bordeaux. A lot of politicians and resistance leaders were doctors.

In Bordeaux, Idrissi had become a friend of the Crown Prince, a mere colonial student whose father, the Sultan, was a vassal of the French. After independence, Idrissi had been named a counsellor to the Crown Prince, who was now King.

When the news was over, he turned apologetically to Smith, "It won't surprise you to learn that the other bids have their friends at court. I can hardly trample over them."

"Who?" Smith's question was one of professional curiosity.

Idrissi waved it away. "That's my affair. However, you may be lucky, dear Anthony. Your bid stands in the midst of disorder. The French may be out because the King wants to keep away from them and the Americans keep insulting people by trying to bribe them the wrong way. Which leaves you—an old friend, with some half decent buses at not a bad price. And everyone will have their little percentage. I hope your clients will be pleased."

Smith shrugged. "I find the Germans don't know how to be pleased."

Idrissi laughed with his deep wheeze and clicked his tongue.

"I have a treat for you," Smith threw in. "An old friend of mine is coming to town tomorrow."

Idrissi said automatically, but with warmth, "Then he must become my friend," as the car pulled into a narrow road with high walls on both sides. At the end was a gate and a soldier, armed with a compact machine-gun. The soldier looked closely, then shouted. The gate swung open and the car drove onto a lane, through a shade casting garden.

The next morning, Saturday, 7 June, was a difficult one for Idrissi. He was driven to the King's entrance of the palace, where he walked past the servants dressed in white djellabahs, and on through to the room where His Majesty ate breakfast.

This event took place at irregular hours. One of the hereditary privileges of the King was to wake when he awoke. His daily schedule began at that moment, whatever the hour. However, Idrissi didn't like waiting around. Instead, a servant telephoned his house the moment the King stirred. Ten minutes later, the Counsellor was at the palace.

That morning, the King stirred, but did not awake. Idrissi found himself waiting half an hour in an ante-room with other advisors.

When eventually they went in, they found the King in good spirits. He sat at the breakfast table eating, a light *gandura* thrown over but not concealing his HOM bikini underwear and his still trim figure. A ceremonial guard with a scimitar stood behind. The Counsellors spread around the room in uncomfortable poses, leaning on walls or tables. Only one of them managed to look at home—Colonel Benmansour. His athletic shape and close-cropped hair slipped naturally into an "at ease" position. He might have been on parade, had he not been in a dark suit.

As for Idrissi, he had long ago established that he would not stand. There was only one chair in the room that morning and the King was on it. With an audible clicking of his tongue, the large Counsellor moved two china figurines off a side table and handed them to the guard, who had to lean his scimitar against the wall to free his hands. Idrissi pulled himself up onto the table. The King looked at him and smiled.

"Comfortable, Sayed?"

They began the agenda in the usual way. Different points were raised for the benefit of the King, who busily assented or dismissed. After three assents, he cut off the conversation and said to no one in particular, "Why is Fatima so fat?"

He was referring to a niece. There was silence, until a household official stepped forward and volunteered, "Perhaps, Sire, it is because she eats two lunches."

"What do you mean, she eats two lunches?" The King pursed his lips when he spoke, verging on a lisp.

The official began to wish he'd said nothing. "She eats one at the Palace, Sire, after which she is driven to the American School and given a second lunch."

Fatima was an element in the King's strategy to strengthen ties with the United States. He hoped the example of his niece would encourage others to give their children an American, rather than a French, education. The King stared doubtfully.

"You mean, she eats one of those American meals?" His tone conjured up white bread, ice-cream, starch. "Tell her not to."

"That would be difficult, Sire," he mumbled. "As I understand it, she feels she must, if the other children eat, that is."

"Look," he pointed a fruit knife at the official, who flinched at this subtle threat to his job, "she must lose weight before the end of the term. She's so fat it's embarrassing. Send her to a clinic. Look, send her to that rice place in North Carolina. Someone else in the family went there. What's it called?"

"The Kempner Institute, I believe is the name, Sire."

"Send her there for two weeks." He waved the man aside. "What about the Sahara?"

Colonel Benmansour walked forward and recited in a mechanical rhythm, "General Kader is in the Sahara preparing a column to relieve Zag." Kader was Commander-in-Chief in the South. "There were a number of minor incidents yesterday. Two short mortar shellings of Smara. One patrol incident south of Zagora." The other Counsellors listened with a mixture of admiration and envy, except Idrissi, whose face betrayed contempt. The Colonel added, "There are indications that a guerilla force may be building up in the south, on the Mauritanian border. If so, they could be aiming for Dakhla . . ."

Benmansour went straight from the King's breakfast to his own office in a wing on the other side of the palace. He arrived to find that his appointment was already waiting.

The man was called Gerten, an ex-Colonel in the American army. He sat heavily in a white drip-dry shirt and a blue seersucker jacket, a peevish, wounded expression on his face and his head held up by his hand. He didn't move when Benmansour came in; his eyes simply followed the Moroccan across the office, expressing automatic dislike. Benmansour sat down behind his desk, glanced briefly at the blunted face before him and opened the conversation,

"I understand you had to come from Paris. We're very grateful. Dr. Menet tells me you are willing to do a bit of work for us."

"Well, I'm doing Menet a favour." Gerten didn't move his hand from his face, so the Midwestern accent was distorted.

Benmansour, in his turn, looked at the man with bemused distaste. "Of course, Colonel Gerten. Dr. Menet and I have discussed how much he will pay you."

"You can't pay for this kind of favour. The charge is for my time." Gerten's expression had in no way changed. He had once been trained to kill in support of a cause and that, he had come to feel, was not only acceptable but right. Violence for money was another matter. It left a burden of shame upon him and a profound hatred for those who bought his skills.

Benmansour wasn't interested in a debate. "Good. As you know, Dr. Menet hopes to close an artillery contract with our army. There is an Englishman staying at the Hilton"—Benmansour handed him a paper with a name and room number on it—"who has a rival proposition. We want you to make it impossible for him to continue the negotiations, while still being able to leave the country." Benmansour smiled engagingly.

Gerten didn't smile back. "By when?"

"Tomorrow."

Gerten nodded, got to his feet and left, a short, tired figure whose strength, although concealed, could be sensed; more like an animal than a man. He had been a reasonably average, ageing officer in Vietnam until he was seconded to a section organizing hill tribes in Laos. It quickly became apparent that not only could he kill, but he could teach large groups how to kill with the same efficiency. Promotion came as a reward. However, the complications of holding the tribesmen's loyalty and becoming their friend got him involved in protecting their opium traffic. Gerten neither approved nor profited, but did what was necessary to keep them fighting at his side. He began by allowing them to use his transport planes and ended up involved in their violence. It was some time before his superiors in Saigon discovered he was killing too well—that is, the wrong people for the wrong reasons. No matter how hard he tried to explain that it had all been done in the good cause, they insisted he retire to save himself from court martial.

His first idea had been to convert himself into an arms dealer. After all, he was an expert in the needs of South East Asia. He went on to do quite well selling small arms to his old friends in the hills, until the war ended and the whole area closed up. Various staff officers threatened to leak his dossier to the press if he went back to the United States, so Gérten retreated to Paris, where his reputation won him little more than a marginal living out of odd jobs of the sort he despised.

FOURTEEN

"I don't sell guns." Smith lurched to a sitting position on his cushions.

"But, Anthony, you don't understand. It's not a question of . . ." Martin Laing was baffled, perched on a chair above his friend. He had been so caught up in working out the steps he would ask Smith to follow that he had scarcely noticed Idrissi's driver, who met him at the airport, or indeed Idrissi's house, outside which the two friends sat in the shade of the trees late on that Saturday afternoon. When Laing had arrived they had gossiped for a moment; then Laing had set out the proposal, without bothering to sell it. The last thing he had expected was a refusal.

"Did you really think . . . ? I'm surprised you came all this way without checking." Anthony Smith's face was flushed. When he was embarrassed or annoyed, he blushed easily, and in this case he was both.

"I thought you'd be interested, Anthony. Don't get excited."

Laing had always heard Smith talk as if he were available to anyone at a price. That was how he financed his itinerant life—without suffering a permanent master. Perhaps self-respect pushed his standards higher when he dealt with friends.

"Anyway, I'm here." Laing tried to ease the tension by making a joke of it all. "You can't shut the door on me like a brush salesman. And I can't walk back to the hotel. I don't know where it is."

They relaxed, but said nothing. After a moment's silence, Smith clambered to his feet, ambled a few yards towards the house and called. A boy appeared a few minutes later with mint tea and a plate of rich shortbread patted into balls, which crumbled if lifted too firmly.

"For someone who doesn't like guns, you certainly display them." Laing pointed toward the gate.

"They play a practical, not a dramatic role. The man they protect has asked me to ask you for dinner tonight." Smith's face was pasty again.

"Then we're speaking." Laing's relief was genuine. He would work out what to do later. "What have you been up to apart from selling train tracks to Hanoi?"

"Run-of-the-mill stuff," Smith said, stretching out again on the cushions. "I'm just closing a deal here. Then I'm supposed to go down to Chad on a uranium kick. An American group have been negotiating mining rights there for three years. Frankly, it's a lost cause. The government offering the leases doesn't control the territory the leases are on, but the rebels won't get off their asses and finish the war. The Americans hired me because I once got a load of grain into the place during a drought and got paid."

Smith hadn't bothered to shave that morning. On his pallid skin a sparse black stubble could be seen around the chin. That was probably the only place he ever had to shave. His nondescript white shirt strained across the stomach. In all, seedy.

"Before Hanoi I was in northern Thailand—a sewage system for Chiang Mai—on behalf of clients who had a Protestant view of honesty, as learned in the sewers of England. Trouble is, the Thais won't move without graft going into every pocket. Well, you can imagine what that was like. In the end, the Thais got their graft and the English didn't realize they'd paid it. So everyone was happy." Smith swallowed two pastries, one after the other. "What have you been doing?"

Laing had now had a moment to think. He'd so far given

Smith no details, as Moffett had instructed. But it was clear his friend could only be won over with the full story, so he began to lay it out carefully, beginning with his frustrations during the last year, trying to break through the corporate maze, held back by Moffett, an ageing egotist who controlled every detail of every interesting event.

This bleak picture was broken by Vietnam. Laing explained how the legal and political problems had forced Moffett to put everything into his hands. He could see Smith was intrigued. They both knew that reviving a dead deal was harder than starting a new one. He described the negotiations in detail, the way he had laid his trap, and Ngo Van Cu's entry into it.

"The MBA defeats Marx," Smith teased, but he was hypnotized as Laing described the warehouses, the money Ngo wanted, their plan to meet in Bangkok after Western-Oriental agreed and, finally, the conversion of Moffett and the Executive Committee.

"The company is going along with that?" Smith raised his voice above its normal whisper.

"One isn't supposed to know the company is involved."

"Just suppose I'd said yes?"

"I'd have been elliptical, even poetic, in confusing you over who was involved." Laing had relaxed, his normal warmth had come back.

"Why tell me now?" Smith knew he was being led on, but he didn't mind so long as there was no frontal attack.

"Now you're not involved, Anthony. This is between friends. We've always told each other . . ."

Smith cut in impatiently, "But why is the company doing it? That's what I don't understand. The risk, well, you must see that."

"We want this deal. We're talking about the best spot in one of the biggest undeveloped fields. Anyway, the company isn't involved. This is an airtight operation with no tentacles leading back to Western-Oriental."

Smith sat back, apparently satisfied. "So here you are, a nice kid all dressed up with nowhere to go."

Laing laughed complacently. "Worse than you think. All the documents for the offshore company are right here." He patted the briefcase lying on the grass. "They're made up with your name as Chief Executive Officer. All I need is your signature."

Smith ate another pastry, grinning. "You won't get it. And

what were you proposing to pay me? My normal fee is five per cent. That would be five million."

"A bit steep, but it doesn't matter. We cut the fee and the costs off the top. The Vietnamese want one hundred million. If it costs us one hundred and ten, we simply sell more armaments. I guessed you'd settle for one or two per cent. That's a lot more than I make walking on the straight path of corporate religion. Now why won't you do it?"

Smith shrugged. "You've never met the dealers. Pariahs. One that I know lives in a nineteenth-century mausoleum in Paris, with a handful of servants. Alone. A fat, bald, half blind old man who trades seventy-five million a year. The first time I went there, he took me into his office. Twenty yards by ten and almost as high, gold leaf everywhere. He scraped his nail over one of the doors and held up the finger, with the gold stuck under the nail. What was I supposed to say? Well, I have a nice clean reputation as a man who gets things done and embarrasses no one. I'm unengaged from everyone's point of view. Selling guns is a marriage contract."

"No one is proposing to you, Anthony. Anyway, this isn't an arms deal. It's an oil package."

Smith shrugged again. Despite his refusal, he was seduced by the complexity of the operation. Apart from the weapons, it was the sort of puzzle he loved. "Let me think about it, Martin. I may have some suggestions for you. Would you mind if I checked with my friend Sayed Idrissi? It may not look it from here, but Morocco is in the middle of a war."

"Don't mention the company."

Smith rolled to his feet. "After all, you mustn't miss the chance to became an important man in the church of your choice. Come on. You've got just enough time to change and get back here for dinner." He put his hand on Laing's shoulder and led him to the car.

That evening, Idrissi received in the European way. Before anyone arrived, Smith cornered him in the vast Moorish-Italianate drawing room with its long, low Arab sofas, designed by a man in Florence, and its elaborately carved traditional tables holding abstract metal sculptures. He told Idrissi the little he had to be told—that Laing was an old college friend, now in the oil business. An independent consultant. The arms deal was a sideline, but not Smith's kind of sideline.

Idrissi's reaction was unexpected. "Why are you so worried about casting the die? Always the extremes. Undying friendship. Unconditional surrender. Your friend needs help, so help him. I know nothing about these things, but crawling around the throne, with a hand stretched out, there are many who do. I'll ask tomorrow."

They looked up to see people arriving. Idrissi jumped to his feet and embraced the man who led them in. He was a young Ambassador—an elegant, lithe man who had come home to rejoin the crowd around the King. His grey silk suit blended into his grey-pink silk shirt, into his soft rose-coloured tie. The Ambassador was an old friend. "You're getting fat, Excellence, fat, in your retirement," Idrissi threw at him. His shoes were of the thinnest calf, his socks a fine silk, which rose in spiral weaves up his delicate ankles and on out of sight. Behind him was his wife, larger, more regal, in a red Dior dress and heavily made up to conceal the approach of middle age. With them was an Englishman whose hair was dyed black. He had a jovial manner and was on the best of terms with everyone.

Laing arrived moments later. Smith crossed the room to meet him and whispered that he had spoken to Idrissi, who was going to see what could be done. "Come and meet him." The Moroccan gave a distracted welcome and turned back to the Ambassador. As Laing's was the only new face, the Englishman came up to him immediately.

"I'm Freddie Bingham, token Anglo around here."

"Martin Laing."

"Do you know these people well?" He indicated the others. "No, you don't look as if you do. Great town for parties, this. Not as good as Marrakesh, of course." He paused to see the effect of these words. Laing was not concentrating, so Bingham asked a pointed question. "You going to be here this weekend? Oh, you should really stay. Come down to Marrakesh. Prince Moulay Abdullah is giving a wonderful party. They do know how to give parties. We"—he meant Anglos—"have forgotten how." He was stopped by the appearance of Idrissi's wife, Kenza. She was tall, and much paler than her husband, with a sensuous, decided mouth. Bingham began, "Do you know her?" but didn't wait for an answer. He slid over and kissed her.

Kenza was nineteen years younger than her husband and did little to disguise the fact that her interests lay in her work as a doctor, not in playing hostess. She wore the expression of a hostage. Idrissi found his wife's public silence enchanting, as he more than made up for her with his own enthusiasm.

Just before they sat down, Colonel Benmansour arrived, apologizing that he had been held up in a meeting. His face was smooth, almost shining, so there had been enough time to shave and apparently to change. The Ambassador's wife took him in hand almost before he got into the room.

When the others were out of hearing, Idrissi turned to his wife and asked sharply, "What's he doing here?"

Kenza pointed to the Ambassador's wife. "A favour."

Idrissi's humour evaporated. He made everyone go into the dining room, which might have been transported magically from an apartment in the sixteenth arrondissement in Paris. When everyone was seated around the long table he began to eat in silence, then called for the second course before most people were ready, then released his anger by shouting questions down the table at Laing:

"Why does the United States import oil with such greed?"

Laing kept his own voice low, forcing his host to lean forward. "Because the government keeps the internal price down. If they'd free the prices, one would find more oil."

Idrissi began clicking his tongue. "If the prices aren't high enough, how do these companies make such large profits?"

"Illusory. Below general industry averages."

"Mr. Laing, Mr. Laing. We have a lot of phosphates, half the world supply. If the President of our national phosphate company—our equivalent of a Seven Sister—made the profits he does and still had to import phosphates, at our expense, we'd shoot him."

"No, Moulay Sayed," the Ambassador interrupted. "He doesn't know you're joking."

"Shh, Excellence. I personally would shoot him." Idrissi leaned towards Laing waving his arm, which just missed the plate of the Ambassador's wife, who was concentrating on Benmansour, at her right. Idrissi shouted at Laing, "Why don't your people demand nationalization?"

"The point is, we are a country of freedom and capitalism." Laing spoke with assurance.

"Freedom! What freedom is it to let a handful of companies bring their own country to its knees? That's not freedom. That's suicide! Anthony. Say something. Tell your friend he's mad." But he couldn't wait. "And how are you going to save the world, if you can't save yourselves?"

Laing replied good naturedly. "I'm restrained by my status as a guest."

"Bah!" Idrissi ejected. "Courtesy not bound by the realities of life is tiresome."

"They've lost faith in themselves, if they ever had it," the Ambassador said smoothly. He turned his eyes on Laing. "You did have faith in your science and know-how. Now it has failed you and you've nothing left except a few cowboy myths. Why? Because your science competed with God. Here they go hand in hand."

"Enough, Excellence. Enough!" Idrissi squirmed about on his chair. "We live in the past and its re-re-re-interpretations. What are we doing to push the great Arab revival? Look at you, Excellence, in your Italian suit. Look at my house, like something out of California. Where is our Arab revival? Everyone talks of it. But there's no leadership."

"The King," Smith threw in, to see what would happen.

"The King, the King. I love him," Idrissi sighed. "But the war in the Sahara blocks everything." Benmansour broke away from the Ambassador's wife to protest. He was cut off. "What have we won?" Idrissi appealed to his guests. "The casualties? A million dollars a day in costs? The national debt? The frozen economic programmes? All that to win some phosphates in the desert, as if we don't have enough. And now we have sixty thousand soldiers tied down in that hell hole by ten thousand guerillas."

Benmansour managed to interrupt, his voice raised, "The land was ours before the colonialists came. And the Polisario aren't guerillas. They're Algerian mercenaries."

"Who cares whether it was ours?" Idrissi hardly restrained his contempt. "Who cares who the Polisario really are? Either we should attack Algeria and have a real blow up, which will be over quickly. Or we should get out. The army is hanging a millstone . . ."

Benmansour lurched to his feet. "I won't listen to this." He glared around the table, already furious at having lost his temper. But he was up, standing awkwardly, his fists pressed to the tablecloth on either side of his half-finished plate of lamb, the others staring at him. It was too late. He kissed Kenza's hand and left the room.

After a moment's silence, Idrissi got up. He left the room through another door, without turning round. The sound of a radio being tuned drifted into the dining room.

Bingham leaned forward, touching his hostess's hand as if nothing had happened. "Kenza, are you coming to Marrakesh this weekend? Prince Moulay Abdullah is giving a party on

Saturday. I was there two weeks ago, when General Kader was up from the desert. What a charming man. I somehow feel, despite the war, that he does enjoy a party. Shall we go dancing when Sayed finishes with his international news?"

"I'm game," the Ambassador's wife said.

"Count me out," Kenza said wearily, "and Anthony hates dancing."

Smith looked relieved.

FIFTEEN

The groundsmen had not yet shut off the floodlights on Sunday morning when Colonel Benmansour cantered round for the first time. His route followed the edge of the golf course, installed by the King inside his walls. He went around again, faster, as he thought about his error the night before.

Of the King's six major palaces, Rabat best suited Benmansour's needs. The town was a bore, but he wasn't interested in those details of life. In Rabat the communications worked. With a minimum of fuss, he could do the jobs General Kader set him.

He left his horse with a servant and walked over to the Palace wing used by the military staff. Sunday was a holiday left behind by the French, so he was alone. He pulled off his riding gear and put on a rigorously waisted dark suit. There was a healthy flush to his skin, which he admired in passing.

No sooner had he sat down in his spartan office than Idrissi walked in, making an effort to look friendly, hands slunk into the side slits of a pale blue djellabah.

"Morning, Moulay Sayed. Did you go dancing after I left?"

Idrissi answered the question as if there had been no scene

the night before. "Once you left, the Ambassador's wife lost interest." They both laughed politely. "Look, Benmansour, I want some advice. Are we in the market for armaments?"

"What kind of armaments?" Benmansour reached into his desk drawer and switched on a tape recorder. He was seated in a half crouch, waiting for something to happen.

"American, second-hand. Pretty well anything you want."

"Moulay Sayed, we get them first-hand from Washington."

Idrissi fell onto a hard chair. "You say that, but they made us crawl for the last lot."

"True. But it's the best anti-insurgent *matériel* in the world." Benmansour came out of his crouch and sat back. "I don't need to describe to you, a peace-loving man, the reconnaissance subtleties of the OV-10 or the terrors of the Cobra helicopter. Who is selling these arms?"

"The American at dinner last night."

"I thought he was an oil man."

"Apparently it's all very complicated." Idrissi realized, with embarrassment, that he didn't understand either.

"Well, what weapons?"

Idrissi pulled out the list. "For looking only."

The Colonel threw his feet up on the desk. Solid black shoes. He examined the two pages in less than a minute and slid them back across the desk. The papers went too fast and slipped onto the floor.

"Of no interest," Benmansour announced.

Idrissi looked at the sheets on the floor and back at the Colonel. "What do you mean?"

Benmansour hesitated. He wished they hadn't fallen. As Idrissi made no motion to pick them up, he felt obliged to do it. Agitated, he got to his feet to come round the desk. While he moved, Idrissi bent over and scooped up the list. The Colonel sat down, humiliated.

"What do you mean?" Idrissi repeated.

The Colonel controlled himself. "The only collection I know of like this is in the jungles of Vietnam. The Pentagon blacklisted them. I should keep clear of it, if I were you, Moulay Sayed."

Idrissi laughed his wheezing laugh. When the General was away, the Colonel forgot he was Kader's shadow, not Kader.

"Dear Benmansour, your advice is always welcomed and shall be passed on. What news from the South?"

"The General will try to break through to Zag tomorrow. The garrison is fine, just lonely. It's too easy for the Polisario to close off a mountain pass. With a few guerillas, they can stop four thousand men from getting through. Have you ever seen the Ouarkziz Mountains?"

Idrissi stood up, wondering when this perfect staff officer could himself have seen them. "Well, I don't understand and don't want to. But I'll tell you, I preferred this war when we were fighting them down in the desert. I don't like it when they start striking up into the country itself."

"Scarcely inside," Benmansour protested.

"Scarcely inside!" Idrissi could feel his self-control sliding as he leaned over the desk. "Is that a soldier's attitude? My friends in the South tell me there was another incident near Tan-Tan last week. You didn't tell the King! They tell me the road's been closed to tourists a hundred miles north of the town. I wish the Spanish Sahara was still Spanish and the great Green March had never happened."

The Colonel was unnerved. He shot back, "Tell me if you like, Moulay Sayed. Tell the King, if you can."

Idrissi cut him off, suddenly shouting. "You can be assured I do! Regularly!"

"But don't talk about it in front of outsiders. Particularly Americans. That's my advice."

"I do not curb my tongue in my own country. That is my own value." Idrissi caught himself before things got out of hand. But as he left, he broke out, "Beware, Colonel, your ambition blinds you."

SIXTEEN

It was ten before Smith awoke. He threw on a *gandura* and went outside to begin a loose version of Tai Chi—an old habit that cleared his mind. He hated anything that smacked of exercise. A few moves in, leaning far to the left, his hand stretched out with the palm up, as if waiting for something to drop, he lost his place and gave up. Since Martin Laing's arrival the day before with his proposition, Smith had been unable to concentrate. He hated to be out of the action.

At eleven, he went to a meeting about his buses. An old-style bureaucrat tried to beat him down on the price, using what Smith thought of as the bazaar routine, but there the man was out of his depth. Fortunately, everyone else knew that they were there on a Sunday because someone up above was pushing.

Smith came back to the house, asked for a brandy and soda without ice, telephoned Laing to say he was free and lay down outside.

Laing had been waiting for the call. He picked up his jacket and went out into the hall, where he found men running up and down, checking rooms. Downstairs in the lobby there was great confusion; everyone who left the hotel was being questioned and searched. Laing waited for his turn and began answering questions about his movements until the concierge told the questioner that he was a friend of Sayed Idrissi. They waved him through. Outside, Laing asked the doorman what had happened. One of the maids had opened a room door, on the floor below his, to discover the guest, an Englishman, lying in the bath in his own blood. He wasn't dead, but his legs were broken and he had severe concussion. They had rushed him to a hospital.

Smith used Laing's arrival as an excuse to have a second brandy and took a cigar from a box he had found in the house. They happened to be Davidoff's, but he hardly noticed so long as they were short and not too fat. Something in plastic from a cigarette counter would have done as well.

Laing looked around for the first time at the garden. He had decided to say nothing more about the arms deal. The more Smith and Idrissi did on their own, the more likely they were to become fully involved. The only useful thing Laing felt he could do was to find out why they needed to buy.

"Last night your friend said they were losing their war. The headline this morning says, "New and Crushing Defeat of the Mercenaries." Says they chased them off the battlefield, killed two hundred and destroyed seventy armoured trucks."

Smith propped himself up on some cushions. "When did you start believing press reports? It probably means the Polisario harassed them, killed a few Moroccans and withdrew. Their strategy is not to hold ground."

"I'd never heard of the war until last night."

"And which others, Martin? I spend my life sliding around the edges of the thirty-four or so current wars, trying to do business with governments that may not be around long enough to pay."

"Hardly wars, Anthony. Skirmishes."

Smith shook his head and his nascent double chin. "Full-blown wars—civil wars, race wars, guerilla wars, neighbour invading neighbour. And everywhere I go, I find our government or the Russians or someone else trying to turn the war into part of their global strategy. They're fighting a world war by proxy, which used to be painless; now it's out of control. A corrupt pig like Mobutu becomes a defender of freedom and capitalism. And a half-mad Muslim fanatic like Gadaffi becomes a tool of Communism. Christ, Gadaffi has more to do with the Mahdi than with Marx.

"As for this war—the Spanish owned a chunk of the Sahara bordering on Morocco, Algeria and Mauritania that was bigger than England. But all they controlled was the Atlantic coast south of Morocco and a few desert outposts. Heat and desolation made the interior untenable, which left the nomads in control—the *Ulad el Mizna*, the Sons of the Clouds.

"The Spanish were happy to shoot game and the odd nomad until the 'fifties, when they discovered two billion tons of phosphates. So while the other empires shrank, the Spanish invested. By the early 'seventies, their mine was producing a few million tons a year, which was just a beginning.

"Trouble was, Morocco claimed the Spanish Sahara along with the nomads, who had a tiny, young elite mostly educated in Paris and ready to fight the Spanish."

Across the garden they heard the gates open. At the sound of Idrissi's car appearing through the trees, the houseboy materialized and Smith waved his empty glass. Behind the servant, two small children ran out of the house, chased by an old woman in layers of hanging cloth. They threw themselves on Idrissi, who picked them both up, a boy and a girl dressed like French children, and hugged them before holding each up into a jacaranda tree to pick a sprig of blossoms. Then he let the old woman take them by the hand and drag them struggling back inside while he walked towards the two Americans.

Laing had watched the pantomime with envy and found himself seeing Cosima in Idrissi's place, with a child in her arms. They had both wanted to have one, but his desire had always been the stronger of the two. They had never talked of why that was so, but he knew instinctively that it was tied to his fear of being alone, of longing to surround himself with people he loved. They had talked endlessly, in the first five years of their marriage, about choosing the right moment and had put it off and off. Now it was never mentioned and the right moment had receded into the mythological background of their daily life.

He pushed the image away and turned back to Smith. "Then why are they fighting?"

"The nomads had no idea of territorial nationalism, but they had always been free. The Sultan of Morocco was just the nearest important man. So they were delighted when he offered to help them and they began agitating from Moroccan territory. Then one day King Hassan decided he could do a deal with the Spanish on his own. He arrested the nomad leaders and the war was on."

As he walked across the grass, Idrissi stared at Laing, wondering how such an agreeable young man had become involved in a complicated arms deal and how to phrase his bad news. He found it difficult to admit failure so easily. The houseboy followed him, carrying two full glasses, one of which he handed to Smith, while Idrissi, who had overheard Smith's last words, interrupted bitterly. "A classic error." He threw himself into a canvas chair the boy had placed behind him.

"Sounds like a calculated choice to me," Laing said.

Idrissi became insistent. "Killing and arresting one part of an elite, Mr. Laing, excites rather than discourages the other part. Next thing we knew, they found a young saviour called El-Oueli and started blowing up things."

Smith interrupted. "Even so, Morocco was all set to take over when the Spanish left. But in '75, the World Court said that the nomads should vote on their future, which meant independence. King Hassan stirred up his people with dreams of grandeur and . . ."

Idrissi came alive. "He really stirred us up, you know. Even I, who saw how it was done, was ready to go down there and die. He gathered up three hundred and fifty thousand volunteers—men, women, children, old, young, poor. The army supplied trucks, tents, water, food and they headed south, with people singing and dancing day and night, people from all over. I went—not in a truck of course—but I went down to Tarfaya to join them in the camps." Idrissi got up, excited by his own story and paced around them under the trees.

"The next morning, we all walked to the border, a sea of people. God, it was desolate. When we came to the barbed-wire fences and gates, we could see the gun positions of the Spaniards but not the soldiers. The signal was given and we walked forward, unarmed you understand. I was in the front line with some peasants, waiting for the machine-guns. You could hear the hearts beat as we crossed the line. But nothing happened. Silence. I thanked God and fell to the ground to kiss it! A piece of Morocco returned to Morocco."

Smith raised his glass. "The Spaniards had pulled out. Overnight, Hassan became a hero. People forgot about his corruption, his extravagant life at their expense . . ."

"Enough, Anthony! Enough," Idrissi shouted from beneath a belladonna tree.

"His palaces, his police. Morocco doubled in size and added nineteen per cent of the world's phosphates to the twenty-nine per cent she already had. Hassan became a one man OPEC in the fertilizer business. Better than OPEC. People have to eat before they drive."

"Trouble is," Idrissi sat and picked up his untouched drink, "it's been all downhill since."

"Why?" Laing asked.

"After our army had occupied the desert outposts, the Polisario appeared."

"The mercenaries?"

Idrissi laughed. "Bravo, Mr. Laing. Now there's a man who learns quickly."

"'Mercenary' means," Smith said, "that they're financed and armed by Algeria and Libya. It also means they're doing well. El-Oueli was killed in '76, but the new leaders are as good. One of them is an old friend of mine from Paris days. Even as a student of romantic literature, he was a disciple of Sun Tzu. Moulay Sayed knows him. They were once professor and beloved student in Rabat. Our friend here used to teach a course in politics aimed at inculcating the young with nationalist fervour. Everyone came to hear the great Moulay."

"You mean Abdullah Lamine?" Idrissi focused sharply on Smith. "Have you seen him?"

Smith nodded. "Last year, in Algeria."

Idrissi looked relieved. "He's in New York right now."

Smith was surprised. "You mean you're talking to him?"

"Ha! Too fast, Anthony. He is talking secretly to the Americans, winning them over, he thinks; only the State Department is keeping us informed. Next time you see Abdullah, embrace him for me. This war will end with words. Tell him."

"Sun Tzu?" Laing asked.

"The strategist's strategist. 500 BC. Everybody who supposedly invented guerilla warfare or rapid mobility copied from him. A few, like Mao and Liddell Hart, admitted it. If the Moroccans would read him, they'd understand how bad things are."

"Enough!" Idrissi jumped to his feet. When they didn't move, he took Laing by the hand and headed towards his car, shouting for his driver. Within minutes they were bundled into the Mercedes, Idrissi in front. No sooner were they moving than he pulled his radio onto his lap and turned the dial, in search of the news from France.

The car sped across Rabat and down the river bank to the bridge over the Bou Regreg. At midday, the sun threw shadows from the cliff onto the fishing barges. Beyond those shadows, people moved in a mass towards the protected beaches. The Mercedes drove north, past the walls of Salé, before turning inland.

"Faster, faster," Idrissi kept saying to the driver, for no apparent reason.

They were soon on a small country road where raised irrigation aqueducts ran beside them. Beyond that were planted fields and geometric orchards. In the air, there was the pungent fragrance of rich farmland.

"The beauty of luxuriant symmetry," Idrissi waved an arm out of the window. He added incidentally, "I asked about your guns," and passed the two sheets of paper over his shoulder to Laing without turning round. "They tell me its blacklisted. If I were you, I'd stick to oil." Idrissi kept talking to avoid any questions. "You see, we haven't wasted our independence. The Moroccan is a man surrounded by a garden." He could feel Laing moving uneasily behind him, wanting to explain the blacklist. As for Smith, Idrissi glimpsed him in the mirror, showing relief that his temptation was over. "The wars fade away, but the burnt gardens grow back. Here we are," he shouted at the driver, although the man had already slowed to turn in.

A wall stretched along the left side of the road. They followed it for a mile to a gate, where the driver honked. It opened onto a dirt track, with orange trees stretching away on either side and water flowing through trenches around their roots.

"Turn right, down here," Idrissi shouted. "Here." He

pointed at a dirt track between the trees. They bumped forward, turning again and again into the maze under Idrissi's instructions. It was ten minutes before the driver stopped at a dirt crossroad, lost. A ditch blocked their path. Despite his djellabah and his slippers, Idrissi jumped out of the car and started to throw large pieces of dried mud into the ditch.

"You look wonderful," Smith called from the back seat. "Wonderful outfit."

Idrissi looked up and started laughing. "Get out, Anthony." He turned away to look for more lumps and shouted over his shoulder, "Get out! Americans never know how to lift mud. Your minds are like machines."

A dirt-stained peasant appeared from among the trees, drawn by the noise. Idrissi called out in Moroccan Arabic,

"Which way to the house?"

The man was so overwhelmed at seeing him that he couldn't answer. Instead he ran closer. Idrissi pointed straight ahead. "That way to the house?" The man lunged at his hand and missed. "No? That way?" He pointed in another direction and the man lunged and missed again. "No? Well, which way?"

They kept dancing their awkward *pas de deux* on the mud track until the peasant threw himself forward. He caught the hand, wrenched it down and kissed it.

"God!" Idrissi exploded. He wiped his fingers on his djellabah. "Go away! Go away!"

The peasant ignored this. He was satisfied and told the descendant of the Prophet to turn right.

In the centre of the property, they found a small pavilion surrounded by roses, an awning on one side. The manager appeared as they climbed out. Idrissi held his hands behind his back.

"Do you have some eggs from my chickens?"

"Of course, Moulay Sayed," the man replied.

"Good. Have you slaughtered anything recently?" He scarcely waited for a reply. "Good. Give us grilled lamb and eggs. And do you have those olives in pepper and lemon? Well, bring them. And a bottle of Gris de Boulouane. And some chairs. And a salad. Ah!" He turned, his arms outstretched. "Well, my friends of the twentieth century, welcome to the meaning of life."

They spent most of the afternoon over lunch under the awning. Idrissi and Smith entertained each other, while Laing ate and drank in virtual silence, dejected partially by Idrissi's bad news but above all by Smith's failure to come to his support. There was nothing left to do but get on the plane back to New York on Monday afternoon and begin again.

Idrissi poured more of the perfumed grey wine into Laing's glass with an encouraging gesture. "So thin and anxious. In Morocco, that's the description of a poor man." He wished he had brought better news. He liked to please people. "How do you know such a serious man, Anthony?"

"I told you that," Smith replied. "We met at McGill in Montreal."

"Two Americans in exile? Wait! The draft."

"Hardly. I wanted to get out of New York." An image of his father went through Smith's mind. A patent attorney—good middle-class stock. Smith's thoughts laboured in a pleasant haze produced by four glasses of wine. At night it took six, although brandy was more efficient.

Idrissi turned to Laing. "Now listen. Anthony tells me you are one of the magical few, with your MBA. Why bother, if you don't enjoy life?"

Laing looked at his questioner, jarred out of his self-pity. "Don't judge the happiness of others on your own terms, Moulay Sayed. For me, this is a pleasant afternoon, not life." Laing shoved his failure to the back of his mind. "As for the magical few, they control everything interesting in the United States. That is reality. They're the cream of the American experience, which is a pretty good reason for me to bother."

Idrissi was surprised by the aggressive answer. He protested, "What makes you the cream?"

"We make a science of probability. We break down the mystery and romantic notions of business and government into practical pieces. We eliminate the need for leaps of faith, because you can do nothing against a mathematical phenomenon." They were arguments Laing had first used to convince himself.

Idrissi fidgeted in total disagreement, but he couldn't marshal a thought.

As a joke, Laing added, "We are the culmination of the age of reason."

Smith surprised himself by coming out of his haze. "We're hardly living in a golden age, Martin. The fatal errors of life come from men being logical, not unreasonable. The States is dying from logic applied like religion, whereas it should be the slave of well-intentioned men. And where are the well-intentioned men? They're relegated to corners, as romantics who don't understand the modern world."

"That's garbage, Anthony. Well-intentioned men have butchered us for centuries." Laing felt his disappointment and anger with Smith come surging back. "And you've become a travelling salesman to avoid reality."

Smith's face, already flushed by the wine, turned a deeper red. He filled his glass and walked away.

"You're very harsh with your friend, Mr. Laing."

"Perhaps because he is my friend, Moulay Sayed."

Idrissi let his eyes follow the shadow of Smith retreating into the orchard. He nodded doubtfully, then went inside.

Laing sat alone for a quarter of an hour. He hadn't meant to insult Smith, but frustration had made him over-react. Smith should have said yes. There was no reason to refuse.

He got to his feet impatiently and walked round the outside of the pavilion. As he came to the second corner, he heard a murmur. A few yards away, Idrissi was kneeling on the ground, praying. Laing turned back, returning to the protection of the awning.

SEVENTEEN

They arrived back in Rabat late that evening, just as the sun finished setting. Smith asked them to let him off on the edge of the old town by the walls of the medina. As he had not said a word on the drive home, neither Idrissi nor Laing argued. When the car had driven away, Smith walked slowly along the ramparts. He hardly knew what had wounded him.

It took him fifteen minutes to reach the Casbah of the Oudias, where he took a narrow street not far from the one leading to Karim Farid's house. The few shop stalls had closed, leaving no one out. He cut through a series of unlit alleys which led eventually to a dead end of high walls broken only by one low door. Smith pounded on the wood. There was a pause, then a grille opened. A boy's face peered through, lit from behind, and Smith put his own face forward to be seen. As the bolt slid back, Smith gave an agitated push. The boy was dark and in servant's pantaloons. "Monsieur Smith," he said in recognition and closed the door carefully before running ahead down the hallway with Smith following. The ceiling and walls were decorated with intricate Moorish designs. Smith noticed they had been repainted in the brightest of colours since the week before and reflected that business must be good.

A short, wide form in black filled the end of the corridor and shouted out, "Cher Monsieur Smith!" This she repeated as she shuffled dangerously on narrow heels towards him. When she was half-way, she stopped, resplendent in a Paris cocktail dress, its abundant lace designed to disguise the quantity of her flesh. She was lightly made up, because her pale skin had always been much admired in Rabat.

"Madame Durand," Smith said as a greeting, but didn't touch her.

She beamed up at him, although the expression on her collapsing face was in fact stern. The teeth were all her own. She turned her back to lead the way in, gossiping over her shoulder as she walked.

Madame Durand held the best house in Rabat and had since before the war. In those days, she had offered the most beautiful in North African girls to the senior officers and colonial officials of the French occupation.

She reached the end of the corridor and made way for Smith. Steps went down into a room that was two storeys high, with blue Moorish tent material hanging on the walls and soft banquettes beneath. Three young men in European clothes were talking to as many girls. It wasn't a big room. There was room for another four clients at most. On the far wall a banner had been hung, carrying a message from the Koran. "Women are your fields; go then, into your fields as you please." The ceiling beams were carved and painted. Large open windows looked over the cliffs of the Casbah, not onto the town of Salé, as did Farid's, but across Rabat itself towards the old French quarter and what had once been Government House. Madame Durand's view had always been the symbol of her quality.

Although French, she had decorated in the Moorish style to please the exotic desire of Frenchmen. She had pleased them so well that her house had never been mentioned in the many colonial studies of rampant prostitution throughout the Protectorate. Madame Durand's policy had always been longterm. During the war, she had not opened her doors to the few German officers in town, even though they controlled the Vichy government in Paris. And when the English and Americans had arrived in '43, her door was as firmly shut. She wasn't interested in the passing trade. She wanted loyal clients. Without Idrissi's introduction, Smith wouldn't have been allowed in.

As the French Empire wound down in the 'fifties, she opened up to the new Moroccan elite. In deference to their taste, she dressed her girls in the latest Paris clothes. It was with a certain sense of history that she refused to change the walls, although she had given in on some of the bedrooms, introducing a Paris look of plastic, chrome and mirrors.

At the bottom of the stairs, Smith put out his hand to help her down and asked if she could get him something to eat. She moved away to organize that and he drifted into an empty corner. A boy appeared with a seltzer bottle and brandy.

Smith emptied the glass and slouched on the cushions. He didn't expect friends to seek out his weak spots. What did Laing expect? Just because he was a friend, he behaved as though Smith's standards were his own. And even if they were, Smith believed the reasons he gave others were sometimes truer than those he gave himself.

No girls approached him, because the rule was that they should wait for Madame Durand to make the choice. Idrissi had introduced him to the place a few days after they first met in 1971. Smith had said he didn't want to go and Idrissi had insisted with an argument that Smith still remembered. "You Christians are all the same. Your sins are negative and evil. Drunkenness, wordly gain, sex, hatred. I want you to know that my pleasures are positive. What's wrong with sex? What's wrong with money? I believe it's a sin to be a beggar. I savour my pleasures. I do not walk with shame in my own shit."

Madame Durand reappeared followed by a boy carrying his dinner—a grilled steak with overcooked green beans.

"A bit of Paris," she said as the plate was put before him. She saw the empty glass and gestured for a bottle. "What would you like?"

Smith had begun his steak and not asked her to sit down. He chewed the tough meat methodically as he looked up across the room at the girls in sight. They all had that placid, to a Westerner's eye, indifferent look on their faces. He swallowed. "Something new?"

She looked pleased and gave instructions to the boy, who ran up a separate set of stairs towards the bedrooms. Madame Durand's good customers always gave her a challenge, but she was sure enough of her judgement to disappear towards the door, leaving Smith alone. He chewed another mouthful of the steak and emptied his glass. What did Lang expect of him? He had no right to expect anything except friendship. A young girl came into the room wearing a yellow silk dress meant for an older woman of another culture. At first she looked ridiculous, but when she reached his table Smith saw that she had a waif-like beauty; her skin, a moody honey colour, framed the expectant look in her eyes. She carried herself with the assurance of a teenager, the silk clinging to her body, rising high around her neck so that the cloth moved with her small breasts. Without a word, she slipped onto the bench beside Smith. There was an expression of life on her face.

Using his bad Arabic, he discoverd that her name was Aisha and that she was fifteen. There was nothing else to do but finish his meat. She slipped her hand onto his crotch and moved her fingers softly until it stirred.

Smith heard his own name and looked up to see Colonel Benmansour, in a grey suit, crossing the room towards him, leaving Madame Durand behind. It wasn't the first time they had run into each other here, but he was the last person Smith wanted to be interrupted by so he went on eating.

Benmansour stared at the girl as he said, in a neutral tone, "I hear Moulay Sayed is giving you a hand on the bus contracts."

"I hope that doesn't mean we're competing," Smith replied amiably.

"We all have our friends to protect."

Smith shrugged, still friendly.

The Colonel was not. "I don't compete against Moulay Sayed." His eyes were still on the girl. "She's very young."

"Beautiful," Smith corrected, looking up at the Colonel.

"Very young," Benmansour repeated; his tone was covetous, not critical.

Smith briefly considered offering her to him, in the hope of smoothing the buses through, but he looked up again and saw the expression on the Colonel's face was one of contempt for the girl, as if she were less than an object.

Smith looked back at her. In her shyness, she had forgotten to take her hand from his crotch, which now lay still. He repeated, "Beautiful," and cut another piece of steak.

"They're never too young," Benmansour said, "to ruin a man's pleasure."

Smith nodded goodnight and the Colonel moved away without smiling. Women were the enemy. Inferior, yet impossible to defeat. Their aim was to destroy man's self-esteem. All of that Smith had heard before from a certain kind of Arab. He dropped his knife and fork and stood up. The girl led the way, past a banquette where Benmansour was talking to a handsome but sour-looking woman. Smith remembered her as being better undressed than dressed. He avoided looking in their direction and wondered how much of Benmansour's twisted heart he himself carried. The girl skipped up the stairs ahead of him.

She had been brought in by her father only a few days before, so Madame Durand had allotted her one of the old Moorish rooms. The moment the door was closed, she dropped her clothes on piled cushions and began undressing Smith. He saw that her sex was shaved, even though there would have been little to take away except a few soft hairs. It was standard procedure for expensive Arab prostitutes, just as it was for rich Arab women. She hardly knew what to do, but Smith guessed that she knew her only hope was to give herself totally to the men in the hope that one of them would make her his mistress or, an almost impossible chance, marry her before her childlike qualities disappeared. When he was naked, she pulled him across the room and down onto a feather divan. He found himself carried away by her innocence and could think of nothing except to get inside and hold her still; but she began moving in a frenzy, trying to make him move. He squeezed the tiny body so that her small breasts buried themselves in his chest and he felt her sex envelop and hold his. She moved harder and harder against him, scratching his back and crying sharply until he found himself rushing to explosion without a motion. He didn't register in that moment what she had done, only that when he had finished she lay still for the first time; and the confusion was gone from his mind, as was Laing and his temptations. It was later that he realized she had left deep scratches on his back.

He sat with her downstairs for an hour, although they had difficulty exchanging more than isolated words. There was a life within her which brought out his affection and made him want to be near, if only to touch her. He thought of approaching Madame Durand to see whether he could reserve her for the rest of his stay in Rabat; then he thought he'd wait and see or perhaps come back the next night.

EIGHTEEN

The pasty quality of Smith's face was a parody of itself the next morning. He told himself he hadn't slept because of the drink and stumbled into Idrissi's library to write a short letter, which he sealed. By shouting towards the servant's area, he raised a boy to drive him to the Hilton.

Laing answered the door with forced civility. There was a half-packed suitcase on his bed.

Smith handed him the envelope. "I thought of someone in New York who might be helpful: Dr. Leonard Menet. We've done other kinds of business together. This is an introduction."

Laing's interest came alive. "Who is he?"

"Menet? God knows. He's in his seventies and theoretically English. My guess is he came out of Central Europe during the war. Not one of your lightweight arms dealers. He's been at it so long he has risen above the odour of the profession." Smith collapsed onto the unmade bed. "Notice the address—he has a big share in that investment bank."

Laing had walked forward and stood over the bed, listening. As Smith explained, he became impatient. "An old man isn't going to put this deal together."

Smith waved him towards a chair on the other side of the room. "Calm down, Martin. Menet isn't for hire. But if there's someone who can help . . . Well, you ask him." Smith restrained himself, as if embarrassed.

That morning's *Matin* was lying beside him. Monday, 9 June. He saw the headlines:

> The Organization of African Unity Will Explode If It Recognizes The Polisario.
>
> The King Addresses a Battalion Leaving for the Sahara:
>
> "We entrust you with our flag. Let your actions be such that it will remain always the symbol of purity and glory."

There was a photograph of him in uniform, Kader's silhouette visible in the background.

"You can't go hard at these people, Martin. They live in shadows. They look like you and me, solid flesh, trading on experience and knowledge. But they're animals of pure instinct. If you do or say the wrong thing, they fade away and become Dr. Menet, investment banker, or they turn vicious. Sayed is sending his car to take you to the airport."

Smith stood up abruptly and left. He was late for a meeting. As he crossed the hotel lobby, the concierge handed him a note sent over by Idrissi. Smith opened the envelope without bothering to wonder how he'd known where to find him. "Bus meeting cancelled. Your contract signed. Congratulations." Smith laughed and mumbled to himself, "Blessed be the Moulay."

Instead of going back up to Laing's room, he took a taxi across town to the Casbah of the Oudias. Karim Farid had no telephone and merely expected people to drop in. As Smith trudged down the dirt alley into the Casbah, he thought about Laing's disappointment. It was a disappointment he felt himself, which was why he needed the distraction of Karim Farid. He came to the turning that led to Madame Durand's and imagined the body of the young girl. Curiously enough, it was an image of her dressed that persisted, trying to talk to him as much with her eyes as her face. Early in the day would be a good time to strike a deal with the old woman. He hesitated, then went on towards Farid's. He could always see the Madame afterwards. The conversations he had had with Laing over the last three days started to run through his mind again, but were interrupted when he noticed a man leaning in the shadow of a doorway, out of the sun. He was in a suit without a tie. His eyes followed the American down the alley until he disappeared behind Farid's door.

The houseboy led Smith through into the garden, where, across the terraces, he could see Karim Farid seated in the gazebo. Two older men were on either side of him and two younger men were sitting on cushions at their feet. They were dressed in white djellabahs and white turbans. All four had full beards. One of them was talking stridently in Arabic, his voice carrying across the garden. Although he was talking straight into Karim Farid's face, only a few inches away, Farid maintained a detached expression. Smith's minimal Arabic was hindered by the accent, but he caught a few words as Karim Farid interrupted the man, quietly and firmly: "No! . . . Why . . . my friend . . . Killing . . ." The man stared at Farid, silent for a moment, then began again, doubly strident.

Smith walked forward until one of the young men caught sight of him and made a sign to the others. They broke off abruptly and twisted about, causing Smith to pause. The four bearded men jumped to their feet, said goodbye to Karim Farid and left the gazebo. As they passed Smith, the leader looked away. The others stared at the American aggressively while Smith smiled and made way.

He walked forward to join Karim Farid. "I didn't know you were in with the puritans." He kissed the hand as it was withdrawn.

"I am not."

Smith had never before seen the old man agitated. His hand trembled. He had been upset either by the visitors or by Smith's finding him with them.

"They came," Karim Farid volunteered, "because I am one of the oldest nationalists and a religious teacher. They said I must speak publicly. They said my words would have a great impact." The old man tried a self-denigrating laugh, but it failed.

"What kind of statement?"

"Condemn the King." Farid gestured hopelessly. "Call for a return to religious purity to save the nation."

"What did you say?"

"To agree with what they hate is not to agree with what they want to do. They are fanatics, not religious puritans. That is what I meant to say. Instead, I said I was too old to fight another battle."

"That's all? I . . ." Smith saw that Farid was angry with him and stopped. The words he had overheard sunk in. Kill? The word had sounded foreign to Farid's mouth. What friend? Smith tried to bring back the words he'd missed.

"You interrupted. They had begun to question whether I was a great nationalist after all." This time he managed his laugh. "Do not tell Moulay Sayed that you saw them here."

Smith showed his surprise, so that the old man added, "He might have them arrested. I could not have that, just because they came to my house." Karim Farid kept his eyes on Smith.

"All right, Sidi Karim."

The old man relaxed. Smith had agreed out of respect, but he couldn't understand. Idrissi would never disobey Karim Farid, so something was being held back.

Smith pulled a worn volume of Anglo-Saxon myths out of his pocket, "I've brought you my bible." Karim Farid looked pleased. "The other day," Smith blurted out, "you told me to go home. I can't. I was brought up in a stable world. No violence. No insecurity. Peace and prosperity. All I had to do was float along, but something made me resist—knee-jerk individualism, I suppose. I'd have gone crazy in a sane society, so I took the easy solution, which was to leave. I became the permanent outsider. The court fool. And that's fine, because your insanity can't touch me—it isn't mine." Smith was flushed.

"Always your dark side, Anthony. The darkness is guilt, which is your invention. We Muslims have never believed in original sin, so I do not carry the burden of my own imaginary evil. Your society may now be one of nonbelievers, but guilt has seeped into the pores of your unconscious—into your buildings and families and business and teaching. Even a tenth generation atheist cannot escape the sin of Adam because it is welded onto his soul. And what is the result? Your alienation. Again, unknown to us. What is that but your revered individualism? The force of the damned man attempting to escape his guilt? How could we or any outsider understand the darkness that fuels your drive or find a way to resist it?"

Smith tried to organize his carefully drawn lines of morality to reply, but found they wouldn't come clear. "Oh, Sidi Karim, if you would work with me, we could run the world."

They both laughed. The teacher murmured, "*Insha allah*",

before replying. "Moralists survive unemployed and strategists live comfortably."

Smith noticed, when he left that the same man was standing in the shade of a doorway farther down the alley. As the American passed, the man looked away, his face meaty, swollen like a frog: a policeman's face. The question was—whose policeman? Smith wished he hadn't promised to say nothing to Idrissi. His mind was in such a turmoil that he forgot about the girl at Madame Durand's.

When Laing came out of the hotel, Smith was waiting in the back of the Mercedes. He leaned across to push open the door.

"My deal closed and I have things to do in New York. If I can't accept your offer, at least I can make sure Menet sees you."

Though they both knew the difference between an excuse and a reason, they also knew how to treat the former as the latter. On the plane, Smith made it clear that he wanted no money for this minor service. Beyond that, he didn't want to talk. He buried himself in *The Good Soldier*, smoked cigars and drank his way across the Atlantic with brandy and soda.

Left on his own, Laing closed his eyes to try to work out what Smith was up to, and how to deal with him. All Laing wanted to do was to sell his guns and forget it. He didn't want to get involved in why someone was buying the guns to kill someone in particular. He guessed that that was why Smith had begun by saying no. Smith's life consisted of becoming involved with people, then selling them something—the web was part of the package. Laing had hoped to trade on that involvement, but he had quickly buried the thought that it was inflicting death by proxy. What confused him was why Smith had half changed his mind. Laing had once been better at understanding both his friends and Cosima. He was still able to come up with logical, rational answers, as he did in the rest of his life, but they left him dissatisfied. And yet, he found himself unable to reach any deeper.

An image of Cosima swelled into his mind. She was naked, gasping with passion in the arms of a man. Laing could smell the sweat. He could see the details of her legs curling around his. He could smell the sex. The man was one of their friends, nothing more. Laing winced and opened his eyes to break the image. The two years at McGill, spent chasing her without hope, had scratched scars of doubt. When he met her again six years later and Cosima decided that she loved him, the scars stayed to irritate him.

He closed his eyes. The images returned. Cosima was the single passion of his life. Should he discover that she was unfaithful or no longer wanted him, he knew something within him would break. He had no idea what. He avoided the question.

PART 3

NINETEEN

People think only of happiness and yet it does not exist. It is an illusion made for idiots. Moffett couldn't remember whether the idea was his. All he knew was that happiness had nothing to do with his success in life.

That morning, his wife had announced she was ready to move up to their East Hampton house for the summer, which affected Moffett neither one way nor the other. He stayed in town and went up for irregular weekends. Over the last few years he had actually enjoyed her absence, as it gave him a chance to collect his thoughts. When she was there, her words were like the buzzing of flies.

Later that same day, Monday, 9 June, he was ushered into Erlich's office for their weekly conversation to prepare the next morning's Executive Committee meeting. As he came through the doorway, Erlich jumped up to greet him. An unusual gesture. Ensconced in an armchair beside him was David Fell.

Erlich called across the office, "Come on in, James."

Moffett stopped in the doorway. "I did not realize I was early."

"You're not. David and I were just going through some crap." He indicated Fell, who glanced up to smile at Moffett and plunged again into the file on his lap. "Turned out a lot of things he had on his list were the same things we'd got to talk over. I thought he might as well stay on."

Moffett wondered who had done the thinking. "A good idea. I am afraid, though, I have a number of personnel questions. It would not be proper to discuss them, even in front of David." Moffett walked past them across the office. "You two finish up," he said, "I have something to read." He sat down on a sofa in the far corner with his back to them.

There was an embarrassed silence behind him. Then Fell got to his feet, "I mustn't make you two late. See you tomorrow morning."

Moffett waved over his shoulder without turning round. On the table in front of him was a mocked-up advertisement.

WHY ARE YOU SUSPICIOUS OF BIG CORPORATIONS?
Profit is not a four-letter word. It doesn't represent ill-gotten gains. It's the money we use to find and develop energy.

The door closed behind Fell and Erlich came over to sit down. Moffett knew he wanted to say something about what had just happened, but didn't give him a chance. If no one said it, it hadn't happened.

Erlich felt himself being squeezed between his two vice-presidents and it was a feeling he detested. The only way he knew to deal with it was to become sulky and uncooperative; when they separated two hours later, little had been accomplished.

Moffett walked to his own office in a funk. On his desk he discovered a Telex from Laing to say that he was flying back with Anthony Smith. For the first time in the day, he felt something good was happening. His sources had taken no time to dig up information on Smith and all of it had been what Moffett wanted to hear–Laing had found them the perfect man. That was just as well, because he could sense that he was going to need a startling success in the near future to hold off Fell's mole-like subversion.

Before he realized it, he found himself dialling Laing's house to let Cosima know that her husband was expected that evening. He reflected that there was nothing wrong with being over-solicitous from time to time, especially if he was in need of a lift in morale.

When no one answered, he felt unnecessarily deflated and guessed that she was out with someone. He did not imagine that, when Laing was away, she worked in the evenings.

In fact, Cosima was standing at her drawing table changing a detail of a sketch, the furry smell of her partner's breath floating over her shoulder. At eight each evening the air conditioning went off, so his odour lay, like stale cigarette smoke, across her office. He had come in to discuss a municipal building they were redesigning.

She changed a passageway with a few moves. The partner was about to take a pencil to show her why he disagreed when the phone rang. He answered curtly and passed it on to Cosima, who was annoyed by the interruption until she realized it was Laing.

"Where are you? Why didn't you phone from the airport?" She noticed the partner listening with curiosity as warmth came into her voice. "I'll be finished in a minute. I'll be right there."

Cosima went back to the drawing board in a distracted mood to see what the partner had changed, but the first hint of his breath cleared her mind. Why bother with a polite withdrawal? It was better to leave immediately.

She found Laing bent so compulsively over a newspaper that he hadn't heard her come in. Without expecting it, she sensed the frailty that he revealed when alone. He looked up and any weakness disappeared as he came alive with a warm open smile and put an arm out to her, saying, "The flower of the species." She threw herself on him. He kissed every part of her face and drew her up onto his lap, where he held her as if he would never let her go.

Laing didn't tell Cosima that he had offered Smith a bed—Smith wasn't one of Cosima's great favourites—nor could he help being relieved that the offer had been refused, leaving them alone. Instead, Smith had gone to the Carlyle, which was expensive enough to be never full. Sometimes someone on the staff remembered him, but generally speaking his ordinary clothes, worn as if he'd been dressed by someone else, helped them to forget.

After sixteen years living elsewhere, Smith's periodic visits to New York were those of a foreigner deprived of all sense of belonging. It was a distance which released him from any need for the sentiment and warm memories he had never felt. Besides which, his parents were dead and his sister had moved elsewhere with a husband.

The moment he was alone in his room, he looked through his address book for the phone number of the Polisario observer at the United Nations and dialled it. The voice which answered denied that Abdullah Lamine, Smith's friend in the Polisario leadership, was there or indeed had ever been in New York. Smith insisted. It went away and came back to ask whether he was free the following afternoon, Tuesday, 10

June. Smith said he would be there at two p.m. and went to bed. He would call Dr. Menet in the morning.

The apartment was in a rundown building near the United Nations. The door was answered by an Arab, who looked like a well-brought-up, middle-class student. He left Smith in the first room, surrounded by walls bare except for one poster of a guerilla with a headcloth wrapped dramatically around his face. Smith dropped onto a cheap sofa that could be pulled out into a bed. A Formica-topped table sat in front of it.

Moments later Lamine came into the room and they embraced.

"My God, Abdullah, they have you dressed up in a suit."

Smith had known him first as a student in Paris and later as a guerilla leader, neither of which role called for a tie. Lamine was shorter than Smith and a solid shape. His face was wide, with a sharp, small nose and a closely-clipped beard; evidence that he did not come from the warrior nomadic tribes with their long, thin features. There was, nevertheless, an aura of command about him.

"Who told you I was here?"

"Moulay Sayed Idrissi."

Lamine showed a second of surprise, then rolled his eyes in mock despair. "So much for the State Department. I keep saying to them—we want to be your friend, we have no ideology, we simply want independence, we will co-operate in any way. Do you know what they reply? Obscurely, of course. The United States is against Communism. You are Communists, supported by the Communist regimes of Algeria and Libya. Morocco represents freedom and democracy in North West Africa. We cannot abandon King Hassan as we abandoned the Shah. Now tell me, Anthony, what can I say?"

"Don't look at me. I only know how to handle wogs."

Lamine sat down close beside him on the sofa and rested a hand on Smith's arm.

"I was staying with Sayed Idrissi until yesterday. He told me to embrace you and tell you the war will end with words."

"*Insha allah*," Lamine said. He tapped Smith's arm with his hand to emphasize the point. "Idrissi and his friends must be heartbroken after fighting so many years for independence, to see the money for their development dreams poured out on a losing war."

"Morocco may be losing, Abdullah, but can you win?"

They had never lost the habit of treating each other as students proving themselves.

Again Lamine replied, "*Insha allah*. We can wear them down. Sooner or later the King will give up or be overthrown. Now tell me, what are you doing here?"

"I'm unloading some weapons. That is, I'm showing a friend how to do it himself." Lamine stared hard, as if dealing with a man much younger than himself. Smith protested, "A favour for a friend."

"What kind of arms, Anthony?"

"Come now. You of all people aren't on the market. You have a supplier."

"True, the Algerians look after us. And so do the Moroccans, the way they abandon weapons on the field after every skirmish. But who knows?" Lamine's fingers tapped Smith's arm insistently. "Tell a friend what you have."

Smith pulled the list out of his pocket. Lamine ran his eyes up and down both papers.

"Expensive?"

"It's American blacklisted. What's your problem, Abdullah? Are your friends holding out on you? That's the rumour in Rabat." Smith was annoyed at himself for producing the list.

Lamine looked up. There was no change in the expression on his face; only a slightly defensive tone in his voice. "Of course not. It's just that I'd like to give a jolt to the war. Wrap it up. To do that, I need more than we're getting. Or rather, not more, better. I don't care about blacklists. They only work against friends and the Americans don't want to be ours."

Smith patted his friend's hand. "Sorry, Abdullah. The deal is pretty well done. Only a fraction of the list is for sale—one transaction of one hundred million net to the seller. That's too big for you. Besides, you have nowhere to receive if the Algerians aren't co-operating."

Lamine shot back, "Don't you think we've had time to build up a fund?" Then he paused and said quietly, "If you don't do the deal, call me. I'm here for another three days and after that in Algiers."

"It's done, Abdullah."

"You said almost done."

Smith excused himself saying he had to get to his next meeting. They embraced again, with less openness, and he found himself in the dingy hallway outside the apartment with just enough time to pick up Laing and get downtown to Menet's office.

Life was complicated enough without arming one friend against another. Had he known Lamine was on the market, he'd have said nothing. And yet, he wondered to himself again why he'd shown the list.

TWENTY

Dr. Leonard Menet inclined his head to Smith and Laing as if taking his hat off in respect. He was a paragon of delicacy; small, modest, exquisitely dressed in black, a reincarnated diplomat from pre-war Vienna. He perched on the least comfortable of the three chairs in a corner of his Wall Street office and gazed at a Dutch crucifixion scene hanging on the wall that faced his desk. He was delighted when Smith admired it. Laing wasn't introduced.

"I should prefer to ask your advice on paintings, Dr. Menet, but my friend has a problem. I hope you'll forgive my taking the liberty of asking your advice." Smith had automatically adjusted to Menet's cadence.

The doctor's eyelids slid slowly shut as Smith finished. He had small sacks on the inner edge of his upper lids which made each side look like one half of a butterfly.

"My friend needs to dispose of some arms. It's a matter of selling one hundred million worth of goods from a longer list. American arms."

Menet's eyes reopened with the same languour. "That doesn't sound like a problem, Anthony. If he has the material, the market is flourishing. It was four hundred billion last year. Of course, the lion's share is government to government. Are these new items?"

"Second-hand."

"I'm afraid only four billion moves privately." He looked apologetic. "Are these small items?"

"A bit of everything," Smith replied. "It would be easier, from his point of view, to sell a few major pieces, but there may be an embargo on the goods."

"There are so many embargoes. I can never understand why." Menet made a gesture with his left hand, like a High Church minister sighing over the minor sins of his parishioners. "They're easy for an enterprising man to circumvent. Two years ago, the United States had an embargo on selling tanks to Argentina. What did we do? Certain friends encouraged Spain to buy new U.S. tanks. They, in turn, sold their not so old ones to Argentina. Thanks to the embargo, there were more commissions to pay." He appealed to Laing as a new soul to be saved. "Everything is a weapon. They can burn down your house with a bottle of gasoline. Sex is a weapon. And all this delicacy about offensive and defensive. All weapons are defensive and all spare parts are nonlethal. Do you have a price list?"

"No," Smith said. "That was one of the things he wanted your advice on."

The doctor came alive, lifting his left hand again. He pushed the melodious cadence of his voice. "Prices! What are prices? They depend on availability. Exotic things are expensive. Gold is expensive. Beautiful women are expensive. Forbidden arms are expensive. Are you asking me to find a buyer, Anthony?"

"No, no. Doctor, unless it interests you particularly."

"I must owe you a favour." His eyes closed again. "Let me see the list."

Smith handed it to him.

The doctor glanced briefly and looked up at Laing, disappointed. "But you don't have these weapons to sell. You left them behind in Vietnam." He had expected something serious.

Laing spoke for the first time. "As a result of a non-related matter, I do have them to sell."

The doctor shook his head, once. "How many people have said that over the last five years. The mother lode, eh, Anthony. If only the mother lode were really there. But it isn't." His expression made it clear that any further conversation was a waste of his time.

Smith interjected. "Curiously enough, he does have them. I can only give you my word."

There was a long silence. Menet ran his eyes sympathetically over a Rouault Christ hanging to his right. This gave him strength.

"No country will touch these weapons, even if you do have them. You must know that. The only solution would be a non-country; someone already excluded by all others, or a subversive movement. These kinds of people are not usually rich enough for what you want, nor are they usually trustworthy, nor are they easy to deliver to. What else? You could sell in small lots, hoping not to attract attention. But the people in this business, like the people who monitor it, know when as little as a thousand rifles are moved. It's not my game, Anthony." He smiled indulgently at Laing. "Very exciting. But I'm too old for finessing." His body relaxed into a reflective pose. "The last time I did it was to sell German arms to Egypt. The Germans said no, we couldn't have an export permit, so we sold the weapons to Jews. That was okay. All the security services knew where they were going, but they let the fiction continue and we landed them in Alexandria. All so silly. What happens when the price goes up? These poor third-world countries starve themselves to buy anyway. They spend three times more on arms than they receive in aid."

Smith looked understanding, which encouraged the doctor to continue, shifting again to Laing who did not appear seduced.

"If governments didn't interfere, the prices wouldn't be what they are. Why don't they leave weapons alone and concentrate on drugs. Those are the criminals. They are destroying our youth. What do arms do? What can they do?"

The doctor considered he had been polite long enough, but as he moved to end the meeting, Smith jumped in,

"Is there some other way?"

The doctor, in his turn, looked understanding. "There must be a way, Anthony. You'd have to find a buyer, then get the goods onto a ship without anyone noticing where they came from. Everything sailing from Vietnam is monitored, but perhaps you could get them out through Bangkok. They specialize in end-user certificates."

Laing looked questioning, but the doctor quickly put him at ease. "Mere jargon. You need a certificate from the country of export stating where you are sending the weapons. We used to get a first certificate to Bangkok, say from Los Angeles. Then we'd get another one from there to wherever—I don't know—North Korea. The Thais don't care, so long as you pay them. But you'd still need a professional to find the buyer, negotiate with him and arrange the details. With all due respect to your friend, Anthony," Menet turned and examined Laing, "you look like a very respectable man, Mr. X." Smith laughed and Laing followed suit. "Of course, this is a very respectable business, like you. But it is also very, shall we say, complicated.

"For example, you cannot sell to everyone, even if they want to buy. Many places are staked out by people who will step on your foot if you try. In the Gulf Emirates, the old British exchange officers have a hold on the market, although the Americans are breaking that up. In Holland and Canada, the Americans have total control. The French tried to break in, but the U.S. knows how to lean on its friends—money, economic pressure, political threats, and the governments fell into line. Or the Central African Republic—you know it, don't you, Anthony? Well, that's an old French stomping ground. The market belongs to Philippe Courman—a political debt paid off by someone. Everything is complicated. I'm afraid you'll have to use someone else's slippers to find your way."

"Can you suggest anyone?" Laing ventured.

The doctor spoke to Smith. "You might try the German, Hauser. You know him, Anthony?"

"Of him."

"There are two Englishmen, Edwards and Turp. Zumback isn't really in the league, although he used to like a bit of excitement. There are a couple of Spanish Princes, but God knows what they'd do. And, of course, Mummings, but he does like publicity. There's an ex–French Ambassador in Bangkok who isn't interested in the nitty gritty. Also a couple of American ex-officers out there, one of them is Mataxis, the general who supplied Cambodia for the U.S. government. When the Khmer Rouge were about to march into Phnom Penh, he reappeared as a private merchant to buy the weapons back. There are a couple of good ones in Paris." He broke off and looked at Laing. "Did you know, Mr. X, that the French government does not tax merchants who sell French arms abroad? The world is such an interesting place. You must know the French names, Anthony."

"Yes I do. That's enough, doctor."

"Don't see them all. Pick a few or the word will get out. And use my name." Laing was about to thank him when Menet sat forward and raised a finger of a remarkably coarse hand towards Smith. "Do not say I recommended they do it, only that I can give them a recommendation on you."

Smith blushed. "I won't be going any farther," he said awkwardly. "It's my friend's business."

Menet looked up with a sharpness that penetrated Smith. "I know you, Anthony. I don't know your friend. You know your friend." He stood up abruptly. "I believe we have finished."

Menet waited until they had closed the door before picking up his telephone. He found a number in his diary and dialled Paris. The number rang five times before being answered.

"Gerten?" he asked, the way a Victorian aunt might have picked up a glove dropped in the mud.

Ex-Colonel Gerten stood in his pyjama bottoms in his two-room apartment in the Paris suburb of Montrouge. On his face there was the wounded look which he carried even in private. Around him were a few pieces of cheap furniture—a sofa in bright green nylon velvet, bought at a store that catered to the local working class. Gerten's Vietnamese wife sat in their kitchen, where he had been drinking.

"Who wants him?" The tone was not friendly.

"It's Menet."

Gerten changed his defensive pose to one of a bully. "Well now, Dr. Menet, I am greatly honoured." The harsh ceiling light reflected off Gerten's face, lined and leathery from too much sun. His chest was covered in deep, dark curling hair, which rose up his still firm chest to his shoulders, then over and down his back like a suit of armour.

Menet cut him short. "Gerten, this isn't a long call. I've just seen two men who have a deal. It's a big deal which won't be done. However, I think there is money behind them."

"You sent them to me?"

"I wouldn't send anyone to you, Gerten. You know that. But I'm telling you, they're on the market. I owed you. Now I don't. They'll see the central players, who won't play. Since they've money, I leave it to you to deal yourself in."

"When does it happen?"

"I'd say they'll be in Paris within the week. And Gerten, it's your territory. Vietnam is involved." Menet hung up without a further word.

Gerten had become used to being treated with contempt since leaving the army. At first he had struck back, but that hadn't made him any money. Now he said nothing and allowed each insult to splash into the rising swamp of bitterness within him. He turned his curling back on the phone and returned to his beer and his wife, to whom he said, in Vietnamese, "Well now we're going to get out of this hole."

She listened, which was her role, and refilled his glass, while looking with adoration at the man who had married her and taken her with him.

Downstairs, in Wall Street, Smith and Laing stood awkwardly among the end-of-day crowds.

"I'm sorry, Martin. That was a waste of time."

Laing seemed indifferent. "Let's not worry now. It'll work out. Come for dinner. Cosima insists."

In fact, Laing had catered everything through his office. That morning, he'd told Cosima that Smith was coming and that she must be nice to him. When asked why, he said that the deal negotiated on his Vietnam trip was at stake, plus his own career. Besides, Smith was a friend.

Cosima didn't mind one way or the other. She had but to eat and to make a little effort.

Although the invitation was for eight, Smith, who had always been awkward in the polite details of life, arrived on the hour. He realized that Laing was softening him up, which was perfectly all right. His own life was made up of softening others or being softened. The sharpness of his original refusal to help Laing had lost so much of its edge that he was now being coy both with Laing and with himself.

Cosima opened the door and kissed him lightly on the cheek, filling the air around him with the scent of her tea rose perfume, then led the way in, chatting warmly about how long it was since they had last seen each other. She wore a black silk dress, bare on the shoulders and gathered in at the waist. Smith found himself hypnotized in her wake. He had forgotten what an effect she had on him, or rather, he had made an effort to forget since she had never had much time for him. Her reserve seemed to have disappeared, but he guessed that she was under instructions to be friendly. Whether it was an act or not, she still emanated a warm, unthreatening light.

The evening floated smoothly along on the back of their reminiscences, without any mention of Vietnam. Laing and

Cosima sat together on a sofa before dinner, with a hand always touching the other. Even in the dining room they spoke as much to each other as to Smith. It was only after dinner, when they were back in the drawing room and Cosima had gone to make the coffee, that Laing brought the conversation around to Vietnam. He wanted to know which of the arms dealers Smith thought would risk taking on a case like his, when American laws stood against them. Smith answered in a roundabout way. He was certain there were enough untouchable governments or rebel groups in Africa and Asia to buy the weapons, the only problem would be reaching them.

Neither man noticed Cosima coming slowly down the hallway, balancing a tray. Laing was rehashing the illegal side of what they were doing and she froze in nervous embarrassment. From the next few sentences she understood it was American arms left in Vietnam that they wanted to sell. She listened in disbelief, gripping the tray as if it were a hold on reality. She expected Smith to be making money out of someone else's tragedy; but not Laing. A distorted, scarred face filled her imagination, blocking out what she was overhearing. Robert Morgan had been one of her closest friends, he still was. He had been a medical student, a bright, enthusiastic boy and, like most people she knew, had been against the war. But unlike them he had been unwilling to use his contacts to avoid going. He kept saying he didn't see how he could not go. So they had trained him to be a medical orderly and he had come back blind. It was as if someone had drawn a steel rake across his face, but she could remember his eyes clearly: brown, gentle, dancing with enthusiasm. She didn't understand how Laing could be illegally selling arms without telling her. It was as if she had been living with someone else and the devotion that their married life revolved around was a twisted joke.

She walked quietly back to the kitchen and stacked the dishwasher to calm herself, then came out to join them. Although nothing was said, they both noticed that she was distracted. After Smith had gone, Laing asked if she was all right and for a moment she thought of confronting him, but she hardly knew how to do it. They had never had to confront each other. Instead she went straight to bed saying she was tired.

* * *

When Laing called on Smith at the Carlyle the next day, Wednesday, 11 June, Smith agreed without much resistance to do a quick survey of the merchants Menet had mentioned, so long as he didn't have to go to the Far East. In any case, ex-U.S. officers were not the right people to deal with Vietnam and their own lost weapons. Smith would recruit the front man in return for Western-Oriental's paying his costs.

They had been so busy since their return two nights before that Laing had stayed away from his office and not reported to Moffett, at least that was his excuse. In fact, he had been loath to surface without having made progress. Things were now moving, so the moment he left Smith, Laing called Moffett's secretary for an appointment. She managed to convey the older man's impatience in the few words she used to say that he was waiting at home for Laing to telephone.

His call came through when Moffett was in the midst of taking down his naïve paintings and packing them in boxes to be sent to Parke-Bernet for a sale. Moffett's wife had left for East Hampton that morning. As he listened silently to Laing's story, he felt his spirits sag, but waited until the young man had finished before asking calmly, "Why is he only fronting?"

"As I explained," Laing replied patiently, "he's going to find us a dealer who will take it on."

Moffett began to lose his temper. "That is not good enough, Martin. Not nearly good enough. I want this deal done. I do not want to be waltzed around by some freelance wheeler dealer you happened to be at college with."

Laing protested. "He's a friend who is doing me a favour. Anyway, I'm sure he's just getting his feet wet slowly until the situation is clear."

"I am not interested in explanations. Just put the pressure on."

Before Laing could say any more, Moffett hung up. It was only then that he realized he had forgotten to warn Laing about his assistant Morley, who had been nosing around and had been seen going into Fell's office several times. But then, Moffett reconsidered, perhaps Laing knew and was encouraging him.

He went back to his windowless, bare dining room and found it lugubrious. Isabelle had left, in a convenient spot, the two oval mirrors that she had already suggested, because she believed that people would do what she wanted if it were made easy for them. Moffett hung the mirrors side by side on the long wall of the room, certain that she would have preferred them at either end.

The year before, he had looked forward to his two months solitude in New York. This year the anticipation had turned to depression. He tried to think of something to fill the evening.

TWENTY-ONE

Smith left for England that evening and once there flew immediately to Birmingham to see Bob Mummings, the best-known of the dealers Menet had mentioned. The talkative little man had his office in front of his store and insisted on giving a tour before doing business. He affected the airs and clothes of a conservative English accountant, although he was originally American. The aisles of his warehouse were spotless, the weapons neatly stacked or in crates.

Smith patiently followed Mummings, who began boasting as he led the way into a second building. "Tell Menet what you saw. This is the biggest private stock in the world. Tell him that."

They were in a shooting gallery used to test the weapons but Smith begged off a demonstration of machine-guns and, once back in the front office, he presented his case.

Mummings said he wasn't interested. Not that he couldn't do the deal—of course he could. But he wasn't about to risk his American government contacts for mere money. What was more, there was no one else who could do the deal. That he knew.

The visit was a waste of time, just as Menet had said it would be. Smith went down to London where, that same afternoon, he saw another dealer—an ex-parachute officer who disliked dealing with anyone other than ex-officers. The impression he gave physically matched his character—smooth and hard in an understated way. He didn't believe the goods existed and he didn't trust Smith, whom he took to be a fringe player trying an old trick.

The trick was deceptively simple. He believed that Smith wanted him to find a buyer, at as high a price as possible. When this was done, Smith would go out and find a seller, at a lower price. The margin would go into Smith's pocket. People were always trying that one, although it rarely worked. Europe was full of believable men carrying identical lists of arms which were for sale, but were not theirs to sell.

Smith took a day off to go through the mail at his office in the West End, across the road from Claridges. There was a Telex from Lamine saying that he had tried to find him in New York after their meeting. He wanted to talk urgently. There was another Telex, from Idrissi, wanting to know when Smith would be back.

He went to Paris the next day, Saturday, 14 June, to meet a dealer who was a ballistic engineer by training. The Frenchman had already heard about Smith on the grapevine. An untidy figure, with pens and pencils sticking out of the breast pocket of his jacket, he came to Smith's hotel in the afternoon to warn him that the word was getting around. The government monitors would soon be following him if he weren't more careful.

As for Smith's proposition, he wasn't interested. He claimed that Hanoi itself had tried to sell the arms through dealers in 1976 and failed. He could see no reason why he should do better.

From Smith's hotel the ballistic engineer went on to the George V, where he had agreed to have a drink with Colonel Gerten. It was the sort of place the dealers liked—gold paint generously applied and expensive tarts preening in the ornate lobby furniture. Gerten made a point of meeting people there. The engineer had accepted because he owed Gerten a favour; there were not many people around so adept at doing unpleasant little tasks. It took Gerten thirty minutes to find out that his pigeon had arrived in town, that his name was Smith and that his hotel was the Lancaster. The added bonus was that he discovered the nature of the weapons; then he knew the rest would be easy.

That evening, Smith sat in his room in the Lancaster working through what he had heard. Curiously enough, he wasn't depressed by his failures. In a confused way, he was elated.

The dealers were discouraged by the elaborate rules governing their trade. But what meaning had the rules when the profession consisted of mere scavengers running between the legs of governments, attempting to steal scraps from a four-hundred-billion-dollar business? They gave themselves airs.

He re-examined his list, looking for one last dealer who might accept. To approach more would be dangerous. As he went through this collection of strange men—because, however banal the appearance, the interior was always strange—he had the impression of walking through a fairy tale in which the characters themselves were children.

The dealers were businessmen or ex-soldiers or salesmen with a flair for strange countries—like Smith. The most successful had never been soldiers. They had never seen what happens when a piece of metal hits an expanse of flesh. They were like money market geniuses who know nothing about mines or factories, but can sense the smallest change of current in the flow of finances around them.

And yet, reality was doing the deal. These men, who lived to do a deal like this, could not; while he could, if he so wished.

On Sunday morning he flew to Madrid, where he wasted two days trying to contact the Prince-dealer who seemed the most likely to accept. When he finally tracked him down, Smith took one look at the man and decided he wouldn't even risk making the offer.

He could think of nothing more to do than to give up. In the bar of the Madrid Ritz on Monday evening, he drafted a telegram to Laing, giving the bad news without being indiscreet. He sent it off from the hotel desk before telephoning his office. His secretary had another message from Lamine; this time from Algiers.

Smith went back down to the bar. He sat drinking and emptying the plates of tapas that succeeded one another. What was it Farid had said? He was becoming the man of other men. Was that true? Why shouldn't he sell the arms for his own reasons? What reasons? They wouldn't come clear. They had to do with wanting to grab hold of something big. Wanting to hold onto it until it had run its course.

He thought about Idrissi and Lamine. There was no real contradiction. Idrissi was against the war and the arms could help to end it. Smith laughed to himself. He was as good at inventing reasons to convince himself as he was at convincing others. Now Cosima was a different kind of person; she invented nothing to fool herself.

He wasn't surprised to find himself thinking about her. She had been slipping into his mind whenever he found himself day-dreaming as he travelled alone around Europe. Her image was without words; a growing desire which he nurtured and pampered to warm his imagination.

This messy situation was just what he expected to fall into, but he remembered her as someone who fell into nothing. She created situations; she chose. When he had chosen to go to university in Montreal, it was to escape his friends who were all lined up on the threshold of a new era. All he had felt was claustrophobia. And McGill had been no escape. There had been just as much talking, marching and striking about everything under the sun. He had withdrawn into four years of solitude. That was what had drawn him to Laing, whose relentless drive was equally out of place. They had been joined in their disaffection, while Cosima was effortlessly navigating her way, embracing all the great events, drawing people to her, appearing at the centre of everything. It wasn't surprising that she hadn't had time for Laing. She hadn't noticed either of them. Smith's only desire after those four years had been to go farther away. Yet, even in her superiority, she was seductive.

He shook her image away and tried again to organize his thoughts, but he found he'd drunk too much. Something made him look around the bar. He had the sensation of eyes resting on him. The room was full of businessmen and Spanish couples, among whom there was no one familiar, so he went back to his drink. One of the men looked up and resumed watching. His face was lined, leathery. His expression was satisfied. For a reasonable sum he had won the heart of a desk clerk, who provided a copy of Smith's Telex to Laing and agreed to inform Gerten of anything else; reservations for example. As for the Telex, a quick look in the numbers directory revealed that Western-Oriental was Smith's employer, which Gerten translated as money.

Ideas were floating through Smith's mind without order. He couldn't marshal them. One thought returned again and again—the deal itself was what drew him. The act itself, standing clear from morality or friendship. He decided to wait until the morning before sending a Telex to Lamine.

TWENTY-TWO

"Nasser means freedom. It wasn't his real name. This place is named after the basic state of man, not the various men who fought to achieve it."

Lamine wore neatly pressed fatigues, the top a loose, open-necked jacket without a shirt beneath. His bare feet were protected by heavy sandals. He had replied immediately to Smith's message, leaving the American enough time to fly to Algiers for a meeting on Wednesday, 18 June.

Villa Nasser, the Polisario embassy and window on the outer world, sat part way up a hill in a French villa, surrounded by abandoned gardens and a high wall. Two men with machine-guns stood out of sight inside the barred gate. The road to it led past government departments and foreign embassies, all making do in former villas. Among them was the Villa Jolli where the Algerian President lived.

Smith sat down beside Lamine on a cracking leather sofa in what had once been the salon. "The Polisario style shows great consistency," he said. They were surrounded by uncomfortable furniture, posters and half-shuttered windows.

"We aren't city people, fat like you, Anthony, from sitting in rooms, thinking about how to furnish them. Apparently your deal wasn't done."

Smith put his hand on Lamine's knee. "What I want to know, Abdullah, is can you pay? 'When the army marches abroad, the treasury will be emptied at home.'" Smith couldn't help but notice his friend's hard but clean feet and trimmed toenails.

Lamine patted Smith's hand. "So you remember Sun Tzu. Read it carefully, Anthony. Our army marches at home. Our treasury is full. For problems of payment, look to the other side. Why is Morocco, a land of plenty, receiving cash gifts from the King of Saudi Arabia?" He got to his feet. "Stay here. I want to include someone else—a political type."

He went into the hall and called up the wooden staircase. A few minutes later, a short man in his early twenties came into the room.

"This is Ahmed Mah. The Central Committee has asked him to follow the matter."

Mah was serious, almost glum, as he sat facing them.

Smith said doubtfully to Lamine, "Are you on the Central Committee?"

"Relax, Anthony, of course I am. Now show me the list."

While Mah watched, the two men went through the weapons, Lamine stopping at any item that interested him.

"Those 105mm howitzers are common garden. We've captured more than we can use from the Moroccans. They can be mounted for firing from the back of a truck. Now these 15mm howitzers are more interesting. The Moroccans don't have them. Problem is, each weighs over six tons. We'd have trouble moving it discreetly, but let's mark it for consideration. Rifles are of no interest; their M-16 isn't very good in the desert. But grenade launchers, how many are there? 47,000. Ten thousand are M-70s. That many we don't need. But a small supply . . . You see, the M-70 weighs only six and a half pounds loaded. It's accurate up to 180 yards. And, dear friend, the going price is two hundred dollars. Grenades, my God, 175,000. You're letting a starved man into a granary."

Lamine checked off two more items—anti-tank and anti-aircraft equipment. He bypassed the planes and heavy helicopters, then stopped, "This is what we want."

Smith read the item:

30 AH-1G Cobra attack helicopters unassembled and crated in their original packing grease

"But you have no air force, Abdullah."

"Exactly." Lamine saw his friend's surprise. "The Cobra's fuselage is only three feet wide, which I assure you the Moroccans could never hit. The turret of this model will have two guns, either miniguns or grenade launchers—450 grenades a minute. The Cobra has amazing talents. For the poor men on the ground, it appears like a dragonfly and then like a snake, whipping back and forth over them. There is a strange coincidence; this is the machine the Moroccans will get from America next year—a newer model with more equipment, of course."

"What are you talking about, Abdullah?" Smith drew back to get a clearer look at Lamine. "This is crazy."

Mah broke in with stiff formality. On one side of his upper row of teeth, a number were missing. "If our fraternal army were able to surprise the Moroccan cowards . . ."

Lamine cut him off. "Don't talk to Mr. Smith that way or he'll laugh at you. Of course it's crazy, Anthony. The Moroccans would have packed it in earlier this year if the King hadn't got his arms deal through in Washington. Now the hot shots in Rabat think they have but to wait until the equipment arrives. When it does, nothing will happen. There isn't the willpower in their army to use it properly. But the war will drag on and I want to end it. War is deception in every way. I want them to believe we'll do more than we can. If I have the helicopters this summer, we'll be ready by spring."

"With whom to fly them?" Smith's voice was tinged with sarcasm.

"Pilots I have. You don't image that just because we have no air force, we have trained no pilots. We've had five years. Our backers are afraid to give us planes, because that might lead to war between them and Morocco, but training pilots is a harmless gesture towards the future independent Sahara State. And you, Anthony, come like a prophet, just in your time. We couldn't buy these on the open market without everyone knowing. I recognize this list. Your middlemen, whoever they are, have as much to hide as us. Our needs for discretion meet—we must deceive even our sponsors. Now what about price? The open market price on the Cobra is $1.7 million."

"I don't know . . . let's say two million," Smith hesitated, "delivered."

Lamine had a way of intertwining his fingers in an expression of great calm which made the listener uneasy. "That'd still be only sixty million. There'll be but one delivery, so we must look at the attachments, spare parts and ammunition. A few of the other items could be useful. The anti-tank equipment. Oh, and the grenade launchers. Let's say 2,000. That'd be $400,000 before ammunition."

They worked out a list and gave it to Mah to have typed. When the young man had left them alone, Smith asked, with a grin, "Are all your guerillas like Mah?"

Lamine made an embarrassed sign for him to stop. "Formulas are the easiest thing to learn. His father was a miserable villager who smuggled contraband past the Spanish. One day, the jargon will pass and he'll be functionally intelligent. Just now, he has certain uses." Lamine hesitated and asked shyly, "What about Moulay Sayed?"

Smith blushed. "Are you appealing to my conscience, Abdullah? I thought you wanted the deal."

"I was curious."

Smith betrayed confusion. "I'm doing nothing against Moulay Sayed. He's against the war." Smith paused to look at Lamine. "You may find that specious, but I can't be expected to take sides in a conflict just because I have a friend who is a citizen of that country."

"And it's all for their own good?" Lamine's tone wasn't sarcastic. He was uncomfortable when he didn't understand his friends.

"We'll see . . . For God's sake, Sayed will never know! That, no doubt, is why you brought me here with the curtains drawn in the car."

"Don't get excited, Anthony. Who's your friend? I mean, who are you doing this for?"

"You'll meet him. He's an independent. Doesn't look like it. Looks like a technocrat. But then you used to like Rimbaud. Where do you want us to deliver? Mauritania?"

"No. Any port will attract attention."

He took Smith into the next room, where a map of the Spanish Sahara hung on the wall. Lamine traced his finger down the long Atlantic coast.

"The north is no good. Too close to El Aayun and their air force. Then there's a stretch of difficult beach where the water covers shifting sands. Below that is the southern capital, Dakhla. It's jammed with Moroccan troops and also has air force. But look fifty miles to its north. Angra de Los Ruivos. The Spanish named it. A good, wide bay. There we would be alone."

Smith stared at the map. He was exasperated. "You mean land on a sand beach? How do we handle the crates?"

Lamine laughed at him. "You haven't read your own list properly. Landing-craft. All you need is a ship that can lower them into the water. When the shuttling job is finished, you either hoist the craft back on board or sink them. Don't look so doubtful, Anthony. You do the selling. I'll do the logistics. It'll happen as in a dream. What are the words? 'When capable feign incapacity.'"

Smith reluctantly finished the phrase. "'When active feign inactivity.' I'd better sleep here if we're after discretion."

They spent the rest of the day working out details, and the next morning, Thursday, the 19th, Smith sent a telegram to Laing—"Place reserved Flight Lufthansa 82, New York—Madrid—Algiers, 20 June. You will be met." As a precaution, he sent it to Amster Yard. It was Smith's first sign of life since Madrid and he imagined that Laing had been sunk in depression for the last forty-eight hours.

That same afternoon a desk manager of Air Algeria telephoned Colonel Gerten in his hotel to inform him that a reservation had been made for a Mr. Martin Laing. Gerten was delighted. Now he was certain that Western-Oriental was at the centre of the deal. He probed the manager to make sure he was still satisfied with his small bribe.

Laing prepared immediately to go, but just before he left his office for the airport, he went upstairs to inform Moffett. That way it would be too late to stop him. In fact, Moffett was delighted and held his peace, so that Laing wouldn't think he was trying to interfere. While the older man found Smith intriguing, he didn't like leaving everything in the hands of an outsider who was bound neither by a contract nor by money. It was strange, but he found he couldn't shake the deal out of his mind. Without meaning to, he thought about it in the middle of negotiations or lunches or through the evenings he spent alone in his apartment. It was the one spark in his life and he found himself wanting it to work more than anything he could remember.

Laing was met at the gate in Algiers airport by a young man in cheap trousers and sandals who led him outside to an ageing Peugeot. Curtains were drawn over the rear and side windows. Laing opened a side curtain, but the driver stopped him with a sharp order. He didn't argue.

It was a long drive up and down the hills of Algiers, winding through the unkempt streets until they stopped halfway down an incline before a high wall and a gate. It swung open on two armed men, who waved the car forward, then closed the gate behind. One of the armed men opened Laing's door and sent him across a stretch of weeds to a villa, the driver following with his bag.

He was met at the door by Smith, who greeted him warmly and led the way to the bedroom they were to share. It was empty except for two metal-framed single beds. The walls were yellowed, the ceiling cracked. They sat on the beds, facing each other. Laing had no idea where he was and understood nothing, because Smith hadn't told him about meeting Lamine in New York. It took an hour to explain the whole deal and Laing reacted with anger,

"This isn't what I planned. What one needs is a clear, neat sale, in normal business conditions. Wes—"

Smith cut him off before he could say the company's name. He had no idea whether they were being listened to. Laing already felt a fool and it upset him even more to have almost shouted Western-Oriental for all to hear.

"Listen, Anthony, I'm used to deals which need discretion. But this is ridiculous." He looked around the room with disbelief. "What we are talking about is a hundred million dollars."

In his excitement, Laing overlooked the fact that Smith had gone much farther than he said he would.

"All right, Martin. You find a buyer. You yourself heard Menet. I've told you about the dealers. They may sound professional, but they're the tacky ones. Abdullah Lamine is a competent man and his ten thousand guerillas have kept the Moroccans on the run for five years."

"What about the Moroccans? We have a lot of business there . . ."

Smith lost his patience. "Martin! You're selling guns! No matter who you sell to, they will be the enemy of a country you have investments in. Why are you doing everything offshore? Why isn't the company involved directly? Why do you think you were brought here so discreetly? Surely the certainty of Vietnam is more important than a risk over Morocco."

Laing was about to mention Sayed Idrissi, but he decided that was a personal question for Smith to deal with on his own.

Smith pulled out a cigar, annoyed that he had been drawn into defending himself. "Do what you want, Martin. Deal with Lamine. Find someone else. Drop the whole business. It's your problem."

He lit his cigar and stared at Laing, who sat absorbed in his thoughts for a good five minutes, perched on the edge of the bed. The only hint of a noise was Smith sucking on his cigar.

Laing abruptly pulled himself together, looked up, and spoke in modulated tones, "I'll go along with you. After all, you're the miracle worker. I'd be foolish to decline your miracle. What about the prices?"

Smith put his cigar in the metal ashtray that sat on his bed. He replied warmly, "We can thrash the final details out with Lamine. I suggest we ask for a first payment of ten per cent. The rest goes into a trust account payable when we present a delivery-release note countersigned by Lamine."

Lamine appeared the next morning with Mah, who took it upon himself to argue the terms with Laing. When that was done, Laing agreed to go straight to Bangkok to get the shipment moving. The moment it was on the water, he would cable Lamine, who would make the first payment. At that point, they would fix a delivery date, probably mid-August. Lamine supplied charts of the coast around Angra de Los Ruivos and that was that. The whole conversation took less than an hour.

When they were alone again in the bedroom, Laing asked nervously, "You are coming with me to Bangkok?"

Smith reassured him. "Of course. It's all right, Martin. You believe everything follows a set plan. I don't. You mustn't try to negate intelligence. Learning applied produces inconsistency."

Laing ignored the comment. He pulled his case onto the bed and brought out a file.

"I have the company papers with me. Why don't you sign? I filled in your fee at one and a half per cent."

Smith put his hand out for the papers. He read them and signed, changing his percentage to two. Laing was amazed that nothing was said. Smith handed the papers back, still without a word.

Laing heard himself agree, "Why should I argue? I have what I want."

Whatever papers were signed, Laing knew he didn't have Smith under control. He didn't believe that possible. What he did have was his own kind of agreement, with his own parameters.

There was nothing to stop Smith walking out or twisting the agreement, but those were acceptable risks because Smith didn't have the kind of motives people flash about under the banner of morality or honour—whatever they really are. At least he made no pretence. In that they were joined, because Laing knew himself to be driven, not motivated. Such a pure state could only be the positive side of man.

Closed up in their room and walking in the rundown garden of the Villa Nasser, they spent the rest of the day working through the next steps. Their first need was to contact Ngo Van Cu in Hanoi and arrange a meeting with him in Bangkok. A message from Algiers might not arrive. It would also be indiscreet, given that the government monitored all communications.

They decided to fly to London, where Smith's secretary could send the message. There Smith would draw funds on the newly constituted Bermuda company and send larger sums to Singapore, to be readily available for use.

For Smith it was the first time in years he had worked with someone. Usually he saw himself as a modern version of the itinerant soldier or scholar of the Renaissance or, for that matter, of ancient China. Like a *condottiere*, he moved from state to state or company to company, selling his expertise; no better and no worse than a Sun Tzu or a Machiavelli. Neither patriotism nor class rules restricted him. He sold himself or any object to anyone to do anything. It was hardly a complimentary image; but Smith didn't need compliments to survive, only reference points. It comforted him to know that others had already lived the way he did.

Now he felt himself being drawn together with Laing, as they had been years before. He had always seen Laing in the same light as himself and felt that this was what cemented their friendship. Smith said as much as they picked over the tasteless white rolls at breakfast the next morning, Monday, 23 June, just before they left for the airport.

Laing was amazed. "I'm not for sale." Then he laughed. "You forget, I'm a conservative, six years in the arms of one all-consuming corporate mother."

"Yes, Martin, but that's because she treats you well. You'd have sold your expertise to any company, any country. There's no greater whore than a hungry man with knowledge for sale. And when order breaks down, the prostitutes hit the streets. Look at me. I'm your common variety. But at least I do know that I'm selling."

Laing looked at himself in his mind's eye and sought the Renaissance scholar without success.

On the flight, Smith's attention was drawn to Gerten, sitting across the aisle from them, studiously not listening to his neighbours' conversation. Smith couldn't place the man and looked away.

They decided not to wait in London for a reply from Ngo, which might take days, while the Vietnamese was only a few hours from Bangkok. If they left immediately they would have time to recover from the trip while waiting for Ngo to appear. Laing sent him a telegram—they could be found at the Oriental Hotel and would themselves make enquiries at the Vietnamese Embassy.

TWENTY-THREE

The ringing of a phone bore into Laing's consciousness until it sent his hand searching in the darkness for the receiver. He heard Ngo Van Cu on the line, asking him to come to the Embassy in an hour. Laing discovered the light switch. He had slept eleven hours and the morning was half gone.

He threw himself under the shower in the marble bathroom, but the water was tepid and did little to clear his mind. It didn't flow cold in Bangkok, not even in the Oriental Hotel. He came back into the room and opened the curtain. The heat could be sensed, waiting outside his air-conditioned isolation.

The Classical Colonial architecture of the East Asia Trading Company lay below, painted in sloping pastels. Behind it were the more aggressive towers of the French cathedral. Soot floated down from a metal smokestack on the far bank of the Chao Phrya River and across the water onto the terrace of the hotel, where he could see tourists eating late breakfasts in the baking sun.

He ordered papaya and coffee, then rang Smith, only to find a message that he would be out for the day. Laing went back to the window and stood waiting. Clumps of tangled green vines, hacked away from the canals they choked, floated down the great brown god to the sea.

Twenty minutes later, Laing was in a car honking its way

through the trucks and tuc-tucs, whose sound was more like an anguished scream. Even with the windows closed and the air conditioning on, the noise and heat washed over him as in a nightmare.

He was driven out of a shopping district and past Patpong, its massage parlours and bars dormant in the morning. They skirted around Lumpini Park onto Wireless Road and into a district that had been country thirty years before, when the city had been more a rural Venice than an urban capital, its canals now covered over to make roads for the exploding population.

The embassies began to succeed one another. They passed the gardens of the American compound, visible through its grill fence. That was scarcely out of sight before his driver pulled up to a wall with a metal gate.

A Vietnamese came out to ask for identification. There was an argument about logistics, which ended with the driver being made to wait in the street while Laing walked in through the garden.

The house had a red roof, yellow stucco reminiscent of vomit and blue trim. The guard led him up some steps, through a hall and into a long reception room with leather sofas down either side, a small glass-topped table in front of each. The room was shuttered in a vain attempt to keep out the heat and the ceiling fans were off. Laing looked up suggestively, but the guard chose to ignore the glance. He indicated that Laing should sit down. Then disappeared.

Ngo startled him when he appeared, calling out across the room in English, "Mr. Liang"—that was how he pronounced it. Laing couldn't tell whether it was a joke or whether he'd forgotten. "Welcome!"

The fans began to turn and the lights came on, like a carnival ride.

"I thought you had disappeared for ever." Ngo settled into the chair next to Laing so that they were huddled in one corner of the room.

"It is the 25th of June, Mr. Ngo. One month is not long if one considers that you tried for five years and failed."

Ngo smiled. "You mean you succeeded? Good. Very good. Whom have you found?"

"As one might imagine, the buyer will remain anonymous. Once we take delivery of the arms, they're no longer your affair." Laing handed him a list. "This is what we want."

Ngo nodded and called across the room in Vietnamese. A

young man appeared, paused to leave a folder, then disappeared. He reappeared balancing, on a tray, enough bottles of Thai orange crush to last two days. While Laing sipped this, his tongue prickling from the sugar added to please the local taste, Ngo made comparisons between his folder and the list. He jotted down numbers and eventually totalled them up.

"You have given good prices."

"Not really, considering the circumstances. They average out at eight per cent below the open market. We need to sell a bit extra to cover costs. There'll be shipping and various other payments, here in particular. There is also a professional."

Ngo looked up. "Are you not a professional?"

Laing was put off stride for only a second. "You will deal with him from now on."

Ngo adopted an agreeable expression. "You are certain they are not in Asia, these buyers? This was agreed."

"There's an ocean between you, Mr. Ngo."

"If you were inaccurate, I would . . ."

Laing flinched, as if stung. "What would you do, Mr. Ngo? Tell me that, just what would you do?" He leaned sharply towards him until their faces were only inches apart. "Tell the world? And who would be the most embarrassed? Western-Oriental or Vietnam or you, Mr. Ngo? I hope that you will ensure every penny makes its way back to Hanoi. One can't be too careful."

Ngo moved his head away and smiled shyly.

The smile was returned by Laing. "I suggest we stick to business. I want to move quickly."

"There will not be a problem. You have made my work easy. The major purchase is already crated." He looked at the list again. "I am surprised to see the landing-craft are wanted. Compared to their other choices, these are of no interest."

"I've no idea why they're there," Laing dismissed. "In fact, I don't care."

"Care?" Ngo said sarcastically, "I didn't mention care. You spend so much time denying emotion."

Before Laing could say anything, he pulled a map from his folder and pointed out where he would deliver. A good road crossed into Thailand from Cambodia just north-east of Chanthaburi, and from there it wasn't more than four hours to decent Thai ports.

The Vietnamese said he could deliver within one week of firm notice. As of that afternoon, the goods would be gathered together in the south. His only stipulation was that the Americans must be precise about the delivery date, because he didn't want the weapons sitting around in Western Cambodia, where the Khmer Rouge were active.

"A convoy of fifty trucks will hardly pass unnoticed, Mr. Liang."

TWENTY-FOUR

Long before Laing had been woken by Ngo, Smith had gone out in search of an ally. He knew that the real work would be organizing each second after the arms hit the Thai border. From that moment, their way would have to be padded with bribery, protection, blind eyes and speed until they were on the water.

He had an idea that led him to the edge of the chaotic alleys of Chinatown, looking for a company called the Siamese Worldwide Trading Company. The owner, like most Bangkok businessmen, was Chinese, not Thai, and he had once helped Smith do a marginal deal. The company was in an ugly three-story concrete block and the owner remembered Smith well; but he was the wrong man. He had no interests in the south-east. His business was in the north—probably smuggling across the Burmese border. Probably drugs.

By the standards of the Bangkok Chinese elite, he was a small man, but he knew who the big men were. For a cash payment of $5,000 he told Smith to see General Krit Sirikaya.

"For a name?" Laing complained when told that afternoon. "We're not even getting an introduction. If we start throwing money around, everyone's price will go up."

"Impoverished men hang around the Bangkok railway yards," Smith explained. "For twenty-five dollars, they'll kill a man. As this is a common occurrence, it's better to pay."

"How do you know Krit is the right man?"

"For twenty-five dollars," Smith pointed out, "the same gunman is available to us."

General Krit turned out to be elusive. He was one of the new rising Generals who had hopes for a senior ministry and, perhaps later, a crack at being Prime Minister. All he had to do was win enough support for a coup. Smith rang his office several times that day and the next—without being able to leave even a message—until he realized there was no point in persisting. He would have to find another way.

At the same time, he began looking for a ship. He knew of a trading company that specialized in off-colour imports and illegal exports, including religious objects such as Buddhas. Unfortunately, they had no ships in port large enough and hadn't had since 1979. Most of the marginal carriers had abandoned the illegal business because they could make unlimited money carrying medical and food supplies to the Cambodian refugees.

Smith decided to ask a friend for advice. He'd spent the first evening with a journalist called John Field, while Laing stayed in the hotel to get over his jet lag. Smith and Field had first met in Montreal when they were both twenty. Smith had been a student, while Field was already grubbing in a newspaper office. He had left Montreal after wresting from his paper the dubious privileges of a roving stringer in the Far East and, once there, he'd stayed put for the last fifteen years.

The journalist met the two Americans that evening on the terrace of the hotel. They sat with a mosquito coil burning under their table to discourage the bugs, while a breeze off the river carried cooler air into their faces, along with the noise from river taxis churning by and people shouting on ferry barges.

Field was classically good-looking, with fair hair and strong features that were marred by an impression of brutality in the lower half of his face. Like a tough child. Smith couldn't remember whether he had always been like that, or whether it was a physical emanation of his life. His eyes were glazed, which could have been the effects of opium or merely a mental state. Because they never focused on the person speaking to him, he appeared distant, as if thinking of something else. He drank Mekong, the local whisky, which he admitted was an acquired taste. In his case, it had been acquired in the days when he wasn't selling many articles.

"Krit won't see you without an introduction." Field looked

out over the river as he talked, his voice deep with a soft edge. "What you must do is whet his appetite. I can tell you where to find him tonight. No big deal. Anybody could tell you. He's sponsoring a boxing evening at Lumpini Stadium to promote recruiting. The way to get at him is to slip him a note, with cash inside. Have you got some cash?" Field came alive at the thought of some action. "Well, go on, Anthony. Get it."

Smith went inside while Field pursued a favourite subject. "Around here, a euphemism is a polite form that reduces cash to friendship." He asked a waiter for paper. "Everybody in this country is for sale. The charm of it is that nothing appears to be. There is a magic formula which removes the sting from acts that would destroy the self-respect of nice Anglo-Saxon Protestant boys like yourself."

Laing was amused, but he asked, "Don't you find that depressing after a while?"

Field hardly let him finish. "If the Vietnamese army marches in and devours Thailand, I'll go somewhere else in Asia. If that doesn't work out, I'll go to Africa. I haven't set foot in North America for fifteen years and I've never been to Europe. That's the last place I want to go. I'll die here or in Africa." He took a drink from his Mekong. "They leave you alone."

He said this without any pleasure and turned to writing Smith's euphemistic note. "You will do me the greatest honour, if you permit me . . ."

Smith brought down five one thousand dollar bills, but Field made him put away two.

"You want to arouse his curiosity. Too much is pushy."

They agreed that Smith should approach the General alone. Field would go in just long enough to point him out, then leave with Laing, to wait in a bar called The Grand Prix.

The traffic around the stadium was jammed, forcing them to walk the last hundred yards, with car lights picking out the crowds of hawkers, the broken pavement and the mud puddles from the afternoon's rain. An army rock band in uniform was playing on a stand outside, while recruiters harangued the hundreds of young men streaming by. Beyond them was the outline of a low circular brick building with a tin roof.

"Looks like a dump," Smith said.

"It is a dump. Come on."

Field dragged him forward to buy tickets. They left Laing outside, listening to the music.

An attendant took them in hand at the entrance and led the

way through a crowd, over which both white men towered, down a dingy tunnel-like corridor under the cheap section. Somewhere, out of sight, was the dulled roar of people. At the end of the corridor, the noise exploded into a mass of undirected shouts.

Smith paused to adjust his eyes to the light and looked around. The small enclosure was packed with five or six thousand men. The tin roof was raised a yard above the wall of the building to let air escape—yet heat and humidity pressed down. A fifteen-foot wire fence protected the centre seats from the cheap sections rising behind, where there were no chairs and everyone was craning to see.

Field and Smith were led down to the edge of the ring and along one side before going back down the next corner aisle to the sixth row. There the attendant found two empty metal folding chairs. Just behind, four men in army uniforms were playing a rhythmic doggerel with small cymbals, drums and a reedy flute.

For the first time, Smith looked up to the ring at two boys dancing face to face, keeping exact time with the music. They occasionally kicked at each other or threw a punch. Field pulled Smith closer.

"There'll be eight matches. These two are lightweight beginners. The championship match is last. Phadetsuek against a challenger called Khaopong. First time?"

Smith nodded.

"I hope you like violence." Field wiped the sweat from his face. "The boxers are farm boys. This is their way out of the rice paddies. What freedom they get, I can't imagine. It's all organized with a religious edge so that the trainer becomes their father figure, which means their god. He takes their life totally in hand, until their brains have been knocked out. Look. On the other side in the front rows."

Smith stood up. Across the ring he saw three officers.

"Krit's the one in the middle. Don't wait too long. He owns a training camp and has a lot of money riding on the later matches. I'll see you at The Grand Prix." Field slipped away.

Smith brushed the mosquitoes off his ankles and watched the fighters in the ring as they danced on their heels, sliding their hips down and forward like drugged men. They kept to the rhythm of the flute band, which Smith found irritating and artificial. With his foot, one of the boxers caught the other's eye. The crowd whistled approval as blood spurted out. Behind the boxers, Smith saw the men in the upper section agitating their arms with finger signs to take bets.

By the end of the match, both boys stood numb, blood streaming from their faces. Smith worked his way to the front and around the ring, past where the winner was brought out, a tiny figure wrapped in a towel. His crew of assistants propelled him through the mêlée.

At the corner of the ring, Smith got a clear view of General Krit and moved towards him. A civilian at the end of the row stood up, blocking his way. At first it didn't appear intentional, so Smith tried to explain that he wanted to get by, but the man couldn't understand a word of English or French. He had no intention of moving.

Smith pulled out his envelope and pointed at the General. He repeated the name Krit until the man took the envelope. The guard indicated his own seat, meaning that Smith should sit down. When he had gone, the man in the next seat put his hand on Smith's arm, smiling, to show that he also would prevent any movement.

Smith leaned forward. He saw the guard hand the envelope to Krit, who turned it over impatiently. The expression was surprising on the General's face, which was otherwise smooth and serene—the face of a young, devoted priest. The guard pointed at Smith and the General's eyes followed. He caught sight of the American and bowed his head marginally before looking away and slitting open the envelope with a fingernail. The money had been placed separately, so that it could be seen when the envelope was opened. The General read the short message, then placed the contents in his side pocket and sat back to watch the next match as if nothing had happened. Smith swore to himself. But the guard returned and ignored him, walking by to sit in the second row.

The man next to him passed Smith a programme. The weights in the second match jumped from 102 pounds to 116. Someone called Yusop, swimming in large pink trunks, kicked someone called Pohsai so severely that Smith wondered how he stood up. Yusop also repeatedly fouled him, by kicking each time the referee separated them from a clinch. As the referee turned to warn him, he automatically adopted a servile pose, his hands pressed together under his chin, begging forgiveness.

Smith leaned forward again. The benign expression had returned to General Krit's face, while his eyes followed the boxers attentively. Smith was drawn back to the match. The rhythm of the music had seeped into his unconscious, until his breathing had adapted to its pace and he slipped into the same semi-drugged state as the boxers and the other spectators. Like the soul of Arab music, it was a variation on a single theme slowly rising to frenzy.

At the end of the match, General Krit caught Smith's eye and beckoned him forward. He didn't rise to meet the American, but told the officer beside him to give up his seat. He ignored Smith's proffered hand, having raised his own two hands pressed together under his chin, smiling.

"Good evening, Mr. Smith. I'm pleased you enjoy our boxing. What did you think of the last match? I think Yusop shows great promise." Krit had been on an exchange course in Washington and felt he spoke English well.

"He comes from your camp?"

"Oh, yes. Pink is my colour. Tell me how I can help you."

He indicated that Smith should move closer, to speak into his ear. His face was even smoother under close inspection. His ear was clean, like an object on display, with an elongated lobe, indicating longevity.

"I have goods to send out of Thailand," Smith said. "They're coming from Cambodia. My need is for safe transit."

The General looked at him, bemused. "There's nothing in Cambodia to export, Mr. Smith, except refugees. If that's what you're after, you don't need my help. The more who go, the better." Smith said nothing. "If it isn't refugees, then it must come from the north or from Vietnam. I hope we are not discussing opium. That's an unsavoury business."

"No, sir. I'm talking about strategic materials and, if I may say so, our exporting them will reduce the armaments on the other side of your border."

The General discounted that gently. "We're not concerned about our friends. They have so many problems of their own. If that were not so, would they be exporting weapons?" His attention was drawn away by the beginning of the third match. "Do you understand boxing?"

"No, I don't."

"Watch the boxer's eyes, the one in pink. His name is Pol. He never looks in his opponent's eyes. Nor does he look where he strikes. The other tries to do the same, yet through inadequacy he is drawn back to the direct approach. I should say he was fascinated by his own inadequacy. Watch."

As he danced, Pol's eyes moved across his opponent's

body in a languorous stare, broken only by his knee flying up to catch the kidneys. Then his foot flew at the jaw. With each blow, Pol expelled a loud breath.

"These boxers aren't entirely men, you understand. We Thais call them *Nakmuay dua*. *Dua* is the word for animal. A very refined animal—he'll act out your dramas for you." Krit saw that Smith was interested. "How large is your shipment?"

"Fifty transport trucks. We would drive them from the border near Chanthaburi to a port."

The General broke away to consider this. Suddenly, Pol caught his opponent in the eye with his foot, staggered him and followed up with a series of punches. The man collapsed to the mat. The crowd screamed its support for the winner, obliging the General to wait until there was less noise.

"You must stay for the last match. I have great hopes of an upset. It will be an interesting example of human will, Mr. Smith, that has to do only marginally with skill." He pointed a finger at the now empty canvas. "Two men come into the ring. Both think they are the best. The one who isn't is the most surprised person in the world. What he didn't know was he didn't have the will. Do you see?"

Smith indicated agreement.

"As to your problem, you've come to the wrong person. I'm a serving officer whose duty lies elsewhere. If it's business advice you want, why don't you see a friend of mine? Write this down. Pong Hsi Kun. You may telephone him at 2827491. He's a man for details. Do you bet, Mr. Smith?"

"Sometimes."

"I don't have a boxer in the next match. Let us wait one round, at which point we might gamble on their willpower. I shall let you choose first."

TWENTY-FIVE

Field led the way through crumbling, interlocking streets lit by the neon signs over the open bar doors, before which pimps and occasionally dwarfs stood, shouting at passers-by to come in. Field knew them all. They joked with him as he passed, offering a free drink or special treatment for his friend, Laing. Neither of them noticed Gerten moving discreetly on their tail, because despite his appearance the Colonel had learnt years before how to move as if he were part of an Asian crowd. Twice Field pushed his way into a bar to accept the drink, while girls in g-strings and number badges crowded around. They obviously knew him well. Western businessmen sat against the walls having their beery forms pampered.

It was a good hour before they got to The Grand Prix, where a pile of garbage had been erected beside the door, which could only be reached by crossing a narrow wooden gangway over a sea of mud. Field led the way. The Grand Prix was his regular bar, so he was greeted on all sides as they plunged into the long dark room past a series of stalls until they found an empty one. Field dropped into it and looked around to examine the girls at the back, dancing in g-strings under strobe lights to blaring music. He came to The Grand Prix because the booths were far enough from the music to make it possible to think.

Field had instinctively liked Laing, but the two men were so different that he hardly knew what to say to him, and he had given up polite conversation years before. Laing was equally perplexed.

Field began to describe how he had first come to Thailand for a short visit on his way to Vietnam, to write stories for a

Canadian paper. He had been delayed by a good story in Bangkok. To pass the time, he had begun an affair with a Thai girl, who bore no resemblance to the Western women he had left behind in the throes of a revolution over what their lives should be and how men should be treated. He was all for them, but had been overwhelmed by the pressure to sacrifice his private life to rebuilding the male-female relationship. Suddenly all of that had disappeared and he had a woman whose only desire was to make him happy, as if it were an obligation; and she asked little beyond kindness and material comfort in return. The complication appeared a few months later when she could no longer conceal her pregnancy. Field reacted with the bitterness of someone who had sought simplicity and freedom and found complications and obligations. He was convinced that she had seen him as a way into North America and used his innocence. He didn't want a wife and didn't want a child. Nor did he want to abandon it.

In the end, he had stayed and given the woman an allowance to look after his daughter, who now went to a good Thai school. Field saw the girl twice a month and considered those few days to be the high points of his life; but he refused to see the mother, even though he could not admit to himself that she had done no more than use him the way he had been using her. The original scar, justified or not, was too large to be erased.

This guileless confession broke down the barrier between the two men and they drank and ate and talked their way through the evening, while the crowds grew around the bar and the women moved among them selling their wares. A girl appeared and slipped her body, bare except for token strings, onto the bench beside Field. By any standards she was exquisite. Field put his arm around her and called her Sam.

She began to entertain them, in an almost incomprehensible English, with a list of her troubles; which seemed to revolve around a German businessman who had promised to marry her but had only been after a cheaper rate. Field listened patiently for a while and then shut her up with a drink. Periodically she would interrupt them to ask if Laing wanted a girl and Laing would say no. The noise level of people pushing around them had become unbearable by the time Smith appeared in the doorway, a frustrated expression on his face, and pushed his way across the bar. Laing slid over to make room.

"General Krit stayed to the end and made sure I did the

same. He also won five hundred off me." Smith looked doubtfully at the girl.

Field reassured him, "You met Sam last night."

"What did he say?" Laing asked.

Smith replied to Field, "He said I should see Pong Hsi Kun. Who's that?"

"That's good. In fact, that's great. Let's get you something to eat, then go fucking." He told a waiter to bring Shanghai noodles and brandy. "In this country, the army has the guns and the Chinese have the money. Until a general marries a businessman, he's only half a man. Krit is sending you to his wife. Pong is his banker, his surrogate on boards of directors, his giver and taker of bribes. One day, he'll finance Krit's coup."

Smith slumped in relief. "All is for the best, in the most arrangeable of all possible worlds." He emptied his glass and ordered another when the noodles arrived.

Field sent the girl off to find two friends, but Laing leaned forward to stop him.

"Not for me."

"Not good enough?" Field didn't understand.

Between mouthfuls, Smith interrupted. "Not up to scratch with what he gets at home."

Laing said defensively, "Not necessary, that's all." He hadn't paid a woman since marrying Cosima, for no other reason than he hadn't wanted to. They were hardly teasing him, yet he felt uncomfortable.

Smith shrugged. "Maybe if you work hard at it, sex is some kind of joy. For me it's just part of life." He resented Laing's attitude and tried to make a joke of it. "I don't have the memory to be sentimental, so I suppose I'll die having wasted a lot of semen."

That only succeeded in making Laing more uncomfortable. The three girls appeared, dressed more like Sunday school students than bar girls. Field paid the cashier the cover charge to free them for the night and Laing found himself reluctantly following the others outside and across the street to an apartment that should have been in a run-down Holiday Inn. It had been furnished by an American general in the early seventies to entertain visiting officers. That was in the days when Bangkok was jammed with the American army.

The girl Laing chose had a smooth, delicate body, with only a few soft pubic hairs, as if on a child's head. She could not have paid greater attention to him, or given him greater pleasure, but after the pleasure had ebbed away, he was left with a sense of waste, as if she had been an elaborate pretence for masturbation.

The girl was running a hand over his body when he got up to leave. She wanted him to stay, but he paid amply to prove he was satisfied and went down into the street alone, where he found a small taxi that charged him triple fare to go back to the hotel.

The next morning, Friday, 27 June, Laing opened his door to a man he didn't know.

"Martin Laing? Yes?" He had an American accent verging on southern mid-west. "You don't know me, but I'm a good friend of one of Anthony Smith's friends. Could I come in?" He stepped forward as he spoke, a small man with a blunted, lined face, carrying with him the odour of sweet cologne soured by sweat. He closed the door behind himself. "Well," he said, as if something had been accomplished, "it sure is hot in this town. Haven't been here for two years." He looked at Laing. "Can I sit down?" As there was no answer, he smiled agreeably and went on. "Your friend, Mr. Smith, saw my friend in Paris about some arms sales and my friend phoned me, thinking I might be able to help. Well, he told me about it all and God, I hate those mother fuckers, but business is business so . . ."

Laing interrupted him firmly. "I'm afraid Mr . . . ?"

"Gerten. Used to be Colonel."

". . . Colonel Gerten, that you must have the wrong person." Laing moved to lead him back to the door.

"I appreciate your discretion, but relax." Gerten sat down on the end of the bed. "I tried to see your Mr. Smith in Paris, only he left town ahead of me, so I found he'd gone to Spain and I just missed him there. Lucky though, his hotel, real helpful, told me he'd sent a telegram to you at Western-Oriental. Well, I thought, if needs be, you might help me. But I found he'd gone to Algiers, so I followed him there. And where should he be, but with some curious types, Commies I'd guess. You'd know better 'cause you turned up too. No. Now don't you go and protest, Mr. Laing. I know you went in and out real quiet, but I was watching the airline reservations."

Gerten unbuttoned his jacket to reveal that he was wearing a shoulder holster. Laing sat down uncertainly, his back to the window. This encouraged Gerten, who became more expansive.

"All I was trying to do was offer my services, you know, friendly and make some money, so I thought I'd just wait and see both of you at the first opportunity. Well, I'd have done it sooner here, but you seemed to be all tied up with the Vietnamese Embassy and the girls. Anyway, here I am and it does look to me as you could do with some help."

Laing pulled himself together and got to his feet. He had to find out what was happening. "Thank you, but we don't need anything."

Gerten didn't move. "Oh yes you do, Mr. Laing. Can I call you Martin? You and Western-Oriental."

Laing didn't move. "Where can I contact you, Colonel?"

"That's a good idea. Why don't I come back here this afternoon, say around three?" Gerten got to his feet. "I did enjoy this meeting and I'm looking forward to getting to know you, Martin." Gerten shook his hand warmly and was gone.

Laing closed the door. His hand was shaking as he picked up the phone to dial Smith.

They spent the next hour running through every word Gerten had said, but in the end they had no idea what he was. He could as easily be a government agent as a dealer trying to cut himself in. The precision with which he had collected information and used it to touch delicate spots showed he had to be handled with care, as did the pistol he carried. But Smith pointed out that that was the least dangerous thing about him. What did he have to gain by using it? There was no room for someone like that in their plans. Nor was paying blackmail money a solution when secrecy was needed, not the hope of secrecy.

They decided that the only way to deal with Gerten was to stall and try to smoke him out. While Smith went to see Pong that afternoon, Laing would concentrate on tying up the Colonel. Then, at least, they'd find out whether there was someone following each of them or whether Gerten was in Bangkok alone. Laing had been unnerved by the Colonel more than he would admit and agreed only reluctantly to be the baby sitter.

They spent the rest of the morning trying to find a ship by telephoning every contact Smith had in Bangkok. Eventually, someone mentioned that a Captain Toller had come in from Malaysia a few days before under peculiar circumstances. His ship was called the *Sophie*. More than that they couldn't say.

Smith telephoned Field to see if he knew anything about it.

Bangkok was such a gossipy town that Field heard most things.

"Captain Toller? Not quite an old friend, but I know him."

"What do you mean, you know him?"

"I tried to interview him. He wouldn't let me on board."

"All right, Field. What's the story?"

"Refugee smuggling. He was trying to get them into Malaysia and was caught. They impounded him and fined him heavily; i.e., could probably do with some cash."

"What's his ship like?"

"Christ, Anthony, what do I know about boats? It was big and freshly painted and it didn't sink when I looked at it."

The moment Gerten was safely with Laing that afternoon, Smith went off to see the captain of the *Sophie*. At the top of the gangway there was a sailor, who ran down and blocked the way. Smith explained that he wanted to see Captain Toller and, when this made no impact, pulled a thousand dollar bill out of his wallet with a sense of repetition and immediately put it away. The sailor led him aboard to a cabin, where he was left with the door locked from the outside.

It was reopened by the Captain, who sat down without a word. He was an ordinary-looking man with marginally swollen features, which gave his skin a flushed appearance; the flush was as grey as it was red.

Smith explained what he was after and then repeated himself slowly until Toller was convinced that he was for real. When that happened, the captain clambered to his feet and brought out a bottle of Mekong, which Smith surprised himself by refusing. Toller poured a tumbler to sip from as he wrote down the ship's capacity. It was clear that the *Sophie* could carry the cargo and that her cranes could both handle the larger crates and off-load the small barges into the sea.

"There is also the question of ignoring an end-user permit," Smith said.

The captain drew back. "You've got your priorities confused. Let's hear a bit about the money."

Smith put two thousand dollars on the table.

"That, Captain, is to pay for your time over the next few days. I want you to work out an exact price, which we can settle at our next meeting."

The captain took up the bills.

"I don't carry no drugs. Do you hear that?"

"Not much danger of that, Captain."

"I wanted you to know."

"What about the permit?"

"That costs extra." The captain had been ignoring end-user permits most of his life.

From there, Smith went to call on Pong Hsi Kun, who had agreed to see him the moment General Krit was mentioned. His office was across the road from the railway station, in the newest building of the Thai Military Bank. The building resembled a tiger crouched to leap on its prey, because the Chinese believed it bad luck to face an oncoming road, to say nothing of the national rail centre. Pong's male secretary appeared almost immediately at the reception desk and led Smith upstairs to a vast over-decorated office, where he was greeted like an old friend by a man not blessed with strong eyes or straight teeth.

"I spoke this morning with General Krit," Pong enthused. "He told me you spent a magnificent evening together. Sit down."

As a compensation for his homeliness Pong dressed and lived to show his wealth. Large, fussy diamond cuff-links matched a diamond stick-pin. He wore a gold watch on one wrist and a bracelet on the other. Both were of the brassy, high carat gold the Chinese liked. There was a set of gold-topped pens, pen-holders and blotter blocks on his desk.

Smith sat down in a deep chair, with a view over one of the few large canals left uncovered in Bangkok, and explained what he wanted.

Pong nodded heavily and made notes. "None of this is a problem," he said with an expansive gesture. "The General's troops can ensure you pass the border. There, I can provide you with men from my private defence group." His cadence matched his elaborate jewellery. "Normally they are farther north, to protect our timber operations along the border. We call them *Taharn lap jarng*. I think you will find them most helpful. They can unload the Vietnamese shipment and reload the crates onto Thai trucks. The General has an interest in a transport company which is always glad to have another job. We might use only ten trucks. That would mean five trips. That would be wise. As for the port, we'll use Sattahip."

"I don't know it."

"Don't know it, Mr. Smith? How surprising. You Americans built it." He wagged a finger in a friendly way. "Such a short memory for your wars. Your navy left it to our navy. We no longer cut the grass, nor does every office have an air conditioner. But it works. Although it's closed to normal commercial trade, we might persuade Admiral Saphit to lend us his facilities. Do you know him?"

"No, I don't."

"No need," Pong reassured. "Absolutely no need. Admiral Saphit is a close friend of General Krit. You might be interested to learn that the Admiral is running for Parliament. I'm sure he'd appreciate any interest shown in his campaign funds. What else?"

"An end-user certificate."

"Oh, Mr. Smith!" Pong laughed like a shy virgin. "Such an eye for detail. Such efficiency. Now let us talk costs."

By costs Pong meant price. The election fund was to receive one hundred thousand. The trucks were fifty, as was the private army. There was a contribution to a private pension fund for selected senior officers, plus twenty-five thousand for the end-user certificate, paid to a relative of Mr. Pong's in Indonesia. There was an investment to make in a new growth fund that Mr. Pong was developing. And that was where the offshore payments began.

They would have to meet again to settle payment terms, but to save time they decided to give the signal to the Vietnamese. The border delivery date would be Sunday, 6 July. Things were more relaxed at weekends.

TWENTY-SIX

Gerten was furious and nervous. He had already been stalled the whole afternoon of the previous day, sitting in Laing's room, trying to coax some money out of him. He had finally agreed to come back at ten the next morning, Saturday, 28 June; and there he was sitting on the end of a bed being stalled again with no money in sight.

He tried running through everything he had on them, phrasing each item as a separate threat, and when that had no effect he began again, his impatience showing through.

What annoyed him was the calm with which Laing sat in an armchair by the window, listening silently to every word. He didn't realize that Laing's nervousness had turned into delight as he heard no mention of Smith's movements the afternoon before. When he was certain that there was no more to come out and that the Colonel was alone, Laing unfolded two thousand dollars, which he reached forward to offer.

Gerten's anger vanished as he accepted the money, but the nascent smile on his face froze when he saw how much it was. Without warning, he shouted. "This won't pay my fucking hotel bill!" Anger began washing over his self-control. Some people weren't smart enough to be afraid. "I'm telling you, Menet won't like this." Dropping the name had no apparent effect on Laing and Gerten tried to calm himself down. "Well, what the hell, Martin, this just won't do, after all the advice I've given you."

Laing started to plead that he was having difficulties with his partner, who refused to pay anyone off. In the midst of the explanation, Gerten stood in a fury, his eyes clouded, unfocused. As if thrown into gear, he rolled forward. At first Laing hardly realized what was happening, then he looked up, his eyes fixed on the place where Gerten's shoulder pistol bulged out. He tried to get up, pushing against his own chair to gain more room, but it was caught in the carpet. He was halfway to his feet when Gerten swung his fist wildly. Laing tried to dodge. Out of the corner of his eye he could see the hand flying towards him. He wrenched his face away, then felt the side of his head being driven through the air as his consciousness exploded. The impetus knocked him back against the chair, which went over, and he lay stunned on the carpet. He had no idea how long it took for his senses to return, but as they did he was invaded by an uncontrollable anger which he hadn't felt since they had tried to beat him up when he was a schoolboy. That same horror of being alone and undefended rose up in him, drowning out the pain. He tried to get to his knees, still dizzy, determined to fight back. Gerten stood over him as he rose and kicked him hard in the gut. Laing collapsed again. He managed to get back onto his knees, but Gerten had retreated to the door.

"You think about that, Martin. I'll see you tomorrow morning."

The door had closed by the time Laing was solidly on his feet. He followed out into the hall, but there was no one there except the floor valet, who smiled and bowed. Laing went back into the room, where his anger grew, blocking out his terrible headache and every thought until Smith returned an hour later from finalizing the payment schedule with Pong.

Laing managed to explain what had happened, almost shouting out, "I'm going to deal with him tomorrow. I don't care what I have to do."

Smith had been upset at what he heard, but now he was horrified by Laing's agitation. "Be quiet, Martin!" His order wasn't even heard. "Listen. This is no time to risk something going wrong. Let's get the stuff on the boat and out at sea, then we'll deal with this man."

Laing stared at him in disbelief. "If you think I'm going to sit around humouring a thug just because he has a gun and some information!"

"For Christ sake!" Smith shouted back. "You're the one who's always preaching about dispassionate acts! Look at yourself. Reason doesn't kill passion. Reason breeds passion. It destroys your common sense and replaces it with logic. Listen to yourself. A crisis knocks you over and all you have left is your passion, which is just what we don't need." Smith blushed and turned away with his last words, "Save us from the tempers of reasonable men."

There was silence behind him before Laing managed to say, "I'm sorry. You're right." He sat down on the bed, surprised at himself, and repeated, "I'm sorry." Suddenly the pain came flowing into his head.

The next morning, Sunday, Smith was driven to Chanthaburi, close to the border. Pong sent him with a chauffeur, who could interpret and who had a military pass. At Chanthaburi, they picked up an officer from Pong's private army. The two men looked around the border areas as well as the stretch of road on the Thai side, where they discovered an endless choice of flat spots. The country was either covered by rice paddies or was barren. They saw few people until close to the border and the refugee camps.

Once they'd found an isolated, flat field, the officer was taken back to Chanthaburi to fetch one hundred of his armed men to clear the ground and build themselves a camp. Smith returned to Bangkok, with a marked map for the Vietnamese.

Laing, meanwhile, was giving Gerten ten thousand dollars, which he promised was just a first payment, and treating him with kid gloves. Laing insisted they have lunch together, after which they went to visit the Emerald Buddha. It was a ridiculous idea, but at least it passed the time. The Colonel accepted because he thought Laing was trying to get rid of him. He was afraid of losing sight of the American and it was easier to accompany than to follow. His instinct still told him Laing was the man to stick close to—the man with something to hide. That didn't stop him asking what Smith was up to. Laing welcomed the question and began fabricating a story.

Gerten tried to digest the story, but it stuck in his throat and was still there when he went back to his hotel late that afternoon. The hotel was a run-down cement block in Chinatown called the Empress. Fifteen dollars a night. In the hallways, vinyl chairs lay wearily, their covers burst open from fatigue and the foam rubber puffing out. There was a plaque on the door next to Gerten's. CHIANG SENG. INTERNATIONAL PALMIST. Gerten stared at it. He knew he was being end run. He knew that if he did nothing, he would miss out on the big money.

He went back downstairs and pushed his sweating way through the crowds towards the railway station. The heat had built up through the day in the cement and the paving of the streets. Now it radiated up at him. There was a bar he remembered, where men in need of money loitered. Once before he had found the right sort of man there—with a motor bike and a pistol. This time he was prepared to pay a little more, perhaps $25 a day, to follow Smith and keep track of whom he saw. Someone who could read and write, but who wouldn't be capable of working out what it was all about. As to the weapon, it would be useful later.

The next morning he agreed to visit another Buddha, where he accepted another $5,000 from Laing with calm and listened patiently to an embellishment of what Smith was meant to be up to.

In the meantime, Smith was at the Vietnamese Embassy, where he was greeted by the same semi-obscurity as Laing, the ceiling fans springing to life as Ngo Van Cu appeared, a tray of orange crush following behind him. Ngo had heard about an American with the same name who was doing business in Hanoi, having made a lot of money in Saigon during the war, but Smith cut him off each time he asked a personal question. Eventually Ngo concentrated on the proposed banking arrangements. He accepted them quickly and without any changes. His signature would be all that the Bermuda bank needed to transfer the hundred million dollars.

Everything was then in place and the two friends were faced with hanging around for five days until the arms reached the border on 6 July. At first this tranquillity confused Gerten. After one report on Smith's movements, nothing more happened. Both men were either at the hotel or off amusing themselves with Field. Gerten went on meeting Laing once a day, collecting five thousand dollars each time—sometimes more if he became menacing. The two men struck up a peculiar relationship, out of necessity. They almost enjoyed playing their roles, which Gerten thought were based on Laing's fear of him, while in fact Laing was obsessed with taking his revenge the moment the deal was in place.

Of one thing Gerten was sure. The final act was imminent. Each night he stretched out on the hard bed in his room, listening to the rats scratching behind the walls and waiting for his vagrant employee. His reports were meagre offerings, but Gerten lay still for hours, thinking through them again and again in search of the smallest opening. The only interruption was the clapping of his own hands as they killed the more adventurous mosquitoes.

He had to wait until Thursday, the third. He was taken out for a long drive by Laing, and while they were tied up, Smith came to life. He went off to the docks to instruct Captain Toller to move his boat down the river to the Gulf, where he was to lie a few miles off Sattahip. That evening, Gerten got a report of the essential detail—Smith's visit to the ship. With that bare fact he could guess the rest. It was a good card. A queen, perhaps even a king.

On Friday morning at seven, Gerten knocked on Laing's door. He began by saying how much he'd enjoyed getting to know him, but now he had to go home and would have to complete their arrangement. He wanted three hundred thousand dollars in return for permanent silence. Failing that, he would go to the newspapers immediately on his return to Europe. He was perfectly conscious that the worst time for publicity came when a deal was only half done. Laing appeared only mildly impressed by his demand, so Gerten added an account of Smith's movements the day before.

"Your games bore me, Martin. If that ship moves, my mouth opens. As for your friend Smith, he is not invisible. And I don't care for him, Martin. If you ask me, there is something dispensable about him."

Laing said nothing, so Gerten suggested they meet for lunch the next day to settle the business and he would take the plane to Paris that evening.

Laing hadn't expected the crisis to come until after the arms were on board the *Sophie*. The moment Gerten was gone, he went to Smith's room and woke him. Smith listened to the ultimatum, but refused to discuss it. Instead, he telephoned Pong to say there was an emergency. Pong showed little interest. He wouldn't discuss anything on the telephone and said he was tied up all day. Smith agreed to meet him at the businessman's house that evening, which meant that Laing had to go out first to give the Colonel someone to follow.

Pong lived in a suburb of Sathorn Road. His house was in the centre of the family compound, surrounded by half a dozen other houses, a tennis court, a pool and a park; all of which was protected by a ten foot wall. On the way there, Smith watched behind, searching in the mêlée of traffic for signs of someone following. But the light was dim and the disorder through which the car moved made it impossible to isolate anyone. The motor bike which stopped in the shadows, twenty yards from Pong's compound was one of thirty or forty within the block. Its rider offered no distinguishing marks, except that he made a quick note of the address. The guard at the gate had Smith's name on a list and directed the hotel driver to go past the tennis court, where four Chinese in white shorts were playing under floodlights while others stood around watching and drinking. A servant waited by an outdoor bar.

The house was elaborate and modern, concentrating more on show than on taste. Inside, Smith was led up several levels, each of which was reached by steps surrounded by flowing water, to a square dining room in which Pong was eating. Beside him was a girl—his daughter or his mistress. She didn't strike Smith as being a wife. The girl disappeared when the American arrived, freeing a place which had apparently been set for him.

"I didn't wait for you, Mr. Smith, but I've saved something. What would you like?" Although he was polite, the cold expression in Pong's eyes was that of a man who resented emergencies as a sign of stupidity.

He was drinking a brandy with soda and Smith asked for the same. It was a favoured drink among the rich Chinese of Asia. The girl reappeared carrying a dish filled with minute rice birds, caught in nets in the paddies and fried without batter so that their skin had stretched over their bodies as if they had been electrocuted. Their fleshless heads seemed human.

"Eat something," he said, "before you tell me your problem. Go on."

Smith described Colonel Gerten and how they had dealt with him till then. Pong ate as he listened, picking up each bird with two fingers, one pressed in each eye socket, and eating it with bites that crunched through the bones. When Smith had finished, Pong's expression was still colder.

"You've been clumsy. Does he know about me?"

"He hasn't mentioned you."

"What does that tell me, Mr. Smith? I find no pleasure in speculation. You must let us take Colonel Gerten in hand for a chat. He is in our country and abusing our hospitality. At what time is your friend meeting him tomorrow, and where?"

"I'll find out and let you know."

"Let me know tonight." Pong pointed a rice bird at Smith, his fingers firmly in the eye sockets. "Please be precise with your information. We cannot have precision in the important matters and carelessness over the details." He ate the bird in three sharp bites, punctuating his instructions. The head disappeared with the finality of a full stop.

"If you don't mind my telephoning late," Smith said.

"I am always delighted to talk to you."

TWENTY-SEVEN

Laing had arranged to meet Colonel Gerten for lunch at a noisy restaurant used only by Thais. It was on Democracy Monument Square, not far from the Weekend Market Grounds. Smith had suggested Laing should be there early, so he arrived to find the restaurant still half empty and was able to choose a place at the long open windows, looking out onto the street.

They brought him a strong beer, which he drank morosely, the liquid sweating away as quickly as it was swallowed. Smith had told him little except that Pong would deal with Gerten. The room was filling up with people and noise, while outside the pavement was cluttered with men waiting for friends before coming in.

He caught sight of Gerten, getting out of a taxi some distance down the street and walking towards the restaurant in his awkward but determined way, filled with good intentions. The Colonel caught sight of Laing ten yards before the door and smiled as he raised his hand to wave. Laing waved back.

At the same time, he noticed a Thai with a sunken face, dressed in dirty clothes, standing near Gerten. The man was fumbling with a bag. He pulled out of it a homemade-looking pistol and put it to Gerten's head. Laing tried to focus on what he saw happening and opened his mouth to shout a warning, but the sound was frozen by an explosion that blew off the back of Gerten's skull and sent it flying against another man's chest, where the gore made it cling to his shirt. Blood rose in a fine shower, filling the air and covering the bystanders. Compulsively the man knocked the piece of skull to the ground as a scream of agony began in Gerten's mouth. It was never finished, and he fell with his mouth gaping open. The assassin leapt on a motorbike and disappeared into the crowded square. Laing started to jump up in a daze to run out of the restaurant, but he felt warm dampness seep over himself. He looked down to see that he had spilt his beer.

For a period that had no time, he was hypnotized by the liquid spreading over his crotch and thighs. When he managed to look up, it was as if the shower of blood and flesh hung suspended before his eyes, and while this illusion would not go away Laing found he had gained enough control over himself to remain quite still. He unfolded his napkin to soak up the beer.

Minutes later the police arrived and rolled the body into a blanket before putting it into an ambulance and beginning to question people on the pavement. Then they came into the restaurant, where Laing was the only white. They tried to question him, but their English was minimal and he kept repeating that he didn't understand. An officer asked to see his passport and for the name of his hotel.

He forced himself to eat a full lunch before returning to Smith's room at the Oriental. There, overcome by a shaking fit, he vomited up the food.

Smith tried to find out what had happened, but Laing exploded. He accused him of having known that Gerten would be shot and not giving any warning. Smith repeated what he'd already told him: that Pong had spoken of taking the Colonel in hand for a chat, nothing more. Laing couldn't bring himself to believe him. Why should he believe the person who'd been telling him, from the beginning, how complicated this business would be? He calmed down and returned to the one thought at the centre of his mind. The police. He was the only person in Bangkok to have had dealings with Gerten—a long line of witnesses could confirm that. He put this to Smith, who went immediately to Pong's office.

General Krit's partner was in a meeting, but he came out the moment Smith was announced. Pong expressed shock at what had happened. His own people, he said, had arrived moments after the murder. Then he smiled apologetically, "At least we can say that whoever did it has solved our problem."

Smith was not in a mood for games. "Hardly. The police questioned my friend in the restaurant and he has spent the last week with Gerten; the only person in this city linked to him as far as we know."

Pong was relieved. "Is that all you're worried about? How delightful." His innocent laugh broke through. "Your friend won't hear from the police, I'll make sure of that. I feared that something important had happened." Smith still looked suspicious and agitated. Pong reassured him. "Trust me. The police aren't expensive. Another five thousand should cover it, if you want to be certain." He reconsidered. "No. Nothing. On the house, Mr. Smith. On the house."

There was nothing more for Laing to do in Bangkok, which suited him perfectly. The sooner he left, the happier he would be. He decided to fly back that evening, via Hong Kong.

Pong's chauffeur drove both men out to the airport, where they dropped off Laing before going on to the border. The two friends sat in awkward silence in the back of the car. Smith felt guilty for what had happened and kept asking himself, was he supposed to care about Gerten dying? Care about what? He hadn't known him, hadn't seen him die. It was an obscure fact filed. He could understand his friend's reaction. What was it he had accused Laing of—nothing but passions to fall back on. And yet, in twenty-four hours the weapons would be on international waters. He said as much and tried to cheer Laing up.

"Why don't you bring Cosima to Morocco? I'm going to be there next week, from the 10th of July."

"You mean you're going back before the arms are delivered?" Laing looked at Smith across the back seat of the car. He couldn't believe what he had heard.

"That's what I had planned on doing. Sayed loves beautiful women. You'll have a wonderful time."

"Don't you think that's unnecessary?"

"Martin, let me do things my way. I agreed to go before we saw the Polisario. If anything, not going would excite attention."

"And you want me to come?" Laing asked sarcastically.

Smith was exasperated. "We have been as careful as we can be. I won't be doing any business in Morocco. Just a little rest. From the security point of view, it won't make any difference whether I'm there or in Iceland."

"I was thinking of your friendship with Idrissi."

Smith blushed, but turned to Laing, "Let me be the keeper of my own morality."

After dropping Laing, Smith got to the border in time to check that all the machinery was in place and spent the night in a sleeping bag at the *Taharn lap jarng* camp. Eighty of them went to the crosspoint with Smith on the morning of the sixth. They arrived at five a.m. and, as promised, there were no Thai soldiers at the post, nor were many peasants up and about.

At five twenty-five, the fifty Vietnamese trucks rolled out of the morning mist and crossed the border, stopping just long enough to have their Thai plates mounted. The eighty soldiers pulled themselves up onto the tarpaulin-covered crates and the trucks rolled forward. Four miles inside Thailand they came to the camp, where the twenty remaining armed men directed the trucks into a prearranged parking system. Fork-lifts began unloading crates. The first ten shipments were put straight onto the ten Thai trucks, while the rest were stacked on the ground. The Vietnamese convoy, now empty, waited until darkness.

Smith went down to the naval port with the first load and sent a signal ordering the *Sophie* to come into dock. Sailors began loading the ship in the early afternoon. The last pieces to leave the border camp were the four landing-craft, which arrived on the coast in the early evening to be loaded under the personal supervision of Captain Toller. They had to be lashed to the deck. Shortly before dark, the *Sophie* sailed out to sea. She would arrive off Angra de los Ruivos on 8 August.

At eight forty-five the Vietnamese convoy left the camp and disappeared back across the border into the darkness of Cambodia. Again, as promised, there were no guards on duty. Smith drove to Bangkok, where he sent off an unsigned message to Lamine. It consisted of a number—"eight."

He flew west out of Bangkok on the midnight flight that same night. There was just enough time for a quick dinner with Field, who wasn't altogether surprised by Gerten's death. That was Pong's style. He said he would have warned them, had they bothered to ask his advice.

The rest of the time he talked about how much he had liked Laing. "It's rare that I meet a white man who isn't bent on self-destruction."

"You don't see many whites any more," Smith said flippantly.

Field replied, ignoring his tone, "Enough."

PART 4

TWENTY-EIGHT

When a woman he found beautiful was nearby, Sayed Idrissi moved in a different way. He stopped throwing himself about like an impulsive marionette and his tall, heavy frame took on enormous dignity—not the rigid, European kind, but understanding dignity. All of which meant that he moved particularly in a well-cut djellabah, with seductive nobility.

Smith noticed the change the moment Cosima was introduced. He teased Idrissi, who replied that women like her were all that mattered in life. He was neither entirely serious, nor mouthing a polite formula.

Laing's Telex accepting the invitation arrived on 10 July, a Thursday, only twenty-four hours before he and Cosima did. This last-minute flurry was caused by Laing being unable to make up his mind, thanks to a fit of indecision brought on by Gerten's death. He couldn't digest it and he couldn't rationalize it, although he knew that that should have been easy.

In the midst of this confusion, Moffett had called him in. It was their second meeting since his return, Laing having been summoned the afternoon of the first day he arrived back and made to recite every detail of what he had done in Algiers and Bangkok. This he did, with the exception of Gerten's blackmail and Smith's going to Morocco.

Moffett listened carefully and let it all sift through his mind. What Laing didn't realize was that the older man had done little for the last two weeks other than think about the Vietnam deal. There had been a time when he had asked for nothing better than to be left alone to muse or to read; but the pleasure had somehow gone from that. Now he felt uneasy alone, and his nonchalant contempt for Fell was gradually turning into an obsession, as day after day he found he had to deal with some minor manoeuvre aimed at wearing away his position. But Fell wasn't the cause of his unease, only a sign of it. Moffett found he couldn't stay alone in his apartment a second longer than he had to, and for the first time in years spent long days in his office, working on a myriad of plans connected with Vietnamese exploration. When Laing left him, it was six o'clock and Moffett went out to ask his secretary to dig out the files on Morocco and the Spanish Sahara. She went without a murmur, even though his recent conversion to working long hours, after years of the opposite, was throwing her own life into turmoil. He wasn't ready to leave until eight o'clock, and then he walked home by a circuitous route that took more than two hours.

The heat and humidity of July had driven most people like him off the streets and out of Manhattan until the ocean breezes were again able to penetrate the forest of city towers. Moffett walked, staring at the upper floors, and found a change in what he saw. The buildings were advanced ruins, disassociated from the people who swam through the thick air around them. The citizens and the real estate didn't match. They ignored each other, the humans merely camping inside the palazzos and the gothic palaces, whose seediness Moffett had once thought amusing but now found depressing. He put it all down to the less generous light of high summer.

As he thought about Laing's story, one thing came clear: it had been too easy. That meant Laing had told him only part of what had happened. Moffett hesitated for a few days, then called him in for a second time, on 9 July. He prodded gently and it wasn't long before Laing revealed the rest. With the description of Gerten's death, a wry smile crept across Moffett's face. He took it as a good omen, but didn't explain about his own experience in Colombia.

Laing watched the smirk with horror and saw it as yet another sign of an irrational character. When he mentioned Smith's return to Morocco and his own mixed feelings over whether to go, Moffett reacted cynically. Why would anyone think that Smith could be trusted to stick to his contract while he was surrounded by people who would pay him any price to betray it? Laing began to protest, but Moffett insisted, "I do not believe he will, Martin, because I would not do it myself; but I am not the one at risk and neither are you." Laing had little choice but to agree to go to Rabat and said defensively that he had thought of taking Cosima with him. Moffett laughed. "All the better. The company will pay."

But the last thing Cosima wanted was to be dragged into Smith's world for two weeks. Although Laing said it was just a holiday, she knew there was something more and resisted, until he admitted that there might be some business and he had no choice but to go. By then he was so miserable that she agreed to go along. There was certainly nothing in her own work to hold her back. For three years she had made her interests known to her partners. Each time a project involving landscapes had come up, she had volunteered her ideas and asked to be included; and for three years they had made her do computer rooms.

Laing's Telex arrived while Idrissi was away on a short trip with King Hassan, opening a new phosphate mine. They had flown part of the way there and driven the last stretch across the arid wilderness in a cavalcade of sixty limousines. Idrissi found the King unusually restrained. On the way back, Hassan overwhelmed the Minister of Planning by asking him to ride in their car. It was a long drive and, for the first hour, the King went out of his way to put the Minister at ease, with what Idrissi knew was his artificial charm. When he tired of that, Hassan began to badger the man without reason. The Minister, falsely relaxed and now confused, argued back.

The King lost his temper and ordered his driver to stop. The rest of the cavalcade stopped behind them. He made the Minister get out and shouted, for everyone to hear, "Try walking!" The cavalcade drove slowly on, the man's friends averting their eyes out of embarrassment as they passed, until he was left standing alone in the desert.

Idrissi glanced at the King—who was staring ostentatiously at a passing rock—and wondered whether it had been a warning aimed at himself. The Minister was hardly worth such a spectacle. Idrissi tried the ground by pointing out that the percentage of the national budget devoted to security—the Sahara War—had gone from fifteen per cent in 1975 to forty per cent in 1980. And 1981? The King was mildly interested.

"We'll have to delay the housing programme again," Idrissi said.

The King looked at him with a wounded expression. "How is your friend Farid?"

"He's all right," Idrissi replied gingerly. He knew that Hassan resented Karim Farid's constant criticism, even if it was in private, and his refusal to accept any honours lest he be compromised.

"What's he up to?"

"I don't understand."

"Sayed, he's up to something." The King's voice was plaintive.

Idrissi laughed openly. "Sidi Karim is past doing anything serious. He's just an old man with a sharp tongue."

"My life isn't serious?" Hassan saw his friend's confusion and was relieved to see it was genuine. He poked his finger in Idrissi's gut. "You find out, Sayed. For your sake, I leave him to you. And listen," he shot his fingers out and grabbed Idrissi's lips, squeezing them painfully together, "keep your mouth shut about the war, unless it's me you're talking to." He let go and burst into a laugh before Idrissi could explode in anger. They knew each other too well.

Early that morning, Smith had gone over to the Casbah of the Oudias and found Karim Farid standing in the garden at the edge of the cliff. The fall from there to the river and the empty beach below was two hundred feet. The old man was staring at the clouds streaked up the far bank of the Bou Regreg, where they were held by air currents rising from the warm water as it flowed into the cold ocean. He turned, on hearing someone approach, and called out, "Were I a Christian, Anthony, you could accuse me of pantheism. But I was taught that paradise is a garden, so man should be one with nature, not conquer it. When your environmentalists discovered nature, I was shocked. Do you have to be a specialist? I assure you, it suffices to be a Muslim." He gave a sharp clap that belied his frailty, and said something to the boy, then turned back to Smith. "Carry two chairs outside, Anthony. The air is still too fresh for us to sit in the shade."

Smith set the wicker chairs in front of the gazebo before the boy reappeared with tea, a fruit cake soaked in rose water and the book of Anglo-Saxon myths.

"Give it to me," Karim Farid said. He'd left a marker in it. "Listen to this, 'I, sundered from my native land, far from noble kinsmen, often sad at heart, had to fetter my mind, when in years gone by the darkness of the earth covered my gold friend, and I went thence in wretchedness with wintry care upon me over the frozen waves, gloomily sought the hall of a treasure giver where I could find him far or near.' What is that?"

"A beautiful poem," Smith shrugged.

Karim Farid dismissed his remark. "What does it tell me

about you? I should like to understand the soul of the wanderer." Smith blushed and said nothing, so Farid looked discreetly down and cut two thin slices of cake, which he passed. "They have begun to watch me again."

"That's hardly a secret," Smith laughed, relieved to have the attention off himself. "Why?" He had meant to ask why Farid was telling him. Was it because he wasn't sure how much Smith had overheard?

"I thought you might know why," Karim Farid replied.

They looked at each other, but nothing was said, so the old man waved the subject away. Later, when Smith rose to leave, Farid held out the book.

"You should keep it with you."

Idrissi didn't arrive back in Rabat and get away from the King, who made him stay for dinner, until late that evening. He locked himself in his library to make a series of phone calls—first, to make sure that someone had gone back to pick up the Minister. One of the man's aides answered the phone in a voice which could only be called cowering. He confirmed that another aide had managed to slip away from the cavalcade when they transferred to aeroplanes. By the time he drove back and found his Minister, the poor man had been in the sun for five hours. That had left him crazed, or perhaps he wasn't very intelligent, because he had wanted to return to Rabat to collect some papers before heading for the airport. Kader's police had been waiting all evening at his front door and he was now under house arrest.

Idrissi decided that it was too late to do anything more, at least until a few weeks had passed and the King's temper with it. He came out of his library and found Smith reading under a weak light in the garden.

Smith immediately sensed his friend's agitation and, as no explanation was given, suggested they go to Madame Durand's to distract themselves. Idrissi didn't say no, so Smith went ahead and organized the car.

The boy who let them in ran faster than usual down the corridor to warn Madame Durand. Before they had finished pushing the bolt back, they heard her panting up the stairs into the corridor. When she saw them, she let out a great whisper of awe, "Moulay Sayed! What an honour!" She somehow moved on her heels at a run towards them, supporting herself in a continuous ricochet off both walls and repeating, over and over, 'An honour, an honour,' until she had blocked their way, grabbed his hand and kissed it.

"Madame," he said weakly.

"It has been so long!" she exclaimed, the structure of her face lifting with joy, and turned to run back down the corridor, repeating as she went, "So long, so long."

By the time they got to the room, she was standing below, out of breath and waving towards a corner, where champagne was waiting on a table. "In your honour," she gasped. Idrissi smiled uncomfortably. The room was almost full and he knew everyone there. Smith asked for brandy as he went by.

When they were seated, she asked them what they would like, but Idrissi cut her off, "Not now." He waited until there was no one within hearing before describing his day with the King and the King's very mild interest in the cost of the war.

"Mildly interested," Idrissi repeated, more to himself. "What lunacy. He surprises me . . ."

"You'd be less surprised if you loved him less."

Idrissi passed the remark off as a joke. Smith shrugged.

"You saw Sidi Karim this morning?" Idrissi asked suddenly.

Smith didn't ask how he knew. He'd seen no one lurking in the alleys, which meant only that they'd found a place to hide. He shrugged again and said, "The old boy is in good shape."

"I wouldn't know," Idrissi replied. "I went there this afternoon and they said he'd gone away for a few days. I don't suppose you'd know where."

Smith shrugged yet again, hiding his surprise. Farid had said nothing about a trip and he rarely moved from his house, except to go to Zagora for the winter.

One of the girls walked by, causing Idrissi to hesitate awkwardly. "Have you ever talked about this puritan business with him?"

"I avoid the subject with everyone." Smith turned the question into a joke. "I find them incomprehensibly boring."

His promise to Karim Farid to say nothing about finding him with puritans was beginning to make Smith nervous. Everyone played the sides in Morocco, but Farid had survived every regime by playing them better than anyone else. There was no such thing as dignified neutrality.

"Come off it, Anthony," Idrissi said, impatiently. "Somebody asked . . ."

Smith smiled at him vacantly.

Idrissi felt like an idiot. He knew that Smith would say nothing, just as he would never repeat what Idrissi himself confided to him. That was one of his values as a friend in a country where there was no one he could speak to openly. Still, Idrissi tried again. "There was a report from the security services. Kader watches everyone. Me included." His voice turned sour as Smith obstinately held his smile, while his eyes turned away.

He had seen Benmansour coming down the stairs from the bedrooms and behind him was the girl, Aisha. The Colonel bowed to them from the other side of the room before sitting down with her. Smith saw that she had already begun to look like the enemy Benmansour expected; and yet, there was still something. Madame Durand noticed them looking around and reappeared at their side.

"The girl," Smith said, searching for her name, "Aisha, how is she?"

Madame Durand said immediately, "This was the girl you had last time you came. You don't come often enough, Mr. Smith." She actually waved a finger that was still surprisingly elegant.

"Is she free now?"

"No, but I have another young girl."

"When will she be free?" There was a childish obstinacy in Smith's question.

"I'm afraid she's reserved."

"I'd like to reserve her for tomorrow."

Madame Durand moved her head in embarrassment. "I'm afraid there is a permanent reserve on her, for the moment." She believed in the long term, but even that had limits.

Smith hadn't intended to become so involved, but couldn't stop himself. "Since when has she been reserved?"

Madame Durand kept her books in her head, although she was confused by Smith's agitation. "Since the night you were last here."

Smith fell into a depressed silence, which she noticed.

"Shall I send the girl I mentioned? I know you . . ."

Smith nodded.

"And Moulay Sayed?" She attempted an ingratiating smile.

He waved her away. "Nothing." When she was gone, he said, "Why do you want that girl? I see nothing special."

"I don't want her."

"You mean you don't want her any more."

"That's right," Smith replied defensively. "Any more."

"He's just a bag of shit, you know. He's nothing, Anthony. A messenger boy. Why do you still come to this terrible place? For God's sake, if you want a girl, I can arrange it without this rubbish."

A pretty teenager appeared with a willing look. Madame Durand had probably told her to soothe the customer's nerves. Smith got to his feet saying, "I won't be long." After he had gone, Idrissi sat for a moment alone, furious with himself for coming. He could feel that something was going on. Farid knew and Smith knew at least part of it. He saw a girl come down the stairs behind an officer he had gone to school with. Idrissi beckoned to her, with scarcely a look, and got to his feet in despair.

TWENTY-NINE

"Get up, Anthony. They're here."

The sound of a car outside the house brought Idrissi to his feet. He pulled Smith from his chair and strode out into the noon sun in a French-cut beige summer suit. Smith followed, jacket in hand. He found Idrissi standing close to Cosima, who had arrived the morning before and was already enchanted by him. Most of the time she acted as if Smith were not there, which he tried his best to overlook. She was in a blue dress that hid her shoulders and throat.

Idrissi told her where to sit—by the window, behind the driver, so that he could turn and talk to her easily without sitting in the back. He left Laing and Smith to organize themselves. Laing ended up in the middle. As they drove through the gate, Idrissi shouted at the guards and told the driver to go faster. Then he turned round.

"We shall have to drive most of the afternoon to get to Fez, but it's worth it. Tomorrow morning we'll go on to Sefrou for the fête."

Smith shifted to make room for himself. "Worth it once, perhaps. The King's friends just don't like aeroplanes."

Idrissi threw his arms up. "Anthony talks nonsense most of the time. I drive because the country is beautiful and I don't fly because I hate flying. That's why I'll never go to America. It's too big."

"Tell them why you hate flying, Sayed."

Idrissi looked to the front annoyed.

Cosima leaned forward and placed her hand on Idrissi's arm, which was enough, although he spoke to the oncoming traffic.

"The King plays golf. A great deal of golf. I detest games that involve the propelling of spherical objects. There are worse—those in which you propel them between two people. Humans find the most extraordinary ways to waste time, His Majesty excepted.

"He and his staff were flying back from France, where he had been playing golf. When his Boeing reached our coast, it was met by an escort of fighters, as is normal, except the fighters broke off, circled and returned with their guns firing. Bullets streaked through the cabin, wounding people. General panic, except the King who sat quiet." Idrissi looked at his driver. "Pass him. Go on! The pilot tried an evasion tactic. What could he do? Within minutes, the pressure started falling and they lost one engine. Moments later, a second.

"The King ran into the pilot's cabin. He told the radio operator to contact the fighters. When the senior fighter pilot came on the air, the King shouted in a panicked voice 'I am the navigator. The King is dead. Do you want to kill a plane-load of innocent people?'

"The fighters hesitated. The King's pilot cut his last engine and dropped twenty thousand feet, where he managed to start up again and land the plane at Kinitra, as originally planned. The control tower had overheard the message that the King was dead and had passed it on to the Ministers and dignitaries waiting on the tarmac. More panic. The plane rolls up, a mass of bullet holes. The door opens. Out he walks. General consternation.

"He asks for General Oufkir, his strong man, who had put down the palace coup the year before. The General has left to rally the troops. Instead of going to the official pavilion, the King walks into a copse of trees with his staff. The fighters reappear and demolish the pavilion. One of the pilots flees to

Gibraltar, where he's held, interrogated and returned to Morocco.

"That evening, Oufkir is still out rallying the troops. The King insists—I was with him—and eventually the General comes to the palace. He's met, in an outer reception room, by Kader. Oufkir asks—'Has the King seen the captured pilot?' No reply. He draws his pistol, saying, 'I know what will happen to me', and shoots himself in the head, three times."

Cosima put her hand back on Idrissi's arm. "Three times?"

"A good story is truth multiplied by time," Laing added.

"Oh, it's accurate," Idrissi replied. "I was on the plane. The pilot is now Chief of the Air Force."

"But," Smith laughed, "General Oufkir's end is less certain."

"Let's say," Idrissi turned to look at them, "having known him, that it's hard to believe he'd take three shots. At least I didn't ask you along for the ride, Anthony. What time is it?"

It was shortly before the hour. He tuned his radio, then had a last second inspiration and shouted at the driver to turn right. The Mercedes skidded off the main highway, across the dirt shoulder onto a country road.

Idrissi looked at Cosima. "A short cut."

The road was wide enough for one car and divided sweeping valleys of grain, still green in the early summer.

"Are you glad you came?" Laing whispered to Cosima.

She took his hand and thought that it had been a good idea after all. Perhaps what they had needed was to get away from their real world.

The driver got them to Fez before nightfall and drove round the King's palace and up the side of the valley onto a plateau over Fez-El-Bali, the original city created by Sultan Moulay Idrissi in the eighth century. They got out of the car and walked to the edge of a cliff.

In the dead light of evening, the city flowed like frozen lava down the long, sinking bed of the valley. The grey geometric forms of the houses were held within the city walls as by a belt that followed the curve of the hills. Beyond the walls, the city ended and the valley rose up sharply, covered with olive orchards.

Cosima murmured, "It's the most beautiful sight I've ever seen."

"Wait!" Idrissi ordered.

Starting in the upper town, lights appeared on the minarets of the mosques. As they were lit, the call to prayer went out from each tower, echoing across the valley until it reached the largest mosque, the Karaouiyn. The lights of the geometric lava flickered, filling up the space between the mosques. Suddenly, the street lamps outside the walls came on, lighting up the whole.

Idrissi was as stricken as someone who saw it for the first time. "This is the heart of Islam in North Africa. Years ago, Malraux came to Morocco and the King made me bring him to Fez, so I brought him to this spot, at this time of day. He was overwhelmed, but when he recovered he suggested we plant trees around the walls, to break the monotony."

"What an idiotic idea." Cosima couldn't stop herself. "Put a corset on a beautiful old lady?" She put her arm around Laing. "Look at the strength. Not monumental. Not impressive. Do you see it? The strength of perfect integration."

Laing kissed her on the neck. That she was happy made him happy.

"We didn't plant them." Idrissi watched her with some wistfulness. "How could we, knowing I'd have to explain myself to you? Besides, Fez is filled with puritans—men who have their own idea about how to run the soul of Islam."

Cosima was hardly listening. She was floating over the city, over human genius fully expressed without a plan, almost without architects. The vision that she knew she would never build passed before her and filled her with a sense of well-being. She wondered how seldom in her lifetime she would see it—a welling up of the human spirit over generations until it melted together into something beyond reality.

As they watched, the darkness became complete, leaving only the city lights below them. The vision became a trance. Although there was nothing left, she was reluctant to go when Idrissi led them away.

THIRTY

The morning sun reflected off the city. Cosima came in from the balcony, her mind clear for the first time in weeks.

She looked quickly in a mirror. There was a hint of makeup to emphasize her large eyes and the line of her high cheeks. Idrissi had warned her to bring a hat, as they would be spending most of the day in the sun—it was Sunday, 13 July—and she wore a pale dress which followed the contours of her body and was covered in lace.

She and Laing found a crowd of men in djellabahs milling around the lobby, with Idrissi in the middle carrying on different conversations in Arabic and French at the same time. He was in a cream djellabah, a red fez on his head and a radio in his hand. Smith leaned against a wall, half listening to an older man. The moment Idrissi saw Cosima, he broke away to put his arm through hers.

"Come and meet these people."

The Governor, short and fat, the Caid and the military commander kissed her hand. Then Idrissi led her outside, where they settled in the car as they had the day before; but Idrissi saw that the officials were coming slowly out of the hotel. He pushed the button to lower the front window and stuck his head through, shouting at them to move faster.

Without thinking, Cosima said, "Moulay Sayed, you shouldn't shout at men in public."

"First," he replied, as if hers had been a perfectly normal comment, "I never shout at children. Second, in this country there are no public versus private manners. Everything is public. We've no secrets whispered," he drew his fingers across his lips, "by ladies in middle-class parlours."

They all laughed. He shouted at the driver to start, but the man objected that the others weren't ready.

"They'll be ready if we start." Idrissi reached across the driver's arm and thumped the horn.

Everyone turned. He waved at the police motorcycles and the cars in front as his Mercedes began to move. The police were forced to leap to their bikes.

They sped out of Fez, two motorcycles a hundred yards ahead, side by side down the centre of the road with their lights on and sirens wailing. They waved their arms to force oncoming traffic into the ditch. Behind came a police car, its lights and sirens also on, the men inside waving people off the road. Another motorcycle followed them.

Idrissi's Mercedes hung just behind—only just, because he made his driver force the pace. This terrified the motorcycle policeman immediately in front. He was third in the line and could go neither faster nor slower. Behind them, a cavalcade of official cars stretched out of sight through the green fields and orchards.

On the outskirts of Sefrou, crowds of farmers built up behind the police lines. Women, wrapped in layers of black muslin until it disguised their shape, wailed the *zqharit*, a primeval cry used for celebrations or funerals. It rose from deep in the backs of their throats and penetrated the senses. In Algiers it had been used against the French, just as the Scots had terrified their enemies with the inexplicable sound of bagpipes.

The cries of the women built up on both sides until they came to a square, large for a country town, where the crowds were thick and an Andalusian band played. The car slowed. Idrissi jumped out before it stopped and strode towards the officials in grey capes, who came forward to take him in hand.

He turned and shouted to the Americans to keep up as they walked towards a stand, draped in carpets, with canvas hung over the top and part way down the front. Idrissi led the way up the narrow wooden steps, stopping long enough at the top to tell Laing to give his wife a hand. Then he sat down, in an old red leather club chair, in the middle of the front row. The officials filled the chairs on either side of him.

"In the second row, Anthony."

Idrissi made sure Cosima sat behind him. In the second row, the chairs were wooden.

Officials arrived and departed. Police cars sped by one way

and minutes later sped back the other. Idrissi examined the crowd jostling around the outlines of the square, his gaze one of familiarity and acceptance, not of critical judgement. He noticed a minor official sitting below the stand and waved him up to congratulate him on an agricultural modernization project; then insisted that the man sit on the platform. They had to pass his chair up from below. After a time, the band got tired and stopped, so someone ran over to tell them to play again.

Idrissi sank into a depressed silence—another stand, another rural parade. His eyes moved aimlessly over the crowd until they stopped abruptly, fixed on something that brought him to his feet. He pointed and shouted at no one in particular.

"Move those cars!"

The officials had parked their cars around the edge of the square. He stood there, repeating at the top of his lungs, "Move those cars! How do you think the people will see? You're on the stand. What do you care? Who's going to move those cars?"

Faced by this harangue, men reluctantly rose and climbed down the steps. Laughter and a murmur of approval went through the crowd.

Smith looked around. Near the stand he saw a small group of bearded puritans in their white turbans and white djellabahs. They were solemn. No. Malevolent. He remembered the four in Farid's garden. Killing, Farid had said. Killing whom? For purity? They didn't go to country fêtes. What were they doing there? Smith looked at the other people on the platform.

Freddie Bingham was in the back row and beside him was Colonel Benmansour. Bingham waved.

The official next to Smith got up to move his car and Bingham good-naturedly clambered forward over people to collapse beside them, an elegant, if ageing, figure in a finely cut beige linen suit and a pale mauve voile shirt. He remembered Martin Laing and already knew about Cosima.

"More beautiful even than the description going around Rabat."

She acknowledged the introduction, but Cosima didn't like gossipy men.

Idrissi, who was still standing, turned, "Not your style of party, Freddie."

Bingham laughed. He pointed to the back of the stand, at the neatly trimmed Colonel in a grey suit; the only man, besides Bingham and the two Americans, not in a djellabah. "The dear boy asked me along for the ride."

"What's Benmansour doing here?" Idrissi asked, not so warmly. He raised a hand to the Colonel, who had seen he was being talked about.

"Bucolic pleasure, I suppose," Bingham replied. He knew it wasn't but he hadn't yet worked out what was going on. All he did know was that Benmansour had brought him along to smooth the way.

Idrissi turned back to point at the cars again. The first had been moved fifty yards to the side of the square.

"Not far enough! Tell them not far enough!"

The crowd laughed again as a policeman ran off to warn the Secretary-General of Agricultural Cooperatives that he must move farther. This exercise had cheered Idrissi, who collapsed into his club chair and said to the Governor at his side,

"We're ready." He indicated the crowd. "Where's the parade?"

This message was carried off down the street and, almost immediately, a mixture of sounds approached. Idrissi leaned forward as a trumpet band came into sight. Behind came three troops of Boy Scouts. They were all in their thirties and carried pictures of the King. As each picture went by, Idrissi stood and the whole stand followed suit, the struts below creaking. Smith heard Bingham say to himself, "Our little King."

A tractor followed, pulling a farm wagon decorated with paper cherry trees. Behind came another Scout troop. They tried to form up in front of the platform, until Idrissi waved them on. The next tractor drew a float of the Green March and victory in the Sahara.

Smith looked for the puritans. Two still stood at the front but the others had melted out of sight. He sank down into his chair, his eyes searching the crowd for white turbans. He found the heat oppressive away from the coast. Bingham was eager to chat and asked what they'd seen on the road. Smith didn't bother to reply, his mind still on the puritans, so Laing replied that Moulay Sayed had entertained them with the story of Oufkir's death.

Bingham's face lit up. "I'll bet the loyal Moulay held back the juicy bits," he whispered.

"What do you mean?" Cosima asked despite herself.

"The rumour, my dear, has always been that our little King

pulled the trigger, which might explain the three shots. That's only the icing on the cake."

Bingham looked up, to be sure no one else was listening. Idrissi was on his feet, insisting that a float move ahead faster, and attention was focused on him. While Bingham's eyes roved, Laing's attention slipped to the man's elegant suit. On closer inspection, it had a few spots that hadn't come out in cleaning, and worn cuffs. The collar of his shirt was also worn.

"What's more, your gentle friend," Bingham indicated Idrissi, "and lover of the people, was at the King's side. They say there was a struggle. Sayed had to fire the last shot, I mean the one that worked, while they held Oufkir down. Kader did the holding."

Cosima looked up at the genial figure of Idrissi, shouting at someone to move on. She glanced questioningly at Smith, but he shrugged. "Is it true?" she asked Bingham.

"Ah, dear girl, the pleasures of speculation are so much more varied than those of reality. That's one of the delights of living here."

The arrival of Miss Cerisette, the festival queen, interrupted them. Idrissi jumped to his feet and leapt down the steps to kiss her and to eat one of the cherries in the wicker tray she held. Behind were two men carrying a woven basket filled with cherries, which Miss Cerisette offered to him. Idrissi shouted to his driver, who appeared from the crowd to take it away.

Bingham whispered to them again, "It all comes full circle. Oufkir was dangerous but necessary. After his death, Kader picked up the pieces. Now the King has his new creature—pity is, Kader hasn't the same style. I was at the palace the other day, when he wore his general's uniform for the first time—decked out like the Milky Way."

Sayed Idrissi heard this as he sat down again, and he turned long enough to say, with contempt, "Kader's just a cop."

The official cars drew up in front of the stand the moment the parade ended. Idrissi led everyone down, then took Cosima's arm and abruptly changed direction, past the cars, up the street into the crowd.

"It's not far. Let's walk."

In the confusion Smith tried to pick out the puritans. They'd all disappeared. He threw himself after Idrissi, dragging Laing by the arm. The officials took a moment to realize what had happened and to jump out of their cars in pursuit.

Behind came the police escort, abandoning their motorcycles and trying to run ahead to form a protective wedge between Idrissi and the crowd.

But he had a head start. Cosima, if anything, walked faster than he. The crowd broke apart in front of them in the graceful way that an Arab crowd can move, some reaching out to kiss his hand, but he was gesturing as he made Cosima laugh at his jokes. She looked around to see that Laing and Smith were right behind them, Smith forcing the pace to keep up.

Laing was saying, "I like your Moulay Sayed. He knows how to amuse himself."

Smith didn't answer. His eyes were searching the sea of people through which they passed as he sweated in the humidity. He saw a man in white pushing forward and lunged to grab him, but it was just a peasant trying to get a better look. Laing was enjoying himself so much that he noticed nothing.

They turned up a smaller street towards the edge of Sefrou, then along a tree-lined lane where the crowd was thinner. Cosima looked around again, to see that Freddie Bingham and the man in the grey suit had caught up. Bingham was jostling his way forward with surprising strength, trying to talk to Laing between deep breaths.

"You remember Colonel Benmansour. You met a few weeks ago over dinner."

Her attention was drawn away by Idrissi, who led her along a high brick wall and through an archway into a formal orange garden. There was a mosque on one side and a hall on the other, with six monumental cedar doors pulled open. Inside were a hundred low, round tables. He led her to one at the front, close to a stage where an Andalusian orchestra played.

Their table was filled by Laing and Smith, the Governor, the Caid and three others. Colonel Benmansour dropped into the last chair, next to Laing. When he had seen there was only one place left, he had pushed Bingham off to the other side of the hall, where he now sat, laughing and talking at a table of young Moroccans, and periodically looking ruefully at Idrissi's group. Smith had not seen Benmansour do this, but it passed through his mind that the Colonel was taking a special interest.

Around them a thousand people milled, choosing places. Cosima was the only woman in the hall, because even Miss Cerisette hadn't been invited.

"Why isn't your wife here?" she asked Idrissi.

"Not done. Besides, Kenza says I waste my time. She has better things to do in her hospital."

Before they were all seated, a hundred large pastilla were brought out—round flat sweet pastry filled with pigeon, egg and spices. They pulled off pieces with their fingers. Idrissi shouted at the orchestra to play a song he liked and the orchestra leader, an old man, shouted back at him, pleased that notice had been taken. The pastilla was replaced by a whole roast lamb, curled up with its legs tucked in, as if asleep.

Idrissi pushed his fingers in and ripped away a strip of the skin. He dug flesh out from underneath and dipped it in bowls of salt and cumin before handing it to Cosima. "The rest you do yourself."

Fingers plunged into the anatomy of the lamb until the Governor stopped eating to sing with the orchestra. From his place, he waved at them in rhythm, his hand glistening with fat. The music had a particular lilt—the blending of Spain and North Africa. Over it the musicians sang a chorus in low tones, to which a soloist replied in a high tenor.

"Again, again!" the Governor shouted.

"What a beautiful voice," Idrissi said to Smith.

But Smith was hungry and nervous. He looked around and could see nothing but absorbed eaters. He didn't like being jumpy when there was nothing to be jumpy about. His fingers were burnt as he pulled off the meat. Nor did he like public events in Arab countries, where no alcohol was served. He thought of saying as much, but there was no one to say it to. Cosima was enjoying herself and Laing was being monopolized by the Colonel.

The lamb was followed by the richest kind of couscous, rolled in rancid butter. It was nibbled at for politeness' sake. Seffa, or sweet couscous, followed that, covered in sugar and cinnamon. Then bowls of cherries were brought.

THIRTY-ONE

The escort led them back to Fez, to rest during the heat of the day.

Laing came out of a cold shower to find that Cosima had thrown her clothes over a chair and was stretched out on the bed. He lay down and rested his head on her stomach. She pushed him.

"Move, Martin. You're lying on the couscous."

He raised his head, laughing. Then flicked his tongue in her belly button, to tickle her. She tried to get away, but he stopped her and ran his hand over the curve of her waist and the rise of her ribcage. He could feel the vibration of her heart against the otherwise still body.

His fingers slipped around her breasts. He pulled himself up, took her face in his hands and kissed her for a long time, his soul melting into hers. She broke away and looked at him from a few inches away.

"Do you love me?" he asked.

She dragged him back down, to be kissed again, her hands on his buttocks.

"Would I be here if I didn't love you?"

He squeezed her as hard as he could, feeling her whole body mould to him.

"That's a question, Cosima."

"I love you."

He pulled away and caressed her. She lay still, on her side, not responding to his touch but staring at him with confused emotion until he noticed and looked at her, aware that something was wrong.

Cosima said, "Why didn't you tell me you were breaking the law and selling guns?"

Laing was so confused that he said nothing.

"I heard you talking to Anthony when he came to dinner."

Laing hardly recognized himself in her description. "I'm not breaking the law." He stopped, confused again.

She saw this. "Why are you letting someone like Anthony drag you into his kind of world?"

"I'm not! It has nothing to do with him. We hired Anthony. I mean, it's not my decision. I'm doing what the company wants." He could see that he wasn't making any sense and pulled himself together as if he were dressed and talking in his office. "The company wants Vietnamese oil. The only way to get it is to sell their arms. The law is out of date and unenforceable. It's a technicality. Come on, Cosima. If I don't do it, I don't have a job."

"And that's all?" She still didn't understand.

He hesitated, but told her no more. "It's just a part of what they pay me to do. Once in your life you come up against something that doesn't fit into any nice mould and you have to deal with it as best you can. It has nothing to do with us." He put his arms around her and drew her close. "Stop glaring at me as if I were a criminal." He kissed her and then laughed, "Criminals can't kiss like that."

She smiled and, in lieu of a reply, told him, "I stopped taking my pills this morning."

He drew his head back to see her.

"I thought it might discourage you from breaking laws if I were pregnant."

They laughed, but she could see that he was moved. He wound his arms around her and held her tight for an endless time, as if the sexual act were a mere detail of osmosis.

They were woken late in the afternoon by a call from Idrissi. He was waiting in the lobby with Smith to take them into Fez-El-Bali.

Smith had already described to them his walks with Idrissi, how he would follow blindly down the alleys and long stairways until Idrissi darted off into a dark opening, to find the tomb of a forgotten, saintly Marabout. Or Idrissi would stop outside a fifteen-foot door and pound on it.

"It's a cousin's house," he'd explain. "They're all in Casablanca making money, except an old aunt I haven't seen for twenty years."

When the door opened, he'd barge in, past a startled servant girl, and search for the aunt. Smith would be left standing in a courtyard surrounded by the great rooms of the house.

Sometimes there'd be a simple fountain in the middle and, in each corner, lemon or orange trees stretching to escape the shade. More often than not, it would be a grand house, the courtyard partially paved with marble that separated trees and rose bushes and water running through in ceramic waterfalls. These houses were always empty. The owners were always in Casablanca or Rabat.

While Cosima dressed, Laing lay on the bed. He said he wouldn't come. Colonel Benmansour had promised to drop in and he was an interesting man—part of the new generation trying to modernize the country.

Half an hour after she left, Benmansour telephoned from the lobby and Laing went down to meet him on the terrace. The sun rose in front of the hotel and set behind, lighting up the city below while leaving the terrace in the shade. Benmansour was drinking Campari and Laing joined him.

The Colonel fiddled with his glass in silence, trying to decide how to deal with his problem. "Amusing folklore this morning," he said eventually.

"Fun to see it once," Laing replied. He looked at the Colonel, dressed in carefully pressed trousers with a slight flair and a tight jersey French shirt that was open too many buttons for Laing's taste.

"I'm afraid Moulay Sayed makes a life out of pressing the flesh," the Colonel said. "He's always telling us we're out of touch with reality. He means the people."

"Is he right?"

"The people follow the King. The Cherry Festival of Sefrou neither helps nor hinders. How do you change people who want to kiss a hand because its owner descends from the Prophet?"

"Yes, I've seen that. One finds it . . ."

"Disturbing," the Colonel provided.

"I suppose your first step is to reform the leaders."

"We can't do anything until this war is over."

Laing nodded. The Colonel leapt a gap.

"Moulay Sayed offered us the arms you had to sell. We weren't interested. We couldn't risk our friendship with your country."

Laing smiled agreeably.

"Have you found a buyer?"

"The matter has been nicely settled." Laing dismissed the subject as unimportant.

The Colonel sipped his Campari, then looked at Laing, "You might like to know that one of our friends in Algiers—we have many there—tells us you spent time with the Polisario. With Lamine, I believe. The friend reports directly to General Kader, who is in charge of Moroccan security, and the General has informed me."

Laing reached forward to take an olive from the dish on the table. He looked stolidly at Benmansour and concentrated on chewing around the stone.

"You see, Mr. Laing, other friends tell us that the Polisario have mentioned to the Algerians neither your visit nor their desire to buy weapons. That's unusual. It implies that these arms won't be delivered to Algerian ports. No. Please. Don't say anything. Let me explain our quandary. Perhaps there is no arrangement between you and Lamine. Why should there be? Mr. Smith has a varied life that leads him up many blind alleys. He enjoys the exercise, although I think even Idrissi would be surprised to hear that Smith went, with the same offer, from the house of his friend in Rabat to our enemies. No. No," he reassured Laing, "which, of course, we don't really know."

The Colonel paused to eat an olive himself. He smiled warmly at Laing, whose face had no expression, before going on, "You see, if there is nothing, there is nothing. So much the better. But if there were something, then we'd find out sooner or later. The name of your company, for example, was quite easy. And these arms, they'd turn up in the war and we should recognize them. At that point, we should inform your government. That would be embarrassing for Western-Oriental—contravening the embargo and supplying the enemy of your nation's ally. Then, we should seize Western-Oriental's franchise here. As for your sales of crude to our government, there would be no more. Perhaps all of that is unimportant. But I think we could make you a proposal, a very positive proposal."

Laing was grateful for Benmansour's soliloquy. He smiled back at the Colonel. "One is always interested in theoretical proposals."

"Good." The Colonel raised two fingers to order more drinks. "Life is so much more interesting than people think. Are you going back to Rabat for the week?" Laing nodded. "Good. You must meet General Kader. He would like to meet you. He's in the South just now, putting the final touches on a mobile column. Four thousand men. The third new column in scarcely more months. We keep them moving around the open desert to unnerve the guerillas. He should be in Rabat later in the week.

"Now tell me about your politics. How does the greatest nation in the world find itself with a choice between sincere inconsistency and bad acting?" The Colonel laughed at his own joke. Before Laing could say a word he added, "I shouldn't mention anything to Mr. Smith. At least, not until you've seen the General."

THIRTY-TWO

Smith followed listlessly, avoiding the donkeys as they pushed by carrying loads in and out of the city. He still sensed that something was wrong, but he could rarely tell what was show, what reality, in the Arab world.

A few yards ahead, Idrissi propelled Cosima through the crowd, keeping a firm grasp on her arm lest she slip on the stone paving. With unassuming gestures, he cleared people from their path or gave a wide berth to a beggar, talking non-stop,

"Three hundred thousand people are crowded inside the walls. No machinery. No room for cars. No motorbikes. Nothing modern except electric lights. This city is almost untouched by time." A puritan came through the crowd. "Look. That man. He belongs to the old school. Watch. As we pass, he'll avert his eyes. Uncovered women. Cosima, you're a veritable sin. Now look." He pointed at an opening in a wall where water bubbled up. "They've had running water since the twelfth century. It's carried inside the house walls, flowing downhill through the town. Every hundred yards or so there's an opening where it comes up and goes back down these ceramic pipes, running into each house twenty-four hours a day and out through a sewer to the river below the city."

"And that's polluted?" Cosima couldn't help teasing him.

Sayed Idrissi raised his shoulders. "Ah, I'm telling you of the twelfth century. In the eighteenth century at Versailles, they were still pissing on the floor, behind the curtains. We've no lessons to learn from your past. For the future, we'll see. But come over here. Anthony!"

Smith waved them on, preferring to wait in the street, which was two yards wide. People were pushing so he stepped into an alley out of the way.

It was curious, he thought, this refusal of a city to die or change or to become a soulless museum like Venice. He noticed a puritan watching him in a doorway on the other side of the alley. The man moved quickly as Smith stared back. Perhaps the force of religion, beating in its heart, had saved Fez.

Idrissi reappeared with Cosima and they headed down the hill, toward the main thoroughfare, the Talaa Kebira. The shop shutters were opening and the streets filling as the air cooled.

Smith caught up with him. "Sayed, there are an awful lot of puritans around."

Idrissi looked at him, surprised. "I hadn't noticed any more than usual."

"There was a man following us," Smith said.

Idrissi began to look about as they plunged into the crowds of the market area and the smells and soft colours of spices surrounded them. He led the way past the rows of ageing merchants, sitting cross-legged on the counters of their stalls. Their skin was paler than an Anglo-Saxon's, with an even white quality as if the sun had never touched them. Beyond the spice merchants were stalls covered with leathers, then more stalls covered with cloths, the sharp colours competing with one another.

The way narrowed, forcing people together, until the crowd came up against the wall of the Karaouiyn Mosque and broke to either side or moved into an entrance, where men could be seen washing their feet in a marble pool.

The mosque was forbidden to non-believers, so Idrissi led the way to the left, through the crowd around the outside of the wall. There they found a minor entrance and a guardian who was waiting for them. The afternoon call to prayer could be heard from the minaret above as the attendant led them into a corner of the main hall. They slid along the wall in the shadows. Between a forest of pillars, the crowd of men kneeling on the rush mat floor could be seen, their legs to one side, bowing to the ground three times before rising to their feet and kneeling again.

Smith saw a man standing against one of the pillars. A puritan. He had been watching them and looked away. Smith moved to draw Idrissi's attention, but the man disappeared into the maze. Words drifted through the vaults in a smooth, unaggressive murmur.

> You alone we worship,
> and to You alone
> we pray for help.
> Guide us to the straight path,
> the path of those whom You have favoured,
> Not of those who have incurred Your wrath . . .

Darkness fell as they worked their way back up the hill on the Talaa Seghira. The crowds thinned and their pace quickened until Idrissi stopped outside a slit in a wall. It was a tea house with a bench for four people down one side and a copper heater over coals on the other. Smith wasn't thirsty and waited outside, leaning against the wall in the wide alley, watching people drift by. It was ten minutes before he heard Idrissi exclaiming:

"Anthony, you missed the best tea in Fez!"

Smith swivelled and noticed, in the fading evening light, that his friend had come out, Cosima behind him. As he turned, a bearded man in a white djellabah ran from the passing crowd and raised a pistol to Idrissi's head. Smith was three yards away, but he froze. Idrissi managed to swing his right arm in a brusque nervous reaction.

The explosion of the shot echoed down the street—out of its time—shocking Smith back to life. The gunman raised his pistol to fire again at Idrissi, who stood dazed by the shattering noise inches from his head. Behind, Cosima was mesmerized.

Smith threw himself on the man. A second shot went off. They crashed to the cobbled ground and the pistol flew loose, clattering along the stones.

Idrissi rushed for it, but Smith was back on his feet and grabbed him, "No. He's not alone."

They hesitated. Idrissi forced himself to pivot round. Beyond the gunman, spreadeagled awkwardly on the ground, men were running towards them.

He grasped Cosima's hand. "Quick," he cried and led them at a run up the street and off into a narrow alley. As they turned, Smith glanced behind. A group of men had gathered, most of them with weapons. The gunman pointed.

"This way!" Idrissi shouted to him. "Quick."

They veered again into a long empty alley enclosed by high walls, their feet echoing on the cobbles. A hundred yards from the corner, Idrissi stopped and pounded on a door, while all three stood panting, their eyes fixed behind them. Idrissi banged again. A girl pulled the door open and he pushed his way in, talking.

Smith followed last, but not before two men appeared at the end of the alley and saw him disappear inside. He shoved the bolt across the door and found himself on the edge of a courtyard of pure white marble, surrounded by pavilion walls painted blue and gold.

"Can we stay here?"

"God, Anthony, no. There's no telephone here. And these houses have too many ways in."

Cosima leaned on a fountain in the centre of the courtyard, trying to catch her breath, while Idrissi went inside to question the servant. When he came out, he took her hand and smiled. He was calm and in command, although the ringing from the shots still reverberated through his head. She managed to smile back.

"I'm all right." Her voice was uneven.

Idrissi whispered, almost laughing, "What a wonderfully inconspicuous trio we make."

He motioned them to follow him up a circular staircase to the first floor, which led onto a tiled terrace. There, they climbed over a low wall and ran around the next terrace, a courtyard dimly visible below.

Behind, in the darness, they could hear men's voices and a woman protesting. Feet ran across a courtyard and then onto echoing roofs. Someone moved over a terrace off to one side.

Out of these distant sounds, one set of running footsteps emerged, clattering up stairs to follow them. Cosima and the other two ran almost silently, but the steps behind grew louder, echoing through the darkness. Idrissi changed directions, climbing across a low wall to the right. Smith heaved Cosima over it and they began running again, around another courtyard. The footsteps followed like a reverberation of their own, gradually gaining. In the darkness, with the low walls and echoing courtyards, it was impossible to know how close they were. Idrissi could hear his friends panting and sense Cosima twisting constantly to stare behind; then he heard her gasp as she slipped on a piece of tile. He managed to catch her before she fell and they ran on, unable to see one another's faces in the night.

Idrissi swerved again onto a new terrace and abruptly stopped at a stairwell. He pushed them in first and followed. They were separated from an unlit courtyard by a narrow terrace.

The running footsteps grew within seconds into heavy sounds. They hesitated once, then began again in the right direction, until Idrissi could hear the heavy breathing of the runner. They shrunk farther into the darkness of the stairwell. Smith put out his arm to press Cosima back and felt his hand against her breast, heaving as she tried to catch her breath. In a weak ray of light shining from the courtyard, he saw her face, an ethereal mask drawn down to hide any fear.

The footsteps were almost upon them. They hesitated, moved on and hesitated again outside the stairwell. The silhouette of a man and a pistol pivoted slowly, peering into the darkness. Idrissi threw himself forward, catching the shadow from the side. There was a wheeze of surprise and the man floated for an instant in the air before crashing down into the courtyard. Idrissi picked himself up and stared at the stillness on the marble paving below, then turned away with a sigh more felt than heard. He drew them on over another wall, around again and over another. There they found stairs, down which he led them, across the courtyard of a house and out through a door into an alley.

"Now we must be careful," he whispered.

They followed him at a trot, his djellabah hitched up to free his stride, through a series of dark alleys. He made them stop once to listen to the steps of people running. In the maze of alleys, it was impossible to know where they were coming from. Idrissi moved on.

Around the next corner they came to the city wall and the darkness disappeared. There was a city gate before them, Bab Mahrouk, with cars driving by on the other side. Idrissi hurled himself into the street to block a car and, after a few words, they leapt in. Fifteen minutes later they were at the hotel.

Smith didn't wait while Idrissi shouted instructions at the

doorman. He went ahead to the bar, where he emptied a brandy in two gulps, then ordered a round of drinks for all three of them.

They were scarcely seated, the glasses before them, when the Police Superintendent arrived. He wasn't invited to sit down. Instead, he was insulted for his incompetence.

"I beg of you, Moulay Sayed, forgive us for this error." The Superintendent would have said anything to defuse the torrent of insults. "If only you would allow us to give you a man when you come to Fez."

Idrissi went into a frenzy. "I don't want your goons on my tail! I should be able to go where I please here. I want this city safe. I don't want bodyguards. Goons! That's all I need . . ."

"Please forgive me, Moulay . . ."

"Tonight I want your goons! You put a detail on the hotel. I want officers on all night outside my friends' rooms."

Cosima laughed, "That's not necessary, Moulay Sayed."

Smith cut her off, "Just do what you're told."

She smiled passively and reached out to pick up her drink, only to find her hand shaking so violently that she couldn't hold it. She placed the hand in her lap as discreetly as possible, but the shaking spread through her body. Smith noticed and said to Idrissi, in English,

"Get rid of the cop. Everybody is upset enough."

Idrissi understood immediately. When the Superintendent had gone he sat down beside Cosima and put his arm around her until she was calmer. "In a country like this," he said, "my way of life carries certain risks. There's always someone who wants to take it away—an assassin or the King or a revolution. I have no illusion of immortality; the risks are too real." He held her tighter and smiled, "What about you?"

Cosima managed to smile back.

"Here!" Idrissi shouted. "Bring us more drinks! Then we'll find that husband of yours and celebrate."

Driving back the next day, Sayed Idrissi fell into a long depression. It was, Smith saw, the low after the high. Perhaps the image of the pistol pointed at his head had come back to him in his sleep. Certainly it had to Smith, who had been unable to make the black barrel go away. If he awoke quickly, he didn't hear the explosion or see the flash of death passing in the night. That was small reward. If he so much as closed his eyes, it was there again.

Idrissi's silence weighed on them all, even on Cosima, who

found after a night's sleep that the whole incident had given her new energy and enthusiasm and even made her see Smith with some sympathy. The silence in the car was broken only by Smith turning the pages of a book he carried in his pocket. He was turning, not reading. His mind was churning over the problem of Karim Farid; what to tell Idrissi.

When they arrived in Rabat, the driver followed the walls to the Palace, where he pulled up before the King's private entrance. Idrissi took the large basket of cherries from the boot. The monumental doors swung open for him and he walked in alone, the basket grasped to his chest.

Twenty minutes later he reappeared. In his hand was a bouquet of garden roses wrapped in newspaper, to protect against the thorns. He came to Cosima's window and thrust them through,

"From the King."

THIRTY-THREE

In the confusion surrounding their return to Rabat, with policemen coming and going, arrests being made and public outcry, nobody noticed Laing's agitation. He disguised it well. Even after four days had passed, and he had heard nothing from Benmansour, he resisted the temptation to confide in Smith; from fear that his friend would back out of the whole deal. Laing was determined to make it work. How, he didn't know.

That left him no option but to wait and to keep his own counsel. Idrissi's ebullience was no longer a distraction. Laing found it tiring, if not imbalanced. Nor were the rich Moroccans of Rabat amusing, grouped in their houses in a state of permanent celebration over not very much in particular. And so he spent much of his time in the hotel. While his performance in public was flawless, in private he was introverted and moody. Whenever Cosima pointed this out, he pulled himself together and apologized, admitting that his arms deal was getting him down and suggesting that she join Idrissi and Smith. He didn't mention that he was happiest left alone at the hotel, where there was no risk of missing Benmansour.

Cosima followed along in Idrissi's wake for three days, increasingly confused and then upset. Her confusion was sensed by Smith in his disordered way and he gave the kind of unspoken comfort that had always come naturally to him. Cosima began to treat him almost as a friend, but it was as if she felt sorry for him, as if he were a lower form of man than Laing. Smith sensed this and resented it. Let her love Laing, but not through ignorance.

Whenever Idrissi was busy, Smith took her in hand on his own, which was how she discovered that he spent a great deal of time with Kenza, Idrissi's wife; that is, whenever she wasn't at the hospital. They made a curious pair which Cosima couldn't entirely understand.

On Friday morning, the 18th, Cosima suggested to Laing that they should go away alone to the Mediterranean at Cabo Negro. He asked for nothing better, but it was impossible, so he delayed by saying that it would be rude to Idrissi and Smith. She pressed him and he retreated into an embarrassed silence until the subject was dropped, leaving a distance between them which she thought had been squeezed once and for all out of their existence.

Later that morning, she was sitting with Smith and Kenza in her garden when Smith was called away. The two women were surprised to find themselves alone and talked politely until Kenza asked about Cosima's work. In New York, caught up in the detail of her small projects, there was always something to discuss; but the details didn't make much sense at a distance. Cosima tried to explain that she was an architect, who worked hard but had never actually built anything. Then she hesitated and Kenza asked what was wrong.

"I was brought up by my father," Cosima said shyly, "to believe that I would succeed as a woman, but in a man's world. When I went away to university, I discovered that most women were fighting to free themselves of their father's disappointment at their not being men. Or from his cloying love. Or from their mother's siege training. All things I'd never known or worried about. Unfortunately, I've since frittered away my advance."

Kenza listened to her sympathetically. Her children appeared from the house and dropped themselves on her lap. She talked to them in French before looking up at Cosima,

"Have you had your children?"

Cosima was taken off guard. "No."

"As you can see, I have two. Now that's done. We have a saying from before the days of modern medicine—"A woman's grave is open forty days before and forty days after she gives birth." Now they should say a woman's grave is open until she gives birth. Until then she is the victim of regret, and regret is a grave which swallows up everything else."

Cosima said nothing.

It was noon when Colonel Benmansour knocked on the hotel room door. Laing opened to find him in a dark suit with a warm smile.

"I was passing and thought you might enjoy a drive."

In the black Renault, which the Colonel drove himself, Laing asked whether they were going to Kader. There was an anxious note in his voice, which Benmansour noticed and replied to with gentleness,

"The General is looking forward to meeting you. I think you'll find him an engaging person. He's not at all in the old style."

Laing reined himself in and said nothing more. The house was in Souissi, surrounded by a large garden. It wasn't a grand house, because Kader wasn't a Fassi, from an old family, with a certain style of living. He was from the country; a man without family, allies or inherited obligations. He was the King's man.

They waited in a small entrance hall, lined by shelves loaded down with miniature statues and porcelain drums—the sort of thing that belonged in the house of a career officer in Fort Benning, Georgia. The door into the next room was partially open so that Laing could hear a conversation in Arabic. He caught a glimpse of a man in uniform.

Two officers came out and greeted Benmansour on their way by. They were followed by Kader, who took Laing's hand firmly in his own fleshy palm and drew him forward with a round smile, his teeth closed.

Although the salon had two double doors open onto the

garden, an odour of cigarettes permeated the air. Kader placed Laing in a modern, European chair covered with wool, which made him sweat. Across a glass table, the General balanced himself on the edge of a sofa designed in the same floating style and waved the Colonel down beside him. He took a cigarette from a pack on the table and put it in his mouth. Benmansour had a lighter burning and in place. Leaning forward to make contact with the flame, the General began talking, without acknowledging the Colonel's kindness.

"You've been getting to know Morocco in the good hands of Moulay Sayed Idrissi. I hope what you've seen pleases you."

Laing said nothing and slouched as far down in his chair as he could, with a relaxed air. The General had small eyes and a wide moustache, trimmed to a sixteenth of an inch. He was a large, slightly soft man with a round face—darker than the pale Fassi—and wore a navy blue silk suit. Very warm, Laing thought to himself.

"Moulay Sayed is my friend," Kader went on. "He comes from a great family and has worked hard for the common good. I personally find he concentrates more on propping up than on organizing the future; but he would disagree. I'm certain there's a great deal we could say to each other on the subject."

Laing wanted to force a quick revelation. "No doubt, General. I understand you have an idea as to how my company could help." Left to his own devices, Kader would weave a tortuous web.

"Exactly." The General jumped a step. "We want to get on with the country's real problems. But we're held back by an interminable guerilla war, the kind that any state is ill-suited to fight. Five men and a mortar in a Land-Rover can roam the desert and harass thousands of conventional troops. You, Mr. Laing, can help us hit them hard and kill some of their leaders—because Lamine will be there the day you deliver. He wouldn't miss it. Their set-back will give us the chance we need to negotiate a settlement with Algeria." Kader moved forward precariously onto the sofa edge, hanging over a full ashtray. "When and where are you delivering?" As Laing said nothing the General continued, "We know it will be by boat. After the Captain has landed the goods and is out of the way, he has but to send us a signal. Our jets can be anywhere on the coast within half an hour. We'd catch them together out in the open. Knock out their transport. Then move in our mobile columns."

Laing whispered from a disinterested sleep, "In exchange for?"

Kader dropped his cigarette in the ashtray and pulled out another. The Colonel's lighter was again there. Kader never looked directly at anyone, perhaps from shyness.

"Survival. Men die so easily, Mr. Laing. You are no different. And not only here. New York is as unpredictable a place as any. And your friend Smith as well. And the embarrassment for your company. There's a Moroccan adage. "He who would eat me for lunch, I eat for breakfast."

Benmansour indicated laughter. The General smiled.

"Of course, we can also talk about future co-operation. Benmansour will have mentioned your franchise. That franchise could grow substantially when those of other foreign companies come up for renewal. All things being equal, we could also arrange for government crude purchases to favour Western-Oriental. Ours is the most sophisticated market in North Africa. Who knows, Mr. Laing? Your company does many things. We have many interests. I'm suggesting we strike up a friendship that will serve us all."

The General got to his feet and walked to the garden doors. "There's so much to be done here. What we need are dispassionate friends who will help us to organize."

Laing's mind broke the proposition down into pieces. He looked for elements to reject while others could be accepted. He tried to restructure the whole thing to get what he wanted without doing as they wished, without betraying anyone. He came to the idea of the Polisario dying. That made little impression, because he didn't know them. Then he thought of Lamine. At first he felt nothing, beyond uneasiness over the betrayal his death would involve. It was an idea. A statistic of war. Then, without warning, revulsion rose from the pit of his stomach and his vision was blurred by the illusion of blood as he saw Gerten slipping to the ground. He muttered resentfully,

"In this case, organizing violence."

The General twisted towards him, surprised. It wasn't the reply expected. He gazed back out at the garden, the cigarette motionless in his mouth. Smoke rose, enveloping his profile against the trees like a morning mist. Raising his fingers to remove the cigarette, he pointed outside with the same hand,

"Look at this garden, Mr. Laing. Colour organized is beauty. Sound organized is melody. Violence organized is strength. The strength of power is what we are discussing, and whether you wish to participate in it."

Laing rose in a sudden movement to avoid hearing any more. "I must ask my superiors." He said it firmly, to drown his feelings.

"We look forward to their reply." The General's tone suggested an invitation to dinner. "Benmansour will look after you and keep me informed."

As they left, other officers filed in. Laing turned to see the General standing at the garden doors, lighting his own cigarette.

By the time Laing got back to the hotel, Cosima had already returned. When she asked, the front desk said her husband had been seen going out with Colonel Benmansour; which confirmed what she had already guessed—that Morocco was buying the Vietnamese arms. The moment Laing arrived, he told her that an urgent Telex had come in from his office, calling him back to New York immediately. That meant flying home the following morning, Saturday the 19th. While he hadn't received a Telex, he had sent one to Moffett, warning him of his arrival and asking for a meeting on Sunday.

Cosima offered to go with him, but he was preoccupied to the point of total isolation. He said there was no point in her coming, as he would only be gone forty-eight hours. He had to be quick, because Smith would be joining the *Sophie* in a little over a week. That part Laing couldn't explain, but he could see that she was annoyed, so he promised that they would go away together when he came back.

She agreed, submerging her feelings. He was the one who had made her come, for reasons which she had never understood, as if she were a dog on a leash. And now he was running off with some personal obsession as if she didn't exist. She made an effort to say calmly, "Anthony wants you to meet a friend of his this afternoon."

THIRTY-FOUR

A police officer fidgeted under a tree, out of the Friday afternoon sun, on the edge of Karim Farid's garden. He was in plain clothes and had been assigned in spite of Idrissi's protests. They kept him out of hearing and spoke English when he was close by, because Idrissi was convinced he reported to General Kader.

"I see," Karim Farid remarked evenly, "that you have saved us from a devil." They were sitting inside his gazebo.

Idrissi was embarrassed. "You shouldn't read the papers, Sidi Karim."

"And why not?"

"They've nothing to teach you."

"Was this man not a criminal posing as a religious fanatic? That was what I read. And that he incited a riot in the streets of Fez; the situation being saved by you?"

"Not exactly."

Smith leaned forward. "They tried to shoot Sayed. There were witnesses. Some explanation had to be given."

The old man stared straight at Smith with what was either a warning or an entreaty. Smith looked away annoyed. He was being treated as an accomplice. Farid took a slender silver pot and poured tea for Cosima, then for Laing.

"Is it not true, at least, that there have been arrests?"

"True," Idrissi grunted. "Seventeen so far."

"Poor souls. They will suffer."

"No doubt, Sidi Karim," Idrissi raised his voice. "No doubt. But these men are evil! If they represented God, you yourself would have shot me long ago."

Sidi Karim stared out at the garden, where the afternoon light threw shadows from the trees into the gazebo. "No doubt."

"I came to visit you last week. You weren't here."

The old man gestured helplessly. "I sometimes go to a mosque just south of the city, to pray and to think for a few days, the Marabout's tomb on the offshore rocks. There I can be alone, except for the woman who takes care of the building. She brings me food, you see."

Idrissi was even more embarrassed, but he couldn't stop himself, "Your prayers did me little good, my friend."

"And yet, I prayed for you."

Idrissi jumped up, furious. "Well, am I safe here? Eh? Tell me that! Am I safe here?"

The old man refused to play. "You have your policeman."

Laing and Cosima had no idea what was going on and could only feel like awkward eavesdroppers. Farid's face was impassive. "As for these puritans, they are not evil. 'Man is exceedingly contentious,' and there is good reason for good men to be dissatisfied. Good men who are simple may find the wrong solutions. And yet, simplicity is a great strength. You, Moulay Sayed, when you kill, are you evil?"

The old man picked up and passed a plate of buttercream pastries—his one concession to the French during the Protectorate. Idrissi collapsed onto his chair, the wind gone out of him, and said vainly, like a reluctant prodigal, "What do these people expect? When the Europeans beat us and colonized us, we all believed they held the secret of the future. We followed them blindly and now, where are we?"

"We did well when we followed the path of Islam," the old man said.

Laing broke in restlessly, shifting his small backside on the wicker chair. His mind was already half in New York. "You're in mid-stride. This is the most awkward stage."

Sidi Karim sceptically examined the outsider who had broken in. "Striding where? The Prophet predicted that near the end of the world most people would follow a one-eyed devil called the Dajjal. 'He will hear what is said everywhere, see infinite distances with one eye, fly around the world in a few days, make gold and silver rise out of the earth, kill and bring back to life. The feeble believers will take him for God. The strong will see he negates God and is a test for man.' Is that not technological civilization? One-eyed, it sees only one side of life—material progress. Life becomes an enigma, man sceptical and isolated. In desperation we search out material allies and give our soul to machines. The priests of this divinity lead us to despair—a world incapable of balancing material and social needs with the spiritual. I remember in 1940, your Mr. Roosevelt said man's machines were out of control. Invented to bring him freedom, they no longer served his liberty."

Laing brushed this aside. "We've learnt how to lock the machines into systems that use them properly."

Karim Farid contemplated Laing with aggressive pity. "Intelligence is far more than the possession of knowledge or a system of application. We have no church, Mr. Laing. No priests. No system. Just five obligations and the Koran. Man and God alone together."

"Be fair," Smith interrupted. "Your religion is six hundred years younger than ours."

Karim Farid averted his eyes in disgust. "Because you are in decline, you believe decline inevitable. How have we survived? Faith, and ethics that are the norm of our society. The civilizations that pass away have codes and systems—things concrete therefore fragile. Were I to shoot Moulay Sayed, what would I kill? Ethic is untouched by personal tragedy or mechanical failure."

Laing couldn't believe what he heard. "If that's how you justify murder, I'm not impressed. The logic of the system that is coming is so strong that your faith and your ethics will have to find their own place within it or disappear."

Cosima stood and walked down into the garden, Farid's eyes following her. He turned back to Laing, unleashing bitterness. "Until fifty years ago, you preached Christianity and materialism throughout the world. Now, you preach the gospel of structure and materialism. You are a people of guilt who must carry your guilt to others." Farid clasped his hands tight on the arms of his chair, straining, his voice becoming shrill. "You train our people to go out and fight for freedom and individualism, for their own good. As you define them, these words mean nothing here. Those who do as you wish are the dishonest men of the developing world! The honest men you will not trust because they will not mouth your formulas." The old man saw the other three were amazed and so he abused them. "Where is the evil in a pistol shot?" He twisted sharply to Idrissi, ordering him as if he were a child, "Help me up!"

Farid walked slowly down the steps into the terraces and called to Cosima, pointing to a wall of yellow wild jasmine at the end of the garden. She took his arm and they walked together, along the middle terrace. From the gazebo, they could hear his voice, calm again,

"What do your architect's eyes see here? We Arabs used to build a marriage of the natural and the rational, while the French put nature in chains and the English surrendered to it. Now we imitate ourselves and others."

The bodyguard looked up, curious.

THIRTY-FIVE

The oppressive humidity of the city chased Moffett across the endless bridges linking the suburbs. He had driven himself so little over the last years that he had to concentrate to keep control of the rented car, its power steering sliding like a pillow on ice, imprecise in its reassurance. He hardly knew why he was going, except that Isabelle had telephoned to say she wanted company; as did he, though he didn't say as much, because he didn't want hers.

The narrow, ageing speedways leading onto Long Island were part of a distant memory that kept him on track, despite the missing signs. A symphony of empty cups, tyre scraps and abandoned cars lined the road until he crossed the last bridge, leaving behind the suburbs and their carloads of Saturday shoppers. Somewhere ahead, the smell of the still invisible sea would cross the road. When it came, it reminded him of the years of driving Isabelle and the children to open their house in early June.

In those days he had spent a week with her before returning to New York, only to commute by train every weekend. She would meet him at the station, just a few minutes from the house, and when he finally walked down onto the rolling miles of beach, empty in the early evening, he always felt as if New York no longer existed.

All of that he remembered without emotion. He knew there must be something—good or bad—yet he could find nothing, and this lack of feeling obsessed him for much of the drive. At last he stopped the car on the sand shoulder of the road and sat for half an hour, his soul like an abandoned icebox, the sour smell of emptiness rising up within him. Eventually he turned the car round and drove back to New York.

From their apartment, he telephoned Isabelle to say he wouldn't be able to come, then paced the rooms for the rest of the afternoon, trying to occupy his mind. He took Laing's Telex from his pocket, unfolded it and read the short message, as he had several times since its arrival. Something had obviously gone wrong. Was it so difficult a task that the boy would fail now? He crumpled up the message and began searching the newspapers for a way to fill the evening. By the time he found a play, it was almost too late to get there by eight, so he decided to go down to Fiftieth by subway and walk across to the theatre.

Moffett rarely went on the subway—not because he had a car and driver but because he had never liked going underground. Years before, he'd convinced himself that he suffered from mild claustrophobia; at least, that was what he told others. He no longer bothered to explain his prejudices, even to himself.

The colours of filth in the station were variations on medium grey and the smell was a natural continuation. By asking questions, he discovered were he had to go to catch his train. When it arrived, labouring under its charge of graffiti, he climbed into a half-empty carriage and sat near a doorway, as far as possible from the other passengers. Protected by this isolation, he eyed the mixture of largely blacks and Puerto Ricans as if either he or they were not really there.

Two teenagers got on at the next stop and stood not far from him, near the centre door. One was Puerto Rican, the other white. Both wore red berets and T-shirts with "Guardian Angels" printed on the front. At each succeeding station, people paused before they got off to pat them on the back or to thank them. Moffett heard one old woman say loudly, "Where would we be if we had to rely on the police? Thank you, boys." So they were vigilantes. This word took on mammoth proportions, crowding everything else out of his mind. They were worse than mercenaries. What difference was there between destruction and protection when it was innocent? They were animals in a world without enforceable rules.

The train slowed for the Fiftieth Street station and his mind as suddenly emptied. He prepared to get up. It was only then that he realized he couldn't move. His hands lay before him on his lap. He thought of moving them to the bench, to level himself, but the arms didn't move. He turned his head. Nobody had seen his trouble. There was a light tremor in his breast; a fine, delicate shaking that spread into every corner of his body. He was surprised, but the surprise passed. He recognized the trembling as something that had been there for a long time, in different forms, but this time it inflated like a balloon, pushing against his frame.

Abruptly, the pressure changed. Something drove against his chest and he felt he would choke, but didn't. He was able to breathe. Nothing happened. He was paralysed, but nothing happened.

An uncontrollable fear swept over him. He wanted to put a hand out to the black workman sitting next to him, so close, if only he could have moved. His body was encased in clear, hard plastic. He felt wetness on his eyelids, where tears wanted to flow, but only a few drops came. He was overcome by anguish. Everyone in the carriage became transparent until he was alone.

The black stepped over his legs at the next stop without Moffett noticing anything, then another station came, then a row of stations, while fear sat upon him. Involuntarily, his hand rose to wipe away the tears and he found he could move again. He tried his other arm, then his legs, then stood carefully, only to discover that everything worked. Whatever had happened, it had not been physical.

When the train stopped, Moffett floated effortlessly out of the carriage, passing in a dream before the Guardian Angels. The station was in Soho. He climbed the steps into the darkness, crossed the road mechanically and descended back underground on the uptown side, from where a train took him up to Fiftieth. He made his way to the theatre. Only there did he discover that it was after ten o'clock and, without any feeling of surprise, he turned away to cut through the crowds like a phantom. It was early in the morning before he arrived home, with no idea of where he had walked.

Laing tried to telephone Moffett as soon as he arrived home on Saturday evening. There was no answer. During the flight he had turned the problem over again and again without finding any answer. Lying in bed, trying to sleep, he went through it once more and still came up with the same blanks. It was the sort of crisis that Smith might have found a way out of and Laing began to regret not having told him anything; then pushed the regret aside. Had he told Smith, everything would have been at risk. They were friends, but Laing knew of no way to predict what Smith's reaction would be. One minute he was for sale and the next he was the philosopher prince. No, for once Laing was sure that Moffett was the person to turn to.

On Sunday morning Moffett's telephone was engaged. It stayed busy all day. Laing tried through the operator, only to be told that the number was in order and engaged, which meant it was off the hook; therefore Moffett didn't want to be disturbed. That left Laing with no option but to wait and go to Western-Oriental early on Monday morning, 21 July.

He handed his secretary a sealed envelope for his personal Vietnam file before going upstairs to Moffett's office. As he stepped out of the executive lift, Cosima went through his mind. She was going to Marrakesh that afternoon for the birthday and circumcision of the King's second son. It was all so improbable at a distance; even Kader with his threats dressed up in businesslike robes.

Moffett's secretary was as distant as ever and told him that the Vice-President wasn't yet in, which was hardly surprising. Laing asked to see him later in the morning, only to be told that Moffett was away for a few days. When he tried to explain how urgent it was, she wasn't even prepared to define what she meant by a few days. He asked whether his Telex had arrived and she admitted that it had, but Moffett still wasn't available.

He had telephoned her early that morning and, in a short, strained sentence, said that he wasn't to be bothered by anyone, including herself. She had never questioned his orders and had no intention of doing so now. When Laing had given up bothering her and disappeared, she went about her Monday morning tasks—changing the blotter pad on Moffett's desk, putting out a new red felt pen, changing the Gillette blade in his old fashioned razor and so on—until she was interrupted by the next nosy caller.

Laing went back to his office in a rage, all the agitation he had felt in Rabat resurfacing. He had to come up with something and get back to Rabat to warn Smith, who would be flying to London on the 27th and then going on to join the *Sophie* in an African port.

He calmed himself. The first thing to do was find out why Moffett was being so unco-operative. Laing called in his assistant, Morley, to see what he knew.

Morley was filled with gossip and was almost ingratiating, which didn't suit his mechanical personality; but he admitted to knowing about what was wrong with Moffett. Laing asked whether he had heard any echoes from their Vietnam negotiations. In the midst of his answer, Morley accidentally let slip that he knew about the arms. Laing showed no surprise, but afterwards thought through the incident again. There was only one person who could have told him and that was Moffett, the one person who didn't trust Laing, who wanted him watched on all sides, who wanted to keep the glory for himself.

Laing telephoned David Fell's office and asked to see him urgently. Fell's secretary said he was busy, but if it was urgent it was best to come immediately. It took Laing some time to explain everything that had happened since their last conversation, including Kader's threats and Moffett's disappearance. Fell listened without interruption, until Laing asked him whether he thought there was a link between Moffett's evasion and Morley's being so well informed.

Fell asked sympathetically, "You mean, is Moffett planning to give Morley your job?"

Laing was astounded. "Is that what it is?"

"My secretary tells me that Moffett has been using Morley a great deal since you've been away. They appear to get on well together. Morley is so much more his style in many ways."

Laing said, almost to himself, "If that's the case, what do I tell him?"

Fell sat very still, staring at Laing in his bald way, scratching from his scalp bits of dry skin which he held between two fingers and examined, then dropped on the floor. The whole adventure was becoming wonderfully complex, while remaining perfectly controllable. Suddenly Fell sat forward, the weight of his eyes fixed on Laing, transmitting electricity. "The question is whether you should tell Moffett."

"What do you mean?"

Fell took off his glasses, intensifying his stare. "You mustn't lose sight of your case—Vietnamese oil rights. Your problem—how to get them. Your solution—raise one hundred million dollars. What we're talking about now is a new case. If you go ahead as planned, everything Moffett sent you to do will be done. But if you tell him about the Moroccan offer, the Moroccan contact will become his. He will be the one who brought in the new bacon; while you will get a reward, like a good junior.

"Now suppose you don't tell him and you go ahead with this Kader proposal. Moffett will never know. What happens to a bunch of guerillas in the Sahara desert after the ship leaves will never reach our ears. Even the Polisario will have nothing to reproach you with. You carried out the bargain and they lost it all, because they were clumsy. Too bad for them."

Laing tried to interrupt but Fell wouldn't allow him. "You, Martin, will suddenly have a new value at Western-Oriental. You will be the man who can deliver deals in Morocco. No one will know how you do it, so you'll get all the credit and proper reward. That's the sort of mystery Moffett used to build his own career."

Laing tried to disagree. He knew he should, but suddenly he could find no reasons. What choice did he have? He could only think of another argument in favour. If Moffett didn't know, he wouldn't have to be convinced. And more important—if Moffett was gossiping, the fewer people who knew, the better he would feel himself.

Fell interrupted his musings. "You might worry that I know and could tell. But first, I'm your friend. Second, how could I tell? People would say—'Mr. Fell, you're a senior executive. You were aware of this insubordination and yet you did nothing.' You see, Martin, I'm doubly your friend."

"He knows I've come back with something important to ask him."

Fell's lips moved in a parody of contempt. "From what you have told me, you have a few days to think of something important to ask him." In the silence that followed, Fell gazed at him, scratching his forehead idly.

Laing spent the rest of the day working out his plan. He couldn't leave New York until he had seen Moffett, and with what he had learnt from Fell, he felt obliged to spend a few days consolidating his position against Morley. He sent a Telex to Cosima to say that he would arrive in Rabat on Friday morning, 25 July. That would get him there two days before Smith left for London. All he had to do was work out what to tell him.

THIRTY-SIX

It was not an expensive taxi fare to the Palace from the former French quarter, where Freddie Bingham borrowed a house on a semi-permanent basis from soneone who couldn't sell it and had gone back to Paris. And yet, every Monday morning, when he went to play tennis with Benmansour, Bingham rented a limousine. He could ill afford the luxury, but he felt it simply wouldn't have done to arrive any other way. Once there, he let the driver go and kept his eyes open for someone who would give him a lift home.

He worked hard at his tennis that morning, to keep Benmansour's interest up, and worked equally hard at making him talk. To set the tone, Bingham offered a few indiscretions of Idrissi's from the night before, plus a rumour that former friends of the King had met to discuss how they might damage Kader's influence on the throne. In return, Benmansour offered little, even when Bingham managed to gracefully lose his advantage at the end of a match he could have won. Bingham already knew the name of Laing's company, that the Sahara was somehow involved and that something was off-colour. When he left the court exhausted, all he had found out was that Laing had been obliged by the Moroccans to return to New York and that Smith probably didn't know why. It was hardly an outline, let alone enough information to work with.

A royal official was on his way out of the Palace at the right moment and offered a lift. Bingham asked to be dropped at the Hilton. He had heard that Smith would be picking Cosima up there and taking her on to Idrissi's where they were all to meet. But Bingham's hope was to catch Smith alone and have a word with him in private.

When the hotel doorman saw the palace car arriving, he rushed down the steps. Bingham greeted the man kindly. Since the Hilton was the only good hotel in town, it did no harm, in the little world of Rabat gossip, for the doorman to see who his friends were. Unfortunately, the concierge dashed his hopes with the news that Smith had already gone out with Mrs. Laing. That meant Bingham had to take a taxi. He considered for a moment whether his finances could afford a big taxi or his reputation a small, scruffy one. He counted the change in his pocket and opted for a small one.

"No need for a big car," he joked to the doorman. "I'm not tall enough."

The taxi took him to Idrissi's house, where he was expected to lunch before they all set off for Marrakesh to attend Prince Moulay Rachid's tenth birthday celebration. He got there early enough to ask for a Martini and to corner Smith alone in the drawing room, disguising his nervousness with banter.

"I was so sorry to see Martin go. It's always great fun to have a new face around here. A breath of fresh air for me, you know. I don't travel like you. Now sit down, Anthony, and tell me, is your deal all set?"

Smith stayed on his feet and stared blankly at him. "The buses? That's been put to bed."

"No, silly boy. Your deal with Kader." Smith showed some surprise. "Now, Anthony, relax. You know me. I'm up on most things around here. Of course, I was pleased as punch to put Laing and Benmansour together the other day."

Smith looked even more surprised. "I don't follow," he said coldly.

"Why, the business that sent him to New York, Anthony." He could see that that gave Smith a bit of a jar. Now all he needed to do was create a need. Bingham tried a small threat, moving about all the time with little shuffling steps. "What a funny world. I did feel an ass last week when the *Monde* came out with all the details on that poor Minister's odyssey in the desert."

"What do you mean?" Smith bit, not yet following Bingham's intricate logic. The houseboy appeared in the door to say that lunch had begun. Bingham waited until he was gone.

"Oh well, I'm such a chatterbox and, of course, the correspondent is such a good friend. You know the silly fellow is always trying to pay me to give him information. But, of course, the interests of my friends come first." He could see that Smith had followed. "I was thinking about your deal and that there must be some way I could be more helpful to you. Some little thing. I might be able to keep you better informed on your friend's activities."

Smith digested these words impassively, now careful to control what he showed, and put a hand out to take hold of Bingham's lapel in a firm but friendly way. He pulled him closer. "Don't ever try to put the touch on me, Freddie." It wasn't a threat. It was more like a mother's sensible advice. "Your existence here is very fragile. You could never win a fight like that. All right?"

Bingham's face didn't lose its joy for more than a second and he laughed as if a joke had been told. But his heart was sad. All he could think to himself was that a few dollars wouldn't have mattered to a big company. He had known from the beginning where the weakness in his approach lay, but damn the man. "Where's my drink?" He pulled loose and put his arm around Smith's shoulders. "Come on, Anthony. They're not going to give us a drink in here."

He drew Smith through to the dining room thinking that he would have to stay up late that evening coding a telegram for the States. He would send it off on Tuesday morning from Marrakesh, but they were never in any rush to pay him, and with the little information he had they wouldn't pay much. Bureaucrats were so cheap. Again he thought wistfully of Smith. That would have been a more profitable course to follow; still, there was more to uncover and then he could feed them a series of reports.

They found Idrissi sitting down with his friend the Ambassador and Cosima. Idrissi peered up at Smith, his tone resentful. "I hear you're not coming, either of you."

"But it's the celebration of the year," Freddie Bingham chimed in, taking the place next to Cosima before Smith had a chance and immediately beginning to eat. "You must come."

"Militant circumcision makes me squeamish," Smith said.

"You don't see the act, dear boy." Bingham needed a good joke. "You just see the King lead him into a tent on a horse. Then everyone makes a lot of noise."

"Shut up, Freddie," Idrissi said petulantly. "If they don't

want to come, they don't want to come. Not everyone loves a party the way you do."

"And Cosima?" Bingham insisted.

"Fatigue," she said.

Idrissi turned to shout at the Ambassador. "Excellence, finish your story."

"There isn't much to tell." The Ambassador moved his arm modestly. The cuff of his cream silk shirt hid a thin gold bracelet. "OAU meetings are all the same. They would have voted the Polisario in if we hadn't applied a little financial temptation. These tinpot presidents are on top for such a short time they have to cash in quickly; so we pay, and yet they hate us. You can never please an inferiority complex. It is a wild beast with an insatiable appetite."

"The revenge of the unloved," Idrissi agreed.

"I usually get invitations to these official dos," Bingham leaned over to confide to Cosima, "thanks to the Prince. Mind you, Marrakesh isn't what it used to be. Not such fun. They don't let the boys parade around the pools in g-strings the way they used to. Found it set the old queers on too much, you know. I used to keep an apartment there. Beautiful, with a terrace above the city walls. I rented the place in the off-season. But how could you get them to follow the rules? Once I walked in to find my *locataires* at breakfast, with four golden lads, naked and covered in suntan oil, sitting on my velvet dining room chairs."

Smith didn't listen. He was trying to work out how much Bingham did know and what he had meant by their "deal with Kader." Laing couldn't be dealing behind his back. No. Smith wouldn't believe it. Bingham had simply got everything confused. Nevertheless, there was something at the bottom of it which had to be explained. After twenty minutes of Bingham's chatter, Idrissi shouted,

"Lunch is over! Up! We have a four-hour drive ahead." He marched out of the room, saying to Cosima, "We'll see you at the weekend."

They heard the car starting, so the Ambassador and Bingham emptied their glasses and left.

Smith turned to Cosima. "What would you like to do?"

He looked after her for the rest of the day, but drank too much and gave the impression he would rather have been reading whatever book was in his pocket. Since Cosima had been in Morocco, the book had changed almost every time she saw him, then sometimes reappeared a few days later. That afternoon, *Metaphysical Poets* was poking out of his jacket. Without his friends, Smith became a quiet, even taciturn man.

She told him that she doubted he read so much, which made him shrug. He said he slept badly—"congenital indigestion"—and read during the night. Why then did the books reappear?

"I can only carry so many on a trip. Fortunately, I forget quickly."

On Tuesday morning, she got Laing's Telex announcing that he would not be back until Friday. She had guessed that something like that would happen, but it still infuriated her. The *Matin* carried two pages of photos showing the massive reception the King had given in Marrakesh before his son's circumcision. Idrissi was in one photo, caught with an arm extended and his mouth open. In the background of two others, Freddie Bingham could be made out, like a ghost.

Smith telephoned late in the morning and asked awkwardly whether she would like to go to Idrissi's orange farm. Cosima suspected he found it difficult to deal with a woman from his own world, unless he knew her well or she were there for her function. She said as much to him when they were walking through the groves.

He didn't disagree. "I'm not out of practice. I was never in."

"So you make do with what you can buy?" She asked the question blandly.

"Not exactly." He could see that she was looking at him with kindness, perhaps even affection; but still with superiority, as if Laing represented something Smith couldn't even understand. He wanted to say that it wasn't true—that he understood Laing and they were the same—but his emotions showed through as envy. "I make do with women who don't expect anything from me. Or I from them. That has made for some long friendships."

"You just don't have much to say to each other." She was smiling.

Two peasants on the edge of the orange grove stared at them. Curious. Particularly of Cosima. Smith's voice became defensive.

"I already know what the people who resemble me think. As for my friends, I don't want to have anything in common with them."

"That's why you've always been close to Martin?"

Her question was in earnest, yet Smith couldn't help laughing. She stopped uncertainly,

"You know, Martin told me about the arms deal."

Smith said nothing, but stopped a pace ahead and turned, waiting for her to say more.

"I mean, I overheard you in New York and made him tell me."

"And what did he tell you?"

"Is this a test?" She tried to joke.

"That's right." He made an effort to smile back.

"Vietnam, illegal arms in exchange for oil."

"Is that all?"

"That must be everything except the buyer." She walked on past him. "I'd guess, given where we are and that Martin has been spending time with Colonel Benmansour, who looks pretty boring, that Morocco must be the buyer."

"You would?"

"Meaning I'm wrong?"

Smith caught up. He could still see the light of superiority in her eyes, to which he replied, "Quite wrong. The wrong side."

"I don't understand."

"The Polisario, Cosima. The enemy."

Cosima was bewildered. She stopped with an irrigation ditch separating them. "Then what are we doing here?"

"Having a holiday."

"And betraying your friends."

Smith shrugged. "I don't look at it that way."

"Well, how does Martin look at it?"

"Cosima, ask him."

"I don't understand. What did you tell Martin?"

"Martin gives the orders, so he must be satisfied. I imagine he wants a promotion or something. I imagine he wants to succeed."

They walked on in silence. Neither of them spoke, apart from the odd word, during the rest of the afternoon or during the drive back to the hotel in the darkness. As he let her out, he could see in the light of the entrance that the expression of her eyes had changed to confusion. He said, "I'll pick you up at six-thirty tomorrow morning."

She began to protest.

"Just be at the door."

THIRTY-SEVEN

At that hour of the morning, an Atlantic chill crept down the river and across the town. Smith drove along the outside of the Palace walls until just before the river bank, where a track led to an earth fortress sitting on the cliff's edge. Cosima had assumed, whenever she was driven past, that it was part of the old city defences.

Smith turned onto the dirt track and stopped outside the Chella, as it was called, before a thirty-foot door that rose in a key form above them. He thumped on the wood. When nothing happened, he shouted until a voice protested from the other side, which only made Smith keep on shouting until the door swung open on an irate guardian.

There was an exchange in rapid French, and Smith pushed into his hand a ten dirham note, only to have it rejected; but the guard let them pass with recovered civility. When the money was offered again, the man accepted and disappeared.

Smith led her along a path that climbed down through a wild garden where the breeze overflowed with perfumes. Jacaranda and banana trees mixed with honeysuckle and roses. Uncontrolled vines and narcissi surrounded them. At the bottom of the path, the sun came into sight and threw rays of morning light across a maze of ruins, of olive and of eucalyptus trees.

He led her down to a copse of eucalyptus, where they threaded their way between the trees until a broken wall blocked the path. Smith found an opening into the ruins of a small mosque. An arch led from there to a roofless room whose pink stone walls were intricately carved and were shaded by a eucalyptus tree growing in the middle. On the ground were the low, narrow tombs of a Merinide Sultan and his wife.

Twisting through more ruins, where trees had pushed between walls, they were followed by the sun, moving quickly at a low angle, changing the shadows. Smith turned to make certain that she was all right and saw that the look of judgment had gone from her eyes, though they were still confused.

They passed a small, shaded pool, carved out of the rock valley. Sterile women came there to wade in the water, teeming with eels, because it was claimed to be capable of miracles. Beyond that was another ruined mosque, its minaret intact, with a stork's nest on top. At the base were two rows of narrow chambers, like monk's cells. Smith sat down outside them, on a marble mosaic in the sun.

"The people who lived in those cells read the Koran out loud every day and night for anyone who was buried here."

"This is beautiful," Cosima said, twisting around. "But if you're dead, you're dead."

Smith shrugged his agreement. "I'm not a great believer in man-induced immortality—mummies, large tombs, food or flowers on top of the grave. Still, I wouldn't be unhappy to know they'd read to me for ever."

"But Anthony!" She swung around again with an arm out. "No one is reading. Eternity isn't an extra hundred years."

"I enjoy my illusions. Here." He pulled two brioche and small oranges out of the pockets of his jacket. "If you won't read, let's at least eat."

She settled down in the sun beside him, leaning against his back.

It was only ten in the morning when he stopped outside the hotel. She asked him if he would like to come upstairs and he followed shyly.

In the room, standing near the open balcony doors, he kissed her and then stopped. She pulled off his sweater and began unbuttoning his shirt, which made him laugh and he embraced her again, saying, "Come and lie down."

The women Smith knew undressed themselves, so it was a long time since he had uncovered a woman, and his hands tasted the skin he discovered as if eating of that dish for the first time. When she was naked, he stood up to pull off his own clothes.

She watched him as he did it, making him blush. Although his face was smooth, he had a hairy chest and stomach. It wasn't important, but she liked hairless men. His belly pushed out below his ribs, like an over-ripe peapod, and melted into a layer of excess flesh which made her smile; but Smith didn't notice. While he was concentrating on himself, superficial thoughts kept floating through her mind. He was circumcised and she preferred uncircumcised men, a taste wasted on a woman married to an Anglo-Saxon. Uncircumcised, the penis looked like a friendly, wizened old man.

Smith finished dropping his clothes on the floor and walked quickly back to the bed. Cosima put an arm out to caress him, but in his excitement he hardly seemed to notice. His hand made quick passes over her breasts and abdomen, formal motions that he couldn't drop, even in extremis—obligatory preliminaries laid down by some church to precede communion. She responded imaginatively, in the hope of setting him off course. When that had no effect, she thought of stopping him and making him do it her way, but his style was clearly a habit, in place for a good fifteen years. She wasn't, by nature, a prophet in search of souls to convert. People were what they were. She thought of getting up, but that would mean explanations and she abruptly decided it really wasn't that important.

His hand moved inquisitively over her sex, to see if it was wet enough for entry. Cosima's body had not yet had time to retract from anticipated pleasure to reality, so Smith slid her legs open and pushed in. Her indifference turned to resentment. She hadn't expected passion. She hardly knew what she had expected; perhaps just the warmth of a friendly body and the minimum of technical competence. He pumped away, breathing heavily, and then came, in a little under two minutes.

Shortly afterwards Smith rolled off. He looked at her and smiled. She smiled back and a feeling of sympathy went through her.

He burst out, "Why did you marry Martin, after ignoring him for two years at McGill?"

It was the last question Cosima expected. "I loved him. When I came back to New York, I got caught up with a man absorbed in his own insecurity, and for the first time in my life I lost my confidence. That went on for a year, until I began working on my architect's degree. Then Martin appeared. I think I already loved him, but by then I knew how to recognize it. In a city of people who don't listen, he knew how."

"I suppose I should feel some guilt."

She looked at him, surprised. "Why? Now, don't exaggerate your importance, Anthony."

He suggested they drive to the coast for the night, before Laing returned on Friday morning, and she agreed, but without great enthusiasm. When they drove to Idrissi's house to pick up Smith's bag, she withdrew into a silent, friendly detachment which he was too happy to focus on.

Smith went upstairs, leaving her in the drawing room, where she caught a glimpse of the front page of the *Matin*. There was a photo of the King, on foot in a white djellabah, leading a white stallion with his son on its back. The empty room was disturbing, with is schizophrenic mixture of Moroccan and Italian taste. She walked out into the garden.

Here was what she loved, the side of architecture that had always drawn her—the setting of the whole, not the designing of buildings with floral appendages. She remembered being taken as a teenager to see Jefferson's University of Virginia and refusing to go inside. Instead, she had wandered through the grounds, awestruck by his weaving serpentine garden walls. The same emotion had come back when she saw her first Georgian garden—Stourhead in Wiltshire—and again at the Bagatelle, on the edge of Paris.

Around Idrissi's house, files of trees symmetrically aligned stretched away for a hundred yards; then the pattern changed, to obscure the view. She walked aimlessly among them, not thinking of Smith, because that made her think of Laing and how little she had understood. The foot-long, cream-coloured hanging bell flowers of the belladonna trees secreted their pungent sweetness.

She caught sight of Kenza Idrissi, stretched out on cushions under the trees, writing. Kenza looked up and beckoned to her.

"Come and sit down."

"I don't want to interrupt you."

"No. This is nothing. I'm trying to write a paper for a French medical journal. Mental exercise really. I don't suppose they'll take it. We have interesting local variations on hepatitis."

"Sayed hasn't mentioned that."

"I'm sure," Kenza smiled. "Anthony has left you alone for a moment." It was a friendly comment. "Tell me what you think of him." Before she could say anything, Kenza waved towards the house. "He is one of ours, not one of yours."

"I don't know what I think," Cosima said dropping onto a cushion. "I think he isn't very real."

"A figment of his own imagination. Why not? I've been to your country once and I found your men scarcely more real. They were regrouping from fear of women into co-operative poses that were more like tactical retreats. I was an expert after two weeks."

"And what do you think of him?"

Kenza sat up and closed her notebook. "Love doesn't exist for women here—only marriage. Our men believe their imaginations so fervently that they can't see us coming. We don't have your middle-class family to stop us or your managerial class. Our own families are so far removed from the future that there's no middle ground on which they can defend themselves."

"Do you really believe that?" Cosima was wondering to herself why she was there. Why she hadn't simply gone home to New York. She felt suddenly like a feather being buffeted aimlessly in the wind of Laing and Smith's ambitions. What was it she had told Kenza a few days before; that she had frittered away the advance that her father had given her. It wasn't that she had done nothing, but she had refused to be panicked or driven and had gone about her life in a calm way.

Kenza was laughing at her question. "Sometimes." Then she asked, "What is Anthony to you?"

"Just another man, I suppose."

"An interesting man," Kenza laughed. "Give him his due."

"At least."

"I wonder what the American right to variety gives you." She stopped Cosima from interrupting. "I'm not criticizing. Just curious."

"I suppose it fills our time in different ways."

"Variety isn't a tradition for women here. But one day, I think our men will wake up and find we hold the reins of power. And they won't know how it happened."

"If you stay calm when surrounded by driven people, you are lost."

"That makes it sound wrong."

Cosima stood up. "I was talking to myself. What time does today's plane leave for New York?"

When Smith came out, Kenza told him that her own driver had taken Cosima to the hotel and on to the airport. He blushed with embarrassment. Kenza put out her hand to make him sit down beside her.

"She said I was to tell you that she enjoyed herself."

But he turned away and went inside, where he sat fidgeting in the drawing room. A sense of failure settled over him. A sense of creased, old clothes. Discarded. To be put on again. Emptiness. What had he expected? Smith repeated that phrase to himself. What had he expected? What right had he to expect . . . but the cloud clung tight to him.

He got up, poured himself a half tumbler of brandy and didn't bother to add soda. He turned on the radio to create sound.

The King was still in Marrakesh. That morning he was reviewing the new Al Arak Column as it left for the Sahara—the last event in the celebration of the Prince's circumcision. "There were hundreds of thousands of people lining the streets," the announcer said. "The King was in his uniform of Commander in Chief. Surrounded by the Princes, the senior officers and the entire government, he addressed the Column." Smith listened without hearing.

"The Prophet—the peace and grace of God be on Him—said that love of country flows from faith . . ."

THIRTY-EIGHT

"What's the problem?"

"The number is ringing right now. If you hang up, Mr. Laing, I'll pass it to you."

The offices at Western-Oriental came in four sizes, beginning at nine feet by fifteen. Martin Laing sat, restless, in his office of the second size, at his desk of the third category on Friday morning, 25 July.

He hung up. His phone rang and he picked it up again. There was a distant hum, followed by the click of someone lifting the receiver. Benmansour had said it was his private line.

"Colonel Benmansour? This is Martin Laing. I have a problem about coming back."

"What about our agreement?" The line was reasonably clear.

"No problem. We're agreed. The point is, I have no reason to come back to Rabat. My wife returned on her own yesterday."

That Benmansour knew. He also knew about the time she'd spent with Smith and, with a minimum of supposition, he knew what had happened between them. Benmansour put that aside and concentrated on whom he could trust in New York. Dr. Menet was the one who came to mind. Because his only interest was money, he was perfectly trustworthy if well paid. "I have a friend who will come to see you to make final arrangements."

"He must come soon," Laing said urgently.

"He will. We wouldn't want to miss our appointment." Benmansour, like Laing, hadn't much small talk and was about to hang up, but he ceded to the temptation to complicate Smith's life. "Your wife got back safely?"

"I told you that," Laing said impatiently.

"Yes. Well, we didn't see much of her after you left. Your friend Smith monopolized her time."

At first Laing couldn't understand what Benmansour was going on about and replied, "Good."

"I had no idea that he was such a close friend."

"What are you saying?"

"Nothing. Nothing. We were just glad to know that she was having a good time."

Laing's head began to feel light. He forced himself to ask, "Are you trying to tell me something?"

"I'm saying we're all of age, Mr. Laing. Good-bye." And he hung up.

Laing tried to clear his thoughts but found them swimming into a disordered mess. What had the man meant? That Smith had made a pass at Cosima? Was that it? Perhaps that explained why she'd come dashing home. The thought that something more had happened went once through his mind and he rejected it. But even that Smith would try, he couldn't believe. They knew each other too well. He sought another explanation and remembered that Benmansour and Smith didn't get on. Perhaps that was at the bottom of it. Laing's mind cleared and he tried to focus on what to do next.

Smith was flying to London on Sunday, before going on to join the *Sophie*. Laing would have to phone him, tell him what had happened and instruct him to send the message from the boat to the Moroccans. Benmansour's words came back. If they were true, Smith couldn't be trusted. In any case, he might not agree to send the message. He might well warn Lamine off. Laing thought of the Captain, but it was too late to instruct him properly and too risky to rely on a man who was little more than a criminal. No, the only way to eliminate every risk was to go on the boat himself. It was the last thing Laing wanted to do, so he went through all the arguments again, only to end up with the same conclusion.

He spent the weekend trying to find a way to ask Cosima what had happened, but each time he gave her an opening, she closed it. It was a dance of the blind, because she was avoiding any mention of Smith out of embarrassment, and from fear that it would lead to her asking why Laing had lied to her and dragged her to Morocco. The atmosphere was so difficult that he was relieved on Monday morning to leave for his office.

The first thing he did was telephone Smith to ask when and where he would be joining the *Sophie*. Smith was surprised by the question.

"What's the panic, Martin?"

"No panic."

"Could have fooled me," Smith insisted.

"Nothing really. I was thinking of coming along for the ride."

"Is that right?" Smith's voice was dried of any emotion. "Listen, Martin, I keep hearing that you're doing a deal with Benmansour." There was silence on the other end of the line. "What's up?"

Laing still hesitated, then started to laugh. "Not exactly a deal. They changed their mind about the weapons and wanted to buy some."

"So?"

"So I said it was too late, but they insisted. I wondered if they hadn't heard something and mightn't get ugly. I mean, they had worked out where the arms came from, so I said I'd go home and check. It seemed to me that absence was the safest way to halt all conversation. I've sent them a message that it is definitely too late."

"But you didn't tell me."

"It had nothing to do with you." When there was no reply

from Smith, Laing became more aggressive. "That's the way I chose to play it and it seems to have worked. I've heard nothing more from them. Have you got a problem, Anthony?"

"No," Smith's voice had relaxed, "but it's too late to join the *Sophie*. She left her last port three days ago."

"What do you mean?"

"Don't worry. I'm going by land."

"But Anthony, it could dock anywhere."

"It is not going into port under any circumstances. I've changed my mind. We can't risk an inspection. Most of these African police love to stick their noses in, looking for an excuse to steal cargo or charge you a transit tax."

"What do you mean, you're going by land?" Smith's words had only just sunk in.

"To spend time with an old friend. I spoke to Lamine last night. When we were all in Algiers, he asked me if I'd like a drive across the desert. Apparently it takes a week and is perfectly safe."

Laing fell silent, then added lamely, "The point is, I wanted to be there."

Smith was still surprised by his interest. "Martin, you sound as if you're having an affair with *Jane's Fighting Ships*. Forget it. You are paying me to make everything happen and everything will happen." There was silence on the line. "I'm flying to Algiers in three days. The 31st. Until then, you can get me here."

Laing put down the phone and sat rooted to his chair. He didn't move until his secretary came in to say that a man was on the line, insisting that his call was expected, but wouldn't give his name. Laing looked at his watch and realized that an hour had gone by since Smith had hung up. He picked up the receiver. It was Benmansour's friend, who wanted to come in the next half hour.

Dr. Menet wasn't disappointed by the confusion on Laing's face. In fact, it was so great that he wondered what other advantage there was to be drawn, beyond earning his fee from Benmansour. When the secretary had gone out, he smiled graciously.

"Good day, Mr. X. I see you have done your deal after all."

Laing came back sharply, "What are you doing here?"

Menet sat down, uninvited, and retained his mellow tone. "Calm yourself, Mr. Laing. I am Colonel Benmansour's friend, so it appears we shall work together after all."

Laing felt a last row of bars come crashing down to cage him in. Menet was hardly bothering to disguise his confidence that the young man was in his hands, and the tentacles of blackmail stretched out across the room to bind them together. Laing's anger at everything that had gone wrong suddenly exploded.

"Gerten is dead."

The butterfly lids of Menet's eyes fluttered briefly, but the doctor turned his own surprise into innocent confusion. "Gerten?"

"Oh yes, Gerten. He mentioned you before the back of his head was shot off." Laing pressed forward. "There is no room in this deal for your seedy games, doctor. If I see one sign of you moving out of line . . ."

Menet found this very funny. "You can't threaten my life, Mr. Laing. I'm too old."

"I won't begin with your life. Your reputation is much easier. I don't think Benmansour would enjoy working with someone who can't be trusted. Or the other dealers. And your bank might find the whole thing awkward if details of your other life were to slip out. If none of that works, then we'll arrange for you to become silent on a long-term basis."

"Enough." Menet withdrew deeper into his cocoon of civility. "We must try to be kind to each other."

Laing took that to be acceptance of a truce, at least until Menet saw another opening. He unlocked a desk drawer and brought out a map of the Sahara, conscious that there was now little other choice.

He pointed out where the ship would land and gave Menet the date. Friday, 8 August. They agreed that the *Sophie* would send a one-word signal—"Cosmos." The message would be repeated. The Polisario could be told it was for Smith's employers—a mission accomplished signal.

In the middle of the day, Laing went home to bed in a deep depression. He waited there until well into the evening, scarcely noticing that Cosima hadn't appeared. She had spent much of the weekend and of that day trying to decide what to do. By the time she made up her mind, the day was almost over. She went across to the office of her senior partner, a highly respected man in his early fifties who sometimes behaved as if he were seventy, and asked to see him.

When Cosima appeared in the doorway, he came slowly to meet her and drew her over to a Bauhaus wooden chair, whose comfort was in inverse ratio to how much he loved it. She waited until he was comfortably seated on his side of the desk, then said she thought she'd resign.

He was taken aback and looked at her, Cosima thought, as if she were Lady Macbeth about to stab him to death. And what was the matter with Lady Macbeth? She was a smart woman who just didn't know how to use her power. The partner's expression turned to dismay, then the machine recovered and he became solicitous, imitating wounded dignity.

"But why? That's what I must know. Cosima, I had no idea."

She didn't tell him why, apart from the fact that they weren't giving her real work. After all, it was buildings built that counted. Architects, drawings, words—they were all filler. She also mentioned that she had another offer, which wasn't true, but she could have made it true by looking.

In the end, he asked her to do nothing for a few days. She came home wanting to tell Laing all about it; but when she saw him turned in on himself, scarcely able to talk, she told him nothing.

The next morning, Laing stayed in bed, saying he wasn't feeling well. In fact, he had slipped into a state of inertia that left him unable to move, and at the end of the day he was still there. On Wednesday Cosima suggested getting a doctor, but he refused and turned his back on her. It was only that afternoon that he managed to sit up and telephone London. He told Smith that he was flying to Algiers that evening.

"Is something the matter, Martin?"

"Nothing's the matter. I want to talk to you."

"Well, talk."

"No. I want to see you, Anthony. Everything is fine."

Smith couldn't understand. Laing was usually in perfect control of himself. He appeared to be suffering from nerves.

Laing pulled himself out of bed and went into Western-Oriental to see Moffett. He found the older man more fragile than he remembered, but just as determined to see the deal through. In fact, Moffett had been spending even longer hours in his office, waiting with detached curiosity for the trembling to rise again from his gut. It was there, he knew, but it was waiting; as was Fell at the other end of the corridor, preparing the autumn campaign. Laing explained that he himself was going on the ship to ensure that nothing went wrong. While it wasn't true, it would explain his absence.

Moffett didn't like the idea, but was unwilling to say anything if Laing felt it was essential; so he told him to use his own best judgment. Laing said he would send a message—"Cosmos"—the moment they had completed the delivery. If Moffett wished, he could have that picked up by the radio unit the company kept in southern Spain to maintain contact with their tankers.

Laing went home to pack—for what, he still couldn't decide—and waited to say good-bye to Cosima. She was late again that evening, because the senior partner had called her in to offer her part of a hotel project in the country in Vermont. On the Bauhaus chair sat the partner who had been encouraged to make this sacrifice. He welcomed Cosima to the project with as much grace as he could muster and took her back to his office to explain what it involved.

She arrived at Amster Yard, happier than she had been in years, to find Laing in the hall with a bag, waiting for his taxi to the airport. He told her that he had to go away for a few days, although it might be longer, and Moffett could get hold of him if there was an emergency. He was so on edge that he hardly listened to her news. Each time his eyes met hers, an inner refrain blocked his hearing—Smith couldn't be trusted, but he had to be told, he had to be told. Cosima saw that he wasn't listening and stopped, all her anger of the last weeks coming back.

The taxi arrived. He tried to kiss her, but they were both upset. The kiss meant nothing. Their eyes didn't meet.

PART 5

THIRTY-NINE

The heat dropped a steel wall around them. Beyond the single strip of tarmac, sand stretched out of sight, shrinking all else into insignificance. Any irregularity on this surface was flattened by the weight of the sun on their eyes. Ahmed Mah led them from the plane, across the sand towards a row of canvas-hooded Land-Rovers that were held back by a line of small rocks.

Smith looked around and adjusted his eyes. He picked out circular walls of sand, piled up like child's castles along the perimeter of the runway. Inside each was a fighter plane. Beyond, he made out double rows of barbed wire, one rolled and the other four yards wide, stretched parallel to the ground, six inches off the sand.

Tindouf had always been the frontier town of warring nomads. Now it was an outpost of the Algerian military forces.

Ahmed Mah, Lamine's political assistant, had picked up Smith at the Algiers airport the day before. He had driven him to the Villa Nasser, along streets sullen with a population dragging its way through the long Ramadan Lent. Mah appeared to have lost another tooth since Smith had first met him a month before. He was still awkward and formal. Smith had asked about Abdullah Lamine—only to be told that he was in the South. As for Laing, he had already arrived.

They were woken in darkness the next morning, Friday, 1 August. The Boeing from Algiers to Tindouf left with the dawn, carrying them two hours south to a frontier town, Béchar. As the plane began a slow, even descent across nothingness, they saw the desert stretching out below, covered in pale green tumbleweed. Caught in the low rays of the sun, it looked like sea foam framed against the shoreline of the mountains that shot up brusquely less than a hundred miles away. On the other side of the Atlas Range was Morocco. Somewhere in the middle was their contested border. In the morning mist, the mountains took on the colours of classical Chinese painting. Béchar itself, a tiny, rectangular imposition of man, sat surrounded by the flat desert.

When the plane took off again, the atmosphere aboard changed. Tindouf was in the war zone. It was closed to civilian passengers, meaning that only people with a reason—and a pass—were going there. Apart from Smith and Laing, most of the passengers were Algerian soldiers or civil servants, doing penance at the end of the world for some failure or for lack of influence. The remaining few were friends of Ahmed Mah—people connected with the Polisario—who stood in the aisle talking as if they were already home.

The mountains disappeared into the distance, while the carpet of sand remained below throughout the second leg of the journey. Without any change in this emptiness, the plane began its landing approach three hours later. There was nothing to be seen from the window except the isolated runway off to one side in the distance. Tindouf was hidden in a depression, where it huddled over the springs of water that gave it life.

They stepped out of the plane at ten a.m. Only ten, Smith thought, and twisted his straw hat to one side in search of greater protection.

Mah led the two men to the row of Land-Rovers and left them standing there without cover while he walked off to greet the people who had been waiting for the plane to arrive. Each of them embraced him and went through a litany of compliments, their khaki and blue robes hanging limp in the still air.

Smith and Laing stood awkwardly, melting in the sun, half turned away from each other. They hadn't really spoken since the day before, except in a disjointed, superficial way. On arrival Laing had said that he was coming along because, in the end, Western-Oriental had ordered him to. The strained expression on his face testified to the confusion he felt and added to Smith's own doubts. Having at first believed Laing's story about Benmansour, he had now begun to wonder whether it was the whole truth.

Only when Mah had said a few words to everyone did he come back to point out a light brown Land-Rover and suggest that they get in, under cover. In the meantime, the temperature had risen five degrees.

The driver was in his early twenties—a thin man, all bone structure and sinew. Mah introduced him as Brahim. He spoke Arabic and Spanish, in neither of which Smith was particularly competent.

The four of them squeezed into the front of the Land-Rover, on Brahim's insistence, and set off down the thin, paved road that cut south across the sand towards Tindouf town. Smith stared at Brahim beside him. He held himself upright, like a dancer, except that he did it unconsciously. His face was dominated by high cheekbones and long white teeth pushed forward, with a moustache and neat goatee as decoration.

This, plus his khaki pantaloons and loose khaki robe, made him a *R'gibat*, a member of the chief fighting tribe of the region. For centuries their raiding parties had materialized out of the desert to dominate the other tribes—that is, until the Spanish came. The only flaw, in Brahim's image, was the pair of zip-up black leather boots he wore.

Smith carefully asked if he were *R'gibat*, but Mah curtly cut off any answer.

"There are no longer any tribes here. None of us have any tribes! We are all Saharouis."

Smith looked at Mah's squat, undistinguished figure. It wasn't surprising that he preferred to pass over the question. His family must have been one of those who worked to pay the *R'gibat* a protection fee, so that the raiding parties would pass their village by.

The Land-Rover came around a bend and dipped down a hill into Tindouf. The old *R'gibat* market town had been rebuilt by the French and their Algerian imitators into a model colonial provincial seat. A miniature main boulevard, dry and dusty, cut through the centre. Tired trees struggled up the middle. Neat, soulless buildings lay on either side. Their only redeeming feature was that they were built from the reddish earth of the valley.

Two minutes later the Land-Rover climbed out of the far side of the town past a radar installation on a bluff and, beside it, a power station. Smith was left with an impression of people in uniform.

Tindouf was the main town contested by the Moroccans—stolen from them, they said, by the colonial divisions. The little town was far more than it appeared. It was the gate to the

Sahara and the old caravan routes south. It was also the key to any invasion of or by Morocco; for there, like slices of a pie, Algeria, Morocco, Mauritania and the old Spanish Sahara faced one another.

The Spanish Sahara, now Southern Morocco on paper at least, shared a border with Algeria for a hundred miles. The Polisario refugees sat safe on the Algerian side of this border. Their guerillas used it as a line protecting a sanctuary where they could rest and train before returning to the other side to fight.

Five miles beyond the town, the paved road ended and Brahim swerved onto a rough track.

"There will be no more roads," Mah said, meaning, now you will begin to suffer.

Smith closed his eyes and his mind to the growing heat as the Land-Rover heaved over the rock-strewn sand. With each bump, he understood better why they were all squeezed into the front. They had become a large sponge, absorbing one another's shocks; while sitting alone in splendour in the back they would have been thrown all over the machine.

A knot of Algerian soldiers appeared out of a small tent ahead and waved their machine-guns. Mah gestured at the two Americans and explained something, of which Smith could make out only the words Red Cross. He whispered their new profession to Laing.

"Whatever makes them happy," Laing replied. He was dealing with his own state of discomfort by minimizing his movements. He would have agreed to anything.

After another mile they came to a second knot of armed men, this time dressed in khaki robes, like Brahim, a cloth wound around their heads and across their faces as protection from the sun. They greeted Ahmed Mah with familiarity, repeating their long litany.

"You will see no more Algerians," Mah said with satisfaction when the Land-Rover set off again. "Only Saharouis."

"Do you mean, we are no longer in Algeria?" Laing asked stiffly from beneath his hat.

"No." Mah conceded. "We have not crossed the line."

Laing grunted and said no more. The Land-Rover bumped over the stony ground for another hour in a seemingly aimless path across the low hills, while the heat rose around the silence of the four men. When they stopped moving, Smith opened his eyes. They were in a small depression, beside a white-washed hut with a tin roof.

"We will wait here for the temperature to pass," Mah said.

They got out of the Land-Rover. Laing pulled his light bag from the back and passed another to Smith, who groaned when he noticed the tin roof. In the shade of the entrance, there was a thermometer, curiously out of place. It read one hundred and fifteen degrees and the time was eleven-thirty.

Inside, the air was still cool. They collapsed on foam rubber mats laid on top of blankets, beneath which was the sand. Mah disappeared into the other room and a man, black rather than Arab, in a simple blue robe, came out carrying cups filled with water. Laing drank all of the sweet well water and lay down with his eyes closed. Brahim stayed with them, spreading his head cloth over his face to shut out the light and occasional flies. The tin roof gradually relayed the outside heat until Smith found he could not sleep and pulled out a book to read. When he saw Laing shifting, bored and uncomfortable, Smith produced another book and threw it over to him. Laing smiled shyly in thanks.

An hour later a blanket hanging over an opening in the wall was pulled back to reveal the other room, where a small group of men sat on the floor, rifles by their side. Mah came through with tea on a tray, followed by the black, who was carrying two mixing bowls and pieces of flat bread.

"Goat," Mah said.

One bowl contained meat and the other innards. The black crouched against the wall, waiting to see if they enjoyed his food; so Smith swung onto his knees and picked at the innards.

"Let me give you an amateur's advice," he said to Laing. "These people live on protein and starch—meat, sugar, fat, bread, milk. In this heat, our system wants the exact opposite—salads, light things; so I'd treat this little holiday like Lent." Smith patted his stomach. "Abstinence can only do me good. Drink the sweet tea. Eat the crust of the bread. Nibble at the old goat and camel or it will destroy your insides. Don't touch the fat. The goat and camel milk is delicious, but in this heat it will curdle in your stomach."

"I always take the advice of friends," Laing said automatically, hiding his resentment. He was able to talk, now that they were out of the sun.

He tore away the bread crust to dip in the sauce. It was greasy, but good. He raised his empty water cup towards the black, who spoke only Arabic, but Smith put out a hand to stop him.

"And drink as little as possible. The more you drink, the more you sweat. The more you sweat, the more salt you lose. A cup of water that tastes cool in your mouth will sit in your stomach until it begins to boil. The desert is extreme and minimal. The way to survive is to minimize intake, minimize movement and save yourself for the few seconds when you have to deal with the extremes. What do you say, Mr. Mah?" He thought regretfully of the cognac he had not brought in order not to be tempted.

Mah kept shovelling pieces of meat into his mouth with a piece of bread. "These are the problems of sedentary people."

Smith looked at him critically. "How often does a political counsellor like you get out of the Villa Nasser and into the desert?"

"I am always here."

"Good," Smith said. "Then you can find us a head cloth."

Mah looked doubtful.

"An *arrza*. Two of them and extra long. These hats," he said to Laing, "are useless. The answer is to cover everything."

He ate a bit of bread and went outside to see if it was cooler on the shady side of the building. Thanks to a small breeze, it was marginally better. He dropped a blanket there and tried to sleep.

FORTY

At six-thirty the temperature was down twenty degrees, to one hundred and seventeen. Although the shadows from the low sun were long, the sand and rocks had absorbed the heat and now prolonged the agony. At seven, Mah came outside to wake Smith. If they waited much longer, it would be dark before they arrived.

Brahim drove up the other side of the depression and they began bumping their way over the uneven hills. This time, Smith kept his eyes open. The colours of the desert came out as the sun receded and in the half light the sand and rocks were awash with pale shades that changed with the Land-Rover's passage like the adagio of a symphony.

Two hours later, they came over a final hill and a sea of tents lay in the plain below them, lit by oil lamps and fires.

"My God," Laing said, "how many are there?"

"Fifteen thousand," Mah announced.

Smith snorted, "Come off it."

Rather than reply, Mah said, in a justifying tone, "This is only one of our camps. There are two more. The people from the north of our Sahara, from Smara and El Aayun, camp here."

Brahim drove through herds of goats searching for food around the perimeter, which the refugees used as a latrine and dump. Their habits came from travelling in small groups. Now that they stayed in large permanent camps, they relied on the heat to shrivel everything dry within hours and on the desert to swallow the garbage as best it could.

There was just enough space for the Land-Rover to manoeuvre through the irregular maze of tents. Crowds of children appeared and disappeared. Women, wrapped in layers of cotton, their faces uncovered, watched them go by. Deep inside the labyrinth, they came to a halt on a rise and Mah pointed towards a large tent made of rough, black cloth.

The Wali of El Aayun, equivalent to a provincial governor, camped there. He was on a tour. Smith led the way, bending to enter the tent, which was lined inside with Indian cotton. The sand was covered by rugs.

A boy came in with tea and they lay down to wait. Much later, the Wali appeared, a tall figure in his thirties, wearing a blue robe over an English string vest. With him were a crowd of men. Some were young politicos. Others were tribal leaders, older and more formal in their manner. They left their sandals at the entrance and sat on either side of the Wali, in an order of precedence self-evident to themselves. Unveiled women drifted in behind them and sat in a row, on the open side of the tent. After a time of polite conversation, one of the old men asked something in classical Arabic, which the Wali translated for Smith.

"What do they say in the United States about our war?"

Smith, with nothing to sell, answered frankly, "They don't know about it. The few who do, support Morocco, because Morocco is our ally."

While the Wali translated this reply, women brought lamps into the tent, throwing de la Tour shadows onto faces which were paintings in high relief even by daylight. Someone offered Smith a cigarette. He refused, instead pulling a cigar out of his jacket.

Conversation died away when the translation was finished. The elder flicked his camelhair fly swat. He was dressed in white and lay on his side, the foot of one leg resting on the knee of the other. He spoke with a lilting clarity of tone and Mah translated.

"All we seek is freedom in our own land. The opinions of others are of distant interest."

The elder pointed his fly swat towards the entrance and asked a question. Food arrived moments later, on large circular metal trays around which they gathered in groups while a woman broke hot, flat rounds of bread into pieces that she dropped in front of each person. The first wave of trays held a thick stew of lukewarm goat fat, in which Laing dipped his bread. This was followed by rare goat meat on the bone, which he nibbled.

He listened as the conversation slipped from politics to general philosophy. Numbers and time, the constraints of specific argument, played no part in the minds of those who spoke, and though he tried, Laing couldn't concentrate on what sounded more like an elaborate stylized performance than a conversation.

But Smith appeared to enjoy himself. He was continually stopping Mah, because he thought his translation ran roughshod over the small classical vocabulary the others used, and making him re-translate. Smith explained to Laing that, with such a concise language, the phrases were all known, so that any alteration in a detail was a sign of a disagreement or of changing times. Laing rested his eyes on Smith—who was lost in arguing some obscure point, the complications of the outer world far away—and tried to dispel the suspicions and doubts that obscured his feelings. Concentrate as he might, Laing could not focus on his friend.

Half glasses of tea were poured endlessly and Laing's mind drifted away. He gazed at the women, wrapped in layers of cotton. The darker-skinned were in deep red, the lighter in mixtures of black, green and pale blue. They were framed in the opening, against a luminous black sky, and he found himself staring, unable to imagine them other than beautiful. When they saw his eyes, they turned away, whispering to one another.

Breezes blew through the tent. They were captured, as in a sailing boat, by small boys who lowered and raised various wall panels at the hint of a change in their strength or direction. Laing lay back against a cushion and fell to dreaming. The scales of reality slipped away.

It was eleven before they all disappeared, including the Wali. Women came in and folded blankets into beds, placing candles with matches beside each. Laing did not remember falling asleep, only Smith telling him to sleep naked between the blankets. Breezes blowing across his face carried the temperature down to eighty-five degrees.

FORTY-ONE

His eyes opened, blinded by a light shining inches away. The light moved off Laing's face towards Smith, leaving him in darkness. Someone lit an oil lamp. He made out Ahmed Mah, crouched over them, dressed in olive green fatigues, a rifle over his shoulder.

"We're going," Mah said. "Get ready."

Laing looked at his watch. It was two a.m. The air was hot and heavy and the tent heaved with wind. Through the one open panel, he saw the night was not clear

He pulled on two cotton shirts, baggy, cotton trousers and the Chinese, cotton slippers Smith had given him. A pair of high, canvas desert boots were tied to the handle of his bag.

The boots were for an emergency, but they hoped not to walk anywhere.

Outside, the Land-Rover's headlights penetrated only a few yards through the sand-laden winds. Brahim sat behind the wheel, wearing goggles, the rest of his head hidden by a white *arrza* wrapped around to cover his nose and mouth. The machine had been stripped down. The canvas roof, the windshield and side windows were gone. Even the back seat was gone. In its place were two drums; one was filled with water, the other with fuel.

The three men piled into the front seat beside Brahim. They tried to cover their faces with their *arrzas* as the Land-Rover set out slowly through the camp, speeding up when they reached the open hills. Mah placed his rifle upright beside Brahim's, in the slot directly behind them. Laing could not forget. Whenever they hit a bad bump, the muzzle brushed against his skull.

"Pray for the safety catches," Smith shouted. He was still trying to wrap his *arrza* in place. Each time he thought it was done, the wind blew it off and his nose was filled with sand. Finally, he managed to wrap it from the top of his head down over his eyes, nose and mouth, fixing it around his neck. Leaning close to Laing, to shout above the wind, he looked like a mummy.

"As we're not going to see anything, might as well be comfortable."

Laing had done the same, stretching the cotton tight so that it wouldn't blow off. He left slight cracks for his eyes. After trying to peer through the hot sandstorm for a short time, his eyes were stung; so he gave up and pulled the cloth down, closing his lids in resignation before the hollow sound of the wind.

From within this blindness, his imagination magnified the stones over which they lurched into boulders. He began anticipating them, suffering twice for each pitch of the machine. Eventually he fell into a fitful sleep, but his eyes jerked half open when they swerved or bumped. Seeing a misty light through the cotton, he would open a slit over his eyes. The same opaque headlight would be there, outlining the rock and sand directly before them, rising and descending to what aim he could only guess.

Smith sat beside Brahim, his arms grasped around Laing's neck. Laing himself had an arm locked around Smith's thigh. Mah, on the outside, had one arm stretched around both of them, the other protecting his body from the metal of the door.

At one point Laing awoke to hear Smith shouting at Mah, "Are we across the line?"

"Of course," Mah shouted back.

Later, he dimly remembered being woken by a scream. He saw the door open, with Mah half out, swearing. Laing pulled him, by his neck, back into his seat.

Through all this, Brahim made no sound. His eyes were fixed to the forward limits of the headlights and somehow he was able to find his way, using obscure landmarks and natural sense. Shortly after three-thirty, they stopped. Over the roar of blowing sand, Mah shouted at the two Americans to get out.

"What do you mean, get out?" Smith shouted back.

"We have to pick up our escort. Outsiders aren't allowed to see where the camp is."

"That's ridiculous!" Smith waved at the darkness. "We don't even know where we are. We can't see more than two feet."

"You must wait here. Those are my orders." Mah opened the door for them and waited until they made up their minds to get out. He handed them a blanket and shouted, "Lie down."

Within seconds, the Land-Rover had disappeared into the winds. They cleared some rocks away and lay down, back to back, with the blanket pulled over them. They were silent for a short time, then Laing twisted his head and shouted.

"My God, what are we doing here?"

"I'm getting paid," Smith shouted back. "What about you?"

"Old times' sake, I guess."

"No greater love. Is that it, Martin?"

Laing didn't answer at first. "How the hell is Mah going to find us?" he shouted.

"Well, if he can't, he's lost himself, so what difference does it make?"

Laing started laughing, then abruptly fell asleep and Smith did the same. The warm wind, added to their exhaustion, made it impossible to stay awake. The next thing Laing heard was Smith shouting in panic as he stumbled to his feet. The Land-Rover shone at them through the sand-filled air like a monster on a dark and stormy sea, while over the wind they could hear Mah laughing.

When they were back in their seats, Smith said to Laing, "I don't know what I thought. There was the light in the storm. I didn't know where I was. I thought I was having a nightmare." He wrapped his *arrza* tight around his head and disappeared into a silence which might have been sleep.

Crouched in the back of the Land-Rover were three guerillas who had offered no greeting. Everyone was concentrating on his own comfort. They had stuck their rifles down the crack behind the seat, so there were now five muzzles permanently pressed against Laing's head.

The dawn came late in the desert. They unwrapped their *arrzas* to find Brahim still driving and apparently oblivious to the passage of time. The wind was gone. Sandwiched together, they had eventually chased the rocks from their consciousness and now they discovered that, somewhere behind, the rough surface had disappeared. In the faint, warm light, rising on their backs from the east, they could make out an undulating expanse of hard sand with occasional stunted leafless thorn trees.

Laing tried to swallow. He found his throat not only parched but constricted. He managed to ask for water and Mah passed him a canvas-covered tin, the size of a pail, with a small screw top. Putting his tongue against the top to protect his teeth against a sudden bump, he took a swallow and immediately felt the cool liquid loosen the constriction. He looked around with greater interest. Brahim had taken off his goggles and unwound part of his *arrza*. He turned his head, greeting Laing with a warm smile of complicity and let go of the wheel long enough to take a quick taste of the water. They drove on this smooth surface for another two hours, when a small copse of bare thorn trees appeared on the horizon.

As they drew near, Laing could see Land-Rovers pulled in tight under each tree—so tight that the driver could not get out without being scratched. The sparse branches didn't offer much cover; at least, that was his impression. But Mah explained that, in the desert, the smallest shadow was like jungle when seen from the air. This leafless copse was a perfect defence.

Up against the largest of the trees, a wooden hut had been built. There were a row of sandals before the entrance and a dozen guerillas squeezed inside, talking and drinking tea.

"Some sort of road station, I imagine," Smith said.

He and Laing threaded their way in, through a low opening, to a chorus of greetings.

"*Salam alaikum*," the tea drinkers called out, meaning peace be with you.

"And with you," Mah replied.

Before he could finish, they shouted out, "*Yak labas*," no evil to you.

And he agreed, "No evil."

The ritual went on until Mah asked, "What is the news?"

Everyone in the hut was crouching beside his rifle, mostly Russian Kalashnikovs, which meant Algerian-supplied. There were also a few old French rifles and two American M16s, no doubt captured from the Moroccans. One Kalashnikov was being cleaned in a corner, its parts spread out on the owner's *arrza*.

The guerillas wanted to know who the foreigners were. Mah explained they were American and a chorus of voices asked what the United States thought about the war. This time, Smith gave a glib answer.

A young man, who seemed to be the innkeeper, was making tea on a tiny wood fire near the door. He passed half glasses to everyone. They were emptied in single gulps, before being gathered together, refilled with sweeter tea, and passed around again. They were refilled a second time, the tea sweeter still. In the group there was an old nomad wearing a shoulder bullet-belt, who said, by way of explanation, "We have a saying: the first cup of tea is bitter like life, the second is sweet like love and the third is cloying like death."

They were passed pieces of hot flat bread, followed by a large, metal bowl that was filled with ground roasted corn meal, sugar and cold water. As it moved around the hut, it was constantly stirred, to keep the corn meal suspended. Laing took two long swallows of the sweet, gritty liquid and felt his adrenalin begin to flow.

By the time they left, the heat was already making itself felt. They raced across the hard sands at fifty miles per hour, which would have been exhilarating had not the weight of the slowly baking air been pressing down upon them. Laing asked for the water can.

"We're not doing much hiding," Smith said to Mah.

"From whom?" he asked. "The Moroccans are locked up inside their towns. They would never dare to come out here, except in large numbers. In that case, we would see them first."

Towards eleven, the sand ended on the edge of a fault in the land and a twisted moonscape broke out below them. Brahim slowed his pace to pick a way down the rock face. In the sunlight, it shone black—moulded into one solid piece like rough cast iron. Long illuminated veins of red and occasionally green shot through its texture. The sand had been empty of people, but far from the heart of desolation into which they now descended. Heat poured into the valley, reverberating from side to side and pushing the temperature above one hundred and thirty in the shade, of which there was none.

Laing's *arrza* and shirt were cut through by the sun. He reached into his bag behind—a young guerilla was sitting on it—to take out a third cotton shirt. This he tied over his head and shoulders, but still could not escape the jagged-edged flame of the air.

When at last they climbed up onto another sand plateau, he felt he must get out of the Land-Rover—what for he didn't know. The moving, baking jelly roll had become unbearable. He asked for the water and took a long drink, which cooled his system enough to bring a hint of clairty into his mind.

The plateau of sand led into a wadi, a dry river bed, down which they raced with one common thought—to get out of the sun. At two, they were still driving. Laing had only maintained his consciousness by regular sips from the water can. He offered it to the others, but they refused. Smith had wrapped his *arrza* around his entire face, as he had in the sandstorm, and shut out the world.

At two-thirty, Brahim stopped on one side of the wadi and Mah asked them to get out. Smith opened a crack around his eyes to examine the emptiness.

"Why?"

Mah explained, as he had the night before, that they had come to a camp. Before taking them in, he had to find out which part they were allowed to see. There was a half-hearted argument, which ended with them crouched vainly under the one thorn bush in sight in search of a hint of shade. The sole result of the argument was that they forgot to take the water with them. When Laing realized this, he began to complain, then stopped and curled up on his side and lay still.

He had the sensation of being transparent, as if the sun could reach any part inside him and cook it to specific instructions. Quite separate from this pain, he felt a pounding within him that slowly focused on his stomach. He sensed it swelling. Someone, inside his belly, began to thump the stomach walls with methodical strokes, bringing Smith's warning about too much water back to his mind.

The only words they exchanged came from Smith, speaking towards the sand,

"Ahmed Mah is a prick."

The Land-Rover reappeared thirty minutes later. Smith had to help Laing to his feet and support him across the few yards of sand. They moved stiffly, awkwardly, as if they risked floating away, sucked up by the rays into some evaporating nirvana. A short drive brought them to a proliferation of thorn trees, where they could make out jeeps and trucks. The evenness of the sand was broken by the humps of covered dugouts. People emerged from them, like earth animals, into the empty landscape.

FORTY-TWO

The dugout had walls made of mortar shell cases. The roof was held up by small logs brought in from Tindouf—there wasn't a straight piece of wood to be found in the desert they had crossed—and sand had been piled on top.

Stooping to avoid the beams, Brahim spread their blankets on the sand floor and made Laing lie down. He covered him, then began building a fire inside, near the entrance, a low, almost square opening with a rough wooden hatch that could be propped shut. There were three other small openings, also with shutters.

Laing lay in agony, shivering and sweating, covering himself and uncovering himself. His eyes shifted about the room past rings of light, like haloes, surrounding the small openings, as the sun attempted to force its way in. He closed his eyes. Smith made him reopen them and shoved a half glass of sweet tea to his lips, forcing him to drink it.

The rest of the afternoon, he slept fitfully. From time to time he groaned and opened his eyes to catch a blurred silhouette of Mah and Smith eating or raising a glass of tea in a slow, even motion, as if draining a magical potion: a vision of calm from a distant world. Periodically, that vision disappeared and he saw Smith reading in a corner. At one point, he saw him shaving near the door. The only constant in these irrational moments of consciousness was Brahim sitting complacently against a wall. His feet were tucked under him and he picked his teeth with a thorn, in long graceful strokes.

Laing stopped shivering in the middle of the night and slept quietly. He retained only a vague memory of Brahim looming out of the darkness to cover him. Much later he felt an almost cool breeze move stealthily through the dugout. His nerves had returned to a state where he could recognize such sensations.

Laing woke to the sound of talking. He focused his eyes on Smith bent over a map, while Mah traced the path they had taken from the refugee camps—due west, until they hit the river bed, the Wadi Timel Lousq, then down the wadi to the camp. From there, it was scarcely a hundred miles north and west to Smara, one of the major towns controlled by the Moroccans. They had been following a path a hundred and fifty miles north of the Mauritanian border.

"The Moroccan minimum need is to hold Dakhla," Mah pointed out, "the southern capital on the coast. In the north they've got to protect this triangle of Smara, Bucraa, where the phosphate mines are, and El Aayun, the capital, where the phosphate port was built. There's a Krupp conveyor belt running sixty miles across the sand from the mine to El Aayun. If they could keep the belt moving, they could pay for the war with their exports."

"But?" Smith asked.

"But they can't, because we can shell the belt anywhere, any time. So they tried moving the phosphates out by convoy, but we mined the sand, every night. Then they gave up. There's only a military guard of five thousand left to protect the line—for the future—so we shell it regularly to keep them occupied."

"And where do we go now?"

"South-west towards Mauritania. I was supposed to deliver you to a place called Amgalla," he pointed it out, "on 3 August, that is, this morning. Thanks to your friend, we've lost a day."

"But we can still reach the coast in time?"

"If he doesn't do anything else wrong. We'll have to wait till evening now and skirt around the triangle of the three towns—the one place we risk running into a helicopter patrol." Mah looked up and saw Laing was awake. "*Yak labas*," he greeted him.

"And then?"

"After Amgalla, the Mauritanian border goes straight south and the full expanse of our country is before you. There are a hundred ways we could go, but I know our route only as far as Amgalla." A guerilla appeared in the opening to call Mah away.

Laing threw off his blanket and sat up, his clothes clinging to him with dried sweat.

"Did you dream of *Jane's Fighting Ships*?" Smith asked.

Laing laughed. "No, but I stink."

"I could have told you that from here."

"What time is it?" Laing peered towards the door.

"Seven. God bless the cool mornings. Come outside and we'll get you washed."

They climbed up through the opening into the inoffensive sunlight. Beside the water tank on the Land-Rover, Laing stripped off his clothing and stood shivering while Smith poured water over him. He pulled on his other trousers and washed his clothes, laying them out to dry on the sand, then he shaved carefully. In the small glass he could see the shadow of strain on his face. He put it down to the sun and turned away. Brahim gave him tea and bread, with a half empty bowl of corn meal water, before disappearing with the Land-Rover to refill the fuel and water tanks somewhere in the camp. Laing settled into his corner with something approaching calm.

They sat silent on the blankets as the heat rose around them. Had it not been for the memory of his suffering, this would have been annoying, but nothing more. By remaining very still, he managed to pretend he was floating in a vacuum, out of which he climbed every two hours to drink half a glass of tea.

In the afternoon, Laing felt an overwhelming desire to shit. Wrapping his *arrza* over his head, he climbed out into the sun to walk a discreet distance across the sand. The rays felt curiously friendly, like the first moments lying on a beach. It was hard to believe what they had done to him the day before. He looked around to see whether the dugout was far enough away, pulled down his trousers and crouched. Just as his insides began to work, something pressed on his neck and shoulders. The pressure grew and was suddenly unbearable.

He turned and saw no one. Nausea spread through him. He lurched to his feet, with nails being driven deep into his spine; and struggled back to the dugout. The sensation would not go away until he had been seated for ten minutes. Without thinking, he said to Smith, "I wish I knew what I was doing here."

Smith's eyes lifted from his book and moved across the mortar-case walls past a ledge piled with mortar shells. Brahim sat in the far corner, his Kalashnikov leaned against the wall beside him. Their cotton slippers and sandals lay at the edge of the blankets. Uncertainly, he looked at Laing and saw the strain of something held back. He hardly knew where to begin to help him get it out. He was conscious that over the last few years his friend had become less and less susceptible to any straightforward approach and more locked into a complicated logic that seemed to rule his life.

"If you're not here to enjoy yourself, you shouldn't be here."

Laing smiled indulgently. "A lark."

"That's right, a lark. Funny. That was why Lamine introduced me to Sayed. Said it would be a lark."

Laing stared with disbelief. "Lamine introduced you?"

"Don't look so shocked, Martin. We were friends in Paris. I was going to Morocco. He gave me an introduction and it worked out."

All of Laing's doubts about Smith returned. If the man was capable of playing close friends off against each other, he was capable of one more step. Why hadn't he told Smith about the Kader deal? It was stupid to have come out into the desert rather than tackle the problem straight on. Then he thought of Cosima and wondered whether that wasn't the real reason he had come.

"You know," Smith said, "this town, Smara, a hundred miles from here, was founded in the last century by a saint-cum-warrior called Ma el Ainin. He was in the great tradition of tribal leader and Marabout, sword in hand. He unified the tribes and outsmarted the Sultan in Fez, but because he was a nomad in a country of nomads, there was no city to be occupied. So he built Smara as his royal capital—a network of palaces and mosques in the middle of nowhere. Poor man. He reached his peak just as the French and the Spanish finally got off their arses and attacked, so he ended up fighting both of them long after the Moroccan Sultan had given up. He even managed to keep the French out of Southern Morocco and controlled Marrakesh. That was in 1910. Yesterday. Of course, it all ended in disaster. His little empire disappeared and the palace at Smara was abandoned and forgotten as if it had never existed.

"Then, in 1930, a twenty-six-year-old, bored, well-bred, Parisian, intellectual called Michel Vieuchange decided he would rediscover Smara. In a world bereft of adventures for the Burtons and Stanleys, he wanted to become the last hero, just as the twentieth century made them obsolete. He spent a year trying to get there. First dressed as a woman, to hide his race. Then by hiring *R'gibat* warriors to protect him. They betrayed him. Took his food and his money. Led him on wild-goose chases. Disappeared for two days before returning to find him panic-stricken and lost.

"Half dead, he finally made it, only to be chased away from the sacred sight by other nomads. Not for the eyes of infidels, you see. On his way back north, he died of dysentery and exposure. His diaries showed that to the last moment he wasn't sure why he was there. In the end, it was clear that he didn't want to be there. He didn't want to be a hero, after all. But it was too late."

"I have no desire to be a hero," Laing laughed.

"Oh, I know," Smith smiled back. "You're just trying to push your way up a few squares, maybe even up the ladder on some magical gridiron. And if you ever reach the top, you'll be president of a company you don't own and that nobody cares about; after which you'll be retired into comfortable oblivion."

"That's not so bad."

Smith shrugged with a smile. "What I want to do is live forever."

"And you're not likely to succeed."

"No. But at least I'm after the right thing. Anyway, it was just a story that came to mind. Not much has changed around here since Vieuchange struggled this far on foot and camel."

"I'm here to look after you, Anthony."

"God knows I need it," Smith said. He closed his book and curled up to rest.

FORTY-THREE

Brahim appeared in the entrance, waving at them to come out, "*Taala, taala.*"

They followed him into the sombre receding heat shortly before sunset. He pointed up the wadi, to the east. In the distance a soft, glistening wall advanced across the desert, rising from the ground to the heavens and lit by the sun, low in the west—a screen with magical colours projected onto it. They stood, mesmerized, as men appeared out of dugouts all around them and did the same.

"What is it?" Laing asked.

"*Alrait,*" Brahim incanted, moving his hand in a sweeping line from sky to earth. "*Alrait.*"

Ahmed Mah reappeared just as they felt a soft, cool breeze rise before them. The wall was less than a mile away and Brahim made them go down into the dugout, where he lit an oil lamp and wedged the shutters into place with pieces of wood. Gentle gusts of wind, filled with sand, began to force their way through the cracks around each shutter and grew until they reached gale force. The constricted air became suffocating. They took their blankets and stuffed them into the openings to block the cracks.

The tumult outside lasted half an hour, then died abruptly, leaving an eerie silence. Suddenly, something crashed onto the sand above them.

"*Alrait,*" Brahim said.

The crashing rolled on, like an artillery barrage, for another thirty minutes before tapering off into a light drumroll. Brahim pulled open the hatch and led them out into the rain that was still falling heavily, straight down. To the west, the sun hung inches above the desert, colouring the entire heaven a rich, luminous red. They pulled off their shirts and stretched out their hands, the water streaming off their bodies.

"*Jamil*," Brahim sang, "*jamil*."

"He says it's beautiful," Mah translated. "Nothing more."

"What more is there?" Smith replied to himself as he smelt the perfumed air between the raindrops and turned to go back inside.

Although the temperature had been lowered by the rain, it was warm enough to dry their clothes on their backs as they lay on the floor of the dugout, in a darkness broken by the oil lamp, waiting for Brahim to produce dinner. Laing had begun picking at the rice and goat meat when he heard shouting. Mah snatched up his Kalashnikov and crawled out. The two Americans followed cautiously.

The darkness blinded them but there was a dull roar on all sides. Mah moved off into the obscurity, then began to shout. Their eyes adjusted to the darkness and they suddenly realized that their mound was surrounded by rushing water. Laing deciphered the outlines of people standing on other mounds, shouting. He looked down. His feet were submerged.

They ran below into the dugout, grabbed their belongings, blankets and rifles, dashed back out and threw them into the Land-Rover. Its wheels were already a few inches deep in water.

Laing scrambled into the back after his load. He saw Smith hung over the hood, his feet on the front seat, holding onto two rifles, blankets and his own bag. The motor turned over. Laing looked behind. Water was flooding into the dugout. Brahim dropped his foot onto the accelerator and the machine plunged into the river, which was at least thirty yards wide. They raced straight down the middle, searching out higher ground. Each time Brahim swerved to one side or the other, the water smashed against the chassis and threatened to drown the engine.

The torrent swirled around the Land-Rover as if it were a bauble, racing ahead of them as Brahim pushed his foot to the floor, his eyes turning in a staccato searching for a way out. Laing suddenly realized that they were going to be drowned. The sound of the engine was lost in the roar of the river, beyond which there was total silence. They careened ahead, melding into the torrent itself.

Brahim abruptly swerved to the right. The water washed up over the sides like dark ink, battering Laing's face. He tried to turn away, but his eyes were held by the rush of the torrent and the sound of the machine losing momentum. The motor began to fail. Through a mist, he saw Smith crouching to leap towards the shore, then there was a crash. Laing was thrown onto his back. The earth rose sharply beneath them and they found themselves arched onto the dry bank.

The Land-Rover skidded up the steepest part of a sandhill to a plateau fifty feet above, where they found a crowd of men spreading out blankets. Rifles were piled on one. Belongings were being sorted on another in the light of oil lamps.

Laing noticed for the first time that Mah was wedged in the back beside him, balancing a tray of food in one hand and grasping a mortar shell in the other. The American began to laugh uncontrollably, which Mah took as an insult, making him drop the tray.

They clambered out, soaking and, for the first time, cold. On the maze of blankets, Laing opened his bag to find dry clothes and Brahim offered him an extra blanket to wrap around his shoulders. In the midst of the disorder, someone had already managed to produce tea. There was an atmosphere of general hilarity, which Brahim fed by declaring, grandly:

"I love this life. We are free to go where we want and do what we want. The only constant is killing Moroccans."

He would have continued but an officer had produced a transistor radio and tuned through the static until he found a news broadcast on the Moroccan French station. The voice of the announcer echoed over the hills in rich tones:

> "The day after tomorrow, Tuesday, 5 August, will be a glorious day in the history of Morocco. His Majesty the King will visit the Sahara for the first time since the people, under his sacred leadership, liberated and regained that beloved soil five years ago. Surrounded by the leaders of our country, he will fly to Dakhla, where we expect the inhabitants will reserve for him a reverent welcome of uncontrollable joy."

"Turn! Turn!" Mah called out. Static filled the air. "Most of the people of Dakhla are in the refugee camps. He'll be greeted by Moroccan opportunists come from their north to steal our property."

A voice in Arabic broke through the crackling as if the words were being transmitted from another planet. Mah translated for them.

"This morning, the forces of the Saharouis people struck another blow against the Moroccan army. Penetrating eighty miles within the territory of Morocco, they overran a tank headquarters at Lebourat, destroying twenty tanks and capturing another ten. Our forces lost one transport and three soldiers, compared to two hundred and thirty dead on the other side."

The soldiers shouted at the two Americans, in their minds witnesses to this victory. Smith leaned over to Laing.

"According to one school," he said, "no action is real until it has been described. According to another school, you have but to describe one for it to become real."

Mah stood up to leave. They gathered their belongings together and crowded into the front seat, their heads swathed and the blankets around them making the fit even tighter than usual. Nobody rode in the back. They would pick up a new escort father south. As they drove off, the guerillas shouted out, "*Besalama*," from between the receding pinpoints of gas lamps.

With their combined body heat to keep them comfortable, they floated across the desert, isolated in a temporary cathartic reverie. The smooth surface was broken only when the Land-Rover swerved, to climb up to a new plateau or down to a lower one.

Laing had thought he would sleep easily in this atmosphere, and perhaps his body was asleep, but his eyes stayed open. They moved across the sky or fixed on the beam thrown by the headlights, waiting for some rock or tiny plant to break the purity of the surface.

Once, their lights caught a long-eared fox. It froze in a half crouch for a fraction of a second before skittering out of sight. Laing turned to see that Smith's eyes were open, staring in the direction the fox had gone. It was the first creature, man or animal, alive or dead, they had seen outside the guerilla camps. The air delicately bathed his face, encouraging him to loosen the *arrza* from around his hair. Their thin line of four men was all that moved in the world.

FORTY-FOUR

Without apparent change, the night turned gradually into dawn, finding them in a valley of soft sand. High ridges enclosed either side. What had appeared to be a rock ahead spread its wings to a span of eight feet and rose before them with lethargic beats. It floated in a long glide, coming back to earth a few miles on. This *Hber*, as Brahim called it, stayed with them for some time, always rising to glide a safe distance in front.

Towards seven, Brahim stood up against the seat, keeping one hand on the wheel. He pointed with the other, while talking to Ahmed Mah. Mah, in turn, stood up.

Laing could make out something moving in the distance. It was coming towards them, framed against the backdrop of a ridge. Mah reached for his rifle. As it drew closer, they saw it was another Land-Rover, the heads of three men protruding. Brahim said something. The two machines raced towards each other like knights jousting, then skidded to a halt, side by side.

"Our escort," Mah said.

It was a battered, old machine, pale brown, almost a sand colour, with a camouflage net tied over the hood. The military plate, showing the King of Morocco's crown, had been carelessly painted over. A young black was driving and beside him sat a man well into his sixties, an extreme replica of Brahim. His skin was pulled tight over the sinew and bone, highlighting a narrow, arched nose and long teeth. They jutted forward in two even arcs like exotic jewellery. Over the teeth, his lips were drawn, to be released with precision when he spoke. His eyes darted, examining the other Land-Rover, while his body remained immobile, gracefully upright, ribcage thrust foreward. His khaki *arrza*, bloomers and loose robe had been washed a thousand times.

Mah and Brahim jumped out and went over. They shook his hand before kissing their own fingers. He questioned them briefly, threw an M16 across his shoulder and walked towards the Americans with a slight stiffness as if he had been riding. His bare calves were smooth muscle without any hint of a vulgar, wasted bulge.

Hama—that was his name—leapt into the back of their Land-Rover and braced himself behind them. He told Brahim to get moving. Through translation, some of the elegance of his phrases was lost, but no matter how hard Mah tried to fit all words into political formulas, he could not hide the elementary poetry in which Hama spoke.

"If this young man drives us well, I shall lead you to Amgalla. You have the good fortune to come now, when the figs are ripe. Ah, the marvellous figs of Amgalla, they are the sweetest, most perfumed figs in the world. If they are left to rot, you can smell their scent over the hills long before the town comes into view."

His fingers moved in sharp sweeps beneath his mouth and nostrils to illustrate the point. He then fell silent, moving only to instruct Brahim in short, precise exclamations. As the heat rose, he drew his *arrza* lower over his dark skin and sat as if in meditation.

Not long before noon, when they had begun to suffer from exposure, a range of high rock hills rose before them. Hama directed Brahim towards a track that climbed, through a valley, up into them. The ground rising on either side was rough grey gravel, and on top of it lay large slabs of slate that gathered in the heat and radiated it in all directions. Their tyres threw up a fine dust that settled on their sweaty clothes and skin before it melted into a stain. There wasn't a hint of a thorn tree or of a dried blade of desert grass. They came over a first range three hundred feet up and looked across a series of black slate hills ahead and on both sides. It was Cain's land. From the top of the next ridge they could see a long arc of rocks, piled up, one on top of the other. Hama pointed the way, along the top of a ridge, to an opening in the wall.

"This was the Moroccan advanced line," he said. "It stretches around the town in a circle five miles across. Over there you can see the machine-gun posts. Those piles of stone are shelters. We harassed them for six months before they pulled back from here."

Laing caught sight of two dried bodies in tattered uniforms as the Land-Rover lurched down into a new valley, past some wrecks of trucks and what looked like mass graves. They penetrated another wall, with artillery positions and more shelters and mass graves.

"There are four lines. When we had taken the second, they could no longer land aeroplanes in the centre, nor could they march out through the hills."

Laing couldn't understand how anyone could have held those positions for even a few days. The conditions in which the soldiers had lived must have been impossible—baking when they weren't shot at, with every exploding shell turning the slate into shrapnel. The Land-Rover struggled over yet more hills and finally came onto a ridge overlooking Amgalla, which consisted of fifty ruins and two fig trees surrounded by stumps.

"To end their madness, two Moroccan battalions were marched in. No sooner had they arrived than they turned around and marched out, with the entire garrison. Drive down that way, young man. We must taste the figs."

They drove down into the valley, where two fig trees grew out of the caked earth.

"There was an orchard here, the most beautiful in the Sahara," Hama said, "which they cut down to simplify their defence."

He leapt from the Land-Rover and led them over to the trees, carefully choosing ripe figs from among those scattered on the branches. Hama handed them each one and ate a small bite from the last fruit himself.

"You see. They are the perfume of God."

Standing on parched earth, trying to ignore his overwhelming thirst, Smith's first reaction was that they were pretty ordinary. He made an effort to smell his and to eat it slowly. He scanned the hills above them. The love of superlatives, in a man like Hama, was a true reflection of his life. Those figs represented all the fruit within a five-hundred-mile radius and his was the purity of the extremes.

"All things considered," Smith said to Laing, "these are pretty good."

They climbed into the Land-Rover and drove to the edge of the ravaged town on the side of the valley. Hama led the way through a series of ruined courtyards, past roofless houses, and stopped outside the least damaged building in sight, before which a Land-Rover sat surrounded by rubble. They went inside, blind in the sudden shade, and a voice called out from the darkness.

"How were the figs, Anthony?"

It was Lamine, reclining in a corner, drinking tea.

"Come now, Anthony, admit you find it terrible."

Smith shrugged. "It isn't New England."

He lay propped up against a white-washed wall. After half an hour in the shade of the stone house, with the temperature down to around one hundred, he was cool enough to pull a cheap cigar out of his breast pocket. He stripped off its plastic wrapper and lit it without offering one to the others. Smith carried only enough for himself, on the principle that sharing cigarettes and cigars was a social civility, not generosity in face of need. They were not, at present, in society.

"No," Lamine picked up, "but we have a small population and we know how to live here. This town, filled with two hundred people, will become a garden in the space of a few months. I know the man who owns this house." They were in a room without a door. There was one other room. "He talks with great pride of his garden at Amgalla."

Hama, who had been following all of this in translation, interrupted. "You must not expect us to 'raise the heavens without visible pillars,' as God did. No one will return to live here until the war is over, because the sky is not ours."

"That's the tragedy," Lamine said. "The country has become a battleground whose only population is soldiers. You have crossed half of it. You have another seven hundred empty miles to go. In the old days, it wasn't only the nomads who came out into the desert. In the winter, the coastal people moved here in tents. They consider it a beautiful land. Look at Hama. My European education gives me nothing to teach him here, which is why I arranged for him to guide you."

As the translation came through, Hama clucked in violent disapproval. He sat like an early Christian saint, his rifle resting against his thigh.

"By the way," Lamine said, "there's a slight change in our plans. The King will be at Dakhla tomorrow and a concentration of soldiers and air force will be with him—a little informal protection. Your ship lands on Friday, three days later, fifty miles from there. We have to draw their attention away, quickly. They expect us to embarrass the King by attacking near where he is. Instead, I'm going to make a sortie against Smara tomorrow morning. Five hundred miles north of the King. We'll catch them off-guard. If I understand my friends well, the moment the King goes home, Kader will rush his men north. Afraid, you see, that we'll strike again. We'll use our men like water, as the Master advises, flowing away from the heights and rushing to the low lands, avoiding his strengths and attacking his weaknesses. There are about five hundred nomads being held on the edge of Smara, in a camp from which they'd like to be freed. I think we can manage that in the process. You may come along with me or wait here."

Smith looked doubtfully at Laing and Laing at him. Eventually, Smith said,

"Well now, Abdullah, we've eaten all your figs and we've seen the sights. The medieval tradition is to move on, which I'm delighted to do, if you promise to take care of us."

"Good God, Anthony. Enlisting is the only risk a soldier should take. From then on, everything should be done with extreme care. So we're agreed. We'll sleep now and move when the evening is fresh."

As an afterthought, Smith sat up from his blanket and asked, "I don't suppose you'll be going anywhere near Ma el Ainin's palace?"

"I'll see what I can do," Lamine said.

They were woken by Brahim, who gave them some bread before disappearing outside. The two men gathered their things together and went out to find the others standing around the three Land-Rovers.

"Here they are," Lamine said, "the zombies. Anthony, you ride with me. I want some company tonight."

Hama's machine led the way, with Brahim bringing up the rear. As soon as they were out of the hills and back onto the sand, they fanned out to avoid sending dust onto one another. Lamine sat on the outside, his arm firmly around Smith, a blanket tucked tightly around both of them. His driver was swathed in at least four robes. They were heading north-west.

"The closer we get to the sea, the cooler the nights are," Lamine said. "But the sea is still a lifetime away from here."

"These Land-Rovers must be the biggest thing to hit the desert since . . ."

"Since camels," Lamine broke in, "the biggest and only revolution since the camels. The old men say the camel didn't need fuel, but Land-Rovers don't need food or water."

They were silent for some time, until Smith said, "I thought you wanted company."

Lamine swivelled his head towards him aggressively, "What's Laing doing here?"

Lamine could feel Smith shrug under his arm before answering. "Keeping an eye on the merchandise, I suppose. Anyway, he's paying."

"You mean we're paying. That doesn't make any sense."

Smith shrugged again. "I don't know. He's a great friend, but that doesn't mean he trusts me. He's a bit of a technocrat, obsessed by detail. I imagine he couldn't let go."

Lamine said nothing for a while, then concluded, "I don't trust him. You shouldn't have let him come."

"I'll watch him, Abdullah. He's my responsibility."

"And he looks terrible."

"He'll be all right. He got some heatstroke the day before yesterday." Smith was soothing Lamine, but his own doubts were growing stronger and had to be dealt with. He would have to find out what was wrong. "Martin's all right now."

"He's your responsibility, Anthony. You know the rules."

"Enough. What's happened to the great chaser of skirt? There's not much of it around here, at least, not from what I've seen."

Lamine laughed towards the sky, his short beard separated into two parts by the wind. "The first thing that goes in this climate is the urge to copulate. Too hot, Anthony. Too hostile. If there were any women, they'd be ignored. Zola was wrong in *Germinal*. People don't want to make love when they're dying. They want to live."

"The death of a romantic."

"What?" Lamine had missed his comment in the wind.

"I said you've lost your romanticism."

"Romanticism has always had more to do with nationalism than with sex. If you consummate something, it will never again be truly romantic. Now, a nation can never be consummated."

FORTY-FIVE

They were left by Lamine on the black hills outside Smara with Hama as their guardian. From the top they could pick out the town, a white spot on the dark ground ten miles away.

It was five-thirty a.m. on Tuesday and Lamine's operation was to begin at six. He had said there were six thousand men defending Smara, spread around a perimeter much larger than that of Amgalla. No reinforcements could be brought in in time to influence a battle lasting less than half a day.

As for the air force, it was a hundred miles away, at El Aayun. The jets, F5s and Mirages, would be called in quickly, but there was no direct link between the local ground commander and the pilots in the air. Everything had to be referred through a senior air force officer in El Aayun.

Lamine planned to have his own troops converge at the last moment, in two slightly separated places on the south side of the town. The Moroccan army was known for its lateness to rise, so the attack was to begin as close in as possible, breaking through their lines in two spots. The guerillas were to clear the space between them and move straight towards the core of the town. Two lines of men would stay behind, to keep the corridor open.

By beginning the attack close in, they would make it impossible for the Moroccan air force to fire without hitting their own troops.

"They're so terrified of our Sam missiles," Lamine had said, "although we have very few, that they fly their jets too high and too fast to hit small ground targets. Especially small targets only yards away from their own men."

On the south side of the core, the nomads were held in

their camp under light guard, in the shadow of Ma el Ainin's ruined palace. There would be just enough time for the guerillas to rush trucks down the corridor, pick up the nomads and rush out.

For the withdrawal, Lamine would first send his fastest groups scattering in several directions to draw the jets away. Then he'd feed out the trucks, loaded with the refugees, and the other Land-Rovers and armoured carriers in a wide fan.

To stop the commander of Smara moving men from other parts of the defensive perimeter to meet the attack, Lamine had five other groups. They were made up of two Land-Rovers each and carried two mortars in each vehicle. These would spread out around the other sides of the city, send in volleys of mortar shells, then change position. He hoped that the local commander would fear a second major attack from one of those sides and hold his men in line.

Finally, to keep the rest of the Moroccan air force in the south for the morning, a few dozen men would harass a fort called Bir Enzarem, one hundred miles from Dakhla. Just for half an hour. Lamine hoped that would be enough to spook Kader into keeping every fighter close to the King while he made his ceremonial entrance into Dakhla.

"Very neat," Smith had said in the Land-Rover the night before. "You combine deception with knowing their weaknesses; you deceive them and you strike where you aren't expected."

Under the blanket, Lamine had turned his small finger in Smith's palm, the sign of a joke among nomads.

"If you move in quickly with the trucks, you'll see your ruins."

Hama had given them khaki smocks to pull over their lighter coloured clothing. They sat on top of a hill, waiting while Land-Rovers moved up from behind, slowly and separately winding around them between the hills and on towards Smara. Hama had lent Laing a pair of field glasses. He could make out the machines coming to a halt a few miles ahead, where some of the guerillas abandoned them and went on by foot.

Laing moved the field glasses as slowly and evenly as he could, a parody of slow motion. He tried to ignore the quiver he could feel in his body. "You don't die of it," he had found underlined in Smith's copy of *Lord Jim*. What? Fear. And what if Smith were killed? The idea seeped into his mind. There would be nothing to tell him about Lamine's necessary death and nothing to ask him about Cosima. He brushed the idea aside, but it came back. The possibility of his own death never entered Laing's consciousness.

At five to six they were called down to their Land-Rover. Brahim was told to follow Hama's driver and, under no circumstances, to use his imagination. Hama was on his knees, washing his hands in the sand and then praying. When he had finished, Ahmed Mah called out a question in Arabic. Laing was so distracted that he reacted as if Mah had spoken to him.

"What is it?" Laing asked.

"Whether you shouldn't have weapons," Mah explained reluctantly.

Before Martin could say anything, Smith exclaimed, "Absolutely not. I might hurt myself."

In any case, Hama had ignored the question. Mah, sitting against the door, pulled his own Kalashnikov from the rear and then Brahim's, which he handed to Smith.

"At least you can hold onto it for him."

Laing's impression was that Smith held it apart from himself, denying any relationship with the shaft of steel.

At six, they heard explosions ahead of them, but saw nothing, sitting as they were at the bottom of a valley. Explosions erupted to the left and right, at a greater distance. Laing guessed that those were the mortars, the beginning of the diversions. Noise behind caused him to twist violently about. A line of empty trucks ground up the valley towards them.

"Shouldn't we be moving," he said to Smith, who looked at him, as if from a distance, and replied:

"It isn't in our hands."

Laing realized he had spoken too quickly, without controlling his voice, and forced himself to slouch into his seat. Unspecific sensations rushed through his body. Why hadn't he waited at Amgalla? And now it was too late. He turned and stared at Smith's face. It was immobile, frozen in an expressionless stare. Was that fear of death? What did he know about fear in others, let alone himself?

Hama's Land-Rover moved forward with Brahim following. The air was filled with hollow sounds, echoing down the valley before them. What might have been shouts or screams or explosions became anonymous static in the air as they accelerated up to forty miles an hour, leaving the trucks behind. Two miles on, they stopped. Hama jumped out and ran up a hill, paused at the top for a few seconds, silhouetted like a giant, and ran back down.

His machine raced forward again, twisting between the hills with Brahim on his tail. Around a corner, a line of Land-Rovers suddenly appeared. Laing jerked uncontrollably. He felt Smith and Mah do the same. But these were the empty vehicles of the Polisario advance group. In seconds, they were passed and out of sight.

The explosions spread to either side,with a silence in the middle which grew like an ominous tunnel, looming to engulf them. Laing felt himself accelerating at an uncontrollable pace and leaned forward in anticipation. Had he been able to, he would have stood and pointed like a madman, rushing towards the unknown but certain end. Their wheels hit a gravel track. Hama increased his speed, disappearing ahead of them, and Brahim pushed his foot to the floor, skidding around a corner.

As if ejected from a narrow throat, they found themselves exposed in a major lateral valley. Brahim threw his foot on the brakes and swerved to avoid a crowd of Land-Rovers stopped in their path.

Ahead, stretching in either direction, was a wall, which resembled the defences of Amgalla. A hundred yards away, on both sides, Laing saw Polisario crouching with their backs turned. Straight ahead a crowd of men were pitching stones to either side, dismantling a section of the wall. Until they finished, the machines could not follow the men's advance.

Nothing moved. Laing's eyes fixed on the men heaving stones. They laboured in absolute silence. Nothing moved. The only sound was that of small explosions, which were unreal because he could see neither the man firing nor the target. The guerillas threw the last stones and jumped into their Land-Rovers to race ahead through the opening.

Still Hama waited, the trucks piled up behind them. When the way ahead was clear for two hundred yards, he moved forward.

On the edge of the wall were two men—one without a head, the other with his chest blown open. Laing's eyes were dazzled by the bright rainbow effect of the innards hanging on display. He instinctively clutched Smith's arm, but saw that Smith was staring straight ahead. As the trucks began through the barrier, four F5s swooped in a wide arc, high above. By the time they had turned, everyone was inside. They swept back and forth over the area, unsuccessfully looking for clear targets.

Laing focused on his watch. It was six-fifteen. They came

over a ridge and he saw men spread out down either side of the corridor, firing. Ahead, there was another stone wall, with an opening already breached. This time he averted his eyes from the bodies.

They passed Lamine, standing by his Land-Rover, giving instructions to someone. He didn't notice them. Men fired mortars from either side of the breach, down the Moroccan line.

"Keep your mouth open!" Mah shouted as they drew close. Each explosion rocked their heads.

Over the next hill, they found a group of Land-Rovers bunched up a hundred yards ahead. There were flashes of light and explosions just beyond them. Hama's machine flew into reverse, back over to the other side of the hill, with Brahim working hard to keep up with him. Behind, they saw the trucks catching up. When the firing had receded, Hama's machine crept forward over the ridge again until he saw the way was clear. They accelerated down a long flat stretch, through yet another barrier, past more mortars.

Ahead, to the right, there were buildings. Men were firing in that direction. Hama cut to the left, along a track away from the fighting, and for a mile there was no one to be seen. Then tents appeared in a small valley, with low buildings behind them on a rise. The nomads were gathered in front of the tents, already organized by a group of Polisario, who stood waiting beside their Land-Rovers.

Hama went straight past them, up the hill, and stopped in front of a multi-domed building which was surrounded by ruined walls. The two Land-Rovers emptied, Laing moving automatically among the other men. Only when his feet were on the ground did he register conscious surprise that he could stand.

Smith was ahead of him, ambling methodically towards the building. It was white-washed and without windows, with a large padlock on the door. Smith turned, looking for something to force it, but Mah came up behind and fired a shot, shattering the lock. Smith pushed the door open and walked slowly in, staring all round. Laing followed, surprised to find cool, sweet air inside.

It was a simple room with a purity of grace brought out by the repetition of identical white cupolas. Beneath these, he saw Smith crouched against a pillar, as if dreaming. Laing turned to look outside. The trucks had arrived and Hama and

Brahim had driven the hundred yards back down the hill to see if they could speed up the nomads.

He revolved again and walked around the mosque, out into a series of cloister-like corridors. Floating in the air of the palace there was a feeling of saintliness that he could not ignore; the vision of one man who had built his soul into the walls. A fixed dream in the morning desert. Without meaning to, he finally understood what Cosima meant when she talked about buildings built being the only things that count, and in that moment he felt very close to her.

There was a row of slit windows down one side of the cloister. He went over and stared out of one, catching sight of the rock and sand and of the town beyond. The smells of the desert wafted through the narrow openings, passing abruptly—distant, particular sensations to be savoured. He moved down the row, looking through each as in a kaleidoscope. At the fifth, his eye was caught by something. He froze and tried to focus on a mass of Moroccan soldiers walking up the back of the hill towards him.

Laing turned and ran down the corridors, only to find himself in a roofless, white-washed room that he didn't recognize. The sounds of the Moroccan soldiers could be heard over the walls. He ran back the way he had come, trying to make sense out of the passageways, but they became more confusing. He stopped and forced himself to concentrate. Suddenly he recognized a turning and ran towards the main mosque. Smith was still crouched, staring around himself.

"There are Moroccan soldiers just behind the building!"

From the door they could see the last trucks pulling away. Their own Land-Rovers were still at the bottom of the hill.

"Run," Smith said sharply.

They began down the hill, leaping over the rocks. Laing heard noises behind them and then shouting. He saw their friends below look up, surprised, and raise their rifles to fire. Run, he thought to himself, run. He heard strange noises close about him. Noises that he couldn't identify. Nor did they seem unfriendly. An explosion in his ear threw him into the air and dropped him onto the ground. He found himself rolling over into a ditch, his body impervious to the rocks it was thrown against. He lay for an undefined moment, half on his side, one leg twisted up underneath.

The ditch ran down the hill, just out of sight of the Moroccans, now crouching to protect themselves. Smith's body lay half in the ditch, half out.

Laing righted himself and crawled forward to where he could pull Smith down into the hollow. He could see no blood and felt him breathing heavily, but he was senseless. Laing looked around, suddenly calm, and saw that it was fifty yards to the bottom of the hill. How could he drag Smith's weight that far? It was impossible. And if he left him there, no one could blame him. No one would know. He looked hard at Smith, whose blotched, pallid face was layered with sweat like a plastic mask. Laing tried to move away, found he couldn't and stared at the face again. The sound of their names shouted in the distance brought him back to his senses. He wrapped his arms around Smith's chest and began to pull his dead weight down the hill, while crouching below the line of the ditch. The firing that continued above remained unreal, of another world. With Smith to drag, the distance was unending, and each loose rock a major barrier. Once Laing had to stop when he felt himself about to vomit from overexertion.

As he approached the bottom, he called for Brahim and Hama in the belief that they were just beyond him to the right. Ahmed Mah's voice came back,

"Where are you?"

Laing called again. He heard the Land-Rover engines turning over and the firing intensified. Moments later, Brahim stopped at the end of the ditch. He leaped out and lifted Smith into the back. Laing followed, lying down behind the metal panels as they began lurching towards the corridor, Hama close behind, giving cover.

Once into the corridor, they were protected by other Polisario, so Hama squeezed past and set the pace. They came out through the last defense wall to find the jets had already gone in chase of the first few vehicles to dash from the site. It was seven twenty-five.

Hama cut off to the Southwest, at maximum speed, with Brahim lurching tight on his tail. Laing wedged himself between a corner and the water drum, pulled Smith up over him and held him tight, hands linked over his friend's chest to prevent his being thrown about. Smith's heart pounded under his hands and a blue swelling crept over the side of his skull.

It was forty minutes before Hama drew up and shouted instructions to go slowly. Speed would raise dust and dust would attract attention.

Laing stared at the livid bruise. A wave of affection swept over him, obscuring his vision with the beginning of tears. He was not a man who had many friends. What other friends did he have, Cosima apart? The body moved in his grasp. Smith groaned and opened his eyes, focusing on Laing.

"What happened?"

"Nothing," Laing replied. "How's your head?"

They drove for most of the day, finding the smooth hard sand again towards noon. A breeze arrived from the distant ocean and took the sharp edge out of the sun, although the temperature still rose over 120°. Vines had sprouted out of the barren sand after the passage of the rain and in a single day they had grown several feet, flowered and produced gourds the size of oranges.

Hama rose, turning to stare behind them. A dark spot, throwing up sand, chased them across the desert at double their speed. Hama fixed his field glasses in that direction and signalled a halt. It was Lamine.

He drew up close to Hama, with whom he talked quietly in Arabic before approaching Smith.

"So you fell in a ditch." Smith's head hurt too much for him to say anything. Lamine surveyed Laing with curiosity. "I'm in your debt."

"More selfish than that," Laing replied. "He's my friend."

"Yes, Mr. Laing. I know. But I lost other friends today. In my business, we count each one saved as a victory."

Smith said nothing.

They began driving again, spread out three across, Lamine in the middle. Some time later, he shouted over the sand, "Anthony, what did you think of Ma el Ainin's palace?"

Smith shouted back, "I was too scared to notice."

At first, Lamine said nothing. Then he shouted, "The pretensions of men don't bind us out here. Only the other rules."

After that, they drove in silence until darkness fell, when they stopped to make camp on the sand near some thorn bushes. At nine, Lamine took his radio out of the Land-Rover and tuned into the Moroccan news. It was the same announcer they had heard two nights before, speaking in rich tones—a declaration of his Paris education,

> "His Majesty the King arrived this morning at Dakhla, southern capital of the Saharan Provinces. His 747 jet, the first ever to land in the town, delivered him safely to the hearts of his cheering people. Dressed in a yellow business suit, he inspected a guard of honour before proceeding to the Prefecture, where he met local dignitaries. Later,

mounted on a black stallion, he rode through the streets of the city dressed in a white djellabah and shaded by a purple parasol, to the emotional cheers of the population. By his side were His Royal Highness the Crown Prince Sidi Mohammed; Prince Moulay Rachid; General Kader, Chief of the Royal Aides de Camp and Commander in the South; Maati Bouabid, the Prime Minister; several noted personalities including members of His Majesty's Personal Cabinet, Ahmed Guedira and Moulay Sayed Idrissi; leaders of the political parties . . ."

Later in the broadcast, a Moroccan victory over the mercenaries in the area of Smara was announced. The King personally sent his congratulations to the army.

FORTY-SIX

Smith lay rolled up in blankets, his eyes open into the night air, crisp in the gauze-like light that preceded the sunrise. He could smell his own sweat, dried into every pore with the dirt and salt from his own body. His hair was sticky with the same mixture, as were the clothes he would have to pull on. Far as they were from any well, water couldn't be spared for superficial needs such as washing. Smith probed the bruise on his skull and found the swelling had begun to recede.

He glanced at Laing, lying a yard away with his blankets pulled up over his face so that only his eyes were visible, and they were closed. Laing had made little of having saved him. When Smith tried to thank him, his words hardly seemed to be heard.

Just beyond the fire and the few blankets, the Polisario were washing their hands in the sand. They lined up, Lamine behind Hama and the others behind them, then knelt to pray, their rifles on the sand beside them.

The noise of their chanting woke Laing. He stared at the row of men, bowed on the sand. The strain on his face had taken on a transparent quality, a blue gauntness, and yet, the expression was generous—that of the seduced. Since the incident at Smara the day before, he had even showed signs of pleasure at being there.

There was a shade of pale green over the desert, brought on by the sparse grass that had sprouted in the wake of the vines. The desert was so sensitive to the smallest change that one blade every hundred yards was enough to cast this softer tone.

Perhaps Laing's silence was the correct reaction. And yet, instead of drawing them closer, Smith felt that a wedge had been driven between them. He looked again at his friend, who appeared held to the ground by some internal pressure. It was probably the heat and the food and the cumulation of almost a week at the extremities of survival. In two days it would be over and the other reality would reassert itself.

Laing saw that he was being watched and sat up, pulling his blanket around his shoulders for protection. Smith smiled, but Laing leaned forward in a deliberate, earnest way.

"You know, Anthony, I almost left you on that hill."

Smith laughed. "I could hardly have blamed you. I don't know how you . . ."

"No, Anthony. I'm not joking."

Smith looked at him quizzically and sat up. "Well, why did you do it?"

"You mean, why was I tempted not to?" Laing's voice narrowed to a nervous edge.

"Well?"

"You know, Benmansour told me about you and Cosima."

Smith was astounded. So that's what had been wrong. "What do you mean?"

"He told me that something happened between you while I was in New York."

"And you believed that pimp?"

Laing appealed to him. "It's not a question of belief, it's a question of doubt."

"The man hates me, Martin. He loathes Sayed. He's just causing trouble."

"That doesn't mean . . ."

"I mean it is a total lie." Smith's words were filled with conviction. "If Benmansour said it, you know it's a lie."

Laing nodded with a childlike relief and leaned farther forward to put his arm around him, "I'm sorry."

"I wish you'd told me sooner. You might have left me lying up there, an innocent bystander."

They both laughed and Laing began to say something else, but stopped himself, unwilling to risk any more. He was less certain than ever that Smith would understand how important this deal was. Anyway, he was there to handle it himself, so Smith didn't need to know about the message to the Moroccans. Why involve him?

Lamine had finished his prayers and walked over to them. He smiled at Laing and tapped Smith with his foot, "Up, Anthony. We're off." Smith began to protest, but Lamine cut him short. "Breakfast later. Hama wants to show us something."

"For the first time in a thousand years, there are no camels to eat this grass."

Lamine was squeezed against the door, beside Smith and Laing, having sent Mah to ride in the other Land-Rover. The green hue over the desert grew stronger as they drove south in the still cool air.

"All this softness," he continued, "is temporary relief. Tomorrow we'll reach the Zemmour."

Hama's Land-Rover drove ahead of the others, shifting direction in apparently meaningless variations over the trackless sand. As the other two talked beside him, Laing sat back in silence with the feeling that he could join their conversation if he wished, but he was happy to say nothing. They continued like this for twenty miles, when Hama stood up, bracing himself against his seat, and pointed off to the left. Lamine stood and stared.

"There they are," he pointed.

Laing followed his hand. He picked out two small skeletons on the sand, then another off to the right. The plateau broke before them into a series of small valleys that appeared at first to be overgrown with luxuriant colour, but that turned out to be only the contrast with the desert. There was little more than sparse scrub grass. The Land-Rovers drew up on the edge while Hama stood on his seat, examining the hollows. He suddenly dropped back into place and his machine sped off to the right, plunging down a slope. Lamine ordered Brahim to follow at a distance.

"Stand up," he said to Laing. "See if you can find them."

Laing's eyes followed an arc on either side of Hama's Land-Rover until, in the distance, he picked out small, sand-coloured objects leaping over the grass.

"Gazelle," Lamine said. "We'll let Hama take the first one."

In order to keep up, Brahim had to force the machine; then they began gaining on the gazelle, who ran in a broken pattern over the grass. The closer the Land-Rover came, the more fragile they appeared.

"This is too easy," Smith protested.

"No, it isn't," Laing interrupted. "They're looking for soft ground. How fast can they go?"

"Very good, Laing." Lamine glanced at him with appreciation. "They can push forty to fifty on hard or soft ground. We can do the same on hard. All they need is loose sand or a bluff to get away."

Brahim pulled up on the left of Hama, placing himself to cut off a range of dunes. Just as the Land-Rover moved forward, three of the four gazelles broke across in front of them with an unexpected burst of speed and were gone.

"You see!" Lamine shouted. "All we have is a machine."

But the fourth panicked, perhaps at finding itself alone, and leapt straight down the valley, making short dashes from right to left and back. The Land-Rover gradually closed on it. At fifty feet, Hama stood up, braced himself and fired one shot.

In the midst of a leap, the gazelle flew sideways and crashed down on its side, the Land-Rover skidding to a halt beside it. Hama leapt out, a knife in his hand, grabbed the writhing, childlike animal by its horns and, with one strong motion, slit its throat. By the time the second Land-Rover drew up, the blood was sinking into the sand. Laing stared at the thick liquid and saw a warm, inviting quality, as if the gazelle had been in agreement with its death.

Lamine attempted a compliment, which was ignored. Hama felt obliged to make sure everyone got their chance, so while the body was being tied to the back of the Land-Rover he was pointing off into another valley, telling them exactly where to go.

They left the other machine and drove slowly down the valley, their eyes searching through the hills ahead. All four were caught up in the game. Lamine took a Kalashnikov from behind and checked that it was loaded.

"In fairness," he said, "these rifles can't hit anything over fifty yards."

"That's an excuse," Smith replied.

"Before the fact," Lamine added.

It was Brahim who sighted them, grazing on the left side of the valley between two small hills. He cut close to the edge, to frighten them out into the middle, and at a hundred yards' distance the six animals froze, then leapt into the open. Brahim swerved behind them to discourage their feints, but not fast enough to stop four of the gazelle from pulling ahead and breaking off into the sand dunes. The distance between the Land-Rover and the remaining two gradually shrunk until they were close enough and Brahim gestured to Lamine. But as he did, a small, dry wadi cut across the valley. He veered and skidded to avoid rolling over. When they looked up, the animals were gone.

Cold disappointment spread through the group, as if they had failed to meet a standard they all recognized. Brahim was unable to look at the others.

"Hama may have another idea," Laing said, but then regretted he had spoken.

Rather than go back, they searched down small side valleys, which led into other side valleys; all of them were empty. Eventually Lamine said they must give up. As they turned, a pair of gazelle appeared from behind a bluff.

The surprise was as great on both sides. The animals leapt, turning in the air, and disappeared in the same direction, with Brahim starting a fraction behind them. He skidded around a corner to find the animals standing still, uncertain whether they had really seen something. They leapt forward again, taking an initial distance that Brahim began to close. The larger of the pair broke off to the left and he let him go, concentrating on the other gazelle's broken pattern of panicked leaps.

Laing twisted back and forth between Brahim and the animal, all his tensions rising from within and burning off. He focused on Brahim, whose head was frozen in place. Only his arms moved. His eyes were fixed on the animal, countering its manoeuvres. The long straight run began to tire the gazelle and the length of its leaps shrank with each minute. Suddenly Brahim shouted, breaking the trance. Lamine stood up, put his weight against the seat and took aim.

The explosion was much closer than any Laing had heard

at Smara. The animal still leapt ahead. There was a second explosion and a third. Lamine began to laugh.

"Anthony, you try." Smith withdrew his hands in rejection. "Laing?"

He reached out to take it, but Brahim shouted again and snatched the rifle from Lamine. With his left hand, he braced it against the outside of the Land-Rover and pushed his foot to the floor. They closed a few yards behind its tail, so close that Laing was sure he could hear the animal gasping for air. Brahim swerved sharply to the right and back left, drawing up beside the gazelle, only two yards away. With one arm, he aimed his rifle and there was an explosion that blew the gazelle into a final sideways leap.

The frail creature lay heaving, its legs flailing spasmodically and its back arched, causing it to turn on its side in a circle. Then Brahim's knife found the throat. Laing expected the blood to be somehow different from that of the last kill, but the same welcoming red honey flowed into the sand.

They threaded their way out of the valley, to find Hama's machine drawn up in the shade of a bluff, where they had lit a fire. The first gazelle was already skinned and cut up. Before he stopped, Brahim reached forward and lifted the small body from the Land-Rover's bonnet. Hama shouted at them with pleasure.

"He says he heard many shots," Lamine translated, "and where are the others?"

Laing looked at the old man, and saw that it was an honest enquiry.

FORTY-SEVEN

Lamine leapt from the Land-Rover and turned to put an arm around Laing's shoulder. "I'm sorry you were cheated of your shot."

Laing reacted with friendly modesty, but the warmth of Lamine's body, so close and so trusting, sent a malaise through him and he managed only a mumbled reply before Lamine slipped away to stretch out by the fire, his head against a rock. His own driver was burying dough in the sand between layers of coals. He had already thrown the gazelle's legs into a pot of boiling water and dropped the innards directly onto the fire.

Pointing at this, Lamine said to Laing, "You see, no matter how sophisticated our war becomes, the basics of life out here stay the same."

"Kalashnikovs are hardly basic," Laing said.

Lamine shook his head. "That's not what it's all about. El-Oueli was a Paris educated boy, like me. I suppose in those days I thought I would have all my life to enjoy the soft, coddling edge of that city, pacing out the days, talking, arguing, the women so devoted to being women, to themselves, like wonderful sparkling self-creations." His wistfulness was never more than a hint. "Of course, I was going to come back here, I don't know, to some exalted job that would recognize my preparation and let me float between the two worlds at will," he kicked some sand at Smith, "the way Anthony does. And I did come back and there we all were, exalted clerks for the Spanish. So a handful of us got together in '73. It was the 10th of May. We didn't know what to do, but we wanted independence. That much we knew. We had no money. Nothing. We separated to raise support in the villages and a few days later El-Oueli was picked up by the police—a troublesome student—and locked in a local jail at a little place called Khanga. We borrowed some First-World-War rifles from our families and raided the station. The police were so surprised that we got away with El-Oueli; but after using force once, we knew of no way back."

He reached out to turn over the innards with a stick. His driver snatched the stick and himself lifted them off the fire on the point of his knife, with a shake to make the coals fall away. He sliced the liver and kidney into thin strips and piled them onto two pieces of bread ripped from the loaf that had come out of the steaming hole in the sand. These were handed to the Americans. Laing tried to pass his on, but Lamine stopped him.

"You are the guests. You get the best part."

Laing put the bloody liver to his mouth and bit off a small piece. It was hot on the outside and warm inside—as much from the fresh kill as from the fire. He felt pressure building within him again, as the exhilaration of the chase wore off, and turned on Lamine,

"A bunch of students can become a guerilla army and these helicopters will give you new strength, but you can't win. What good is a momentary advantage? They'll still hold the towns. You'll still be stuck out here."

"The nomads hate the Moroccans," Lamine said complacently. "They hate them as city degenerates, as poor Muslims, as the known oppressor. Brahim's father was killed in one of their bombing raids on refugee camps. My father was blinded in the same raid. There's no Western sense of time here. Hama has been fighting for almost all his sixty-five years and would fight for another sixty-five. Victory isn't overdue, it's a goal. Our people have always had a sense of their freedom. That comes with the clarity of our life; the thing you don't have in your world any more. The Western romantic view of desert life is just envy of our clarity."

"'A certain people despising doubt,'" Smith broke in, "'our modern crown of thorns. They do not understand our metaphysical difficulties. They know only truth and untruth.'"

"That is your Lawrence." Lamine stretched to take a piece of boiled meat and passed it on to Laing. "This is your part." The taste was sweet, like kid, with a gamy edge to it. "If time must be counted, Laing, let the Moroccans count. They're the ones with sixty thousand men in the field at a million dollars a day. Their economy is at a halt. No country has ever profited from a protracted war."

Hama broke in and asked what people in the United States were saying about the war. Laing said aggressively that Americans didn't want to know about the violence of others. They wanted to maintain an impression of peace at home. Hama took the words as a reproach of the nomads' violence and concentrated on chewing a piece of leg.

"You don't understand us," Lamine said. "Why did Moses and Christ and Mohammed come out of the desert with their gospels? Why has every new dynasty in Morocco arisen, like us, in the sand beyond the Atlas Mountains, before marching north to clear the degenerate Sultans from their thrones? Over the last five years, a mystical wave has swept across the desert—not just the old Spanish Sahara—we are not a people of colonial borders—but northern Mauritania, southern Algeria, southern Morocco. In these empty spaces, people talk, people know something is happening. They are drawn to our camps because we are their spirit in action."

His words were blocked out as Laing shook his head. Lamine was wrong. He would be dead within forty-eight hours. His was a hopeless cause. "The reality is that you are ten thousand soldiers," Laing said doggedly, "who cannot win a war."

Lamine stopped eating, exasperated. "What is reality, but imagination added to willpower and applied?"

Hama raised himself on his thighs, shifting his weight onto his knees, and broke his brooding silence, "What Christian has ever turned the other cheek?"

Before anything could be said, Smith tapped Lamine on the arm and insisted, "No, listen, Abdullah. Martin isn't wrong. How can you end it?"

In mock servility Lamine bowed, "Sun Tzu says, the best strategy is to attack the enemy's strategy—we've blocked the phosphates, the reason they came. The next best is to attack their alliances—we destroyed the Mauritanian government and won twenty-six African nations to our side."

Hama interrupted with precise modulation of his voice, still following his own reasoning, "If Christ were the Son of God, God would not have let them kill him. The time will come when Jesus will repudiate those who treat him as divine." Having reached the end of his logic, he sat back to clean his teeth with a thorn. His widespread toes were folded under him, hiding the deep ridges in the soles of his feet, whose texture did not resemble human skin.

The interruption was ignored by Lamine. "The next best, is to attack their army—we harass them, here and inside Morocco. We keep them constantly on alert. We inflict minor defeats. Their morale is low. They never know where we will attack and when. They fight badly, surrender quickly. The worst policy is to attack cities—we don't. We don't kill civilians or destroy their livlihood. Listen, Anthony. Don't take your comfortable boat ride home. Come back with me. I'll show you what we're doing."

Smith ignored him. "Given all of that?"

"The King will make a deal or he will fall."

Laing sat, nodding nervously. "You've just described"—he almost shouted to drown out his own thoughts—"the creation of a Saharan nation. You have an army. You have towns you cannot defend. Like the Moroccans, you need an economy to pay for your war. The bigger you get, the truer that becomes. The clock is ticking for you as well. And if it's a matter of holding on, the Moroccans are better placed. Your very successes lead you to a fatal weakness."

Lamine was surprised by this outburst. He glanced with interest at Laing, who appeared fragile, like thin glass, which he took to be a sign of exhaustion.

They slept through the heat of the day, in the shade of blankets stretched between two thorn trees. When they awoke, Lamine was gone.

A short drive, in the late afternoon, took them across the undulating sands and up a small rise, onto a plateau of flat, hard sand. A vast, empty stage where they paused.

"The Zemmour," Hama called out from his Land-Rover as he swept his hand across the horizon. "It stretches west to the sea and east to the centre of Africa. One thousand miles long. Now we must watch all the time, lest we be seen moving and be run down like gazelle."

They drove at fifty miles an hour until darkness came, without any living thing having broken the horizon. With the night came a bitter cold. Hama would permit no fire, so Laing pulled on three shirts and wrapped himself in two blankets, all of which the cold penetrated, keeping him awake for most of the night.

On Thursday morning, 7 August, the sun appeared, a red monster sitting on the flat horizon. Laing awoke and lay still, while warmth crept patiently across the sand.

Smith was already up, a cigar in his mouth, sliding through his Tai Chi contortions. Beside him, the plastic wrapper from his cigar lay crumpled, reflecting the sun from a myriad of tiny angles. It appeared to dance on the virginal sand as if it were an object from outer space. Smith hadn't shaved since Smara and the filthy state of his clothes made Laing look at his own with discomfort. He pulled them on gingerly and went over to their Land-Rover to draw enough water for a shave. He noticed again, in his small mirror, the shadow across his face. He washed thoroughly and took care to shave his skin absolutely smooth, but the shadow was still there.

After eating some cold, hard bread, they drove on, gradually peeling off their layers of clothing as the heat rose and then putting them back on for protection. The temperature rose to over one hundred, then over one hundred and ten in the shade.

The two Land-Rovers drove side by side, a hundred yards apart across the unrelenting flatness, passing through wave after wave of heat shimmers that washed away all sense of distance and time. They tried to concentrate on watching the horizon for movement, but found themselves withdrawing into a zombie-like state as their machines floated endlessly through the heat.

By noon the temperature was unbearable, but Hama refused to let them stop. He wanted to cross this stretch, so close to Dakhla, as quickly as possible. He had propped himself up, with his fieldglasses before his eyes, and swept the horizon continually. In mid-afternoon, they slowed to thirty miles an hour to avoid sending dust into the air, and it was then that they first picked out the line of cement poles that marked the main track from El Aayun in the north to Dakhla in the south. The sea lay only a few miles beyond that road. Their speed began to creep higher as anticipation drew them on and it was at first without thought that their eyes were drawn to a ball of dust rising in the south. Without a word being said, both Land-Rovers stopped and they all stared as the ball grew larger on the horizon.

At last, Hama broke the silence, ordering them to turn and drive back very slowly. This they did for two miles, then stopped their Land-Rovers side by side and covered them with blankets, stretching one between the two machines to create shade.

They slid underneath, where Hama told them not to move, and lay watching as the dust approached and lengthened into a military column several miles long, with helicopters hovering over it on all sides and breaking off for sorties into the desert each time they thought they saw something unusual.

"So Abdullah guessed right," Smith said. "They're sending their army north."

Laing nodded, but felt certain that it was a feint by Kader to reassure the Polisario. He wondered how far the column was going.

Almost an hour passed before one of the helicopters made a sweep in their direction. At first it flew in a zig-zag, trying to find what had attracted its attention. Then it stopped above them, hovering in a small circle. The hum of the rotor blades was like a chain saw waiting to slice a log, and first Mah, then the others, began to fidget in an unsettled way. Hama saw this and said, with contempt,

"They will see nothing at that height. They are afraid to come lower."

Ten minutes later the sound disappeared and they looked out to see the column drawing away towards the north. They waited until the ball of dust had disappeared, then set out again. When they reached the row of cement poles, the only other signs of a highway were the tyre marks in the sand. The two Land-Rovers followed the tracks for twenty miles before cutting across them towards the coast. Like runners carrying messages, small breezes brushed by as they advanced.

An hour later, the desert fell away before them down a series of long canyons. Their eyes moved from the thousand miles of cream-coloured sand behind to the crude sweep of blue below. A heat mist hung over the ocean, washing out some of its intensity.

The two machines stopped. They all rose instinctively in their places. Laing unwound his *arrza* and placed it on the seat beneath him. There was a silence of discovery, as if they had never seen the ocean before.

Hama shouted to the drivers to move on. The trance was broken. He was the only one among them to have been as far as the coast since the war began and he led them north, along the cliff a short distance, to a good gravel track winding down to the shore. Between the desert and the ocean, nothing grew. It was a clear, unsullied meeting between two extremes. A sea breeze curved up the track, taking the edge off the oppressive heat. At the bottom, there was a wide, flat rock, which Laing calculated could hold a hundred trucks. It was raised only a few inches above the smooth white sand beach that stretched four miles in a slow curve, broken only by a worn rock ledge in the middle. Red cliffs climbed sharply out of the water at either end of the beach, turning the fairly calm sea into breakers.

A windowless, one-room stone hut with a tin roof and an opening without a door stood on the edge of the sand at the end of the track. Empty bottles of Spanish beer, with tattered labels still there after five years, were scattered around outside. The two Americans dumped their blankets and bags inside before going down to the water to join the guerillas.

Hama stood on the worn rocks, his rifle slung over his shoulder. All the others had stripped to their underwear, with careful Arab modesty, and were throwing themselves into the small waves near the shore. Unable to swim, they could go no farther. Laing glanced curiously at Smith, who had taken off his cotton slippers, rolled up his trousers and was wading in shallow water. A moment later, he gave up even this and retreated to the shade of the hut.

Laing stripped off his clothing and swam straight out from shore, while the nomads watched his strokes with wonder. He felt in control of his destiny again as the cold water seized his skin, scraping away the dryness of the last seven days. He floated in a vacuum. The people on the beach dissolved. Smith dissolved. The memory of Lamine dissolved. He was there alone, swimming as far as he wished to swim. There could be no limit.

His solitude was invaded by an apparition. He turned and wished he saw Cosima. Her long clean strokes carried her naked through the water beside him, the curve of her body one with the waves. They swam far out into the bay.

The sound of Smith's shouting broke this isolation. He was forced to turn. His eyes were filled by the panorama of the cliffs and the desert above. Beside the small hut, he could make out a third Land-Rover and a man in uniform standing beside it. He swam back to greet Lamine.

FORTY-EIGHT

The morning light cut through the mist, to reveal the first yards of an empty sea. Beside the hut and along the shore, small groups of men stood, staring out at the waves. Blankets hung over their shoulders to keep off the chill of the shade thrown by the cliff. When the light was perfectly clear, they could make out a black spot on the water.

Lamine passed his fieldglasses to Smith, who stared for some time. He said he thought it was the *Sophie*, after which he lost interest and sat against the wall of the hut, facing the sea, smoking. Half an hour later, the ship was visible to everyone.

Lamine had chosen Angra de Los Ruivos because the bottom dropped away quickly. The ship crawled to within seven hundred yards of shore and, as it neared its limit, Lamine radioed once again to look-outs spread along the coast above. There was no sign of Moroccan movement. He sent the signal for the trucks to come in from the desert, where they sat separated one from the other. They began to converge, driving slowly to avoid raising dust.

Lamine walked down to the water's edge to get a better view of the desert above. The entire shore was still in the shade, but the cliff edges above them were outlined in light. They would highlight the slightest movement.

At his most calm and ordered, Laing came down to join Lamine on the beach, flicking sand with the toes of his cotton slippers. He borrowed the fieldglasses and trained them on the cargo ship, whose cranes were already lifting the first landing-craft over the side. Lamine tapped him on the shoulder.

They turned towards the red cliffs to see the first truck, painted in a pale camouflage pattern, coming down the track. There were ten men in the back and along with them were four small fork-lift trucks.

Lamine was delighted that these had arrived first, as planned. They and four others, coming in another truck, were fitted with deep-tread tyres to handle the sand on the beach. The noise of the diesel engine working its way down the steep track reverberated along the base of the cliff and out onto the beach with such force that it was hard to imagine that nothing could be heard in Dakhla.

Over the next hour and a half, truck after truck wound its way down, until fifty were parked on the rock shelf, side by side in a double row, their tails turned towards the beach. The stone hut was suddenly lost in a sea of five hundred men, milling about, waiting for the landing-craft to reach shore.

At either end of the beach, other guerillas sat in Land-Rovers as lookouts. They were reinforced by a series of roving patrols, out of sight above. If the Moroccans appeared on the Guelta, Lamine hoped to pin them down long enough for his men to escape from the beach.

Among the men were a handful of Polisario officers, who greeted Lamine warmly. He gathered them together to give last-minute instructions. By the time he had finished, the first load of crates had started towards the shore, where soldiers were forming up into four work parties.

The sun, rising on the desert, had just reached the shore when Smith dropped his cigar and left the shadows. He jumped into the first landing-craft as its front dropped onto the sand. The load was made up of small crates—anti-tank equipment and ammunition. A work party pushed around him, trying the weights until they decided two men were needed to carry each crate. Smith came off the craft with a large smile. He went over to Lamine, saying, "Nothing to do but wait."

They stood there until all four landing-craft had beached once. Lamine broke away to ensure each crate was marked off against the list and placed on the appropriate pile, according to its contents. Once the first craft was empty, the men began loading the crates onto trucks and the two Americans left the beach to take refuge from the growing heat in the shade of the hut's western wall. There was not much to be said, so they waited in silence. Lamine came over from time to time and then disappeared to encourage his men to greater speed. The first truck was filled by ten-thirty and ground its way up the track to the desert.

Smith noticed Laing rise and walk out into the sun to stare after the truck. He came back and said, "I'm surprised they're leaving separately."

"Why?"

"Well, I suppose I thought they might need protection." Laing was talking to himself.

"Their best protection is to spread out," Smith said. "You must have realized that by now."

Laing was distracted. "I suppose I didn't think it out." He sat down again in the shade and said no more until Lamine came up. Laing asked how much longer it would take.

The answer was vague. Each time Lamine reappeared, he repeated the question, which Smith put down to tension and heat. Eventually, Lamine lost patience.

"As soon as your people get the crates to shore, we can go."

In fact, that wasn't so. The ship's cranes unloaded much faster than the soldiers could load. After the first beaching had gone smoothly, the landing-craft moved quickly over the short distance of water. Crates began to pile up on the sand and the soldiers were too busy unloading the craft to load the trucks waiting a hundred yards up from the shoreline.

Lamine tried to hurry them on, with little success. The four groups were working as fast as they could. By noon only three more trucks had been filled and had struggled their way back up the track.

There was some argument between Lamine and the Americans about this build-up. In the end, the other two conceded to Laing that the crates on the beach were out of sight from almost everything, while the ship lying offshore was a major giveaway. Lamine went down to the water to order that priority should be given to unloading the landing-craft. He came back to say that the men were faltering in the sun. Two of the fork-lift trucks had overheated. The temperature was already well over one hundred and ten and the beach was becoming a suntrap. Smith looked at his watch. It was just twelve-thirty.

When Laing suggested they might wait on board, where it would be cooler, Smith was ready to agree, but Lamine said no. They were welcome to go ahead, but he couldn't possibly leave the beach.

The two Americans sat down again. The sun was directly overhead, forcing them to sit in the sunlight. A few minutes later, Smith got up to see whether it was cooler inside the hut. The tin roof had made it even hotter, so he went down to the beach, pulled off his trousers and waded into the water to dunk his head. He was surprised that Laing stayed seated against the wall of the hut, baking in the reflection of the stone. Coming back from the water, he cut through the four lines of sweating men, struggling with crates.

Laing was white and shivering slightly. He looked up as Smith arrived and said, "I really would like to get onto the ship." His voice had a plaintive edge.

"Well go, Martin. No one's holding you. You look terrible."

"Lamine has to sign the release paper."

Smith was surprised. "Lamine won't do that until everything is on shore. He's very particular about details. Give me the paper and go to the ship. I'll bring it out with me on the last trip."

Laing's *arrza* was twisted carelessly around the top of his head. An aura hung over him. He stared at Smith, unable to make up his mind.

Smith raised his voice, "For God's sake, Martin, you're paying me a fortune to organize all this. I think I can manage a little signature."

Laing looked up at him, with what was meant to be a smile. "Don't worry, Anthony. I'll wait with you." As Smith said nothing, he added, "Lamine would think me a poor guest if I walked out in the middle of the party." He pulled his *arrza* down around his face and sat immobile.

Smith moved away and walked down to join Lamine, who was directing a fork-lift truck as it tried to manoeuvre a large crate containing part of a helicopter through the piles building up along the beach.

"I know what we decided, Abdullah. It just seems to me we're risking a lot. Don't you think we should get some of this stuff into the trucks?"

"No, Anthony. I want the ship out of here."

At one o'clock, Lamine climbed up on a pile of crates. He shouted to the men to strip and get in the water. They didn't really need an order. The shallow water was teeming within seconds, as shouts and laughter drifted back from the shore to Laing, sitting alone. Then they were out again, dressed and unloading at a faster pace.

Lamine stayed down with them, calmly pushing the pace. Occasionally, when he saw men struggling, he helped to lift.

Smith noticed that he didn't sweat. Desert people don't sweat a great deal, but he didn't sweat at all. And he always moved in clear, smooth motions, no matter how great the pressure.

It was two-thirty before Lamine came back up the beach to the hut. "Good news. Another half an hour and everything will be on shore."

Laing was white and his eyes were locked half closed. He revived enough to say, "Then come out to the ship to see us off. You can go ashore with the last load."

Lamine looked at his sweating face. He turned to Smith. "I think you'd better get our friend to the ship."

But Laing spoke up, "I'll only go, if you come out."

Smith shrugged and said nothing.

Lamine hesitated. "It's almost done." He abruptly smiled. "Why not?"

Smith and Laing fetched their bags and followed him down to the beach, weaving between the hundreds of crates piled up. While the Americans waited in an empty landing-craft, Lamine shouted an order to one of the officers, then jumped in as its front began to go up. They stood awkwardly, hidden from the sea, as it swayed slightly and gathered speed.

"What are you going to do with these?" Lamine patted the inside wall of the craft.

"Whatever's quickest," Smith replied. "Sink them, I suppose. We'll ask Captain Toller."

They were by the ship in less than ten minutes and climbing up the companionway. They found Captain Toller on deck, flushed and nervous, trying to move his crew faster, sweat pouring off him. He reluctantly led them to his cabin and produced alcohol.

"Later," Smith said. "What about the landing-craft?"

"Haul them back on board? That's an hour's work. Couldn't we . . ."

"Sink them!" Laing cut in, with surprising vehemence. He was, if anything, whiter and shivering heavily.

Smith shrugged and agreed that they might as well be sunk.

Lamine drew him aside to say goodbye. When they were at a distance, Laing took the Captain urgently by the arm, "Can you send a message without delay?"

"We've got a radio."

"Now listen. This is very important. The moment the last craft leaves shore, I want a general message sent out five times. Just the word 'Cosmos.' That's all. But it must go immediately."

"What must?"

Smith had come back towards them in time to hear the end of the instructions.

Laing gaped, then replied, "A safe arrival message to my employer. They insisted I send one. I'm afraid that if I delay too long, they might get nervous and do—well, whatever people like that do." He saw Lamine was looking hard at him. "It's just one word. 'Cosmos.' No risk."

"For Cosima," Smith smiled.

"She's always good luck."

Lamine broke away, saying he had to get back to shore. Laing searched in his bag for the release document. He pulled it out and handed it to Lamine, who looked at it and back at Laing before folding the paper and putting it in his pocket.

"I'll sign it on shore, when everything is there."

"But . . ."

"You stay here. Anthony's coming with me. He's going to keep me company back to Tindouf. He'll make sure I sign and will give it to the crew of the last craft."

As Lamine walked towards the cabin door, Laing cried out in an uncontrolled voice, "You can't make a sailor responsible for something so important. I can't accept that."

Lamine stopped and examined him quizzically. "Well, I'm going ashore, Mr. Laing."

"I'll come back with you to get it." Laing spoke with a shrill edge.

He desperately held the lid on an attack of nerves, which in turn paralysed everyone in the cabin. Lamine broke the spell by simply walking out, Smith behind him. Laing twisted to Toller sharply, "Send that message the moment the last craft leaves shore."

"I'm not hanging around here."

"Just send it!" Laing blurted out and left the cabin.

FORTY-NINE

Nothing was said on the way back. They avoided one another's eyes as they stood, balancing on top of the packed weapons. The shore loomed before them, piles of pale wood crates on the sand, the cliff shining red behind. Laing had forgotten his *arrza* on board. When they landed, Lamine told them to wait behind the hut, where there was some shade.

Brahim was crouched against the wall, talking to Ahmed Mah and Hama. They shifted to make room for the two Americans and kept talking. Laing sat, closed in on himself. He tapped his own right knee with the knuckles of his right hand.

His anger seemed exaggerated to Smith, but he was hardly thinking about Laing. Instead, he was wondering why he had agreed to travel back across the desert with Lamine. Perhaps because Lamine had insisted. Smith always reacted to strong shows of friendship. He felt free to go. Everything Laing was paying him to do was done. Lamine wanted him to come. A want was a need.

They sat in silence for another half hour, out of sight of the agitation on the shore, with only the cliff rising up in front of them. Then Lamine reappeared, pleased with himself.

"Everything's ashore. The craft are all gone except yours, Mr. Laing. Now all we have to do is load up."

Laing got to his feet and walked towards him. "I'd better be on my way then."

But Lamine looked over his shoulder. "There's lots of time for that. First, let me make sure they're loading the trucks properly." He disappeared towards the beach.

Laing went over to Smith and clutched his hand. "Come

into the hut with me." His eyes darted, out of control.

Smith followed him around the corner and inside. The heat there was stifling, so he stood near the door. Laing stood very close to him and erupted,

"We must get out of here, Anthony! You have to come with me!"

"Why?"

"Because he's stalling."

"He'll sign."

"It'll be too late then!"

"What do you mean too late?"

"Too late, Anthony. Too late! He's got to sign before the crates leave the beach."

He was swinging his arms as if seized by a fit. Smith looked at him aghast. This only encouraged Laing to greater agitation.

"The moment Toller sends the message, the Moroccans will be on their way here."

Smith didn't move.

"Anthony, listen! They already knew. They were going to do things against us."

"Us?" Smith managed to ask.

"The company. You. Me. We have to get out of here."

Smith made him sit down in a corner of the hut and said he would be right back. He walked quickly outside and then stopped. He turned his head slowly around in its socket, straining the sinews, his eyes wide open, the sun blinding him. He shut them for a moment and tensed himself until every part of his body ached. He let go and walked down to the beach.

Smith grabbed Lamine's arm. He looked up from a group of men lifting cases.

"It's a double-cross. The Moroccans have been warned."

Lamine hardly let him finish. "I knew there was something."

"Martin just told me. We've got to get out of here."

Lamine shouted orders. Men put down the cases they were carrying and ran up the beach towards the trucks. Lamine swung around, staring at the crates on the sand, his fists clenched at his side, trying to think of something to say.

Smith grabbed his hand. "It's too late. Come on."

As they turned to leave, they saw the landing-craft close its door and pull off the beach.

"The message," Smith said urgently. "They'll send the message."

Lamine understood immediately and looked about him. "We can't stop them. Come on."

He ran ahead across the sand towards the trucks. Men were swarming into them. Some machines had already begun grinding up the track towards the desert. Lamine ran to each driver, telling him to scatter as soon as he was above, then stopped and looked at the jam building up on the narrow, steep track. He turned back, suddenly overwhelmed with anger.

Smith caught up and Lamine shouted at him, "They'll never get out in time."

He ran to the back of the column, shouting to the men to jump out and catch up with the trucks at the front. They would lose forty pieces of machinery, but at least the men would get away. There was a rush of bodies around them, leaping out of trucks and running forward to those already part way up the cliff. For a few minutes, the track was a scene of dust and noise. Then there was no one. The beach was empty except for a maze of piled crates and a parking lot of abandoned trucks.

"Now, let's go, Anthony."

Smith held him back, "What about Martin?"

Lamine looked at him amazed, "What use is a man whose word can't be trusted?"

"We can't just leave him here!" Lamine said nothing. "Abdullah, we can't."

Lamine stepped back, moving his right hand across his chest before pointing at the shore. "When Oqba conquered the last part of Africa for Islam, he rode his horse into the Atlantic and raised his sword to heaven, shouting for his army to hear, 'As God is my witness, I can go no farther.' Don't ask more of me."

Smith broke away and walked towards the hut. He heard Lamine call behind him, "Brahim will wait ten minutes. No more."

He found Laing standing at the opening, unable to move. His face was transparent. His voice came from a separate body, "Where have they gone?"

Smith took him back inside and sat him down.

"They've gone, Martin, that's all."

"What about the landing-craft?"

"The crew panicked when the soldiers ran. It's gone too."

Smith walked to the other side of the hut, where he looked out of the door.

"I had to tell them, Martin. I had no choice." He hoped that Laing would say something, but he didn't. "Ambition isn't a religion."

Laing spoke to him out of the shadows, "We must go before the planes arrive."

Smith didn't look round. "I can't take you. They'll just kill you."

After a moment, Laing tried to begin a sentence, but failed. Smith went out, saying he would be back. In the heat shimmer, Brahim stood alone beside his Land-Rover, his face twisted away from the sun. Smith walked slowly across the sand, the emptiness of the beach rushing about him. He took the water can and returned to the hut. Laing was standing in the middle. He handed him the water. Laing's eyes glued onto him, burning like white fires, too frightened to plead, too confused to understand.

Smith turned and left. Outside, his face contorted. He got into the Land-Rover and waved Brahim forward. They churned up the track, cutting close on the corners until they came to the top. Brahim pressed his foot to the floor and drove straight east, the sun at their backs. Five minutes later they heard a roar and then saw fighters flying low up the coast.

Smith wrenched his bag from the back. He shoved his hands inside, searching convulsively until he pulled out a book, which he held close before his eyes and read, skipping through the pages until he found,

> So I, sundered from my native land, far from noble kinsmen, often sad at heart . . .

In the distance behind them, a series of explosions erupted, followed by a violent crescendo as the ammunition in the crates was struck. Brahim glanced round, swerving marginally to the north.

> . . . Comfort me, left without friends, treat me with kindness.

Smith averted his drowning eyes and waved at Brahim to go faster.

PART 6

FIFTY

James Moffett had woken early on Friday morning and gone to his office to phone the communications in Spain, to make sure they were listening carefully. Spain rang him back shortly after eleven a.m., New York time, to say that the word 'Cosmos' had been received. He felt a surge of relief, as he always did when tension passed, but told them to stay in their places until midnight.

At noon, he rang them again and asked that a message be sent to the *Sophie*: "Confirm all okay."

Spain came back to him half an hour later. They had received an answer: "Package delivered but messenger not on board." Moffett told them to instruct the *Sophie* to go to the nearest European port and to contact him by telephone. He thought the messenger was Smith.

It was Monday before a call came in from Captain Toller, in Gibraltar. Only then did Moffett discover that Laing had gone to the rendezvous by land.

The Captain described the confused conversation, overheard when the three men came briefly on board. He described Laing's state and his instructions about sending the message. Finally, he explained how the soldiers on shore had suddenly dropped everything and fled, causing his own sailors to panic and rush off. As instructed, he sent the message. It wasn't until the craft arrived that he realized Laing wasn't on board.

What Moffett wanted to know was whether Laing had got away. Toller said he had hesitated before sinking the last craft. He had searched the shore with his binoculars. For a moment, he had thought he saw a figure moving among the piles of crates on the beach. He had been trying to make up his mind whether to send the craft back to shore when the fighters appeared. He had no choice but to pull up anchor and get away as quickly as possible. Toller had been amazed that the jets left him alone. There had been a terrible explosion on the beach as they sailed away.

There was very little Moffett could do, except wait to see whether anything else would happen. Probably Laing would turn up in a week or so and they could begin redrawing the Vietnam scenario.

There was an Executive Committee meeting the next day and he felt obliged to give them a short report, outlining the little he knew. At worst, he reported, they had failed. But there was no reason to expect anything would leak out.

He was surprised by the vehemence with which Fell asked, "What about Laing? That is worse than your personal failure, James."

After the meeting, Moffett went to Laing's office to question his secretary. He sensed that there was something missing. She seemed to know nothing, except that Laing had had a visit shortly before he left from a man who wouldn't give his name. Moffett asked her for the complete Vietnam file, which he carried back to his own desk to examine. There was nothing in it except the corporate reports. He knew there must be more, because Laing had prepared a private report for him on the arms deal. He went back to the secretary to ask what else she had. At first, she said there was nothing. He bullied and confused her until, finally, she gave up Laing's personal file.

It took the rest of the afternoon to read the notes. He reread them with horror. He was horrified by the fragility of Laing's plan, to double-cross both the Polisario and the company. But it was Fell's actions that shocked him most. He could never have imagined that a man would go to such lengths to wound him—James Moffett—an important employee perhaps, but still merely an employee, who would be gone in a few years. Then it struck him for the first time. Laing was dead. He had to be dead. Who would have saved him? Who would have saved the poor boy?

His first reaction was to destroy Fell—to take everything to Erlich and then to the Executive Committee and destroy him. But then he felt a tremor somewhere within him. He realized that he wasn't interested in destroying Fell. He didn't care about him. He didn't care period. Perhaps he cared about Laing. Moffett remembered how he had pushed the young man. Had he judged so badly in believing him strong enough to break away? Had he pushed him into the turbulence that killed him? That thought drove him to read the file again —trying to trace the gymnastics of the young man's logic. He couldn't understand.

A call, from their Paris office, interrupted him. An article had appeared in *Le Monde* that afternoon. The article suggested that an American oil company had broken the Vietnam arms embargo by acting as middle-men selling to an African guerilla movement. It was rumoured that Western-Oriental was involved. The article was filed from Rabat.

Moffett pulled himself together long enough to reassure the manager. Rumours like that could be easily squashed—just pay the journalist and, through him, find the leak and plug it; usually with more money.

He hung up and slipped back into reading Laing's notes, trying desperately to understand. Then he threw them down in disgust. How many times had he been through these crises? How many Laings? So eager. So pathetic. But not dead. He thought of going home. The tremor grew within him and, having waited for it to return, he no longer wanted to do battle. There would be nobody in his apartment. Perhaps there was someone he could spend the evening with.

He got up from his desk and opened his office door to discover that his secretary had left. It was already past seven. He came back into his office and crossed to his bathroom, with the idea of shaving before going out.

He picked up his razor and looked at himself. Laing's reflection was in the background, staring at him. It was a reminding stare, not an accusation, yet Moffett felt accused. He took out the blade, which made the tremor disappear. Returning to his office, he locked the outer door, took off his jacket and rolled up his sleeves. Laing's reflection followed him as he sat down behind his desk and leaned slightly forward, resting his elbows on the blotter.

He examined his arms for a few minutes. Then, taking the blade in his left hand, he cut two deep troughs across the underside of his right wrist. He watched the blood spurt out in a warm, friendly flow that provoked an afterthought. He paused and picked up the felt pen from his desk, trying not to drip blood on his clothes while he wrote a short note on the side of the blotter, instructing his secretary to give Laing's file to Erlich. Then he transferred the blade to that hand and cut two troughs across his left wrist, this time with all his weight, slicing deep enough to sever both arteries and release an explosion of blood. He put the razor down and placed his hands carefully on the centre of the pad. In the flow of the ocean that followed, all reflections were washed away.

On Wednesday morning, 13 August, his secretary unlocked the office to find him, a porcelain-white figure, slouched forward in his own dried blood. She did not see the message, because the blotter was entirely stained dark brown red, as were his trousers and some of the carpet.

She did not scream. She turned round and walked out, locking the door behind her. There, she thought for a moment, before walking down the carpeted hall to the President's office. Erlich's secretary said he was out of town for the day. She thought again and walked to the other end of the hall, to David Fell's office. It was too early for people to be waiting, so she walked straight in, ignoring his secretary.

Fell followed her back, allowing her to usher him into Moffett's office. He asked her to wait outside and shut the door. Walking around the desk in one full circle, he appraised Moffett as if he were slain game. There was a smell of urine in the air.

He noticed the blood-stained file on Moffett's otherwise empty desk and picked it up, holding it at a distance. It was tagged Laing-Vietnam-Personal. Opening the file, he caught sight of a memo referring to his own conversations. He closed it and, as the blood was dry on the cover, slipped it under his arm.

Outside the office, he told Moffett's secretary to find the President, wherever he was.

FIFTY-ONE

Because he did not understand them, Robert Erlich hated politicians. He had been chosen as President because he was bluff and friendly and warm. But it had been James Moffett's job to deal with politicians. Moffett had been dead only three months, but already he, Erlich, was sitting in a room filled with the breed he hated most.

Erlich knew, in his heart, that nothing too terrible would come of what had happened. Mr. Reagan, the president-elect for the past two days, would not be chastising the guardians of free enterprise during his term.

Erlich had come to Washington that afternoon, 6 November, to meet informally with members of the Senate Foreign Relations Committee. The idea was to avoid Western-Oriental's being called before it officially. Again, the election had been kind. Two of the Senators calling loudest for hearings had been defeated. Those who questioned Erlich were, in general, sympathetic. There was one surviving liberal, who had not been up for re-election, and he had been badgering Erlich for an hour.

"How, Sir, could your Mr. Moffett obtain these millions upon millions of dollars to contravene a law of the United States, without your knowledge as President of the corporation?"

Erlich shifted and thought of attempting a joke. Instead he assumed an apologetic expression and replied, "An arrangement was made by certain people by which these funds could be made available, and the authorities were established and the mechanism was established, and it was simply like any other authority that gets established in a company. There are thousands of authorities, if not hundreds of thousands. And this one kept right on going and everyone that was involved in it, quite apparently from the investigation that has been made since, was acting within his authority."

"Well, gentlemen," the Senator said to his colleagues, "I find this most extraordinary. For myself, I think this matter should go before the Committee."

Erlich tried to smile and shifted in his seat. However it turned out, he knew he would be gracefully retired within the year, with a generous golden handshake—there would have to be one sacrificial lamb. And Fell, if he made no mistakes, would inherit.

FIFTY-TWO

Cosima watched, through the side window of the car, the jagged fissure that fell sharply to a ribbon of oleander below. Without Idrissi, his driver was a silent shell beside her, intent on the climbing hairpin turns. Her spirit was suspended, constricted, searching for a way out.

Ahead, cold rain clouds hung across chasms between sheets of black rock that dropped hundreds of feet.

Sayed Idrissi had not encouraged her to come. He had sent his car to meet her at the airport and the driver had taken her straight to the house in Souissi. She had arrived on 6 November, the anniversary of the Green March. Idrissi was waiting at the house—in his official djellabah, as he put it. He embraced her warmly.

"When you come back into a room, I realize that the room has been empty."

She had steeled herself to insist on what she wanted. "I'm certain that Anthony is in Morocco. You must know where he is, Moulay Sayed."

"I waited for you, but now I must go. Today we are celebrating. I'm late for a reception at the palace."

"I came to find Anthony."

"You're staying here tonight. I'll see you at dinner."

Cosima had prepared this scene for weeks and could see him seeking a way to defuse her emotions.

"Your husband's employers came to see me last week."

She recognized it as a question aimed at ferreting out her position and asked in return, "Fell?"

"Someone from Mr. Fell. A Mr. Morley. He brought a proposition. The whereabouts of Anthony in return for the love of Western-Oriental."

"You didn't tell them?" Her tone was nervous, which reassured him.

"I have nothing to tell, so he went on to Kader. Go to see Sidi Karim. My houseboy will drive you." Idrissi scribbled a few words on a piece of paper, "You'll need this." He turned to leave but paused, watching carefully for her reaction as he said, "My driver tells me you have been followed from the aeroplane by two men. I shall have them picked up." She was not surprised and showed as much.

Holes broke through the rain clouds, revealing peaks covered in snow. They came to a pass. The cold wind was compressed through it. Cosima felt surging up the formless frustration and anger that had held her prisoner since Laing's disappearance three months before. He was dead, certainly that, whatever that was. But where was he dead? How was he dead?

She had sat in New York, surrounded by the physical details of her life. They made his absence as trivial as their presence. She wanted to destroy them, to destroy everything they had shared. She wanted to hold onto him, even dead. He had slipped into non-existence. She knew nothing more. In place of something, there was nothing; only her love left burning in a void.

A platoon of soldiers blocked the alley to Karim Farid's house. They saw her surprise and an officer stopped her with a curt wave of his hand. She fumbled for Idrissi's note and was allowed to pass. Karim Farid was in his garden, wearing wool robes to protect against the November breeze. He smiled kindly at her confusion.

"My guards? Courtesy of Moulay Sayed. They were about to arrest me, but Moulay Sayed beat them to it by having me put under house arrest. The soldiers are loyal to his friends, not to Kader." He took her hand and led her to the gazebo. "Why do you want to see Anthony?"

"My husband is gone, Sidi Karim, apparently dead. No one will tell me anything. Anthony was with him, I'm sure of that, and I have the right to know something."

He leaned forward. "What can you do? Why not wait . . .?"

She cut him off with a burning urgency. "I don't need time. I am exploding inside. The pain I feel tells me there is nothing I can do. But I have a right . . ."

He leaned back until he could see her eyes clearly, then dropped his own gaze in resignation. "This is a bad time for gardens in Rabat. You should go south. Ask Moulay Sayed to come and see me."

She rose to leave, but he leaned forward abruptly, his weight on her arm with surprising aggression, forcing her to sit down.

"The greatest ability, Cosima, after the ability to remember, is the ability to forget."

She left the next morning in Idrissi's Mercedes. They drove south past Casablanca, across the increasingly arid plains that led to the low, peach-coloured city of Marrakesh, where she spent the night. The next morning, they began across the Atlas Mountains that rose thirty miles beyond the city. The road curved up through a wide, green valley, until the way narrowed into lifeless gorges.

The landscape echoed despair, bringing out the confusion within her. She asked herself again why she was there. The answers were so indistinct that they drew her into greater depression.

The heights divided two worlds. From the Tichka Pass down, deep mauve hills glistened against green slate hills, against coral peaks. That night they spent at Ouarzazate, where the mountains opened up into a series of valleys. The Pasha El Glaoui had once had a fortress there. The next day, they followed the River Dr'aa down on its long curve south towards the Sahara, winding past crumbling, dirt fortresses, with multitudes of towers rising in twisted forms. The barren hills and desert crept up on one side. On the other, were the date palms and the river. The desert lay on its far bank.

For the first time, she found herself alone—cut off from her friends and her world, driving without knowing where she was going. She slipped in and out of her life with Laing. Each moment recalled turned into a nightmare. Something had to be buried, that was all she knew.

The heat returned as the other cars and the Western clothes disappeared. People rode on asses or walked by the road, wearing the loose djellabahs of the region. Cloaks were flung over their backs and unconsciously thrown around and over a shoulder.

At the end of a long line of mud fortresses they came to the village of Zagora, the last real settlement before the desert. On the main street, a group danced to flutes, welcoming a *hajji* back from his pilgrimage to Mecca. The driver stopped at the far edge of the village and, while a crowd gathered, he went into a small carpenter's shop where he gave a coin to a young man who ran towards the river and the date palms. The crowd stared at her through the windows. Something grew within her—expectation or tears—but it was blocked as everything had been blocked.

Twenty minutes later, the man came back leading a small boy, with a gilded Botticelli face, in a worn blue robe, whom she was told to follow. The driver waited where he was.

The boy led her down a red dirt path, hemmed in by rough dirt walls. He spoke some English and asked if she were Monsieur Smith's wife. When she answered no, he showed childlike relief.

The walls rose above her head with gardens spilling over them and the path cutting right and left beside irrigation ditches filled with rushing waters that, from time to time, she had to leap across. The boy watched, with distant amusement. Ahead, the worn mountain peaks that lay on the other side of the river came into view and disappeared. He asked her if she were staying the night and she answered no. Again, he showed relief. They followed the twisting garden walls for ten minutes, Cosima brushing away the flies drawn by her rose-scented perfume.

He stopped to push open a metal door in a wall and motioned her through into a grove of date palms that towered over fruit trees and flowers. In the centre of the grove was a low house, the colour of the earth, without windows.

The boy led her into a cool room. The floor was paved

with mosaic, the walls bare. She left her sandals and followed him into a large, central courtyard, the outer edges of which were paved with a green and salmon mosaic. All the rooms opened onto the courtyard through wide double doors and there was a fountain in the centre, surrounded by vines. The boy pointed to a room in the far corner. Cosima walked around the square, staring into the rooms, filled only with long cushions and occasional low tables. As she reached the open door in the corner, a murmuring noise could be heard, but she waited on the edge of the room until her eyes adjusted to the shade within.

She saw Smith on a low bed, on top of a woman much darker than himself; both of them moving at a slow rhythmic speed. The woman played her hands over his back, groaning heavily as she attempted to writhe under his weight, but he was silent, simply following in a circular motion, his hands cupped tightly under her buttocks. It was hard to tell whether she felt any pleasure or was just performing. Their rhythm increased into a melded gyration; Smith's fleshy back glistening and the woman moaning with her mouth open, revealing black teeth. Suddenly, Smith breathed heavily several times and she cried out. They lay still, the woman caressing the back of his head and his shoulders.

She tapped his shoulder to make him roll off her so that she could get to her feet. Her breasts were small and firm, like apples. She was very young. As she got up, she saw Cosima and threw a caftan over herself, before saying something in a guttural voice to Smith and slipping by without looking at the intruder.

Smith looked up to where Cosima was outlined in the light. He pulled on a loose, grey *gandura* without showing surprise or embarrassment, although she was certain he was overwhelmed by both. It was fear she wanted him to feel, believed he felt, but he hid it in expressionless silence as he led the way out into the garden. Under a copse of date palms, there was a low chair and a collection of cushions. Some notebooks and a half empty bottle of wine sat beside them. From there he had a clear view of the Dr'aa, flowing towards the barren rock hills and the desert, through which the water ran for a few hundred miles before sinking into the sand without a trace.

Smith indicated the chair and she sat down without thinking, while he wandered a short distance away to pull a pomegranate from a tree. The fruit had split open with ripeness.

"The end of the season." He broke it in two and handed half to her, then lay down on the cushions.

"Sidi Karim sent me," she began defensively, but caught hold of herself and threw out, "I made him. I want to know what happened."

Without hesitation or justifications Smith told her the story as if it had been rehearsed. She fixed her eyes on him and held them, whatever he said. She had come prepared for something terrible. Every word was registered and buried within her. She was certain that he expected her to abuse him or to break down, instead she picked the seeds from the pomegranate and ate them one by one. Her eyes did not leave him, but they carried no apparent judgement. She had come to endure, not to find comfort in others.

By the time he had finished, she felt certain his expression, his whole body, had become an appeal. An appeal for what, she asked herself sharply and looked away. He poured and emptied a glass of wine. She knew that he felt she was dividing him into small pieces, but in fact, he had merely ceased to exist while she tried to digest his words. Eventually Cosima dropped the pomegranate on the ground and focused on him again. "What people do has little to do with how they are loved."

He blushed, unable to agree or disagree.

"So you are hiding here?" She could see that he read bitterness into her voice. It was closer to disinterest, but she found herself unwilling to correct his impression.

He shrugged. "For the moment I'm resigned to my solitude."

"Moulay Sayed gave me a message. He has spoken to General Kader."

"Martin's company don't like me," he tried to explain. "They approached . . ."

"I know about that. Fell telephones me regularly to see whether I've heard from you. Why is Kader leaving you alone?"

"He could find me if he wanted to. Maybe he sees me as a pawn in negotiations with the Polisario. God knows."

"What are you going to do about it?" she taunted.

"Revenge holds no interest for me."

Cosima became agitated, at first without realizing it and then without understanding why. "You can't just sit here. You have to come to terms with . . ."

"The world?" Smith blushed. "I decided not to do that long

ago. Have you only just realized?" He forced a smile. "You'd be surprised how many qualities of dates there are here. The best are long and black, like soft meringues. They rot within an hour of being picked. How have you managed?"

She moved her hand to dismiss any significance from her words. "I'm pregnant."

"Did Martin know?"

"He had left by the time I found out."

She wanted the child more than she had ever wanted one and yet, once it was there it would always be a reminder of Laing. The feeling that she should cut off that past had rolled through her heart again and again; that she should begin afresh. Cosima looked around the garden at the yellow flowers of the cotton plants, the apricot trees and the palms throwing shade from above. There was a feeling of sympathy somewhere within her for Smith. She could feel it rising slowly.

Smith suddenly appeared excited. It was the nervousness of someone who feared that he was not being given credit for his feelings. "Martin didn't understand the rules. Had I realized . . ."

Her pity dissolved until she cut him off. "What use is your sentiment?"

He blushed and replied sharply, catching her tone, "Then why did you come?"

"I thought I might find something. I was a fool. Why should I expect you to have . . . ?" She could feel the walls breaking down. She didn't want it to happen there and then and fought it back. "What if they find you?"

Smith shrugged. "At the end of the main street of Zagora —where the dirt track begins—you'll see a chain across the road. Last year, anyone could drive into the desert. But there have been Polisario attacks. There is even a sympathizer here. Lamine sent him to see me. If I have a problem . . ."

"There is always somewhere to hide."

"That's right."

"I wish I knew how," she said. "Now it's too late." As the words formed, she realized that a weight had been lifted from within her. The binding cords had been cut. She was overwhelmed by a sense of her freedom. "I don't want to learn. I know what I have to do."

Smith nodded, bemused. "Today is the first day of the Muslim fifteenth century. Did you know that?"

She said nothing. It was curious. She could sense him making an appeal to her again.

"Good news is the right way to begin a century."

"Good news," she echoed as she rose, turning away from him and walking towards the garden door where the boy was waiting to guide her back.

Zagora

About the Author

John Ralston Saul, an inveterate world traveller, journeyed with guerillas in North Africa, with the Shan rebel war-lords in Burma, and to the jungles of Thailand. His explorations and adventures have formed much of the background for his widely published and bestselling novels *The Birds of Prey*, *Baraka*, *The Next Best Thing*, and *The Paradise Eater* which have sold in excess of three million copies and have been translated into more than ten languages. He presently lives in Toronto, Canada.